RON RICHARD

GROUP SIX AND THE CRATER

MAGIC IS BORN

—

GROUP SIX SERIES

GROUP SIX AND THE RIVER
Of Water and Brimstone

GROUP SIX AND THE CRATER
Magic is Born

RON RICHARD

GROUP SIX AND THE CRATER

MAGIC IS BORN

CHRISTOPHER MATTHEWS PUBLISHING

Group Six and the Crater, *Magic is Born*
by Ron Richard

 Christopher Matthews Publishing
Gleneden Beach, Oregon
ChristopherMatthewsPub.com

ISBN:
978-1-944072-79-7 (hc)
978-1-944072-80-3 (pb)
978-1-944072-81-0 (epub)

Library of Congress Control Number: 2023900956
Genre: *magic, fantasy, adventure, humorous, mythical creatures*

Cover design and formatting by Suzanne Fyhrie Parrott
Cover art by Gaurav Srivastava (@hephaestusart, Fiverr.com), © Ron Richard

Please provide feedback

10 9 8 7 6 5 4 3 2 1

Printed in U.S.A.

For Healers
Everywhere

TABLE OF CONTENTS

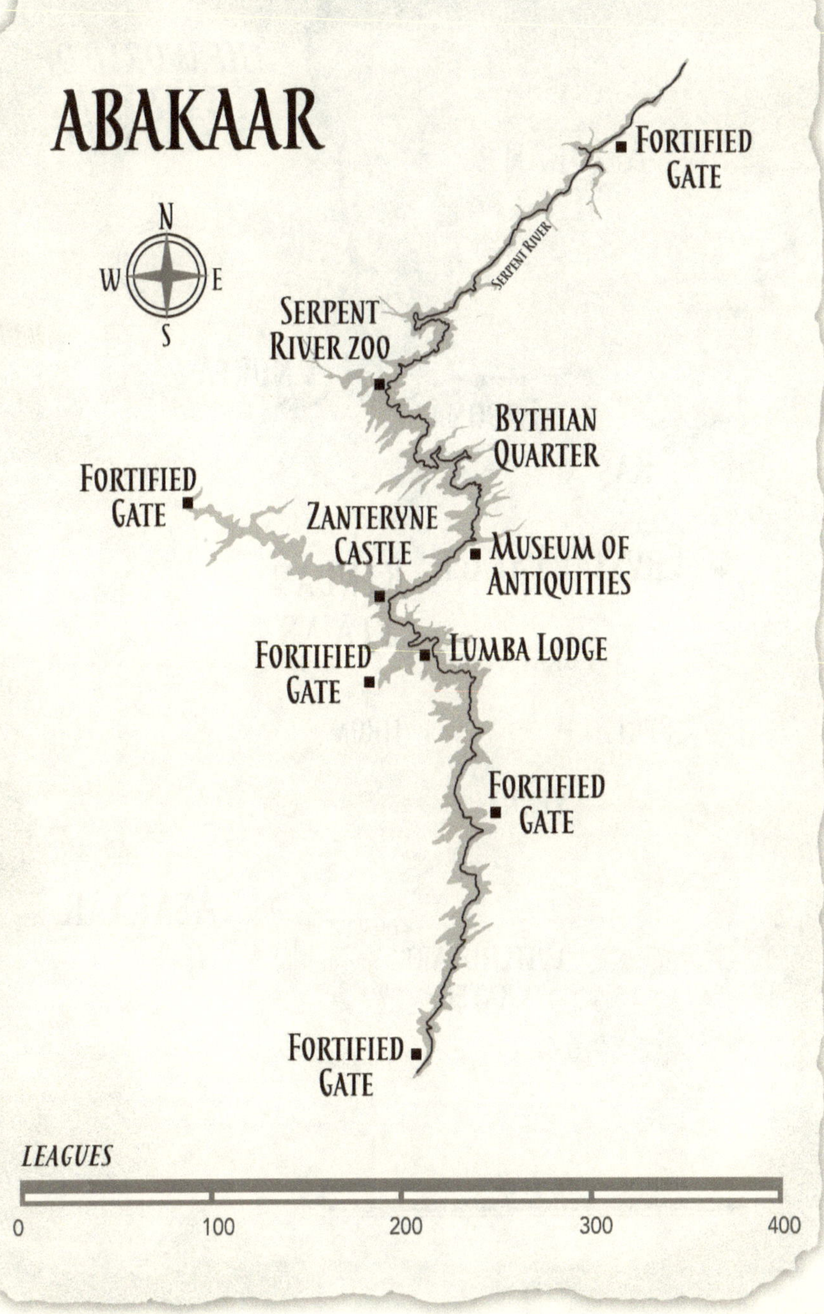

ABAKAAR
N
W E
S
SERPENT RIVER
SERPENT RIVER ZOO
BYTHIAN QUARTER
FORTIFIED GATE
ZANTERYNE CASTLE
MUSEUM OF ANTIQUITIES
FORTIFIED GATE
LUMBA LODGE
FORTIFIED GATE
FORTIFIED GATE
FORTIFIED GATE
LEAGUES
0
100
200
300
400

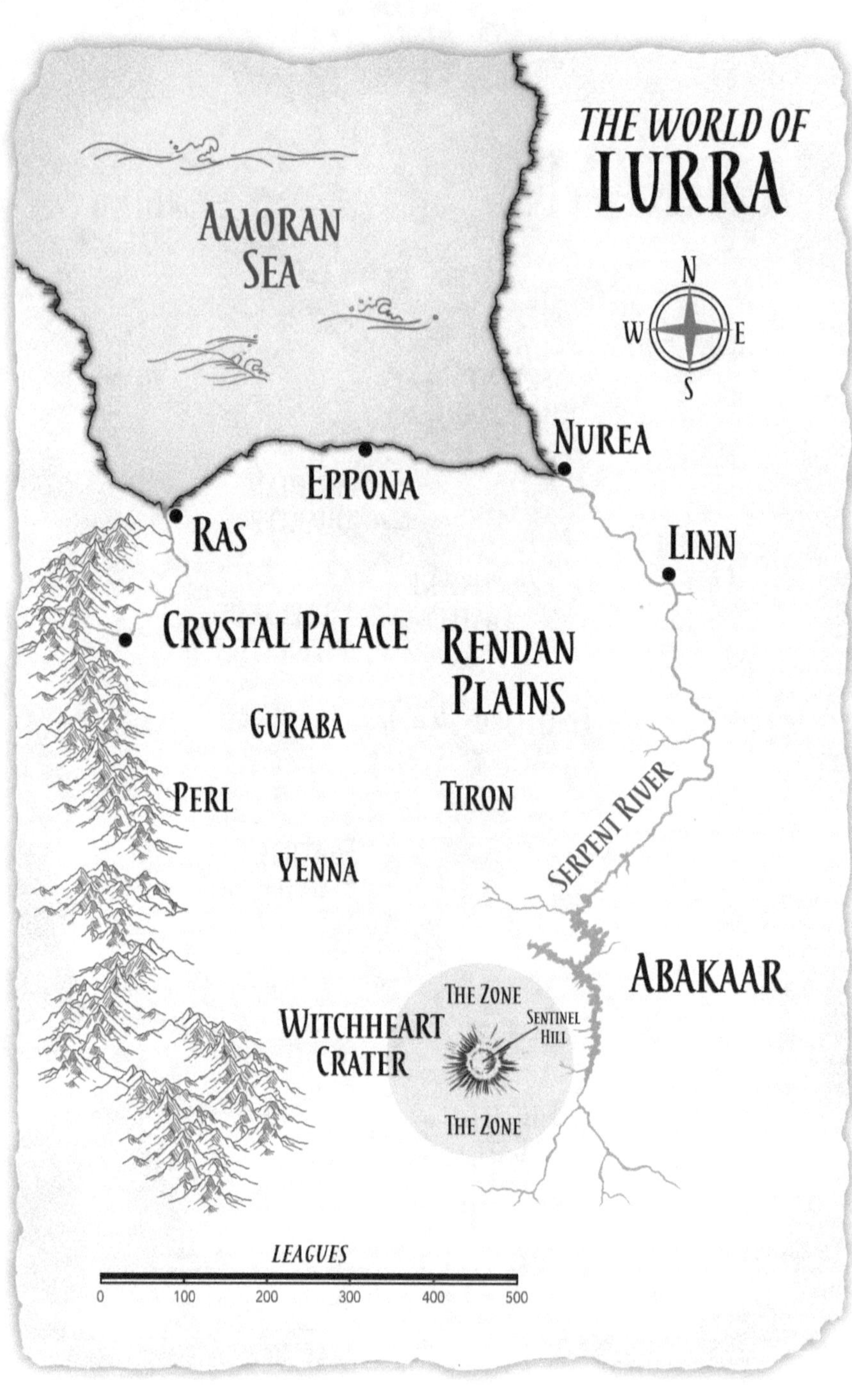

THE WORLD OF
LURRA
N
W E
S
AMORAN SEA
NUREA
EPPONA
RAS
LINN
CRYSTAL PALACE
RENDAN PLAINS
GURABA
PERL
TIRON
SERPENT RIVER
YENNA
ABAKAAR
WITCHHEART CRATER
THE ZONE
SENTINEL HILL
THE ZONE
LEAGUES
0 100 200 300 400 500

MAJOR CHARACTERS

GROUP SIX

SERENA

A 27-year-old Macai Northlands Warrior. A fierce fighter, she values honor in battle above all else.

ORCHID

A 30-year-old Macai. Raised by Eryndi foster parents, she practices the nature based Worldly Magic, which is unusual for a Macai.

FOXX

A 33-year-old self-taught Macai Magician, inventor of the Knowing Spell, which allows him to read moods and influence others.

TRESADO

A 45-year-old Eryndi Magician who practices the more powerful Absolute Magic.

50,000 YEARS AGO

FRADER MANERET
Ma Kahy space traveler from the planet Casal

COMISA MANERET
Ma Kahy medical practitioner from the planet Casal, wife
to Frader

TELLA
Son of Frader and Comisa

JALEX
Prehistoric Ern hunter and leader

DORAN
Mate to Jalex

MUTA
Medicine Chief – Tribe of Doran

TARL
Male child of Jalex and Doran

SHONA
Female child of Jalex and Doran

CORMA
Close friend to Jalex

CHIEF DURAT
Leader of a tribe of Ern

DREN
Villager killed by Senfall

TRU
Villager

GAREN
Villager

YULO

Villager

MYELA

Aged Wise Woman – skilled in herbology

TRAKA

Son of Yulo and Tru

GARNA

Villager

SODAK

Chief of the Hill Tribe

KARROL

Hunter from the Clan of Tarben

DROOK

Brother of Karrol

SHEMIN

Mate to Drook

ARMA

Mother of Shemin

TARBEN

Leader of the Clan of Tarben

KRAY

Sister to Yeni

YENI

Sister to Kray

TAK

Daughter of Tarl, Granddaughter of Jalex

AURAN

Assistant to Tak

THE CRYSTAL PALACE

JAKUNDARANA SLIVERSHKANENT TRYSTELLIAR aka JAKKI

Steward of the Crystal Palace and a powerful Magician. She enjoys the fast-paced style of life within the Palace.

SPARKLY

Assistant to the Steward. His clothing, hair, and even his teeth are sparkly.

GLEAM

An enormous silvery dragon. He and the Palace have a rapport together. The palace provides a home with comforts and Gleam gets a chance to show off his magnificence to his adoring public.

ABAKAAR

TARBOR

Soldier of Abakaar

LIEUTENANT SENSIS

Soldier of Abakaar

CORPORAL NARBO

Soldier of Abakaar

NAOMI

Admissions officer

PELONKA KE DOR

Riddlemistress of the Court Of Abakaar

GREL FONDREN

Depot Manager

FLOOZY
Owner and operator of Floozy's All-Haul, a waste
transportation barge on the Serpent River

QUEEN MINORE ('mĭn-or-ē)
Ruler of all Abakaar

CHINTZY and GRACIE
Owner/operators of Re-enchantment Station 12

RASTABAN ('ṛäs-tə-bän)
Grand Vizier to the Court of Queen Minore

HAROLD
Herald to the Court of Queen Minore

KURREAN
Ambassador from Linn

ZUKO and LEEFEN
Healers in the service of the Queen

THE TRESKAN IMPERIUM

IMPERATOR MERAK (mě-'räk)
Ruler of the Treskan Imperium

GENERAL PRIXUS SCAPULUS
Commander of the Treskan 12th Legion

MISCELLANEOUS

PROFESSOR ABADIAH GENERAX
Owner/Operator of Professor Generax's Traveling World
of Wonders, mentor to Foxx

MISHANNA and REVINAL
Eryndi foster-parents of Orchid

TRIANNA OF SYLVAS, POETESS TO THE GLADES.
Mysterious denizen of the Glades

PROFESSOR HARIEL
Dean of Kadizio University

DEMENTUS, THE MAD TRESKAN
Noted traveler of the world – considered semi-mythical

HROLVAD, THE BERSERKER ('rōl-väd)
A legendary hero and founder of Northlands culture

FUTURE TIMES

VINNIE and DEREK
Jamba heads

GARRETT SONDCHI and JULES BLACK
Reporters

<hr>

PROLOGUE

Just Over 50,000 Years Ago

The steady stream of people came from many sources: the aerodrome, the clogged highways, the three nearby towns, even cross-country through the hills for those without vehicles. Those that did come by car simply abandoned them in the vast parking areas that surrounded the complex. No matter – they would never be driven again. It was estimated that over three million refugees arrived over a five-day period. But only a small fraction of those would actually make it past the screening posts, which were heavily defended with fortified barriers and numerous armed guards.

Frader and Comisa Maneret were in line for one such post. When they had arrived early this morning, there were a few hundred people in front of them. It was now well into the aftermidday and finally it was almost their turn. The line of refugees behind them still stretched nearly a kilometer. Most of those poor people would not be tested today.

"Good thing we brought those granola bars," said Frader, easing his heavy duffel pack off his shoulder. He winced as the strap scraped across the irritated skin. "We'd be starving by now, otherwise."

Comisa looked back in sympathy at the multitude of misery behind them. Hundreds of families waited in the hot sun, some of them in ragged clothing which hung upon their emaciated frames. Many of the children and older folks could not stand any longer and simply lay down on the hot asphalt, which made conditions even worse. "I'm afraid a lot of these others aren't so lucky. They said that there would be rations in the shuttles. If we get accepted, maybe we can toss our excess back into the line."

"Yeah . . . well, we'll see. Okay, finally we're next."

Frader hoisted his pack back on his shoulder and Comisa took up her heavy suitcase. Each person was allowed only one piece of luggage. Weight had not been a factor. Gravimetric control made that moot. It was volume that had to be regulated. No more than point three cubic meters of baggage per person. It wasn't easy to fit one's entire life into a single bag.

Comisa was doubly burdened by the small life growing inside her. Their two previous children had succumbed to the *syndrome*, as had Frader's brother Tella, his last remaining family member. This pregnancy was probably the Manerets' last chance at a family.

"Next group."

The guard at the gate waved them through after giving them a quick once-over. He was watching for anything overtly threatening. The scanners within the screening post would be much more thorough, of course, but better too much security than not enough. The first section consisted of blood draws and breath tests. These went relatively quickly. Out of necessity, the technology had improved immeasurably in the last few months. It was a simple matter of running the samples through the machine and waiting for the *approved* or *not approved*.

Being a medical practitioner herself, Comisa wondered how many would make it through this test on a false negative or be rejected by a false positive. Sadly, many applicants had waited in line all day only to be turned away immediately. Their dazed look of disbelief as they slowly shuffled back out the gate to face the end of days was heartbreaking.

Now the rigamarole really started. Once the medical tests were complete, Frader and Comisa had their identities and backgrounds checked, their belongings searched and catalogued for inventory, and any contraband items confiscated. Any *vorennium* found among the refugees, whether they were accepted or not, was of course immediately seized. The precious material, no matter how small the amount, was simply too vital to the mission. Comisa had a small recharging servo in her bag powered by a tiny purple pellet of vorennium that she was required to surrender immediately. She sighed and handed it over. The charger had been a gift from her parents upon entering medical school. Weapons were allowed on board, but had to be locked up until journey's end, at which time they would be returned. The screening process took about an hour and a half, but at last they were classified as accepted.

The last few meters of their foot journey began as they were guided up the boarding ramp and into their assigned shuttle. The rest of the trip would be measured in light-years rather than footsteps. A high-pitched whine sounded as another craft closed up its hatches and lifted off to eventually enter the great spherical Arkship orbiting like a second moon above their disease-ravaged world of Casal. Soon their shuttle would also be full and the Manerets would begin the next phase of their lives.

Project Arkship began over five years ago when the syndrome was finally accepted as fact and inevitable. Every resource on the planet and every remaining supply of vorennium was dedicated to the task of transporting the maximum number of colonists, livestock, and supplies possible. Construction was at last complete, or at least enough to launch. Many of the finishing details would take place during the eight-year journey out of the Sling gate.

A scouting and return trip was not possible. The massive Sling could only produce the *vortunnel* from the home system and the vorennium engine core of the Arkship would keep it open for the entire eight-year trip. That was the hope of the ship's designers, anyway. The meteoritic ore that had powered and transformed Ma Kahy civilization for over a century was running out.

The newly discovered exoplanets had been christened Segonallar Major and Minor. Little was known about their hopeful new home, other than what the observatories could record. A twinned pair of bodies within the life zone and the spectrograph indicating the necessary liquids and gases on both. But it was a one-way and one-time trip. If you went through the Sling, you stayed where it sent you. It didn't matter anyway. There was no other known place to go.

PART I: THE CRATER

CHAPTER 1

Today – Vinday, Awan 31-21876

Foxx wandered the halls of the Crystal Palace. Actually, he was taking the long way through the casino and exhibition rooms because there were more hot women to look at on that route. Aside from that reason, he really didn't need to wander. Foxx knew right where to look for Tresado. Anyone with a nose knew where to find him. The noxious fumes, reminiscent of burnt dung beetles and ammonia, rolled up from the lower levels. The complaints started coming in when the fabulous entrance lobby to the fabulous Crystal Palace got downright foggy. Earlier, the steward of the Palace, Jakundarana Slivershkanent Trystelliar herself, or *Jakki*, had asked Fox to please rein in his friend.

"*Now hon,*" she had said with her usual gum-chewing grimaces, "ordinarily, it would be a four-hundred *dauric* charge to use the Magic Lab, but a deal is a deal. We made the agreement that you're all welcome to use any facilities you want for free while you're here, but . . . *damn!* I mean, *you do smell that, right?*"

Foxx was at his most charming as he explained the situation. Tresado, he said, was diligently working on a Magical experiment that he needed to finish before the three weeks of their free stay ran out in a couple of days. The story was embellished by plenty of histrionic gestures which Foxx had learned during his time with Professor Generax's Traveling World of Wonders combined with a healthy dose of *The Knowing Spell*. It was a self-taught invention of Foxx's.

In his younger days, his goal of being trained in Magic to become more persuasive and intuitive was rejected by one sage after another. No one had wanted to accept the young Macai into a training school, because it seemed they all possessed those damned *ethics!* They all refused him on the grounds that he sought Magical ability to use nefariously. All these sages apparently saw him as a cheap flim-flam Macai who only wanted to cheat and steal. Finally, to combat this prejudice,

Foxx was forced in desperation to abscond with several text books from old Sage Marison. That showed 'em.

It took years, but the young Foxx managed to comprehend the books and study Magic without formal training. He eventually was able to teach himself his own style, which he christened *The Knowing Spell*. It was a combination of Influential and Intuitive Magic with a dash of Foxx's natural charm. In essence, he could convince a guy that his own feet were purple if he wanted. Mostly though, he used the spell to read the emotions and needs of whomever he was dealing with. It worked wonders playing cards.

But Jakki was an extremely powerful Magician and saw right through his BS.

"All right, all right. Just get him to contain those fumes, *please!* One of the fan dancers just puked during her act. Kind of puts off the customers, you know?"

The oily streams of aerial funk led Foxx below the ground level to the Magical research laboratories, where Tresado had locked himself in for the past five days.

BANG, BANG, BANG!

"Tresado, what are you doing in there?"

Tresado was an Eryndi, an ancient race on this world of Lurra. Eryndi were generally a handsome species with their long, pointed chins and cone-shaped ears. They also tended to be very sensitive to the environment around them, always knowing which way they were facing and what the weather was about to do. All Eryndi were nimble, fast, and athletic, except Tresado. His pudgy middle, flabby muscles, and general lack of coordination made him an exception. This mattered little to him, though. Tresado was a Magician, and a damn good one.

His particular specialty was kinetic energy. While he

could scarcely lift a child over his head using his arms, Tresado could Magically levitate a *lumba* up a hundred-reach cliff. This was actually unusual for an Eryndi. Most Magicians of his race practiced the nature-based *Worldly Magic*. It was a non-invasive, passive way to utilize the ever-present Magic in the air. Most Eryndi, with their deep connection to their world, are a spiritual, conservative people and their Magicians tend to be healers or shamans.

Not so with Tresado. He practiced the more direct and powerful *Absolute Magic*. While a *Worldly* Magician would produce fire by politely edging cold out of the way and allowing the flame to ignite, an *Absolute* practitioner could pull the power of flame directly from Magic itself. It was a matter of great debate as to which was more ethical.

BANG, BANG, BANG!

"TRESADO! Open up, man!"

The initial response Foxx got from the locked blue crystal door in front of him was some muffled shuffling sounds followed by a loud thud.

"OW! Gods flunk it! Just wait a beat, I'm coming."

There were more sounds of sliding and shuffling and stifled curses before the door opened slightly. An oily, grey-green cloud of vapor rolled out of the crack followed by Tresado's right eye. After an initial check to make sure it was only his friend Foxx, Tresado opened up the rest of the way.

"What? I'm busy!"

"Just wanted to . . . *oh, shit the bed! What IS that SMELL?"* Foxx held a hand over his nose after getting a full-strength whiff.

"Just working on a project," said Tresado, who smelled much like the cloud.

Foxx tried to peer past Tresado, who kept the door carefully blocked. Even so, he caught quick glimpses of bubbling glassware and a transmutation furnace in operation.

"Did you need something?" snapped Tresado.

"I am here to deliver an important message, My Liege," intoned Foxx in a sarcastic baritone. "It seems there is a small problem that management has taken issue with."

"He means you're stinkin' up the whole friggin' place with your mumbo jumbo crap!"

Two women stood down the hall. The taller was the one who spoke. Her name was Serena. Her fined-toned, muscular frame was complemented by the mane of blond hair that was combed about as much as it ever would be. Her eyes were a deep lapis color and were at the moment flaring in anger. The most striking feature about her was the impressive diamond that was imbedded in her sternum. Serena's blue leather jerkin was custom designed to complement the jewel, resulting in an equally impressive display of cleavage. A wicked-looking, curved sword of fine layered steel swung at her left hip, completing the ensemble.

"You *Absolutes* with your evil potions. What you need is a good herbal enema to clean out your brain."

That witticism came from Orchid. She was a Macai, as were Foxx and Serena and most other people. In fact, in these parts, Macai outnumber Eryndi by four or five times. Although most Macai are much huskier and stronger than Eryndi, Orchid was a small woman. Her chocolate-brown hair and bright green eyes were all that could be seen of her face, because both tiny hands were clamped over her nose and mouth. In the crook of her arm was an ornate, carved wooden staff. The head of it flared with sparks and Magical green rays of light . . . unpleasantly green.

"Eww."

"Yuck."

"It's coming from down here."

The approaching voices and footsteps were coming down the staircase. Tresado swung the door open wide and hurriedly motioned his companions in.

"All right, get in here quick, before every spelljumper in the place beats you to it. *C'mon!*"

Foxx, Orchid, and Serena held their noses and hurried through the door. Tresado quickly closed and locked it behind them. The source of the putrid fumes was the transmutation furnace at the other end of the room. They were leaking out from around the closed metallic door. The little window in the center was glowing with Magical luminescence.

"What are you doing? Making some kind of gas weapon?" asked a watery-eyed Orchid.

"Hell, that ain't so hard—a little cabbage, some goat cheese—but I don't have the range you're getting," said Serena. "Did you know you can smell that up on the fifth floor? Your stink even drove out the dragon."

"Oh please! It can't be that bad."

"Tresado," said Orchid, "there's an angry mob gathering out there. They don't have torches and pitchforks yet, but we thought we should come down here and tell you anyway."

"Tell them not to worry," said Tresado while looking at the hourglass near the furnace. "I'm almost finished. In fact, there, it's done. Time to take the goodies out of the oven."

Tresado donned a pair of heavy gloves and opened the furnace door. A final cloud of noxious vapor spewed out into the room, almost gagging Orchid. The Magical glow had run its course as planned and was just fading away. The finished product sat bubbling in a ceramic crucible. Tresado picked up a set of tongs and transferred his experiment to a cooling rack.

"Let me ask you again," Foxx said patiently, "just what are you doing?"

Tresado's face lit up with excitement. It even showed through the layers of grime.

"You remember when we first arrived here? How those people's carriages and horses *disappeared?*"

"You said that was some kind of teleportation spell," Orchid replied.

"It was," said Tresado. "I found out later that they were sent to some stables where the animals were groomed and fed and the carriages cleaned up. It's a service the Palace provides."

"I think that's the same spell the Palace used on cheaters," said Foxx. "I saw that woman in the casino vanish after she tried the old double shuffle in a card game. They said that cheaters are sent away to some no-man's land as punishment."

"But the Palace doesn't do that anymore. Now that it got all warm and fuzzy and lovey-dovey from my diamond spirit, it's more tolerant of douchebags," replied Serena.

"But that spell still exists," said Tresado with a greedy look in his eye. "And I'm going to find out how to do it."

"Why don't you just ask Jakki?" inquired Orchid. "She can do it. She blipped in and out of the fight cage before Serena's bout."

"I did ask her. She wouldn't tell me. 'A girl's got to have *some* secrets,' that's what she said."

"What does all this have to do with your stink factory?" demanded Serena.

"Okay, but you guys have to promise not to talk about this to anyone, especially not to those stickfish Magicians out there.

Teleportation is a powerful and dangerous spell. It shouldn't be available to just any third-rate spellcaster."

"Which is why Jakki wouldn't tell *you,*" smirked Orchid.

"Har-dee-har. Now this compound I'm preparing should be able to break down the ephemeral buffer layer and expose the coding. Then an erudition spell can absorb and map the pathways. All I have to do then is let Magic reprocess the . . ."

"*Great Blood-Dripping Gods!*" exclaimed Serena. "You and your gobbledygook! Can't you just wave your little fairy wand, or something?"

"I don't have a little fairy wand," said Tresado defensively. "Besides, you know that's not how Magic works. You summon it with your mind."

"And what do you do with the *goo?*" asked Orchid.

"The Palace is essentially grown out of one big crystal. Any surface at all should be interconnected through and through, I should think."

Orchid's eyebrows shot up. "You're trying to gain access to the Magic in the Palace, aren't you?"

"It's gotta be in there somewhere." Tresado looked downright maniacal for a half-beat.

"So, what, you're going to splash this stuff onto your bathroom mirror or something and then ask the Palace to please give up its secrets?" asked Foxx.

"No, it'll be a controlled experiment. I'll start with small amounts first and check their efficacy," explained Tresado. "I'm a professional Magician, not some two-bit carny trickster like some people I know."

Orchid looked very skeptical. "I don't know. This is making my hackles stand up."

"You say that about all Absolute Magic," scoffed Tresado. "I think you're just scared of it."

"Because Absolute Magic *is* scary," she returned. "It's unstable, unpredictable, and . . . *unacceptable.*"

"Weiner."

"Prickweed."

Foxx stepped in, as usual. "Children, don't make me separate you two. Don't forget, the Palace uses both kinds of Magic — *Worldly* to grow the fruit trees and tame the pet razor lions and *Absolute* to run the lift platforms and all the lights. If a big piece of blue crystal can learn to accept both kinds, I'm sure you can too."

"Okay."

"I suppose."

This was an old argument between them. But as usual, Foxx had squeezed out a bit of his *Knowing Spell* when calming the two continual combatants. Tresado and Orchid were not even aware that they were being manipulated into a truce.

"It's okay," said Tresado confidently. He picked up the rapidly cooling mixture in his gloved hands.

"I've studied the composition of the Palace's crystalline structure. It's very complex and sophisticated, but that makes the variables easier to measure. This formula is correct. I just don't know what potency and amount I need to make this work. But I will, and then I'll be able to reverse engineer the spell and learn to teleport myself or anything wherever I want."

Foxx licked his lips. "Imagine the possibilities — being able to just *appear* inside someone's treasure coffers . . . or someone's boudoir, for that matter."

"How noble," said Serena. "Tresado, you just be careful with that crap. You said yourself you don't know what it can do."

"Relax," grinned Tresado. "Nothing is going to go wrong."

At that moment, the locked door was kicked in with a loud crash.

"Here it is."

"What the hell is going on in here?"

The annoyed mob of gamblers and partiers, who had had their gambling and partying disrupted by the horrid fumes, burst into the room. Tresado, easily startled, shrieked like his ten-year-old great-niece and instinctively threw up his hands. The ceramic crucible he was holding tumbled to Group Six's collective feet and shattered, spreading the noxious compound onto the crystal floor.

A familiar, bluish glow emanated from the far wall. They had all seen it before, like last month, when Serena had been teleported out of the fight cage for cheating, or so the Palace thought. A moment later, the light coalesced into a broad beam and enveloped the four. Then there was a bright flash and Group Six was gone.

* * *

Tresado – "Relax, nothing is going to go wrong."

- Orchid's 'List of Stupid Things
People Have Said'

About five hours later – The Crystal Palace

Sparkly knew not to enter the Steward's sanctum when the large double doors glowed blue. It meant that the boss was deep in some kind of Magical act, but this was important. He hesitantly reached for his seashell *converser* to call Jakki, but before he could use it, the glow suddenly ceased and the doors swung open on their own.

Jakki's normally jovial face was filled with concern.

"There's something wrong."

"Yes, Ma'am," answered Sparkly. "The customers have left the gaming tables and the floor shows. They've mostly headed to their rooms or the bar, which is now full. They seem depressed and glum. And worse than that, *they're not spending money!*"

Jakki nodded as though this explained a lot.

"Mmm-hmm."

"What do you think it means, Boss?"

Jakki looked about her at the walls and ceiling.

"The Palace is sad."

CHAPTER 2

Meanwhile, 950 leagues to the southeast

Tresado's school was in ruins. The ancient stone walls lay crumbled in huge piles while flames licked up between them, consuming what remained of the wooden desks and the books of the great library where he had spent so many difficult hours poring over his lessons.

A piercing scream cut through the acrid smoke. Jokalar, one of his classmates, staggered out of the rubble. The silky material of his athletic jersey had melted to his skin. His once long, lustrous hair was gone and only a charcoaled scalp remained. His blackened lips opened for a final scream that never came. Jokalar was dead before his body collapsed onto the ground.

Tresado grinned broadly at the sight. He felt immense satisfaction at the idea that *he* had caused this. This whole incident was *his* doing . . . and he would do it again. He *longed* to do it again.

Something tickled his face. He reached up to brush it away and found his hand in the painful grip of a fist-sized beetle. The thing had its large mandibles clamped onto his thumb and was chewing away. Tresado yelped and flung the beetle away in disgust. He sat bolt upright, slowly recovering from the pain of the bite and also from the strange, disturbing dream. He looked around. The first thing he saw was the beetle scuttling away. The second thing was nothing as far as the eye could see. Nothing but sand and rocks. His memory slowly returned. The last thing he could recall was the Magic lab in the Crystal Palace, along with . . .

Shaking his head to clear the cobwebs out, Tresado stood on unsteady feet and looked desperately around for his friends.

There, by that big rock.

A patch of blue caught his eye. As soon as he could make his feet work again, Tresado scurried over. It was Serena. The shield maiden was lying on her stomach, her open mouth half-full of sand. Tresado quickly gripped her by the shoulder and turned her over. Just as quickly, her fist swung around and caught Tresado on the side of his pointed chin. He stumbled back onto his plump ass and dazedly looked at her.

"Ow."

"What in Crodan's name is going on?" she demanded, while leaping unsteadily to her feet. Her hand was on her sword hilt, a natural reaction.

"You're all right, I take it," Tresado winced, rubbing his chin.

Serena crouched defensively and looked around her.

"What did you do? *What did you do!*"

"It . . . I think . . . it wasn't . . . *nothing!* I didn't do this. *The Palace! It was the Palace!*"

"The Palace. Where *is* the Palace? *And where the hell are we? Talk!*"

"Habba, habba, habba . . ."

"You babbling idiot!" fumed Serena. She balled her fists menacingly.

A hot breeze, kicking up dust devils, rolled in from the north across the barren landscape and brought something bright red with it. Tresado and Serena immediately recognized the garish, feathered hat as belonging to Foxx.

Serena shaded her eyes against the dust. "It came from that direction. Let's go."

She started walking, but Tresado stopped her. "Wait a beat. Let me take a look."

He concentrated on a simple levitation spell, one he had done a thousand times. It was designed to form an invisible harness about his chubby Eryndi body and gently lift him to altitude. That was not the effect, however. When his spell took hold, Tresado found himself launched into the air as though he had been on a springboard. Were it not for the thin suspenders under his shirt, his pants would have stayed on the ground. His stomach didn't quite keep up with him though. It took him a moment to stabilize his levitation (and his nausea) and then look around. Far off to the north, he spotted movement. It only lasted a moment.

But wait. Is that north?

The power of Magic was coursing through his body, giving Tresado a tremendous and giddy sense of invulnerability and confidence, except for the fact that his Eryndi connection to the natural world seemed . . . off. He shook off the feeling and concentrated again on the fleeting movement.

Whatever it was, it disappeared behind a rock outcropping. As he hovered over the barren landscape, Tresado began to realize the trouble they were in. There was nothing but wilderness in all directions. Far to what he vaguely thought was southwest he could see the silhouette of a mountain range.

Tresado felt strangely good. There was a powerful potential all around him.

Power to be used. Power to achieve what he wanted. Power to . . .

Tresado snapped his focus back to the problem at hand. His other two friends were still unaccounted for. He lowered himself back to the surface where Serena waited.

"I saw something about a league to the north," he said, pointing.

Serena squinted around. "How do you know that's north? With all this cloud cover I can't see the sun."

"I'm an Eryndi," said Tresado, puffing out his chest. It was a good act, but privately, he just wasn't sure.

Today – The Crystal Palace

"Milady, could this be it?"

Jakki looked up from the set of blue crystals on her desk. "Send it over, hon," she said with a pop of her gum.

Arnega, one of her Principal Casters, who were all studying similar crystals, released his viewing spell and transferred it over to her. Jakki Magically connected to the fabric of the Palace via her crystals and nodded at the results.

"That's it, all right. It seems that the Palace's teleportation spell was activated about six hours ago, right about the time the witnesses reported seeing Group Six disappear."

"I thought the Palace wouldn't use the punishment spell anymore," said Arnega.

"It didn't, hon. The spell was activated by an outside source. That means I have a job for all of you."

Jakki paused and looked at the confused faces of her staff.

"Since the Palace joined with the Spirit of Love, it now is under the influence of emotions the same as any of us. These new distractions caused it to drop its guard, as it were. Someone, and I assume it was Tresado, managed to access the teleportation spell contained within. The Palace didn't cast the spell of its own volition, but now feels responsible. That's why the sadness and remorse it's feeling are being transmitted to the guests."

Jakki put in a fresh stick of gum.

"I want you folks to work on installing security spells around all of the Palace's stored spells. This can't happen again."

"What about the people it sent away?"

Pop went her gum.

"We can't bring them back because we can't Magically acquire them from this end," Jakki sighed. "The only thing we can do is to send supplies to the same location and hope they're smart enough to remain in one place."

Today – the desert

"Let's head in that direction and hope we run into them," suggested Tresado.

"Gee, why didn't I think of that?"

After about fifteen minutes of walking, Tresado and Serena arrived at the rock outcropping where he had spotted movement. There was no sign of Foxx or Orchid, but there were some kind of tracks in the dust.

"I don't see any footprints," said Tresado.

Serena knelt and examined the ground.

"At least not any people prints. Whatever made these marks was like nothing I've ever seen. It looks like . . . I don't know *what* it looks like!"

"Like *that,* maybe," said Tresado, pointing.

They almost didn't see it. The creature blended in with the yellow boulder so completely as to appear to be a part of the rock itself. Its armored body looked like an overturned bowl nearly a full reach wide. The edges were ringed with seven stubby, spearpoint-shaped. . . legs, maybe? Whatever they were, they seemed to grip the top of the boulder.

Instinctively, Serena quickly rose to a crouch and her right hand went to her sword hilt. The thing on the rock wiggled for a moment in response to her movement.

"At least we know it's alive," whispered Tresado.

At his words, the thing's pointed feet started scratching across the rock surface like paddles. The creature slid itself down the side of the boulder and flopped onto the sand. It began slowly crawling away from the two uncertain bipeds.

"Well, it's as ugly as a pimple on a pig's ass, but it doesn't seem dangerous," observed Serena.

Right about then, the walking soup bowl stopped.

"It must have heard you."

Serena slowly drew her sword. "I got an apology right here, if it wants."

The creature again lifted itself on its stubby, pointed feet and crawled away another reach or so. The central body then lowered itself into the sand and raised one of its appendages, pointing it at Tresado. A yellowish glow emanated from the shell. There was a flash of light as a powerful bolt of energy erupted from the thing's foot and struck Tresado on his ample belly. He was enveloped by a shocking, painful ring of pure Magic. Tresado went to his knees, his mouth open in an agonizing silent scream.

Before the glow had even left Tresado's crumpled body, the creature spun its bowl body around and drew a bead on Serena. But as fast as the thing was, Serena was faster. By the time the second Magic bolt was fired, she was already recovering from the somersault that got her out of harm's way. She leapt to her feet and sprinted to Tresado's side. He was laboriously trying to get to his feet, but not making much progress. Serena grabbed the Eryndi by the collar and dragged him behind a large rock for protection.

"It . . . it was . . . ouch!"

Tresado's limbs had stopped twitching from the shock and the color started returning to his cheeks.

"Take it easy for a beat and get your wits back, or at least the half that you use."

Serena took a quick peek over the top of the rock to see what the thing was doing. It hadn't moved, but had burrowed itself deeper into the sand. The shell started glowing again, this time taking its time and getting brighter. One of its feet started to rise.

"C'mon, we've got to move. *NOW!*"

Serena grabbed Tresado again and pulled him out from behind the rock. The two of them retreated to their left just as the boulder exploded with a loud *kaboom*. A small piece of rock shrapnel grazed Serena's butt as they ran.

"Keep moving in that direction!"

Serena pushed the still woozy Tresado away. He stumbled for a few steps and then turned defiantly, trying to gather Magic into his mind for an attack of his own. He felt very powerful, but was still having a hard time concentrating.

"Tresado, get to cover!" Serena shouted.

"Get behind me! I can handle this!"

He stood there, drunkenly weaving, but not casting any spell.

"You moron!"

Serena sprinted toward the creature to try to prevent another attack, but arrived a beat too late. Another bolt of energy burst from one of its feet and bulls-eyed Tresado again. He went down without another sound.

The Northlands warrior launched herself into a somersault and alighted on top of the thing's bowl-shaped shell, sword swinging even before she landed. The fine, layered steel in her scimitar bit only slightly into the creature's body, leaving a shallow groove. This thing was hard. Her arm rang with the impact. It was as though she had struck the stone itself. She tried another blow along the edge where the 'feet' attached, but found it just as dense.

She reversed her grip and tried to jam her sword point underneath the rim, but the creature spun its shell around so quickly that Serena was flung off. She twisted in the air and landed in a crouch, staring face to no-face with her foe. It immediately began to retreat. Serena followed, easily keeping up with the thing and staying close. She realized from this and earlier behavior what it was doing. It needed a bit of distance before launching its Magic bolts. Maybe it didn't want to blow itself up with its own weapon.

The thing tried crawling toward the unmoving Tresado, but Serena was able to keep it away by just staying in front of it—not that this monster had a 'front'—always blocking its path. After a minute or two of this play, it finally stopped as though considering its options. It then scuttled surprisingly quickly away and disappeared behind another outcropping.

Serena ran over to Tresado. He was still unmoving. She

squatted down and carefully turned him over to check for life signs. His face and hands were blistered in places, but his eyelids still fluttered. She raised him up to a seated position. With those blisters, Serena didn't want to slap him to bring him around, so she just gripped him by the shoulders and shook him.

"Tresado. *Tresado!* Come on, wake up. Wake up, you pain in the ass, you friggin' Ernie! Give me a sign, here."

"*HOORRRKK!*"

Tresado's stomach contents were the remains of his breakfast of asparagus in snail sauce that he had eaten in the Crystal Palace this morning. The color scheme didn't really match the blue shade of Serena's jerkin.

"*Gods' Crap!*"

Serena jumped up in disgust, releasing Tresado. He flopped back down, his head missing a sharp rock by only a couple of fingers.

Serena stared down furiously at herself. Tresado's vomit was dripping down the deep V-neck of her jerkin, obscuring the fabulous diamond implanted in her sternum.

"*You bumhole! WHAT THE HELL IS WRONG WITH YOU?*"

Tresado looked blearily at the tall, blonde woman he had once insanely loved. Did he really just puke on her?

"What happened?"

"You just yakked all over me, *that's what happened!*"

"Wait a minute. Where's . . . ?" Tresado looked quickly around as his memory returned. "Where's that *thing?*"

"It took off."

Serena focused her most intimidating stare at Tresado.

"Now, turn around."

His open mouth indicated that Tresado did not understand.

"You heard me. Turn around. And if I catch you peeking, you'll curse your mother for not smothering you as a whelp."

Tresado still looked confused until his eyes took a habitual glance at Serena's cleavage and noticed its drippy condition.

"Oh man! I'm so sorry. Here, let me help with . . ." His step forward caused Serena's sword tip to be leveled about neck high.

"You'll help with nothing." Serena's tone became deadly calm. "Now, you step over there, and turn around! *Understand?*"

Tresado knew when his life was on the line, so he quietly complied. From behind him, he heard the swishing noises of clothing and skin being wiped clean. The mental image of what was going on back there was steadily overwhelming his control. The urge to turn around pecked at him like a raven with a dead rabbit.

Oh man, he thought. *She's probably dropped her top by now. I bet she's too occupied with cleaning herself up. She won't notice if I take a quick peek. Why shouldn't I get to look? I saved her life on more than one occasion. Who does she think she's dealing with, anyway? She doesn't realize just who I am . . . and what I can do. I have the POWER to do . . .*

His head began to swivel ever so slightly.

"Ah-ah. Another turn of that Ernie chin and you'll be able to carry it in your hip pocket."

"Serena, I just wanted to say something." He kept his back turned and pulled himself together. His recent disturbing thoughts were really . . . *disturbing.*

"I wanted to say thanks. I saw the way you charged at that

thing and that was the last thing I remember. What happened? Did I get hit again? How did you get rid of it?"

"I told it how greasy and nasty-tasting Eryndi are."

"Ah. Well anyway, thanks."

"Shut up. All right, you can turn around now."

Serena shaded her eyes and looked toward a distant glow on the horizon. "It's gonna be dark soon. We better keep looking for Orchid and Foxx. And," Serena's features softened for half a beat, "*you're welcome*. But if you ever puke on me again, I'll . . ."

"Gotcha. Puke bad." Tresado also looked in the direction of Sensang as it neared the western horizon. The sun was only visible as a dim glow behind the heavy cloud cover.

"That's funny."

"What?"

"The sun seems to be setting way too early. I'm pretty sure it's only about four in the aftermidday. At least that's what it feels like to me."

Serena squinted. "Are you sure? I think we were out for a little while after we got here."

"No more than an hour," Tresado said, suddenly testy. "I know what I'm talking about."

Serena was in no mood to argue.

"Fine, whatever. We've still got some daylight left. We'll just keep following the wind. It hasn't shifted at all and this stupid hat had to come from somewhere. Now let's get moving before that rock crawler thing comes back."

"Yeah, okay." Tresado fell in behind Serena as they set off. "That thing was fascinating, though. Internal generation . . . or maybe channeling."

"Say what?"

"It used Magic as a weapon, but it didn't coalesce it from the environment the way I do. Those energy bolts came directly from the creature's body. It stored Magic and then released it on command. That's impressive!"

"Glad *you're* so impressed."

Serena had suddenly come to a halt, the tip of her sword tracking back and forth. Ten of those weird, yellowish rock crawler things surrounded them, and they were moving into position at the optimal firing distance.

CHAPTER 3

The same area, not quite 50,000 years ago

Jalex moved stealthily, subconsciously noting the wind direction and sun position. She also kept a wary eye on her own back, in case something was stalking *her* just as she was after the young grassbuck. She gripped the handle of her arrow stick loosely as her quarry emerged from behind the stand of trees. Its soft wide eyes and quivering nostrils scanned the neighborhood for danger. Jalex froze and held her breath. She was mostly concealed by the tall prairie grass, but any movement would betray her position and the deer would flee.

There.

The timid creature turned its head away, intent on munching the bark off a bush. Jalex tensed her muscles and readied herself. She would have to rise up and cast her arrow in one movement. Any wasted time would be that many heartbeats for the deer to escape.

Suddenly, the grassbuck raised its head in alarm. Jalex sensed it a moment later. It started as a kind of rumbling vibration that she felt deep in her bones. The deer sprang back into the trees, ruining the prospect of dinner. A flicker of light and movement caught her eye. In the sky to the southwest was a fearful sight. A ball of light, trailing streamers of flame and a great, gray cloud, was slowly descending toward the horizon. It was as though Sen Herself was falling out of the sky. Jalex counted nearly two hands' worth of heartbeats before the flaming object disappeared behind the distant hills. A moment later there was a brilliant flash of light that left spots before her eyes. Then, an ominous white glowing dome appeared and slowly grew until taking up nearly half the sky.

That was enough for Jalex. She felt an urgent need to get far away from this strange event. She turned to the north and started on a run for home. Her village lay behind Sentinel Hill, an immense slanted upheaval of rock. It wasn't far, so she sprinted the whole way. Jalex didn't worry about the predator-filled countryside she had to cross. She caught sight of a fleeing pride of spearcats that were just as intent as she was to get away from that light. They were not interested in hunting.

Jalex ran around the east side of the hill. The village was in sight just ahead. Suddenly she heard the fast-approaching roar of a huge storm. This prairie terrain where she lived had seen its share of windstorms, but nothing like this. It hit with the impact of a stampeding herd of lum. The wall of wind swept over Sentinel Hill carrying debris with it. Uprooted trees and thick clouds of dust and rocks careened across the landscape causing destruction. Jalex flung herself to the ground and covered her head. The rushing wind tore at her hair and hide wrap. When it calmed, Jalex picked herself out of the sandy powder that half buried her, shaking herself like a young lioness to get rid of the dust layer.

Fortunately for her and her village, the slant of the hill deflected most of the shock wave that raced across the land. Even so, many of the dried mud dwellings were either destroyed or covered with a choking dust, and the pitiable sounds of crying victims emanated from the village.

Today – the desert

A sword, no matter how well forged, is pretty inadequate against rock-hard crawly things that fire bolts of energy at you. Nonetheless, Serena stood poised and ready. Her warrior's training quickly assessed her enemies.

Fortunately, the creatures didn't seem to be working together. There were simply a bunch of them and they were all starting to glow hungrily. When the first one launched its attack, Serena was no longer there. As she had learned, she could do nothing to harm these things. But their weakness was that they had to be a certain distance away to attack. All she had to do was to keep moving.

Serena leapt about like a mountain grilk, avoiding the deadly bolts of Magical energy that the creatures fired. She did well for a short time, until three or four of the crawlers fired at once. Despite her agility, Serena couldn't avoid them all. The last bolt impacted on the steel blade of her raised scimitar, knocking the weapon out of her hand and numbing her entire arm.

Serena dropped to her knees half stunned, as several crawlers converged on her and prepared to fire. She tried to struggle to her feet and focus on the crawlers, but her head and vision were swimming in a swirling mist of befuddlement. Several crawlers glowed ominously and released their bolts at once. Serena winced in anticipation of death, but it never came. A half-reach from her face, the deadly energy splashed against an invisible wall. More Magical attacks came from behind, but also never reached her. She looked about for a reason. Tresado stood behind her, tendrils of Magical energy playing about his body. His Eryndi face was grim with concentration as he focused on maintaining the Magical shield erected around himself and Serena. The crawlers had by now surrounded them both and were launching a relentless assault. The bolts of Magical mayhem exploded against the ethereal dome with massive bursts of light and sparks.

Stray filaments of light bounced off his shield at weird angles. One of the creatures was struck by another's reflected bolt and hurled against nearby rocks. Its hard shell fractured, exposing the soft, chewy insides. The nearest ones immediately abandoned their attacks and pounced on this sudden ready-made meal. Apparently, rock crawlers aren't fiercely respectful of their own species.

Serena was certainly no expert, but she had seen enough of Tresado's Magic over the past few weeks to know what he was capable of. The amount of power he was calling down from the heavens was unbelievable. Her little hairs were standing up from the energy around her. But Tresado was weakening. Beads of sweat shone on his forehead from the exertion. And things were only getting worse. Apparently, the dinner bell had been rung. Dozens and dozens of the crawlers were approaching or burrowing their way out of the sand to join in the attack. Tresado couldn't hold out much longer and his invisible shield started to sputter and fail.

When over a dozen creatures fired simultaneously, it was too much for Tresado to maintain. The shield collapsed and he fell to his knees, his head pounding with the feedback of conflicting Magical energies.

Serena stumbled over to Tresado and helped him to his

feet. They stood together and peered into each other's eyes. Tresado's were foggy. Serena's were full of fury.

"I'll be damned if I'm going to die from a bunch of stupid rock things!"

She growled furiously and spun about to face her attackers. If necessary she was ready to wrestle them to death. As if reflecting her furious mood, the sky darkened with gathering clouds.

"Serena, get out of here. Run!" shouted Tresado.

Apparently sensing their vulnerability, the crawlers raised their weird foot things and prepared for the final assault before dinner time. The gathering clouds cast a dark shadow across the barren landscape. Surrounded with no place to retreat, Serena roared defiantly, inviting a face-to-face reckoning with Crodan, her Northlands god. Before the fateful moment, however, a furious volley of lightning bolts rained out of the sky, striking the crawlers. Shells cracked like porcelain dishes and foot appendages spun across the desert sands. The intense electrical discharges continued to pour from the heavens until the last of the crawlers were nothing but shards of debris with bits of red goo clinging to them.

"Are you two all right?"

The voice came from above. A swirling dust devil spun on its axis, supporting the slight but magnificent figure of Orchid, who hovered over their heads. The angry storm clouds rotated about her, rumbling with potential energy and obeying her every whim.

A pair of eyes appeared slowly from behind a nearby rock formation. Foxx carefully emerged from cover and looked about at the carnage.

"Can I have my hat back?"

* * *

- Trianna of Sylvas,
Poetess to the Glades

Not quite 50,000 years ago

The last of the dead had finally been buried, their faces to the ground as Ern tradition demanded. Jalex's arms ached from the constant exertion. There was still much to be done in the village. The sick and wounded needed tending and shelters had to be rebuilt or repaired. But there were precious few able-bodied people to perform these tasks. Most of the hunters had been afield when the sun fell from the sky five days earlier. Jalex was the only one who had returned.

Food and water were growing short. Parties would have to go out soon, but the terrible storm that swept across the land was not finished. Violent, spinning furies of stinging debris capered across what was once green prairie. The grass, buried under the thick dust, was dying. If there was no grass, there would be no herds.

There was still day and night, but little difference between the two. The faithful blue sky had turned a dismal brown and the night lights were all gone, including Nyme, the moon. When it was dark, it was very dark. The only respite from that terrifying blackness was the violent dry lightning. Storms appeared without warning and eerily without rain, shattering the darkness with terrifying glimpses of reality. One night, a bolt lanced across the sky and momentarily illuminated the crouching figure of a huge clee-at. The furred horror was creeping up on the village, using its fine sense of smell to guide it in the blackness. The startled creature fled upon discovery, but the incident didn't calm any nerves. Old Glebal had theorized that, had it not been scared off, it would have come amongst the hearths, seized several poor Ern with its giant finger spines, carried them off to its burrow, and devoured them. That terrifying image was imprinted upon Jalex's brain like an after-flash of lightning.

The black nights, the dark days. Sen was gone from the sky. She had fallen to her death. Nyme and her brood must have fled. There was only the cold, brown sky in the day, the frightening blackness of the night, and the dust.

Jalex and her half-grown friend, Corma, were helping an older man to the common lodge. His dwelling had survived the initial great storm, but despite hasty repairs, had finally collapsed the night before on top of its occupant. It wasn't until morning that he was pulled from the debris with a broken leg. Corma went to fetch some water to clean the man's wound. Jalex noted the jagged bone splinter protruding from his shin. She knew what that meant. He would probably die from wound rot. At the very least, he would never walk again.

Corma returned with a moistened bit of pera leaf. It was all the water Chief Durat would spare. Jalex nodded in understanding and took the swab from Corma. She gently wiped away the dried blood and caked-on dust. The man squirmed in pain.

"Hold yourself still, Dren."

The old hunter was no stranger to discomfort and bore it stoically. The main cause for the tears in his eyes was his own knowledge of his condition.

"Leave me, Jalex. Tend to the others first, or better, release me to ground now."

"Do not speak those words, hunter. You only sound foolish," she replied gently.

"Listen to me, young one. The water is nearly gone. The food will follow upon its heels. I cannot hunt. I cannot dig roots or gather cherfa. You can. You must. Go, or more will die."

Ern were a practical people and Jalex knew old Dren was right. Another black night would soon be upon them, but tomorrow she vowed to brave the dust storms and venture out to forage. It must be done or the village would perish.

The next day, the small party of hunters struggled across the decimated landscape. Their first destination was the stream bed that had provided water for the village for longer than any Ern could remember. The once babbling brook was now a snaking trail of thick mud. Jalex and the others discovered that water could be obtained by laboriously digging a basin in the mud and allowing liquid to slowly seep into the hole. But it was a long, tedious process and the water retrieved was still thick with dissolved dust particles.

Three of the older villagers were left here to harvest as much of the precious water as possible. Jalex, Corma, and the remaining few hunters set out further afield to gather what they could. They all masked their noses and mouths with a strip of hide to keep out the choking dust. They could do nothing about their eyes, though. The stinging, blinding particles swirled about their faces. They headed out around the sheltering bulk of Sentinel Hill, which had shielded the village from total destruction. The devastation that greeted their dust-filled eyes was unbelievable. The patch of woods where, only a hand's worth of days ago, Jalex had hunted the grassbuck was nothing more than several twisted stumps. The great tree trunks had been ripped from the ground like fistfuls of dandelions.

Corma hooded his eyes with his hand and painfully peered to the southwest. An eerie glow emanated from the far horizon.

"There. That is She!"

"Who?"

"Sen. Did you not say you saw the sun fall from the sky, Jalex?"

"I said it *looked* like the sun fell. But how could that be?"

"Corma is right," offered Tru, one of the villagers. "Look to the sky. Sen is nowhere to be found. You said you saw Her fall and there she lay."

"Corma has but two hands and two fingers of seasons. He didn't see the strange light. I did."

"I saw also."

"And I."

The other villagers who had witnessed the event were of a mind.

"The light was round, as Sen was round," insisted Garen. "I saw Her burning flames and smoke. She is gone from the sky and now lies wounded."

Garen pointed to the glow on the horizon.

"We must find the sun and rescue Her!"

Today – the desert

Group Six was once again a group. The four of them related their adventures. Foxx, in his histrionic way, told of how he and Orchid had found themselves teleported onto a small hilltop, where they were almost immediately beset by a swarm of immense locusts. The insects were over twenty fingers in length and numbered in the many thousands. The two Macai would have been stripped of every morsel of meat on their bodies, had it not been for Orchid. She had called upon her Worldly Magical talents and simply told the toothy grasshoppers to go home and leave them alone.

It had been ridiculously easy for her. There had been practically no effort required on Orchid's part. She had never possessed such power as in this place. She felt as though she could command the sun and moon, which she just realized was a disturbing thought. Worldly Magicians did not command. Their use of Magic was passive and conservative. She humbly offered a silent apology to the universe, while at the same time, the urge to misuse this power nagged at the back of her mind.

Serena looked about her. The shadows were growing long.

"Okay, now that story time is over, we better find someplace to camp. It's going to be dark soon."

"There's nothing but sand and rocks for as far as the eye can see," said Foxx, looking around. "But let's at least get away from all these crawler guts."

Five minutes of walking and they came to a large rock outcropping that they could shelter next to. It was better than nothing. As they approached, several rock crawlers burrowed their way into the sand or squeezed into crevices.

"Look at them. Now they know who's boss around here," said Tresado, throwing out his unimpressive chest.

"My hero," scoffed Serena. "Those things are too stupid to be scared of us. I get the feeling they just don't like the dark."

"Well, let's make camp," said Foxx. "I don't know out of what, but we could at least pull some of those rocks around us for protection."

"I'll see if I can get us a little water," said Orchid in an odd voice.

She focused her psyche on the environment and once again found it easy to manipulate. Dark clouds, like the ones that she had summoned earlier, began to gather in her immediate neighborhood. Persuading what little water there was in the air to condense into rain was child's play. Moments later, a very localized drizzle began to fill up a natural cavity she had selected on top of one of the boulders.

Serena searched about for anything resembling food. There was no plant life of any kind anywhere in sight. Even though earlier they had all seen signs of lizards and insect life, now there was no trace of anything living. The fact that everything that crawls or flies had disappeared set her warrior's senses tingling.

Foxx was examining a strange, dark-colored patch of stuff partially coating a boulder. It was not rock, but seemed organic, somehow. It had a faint smell like that of naphtha. He pulled at it with all his strength and managed to break off a small slab of it.

"I don't know what this stuff is, but it might burn."

Getting no response, he looked up and saw Tresado not helping with any of the camp prep. Instead, the Eryndi was staring glassy-eyed at the landscape.

"Anything I can bring you, Your Highness?"

"What? Oh, sorry. Here, let me give you a hand."

Tresado's eyes narrowed as he focused on the task. A spectral glow of Magic rose up from the ground and formed itself into the shape of an enormous hand. It floated across the desert floor and began picking up the surrounding rocks as though they were pebbles. Using his own hand as a vicarious guide, Tresado moved his floating appendage over to the base of the outcropping and started arranging the stones into a perimeter fence.

Orchid and Foxx simultaneously whistled through their teeth at the impressive levitation Magic being displayed by Tresado. The floating hand accelerated. The boulders swam through the air like a swarm of gnats and arranged themselves into a cozy fire pit and protective wall, all mimicking the movements of his real hand. It then gathered a large pile of the stuff Foxx had discovered and stacked it in the hearth. When all was done, the hand dissipated into the air.

"Not bad," admitted Orchid, who normally loathed what she considered an obscene use of the power of Magic.

"Taught him everything he knows," smirked Foxx, who squatted next to the hearth. "Now Master, if you wouldn't mind lighting a fire."

"As you speak."

Tresado simply blinked. Organizing the power of Magic into a flame was one of the first and most elementary things one learned in the study of conjuring. The stack of tinder should have just gently ignited. Rather, an intense column of blazing flame leapt more than three reaches straight up from the kindling. Foxx tumbled back onto his butt and put his hand to his face.

"That was my eyebrow!"

* * *

Everyone searches for what they've never had, but true joy comes from finding something you thought you'd lost.

\- Hobo who lives under the
wharf at Yaneva (name unknown)

Not quite 50,000 years ago

It was many days before enough food and water could be gathered and stored away for the village. The herds had not been sighted since the storm. They had apparently fled or perished. Luckily the underground lair of the clee-at that had visited the village one night was located. Burning bundles of jamba bushes were placed at the entrance to the burrow and the giant carnivorous rodent was soon rendered stupid by the intoxicating fumes. Before it fully registered what was happening, the clee-at was butchered and the meat sent to the drying racks. It was tough and tasted awful, but it was food enough for the injured in the village and for the hunters to take upon an extended trip.

Jalex, Corma, Garen, and Tru set out two days later. Chief Durat would only allow these four to go on their foolish errand. All other able villagers were needed to continue the difficult process of surviving.

Despite the difficult traveling conditions, the hunting party made good time across the ravaged prairie. Usually hunters crept slowly along, watching for signs and predators. There was neither. Footprints did not last many beats in the fine dust on the ground. The swirling storm winds obliterated them as quickly as they were made. It was obvious there was very little to hunt. There was no fresh scat, no gnawed-on kills, no indication that anything still lived out here.

The strange glow was nearer, but the hills that the sun had disappeared behind were still not visible on the dust-filled horizon. Firewood was plentiful. The torn remains of trees lay scattered about, half buried. Each night, they made a blazing fire. It did little more than illuminate the party's immediate area. The blackness of the night and the moaning of the wind hovered beyond the reach of the firelight, whispering to the hunters of evil things.

Each morning, there was no sunrise. The sky would lighten to a pale brown, bringing no warmth or comfort to the hunters. Even their shadows had been stolen from them.

On the fourth day of travel, Jalex was taking her turn in the lead. She shielded her eyes from the dust and peered ahead. Something was there. A faint, jagged line of color hovered over the bleak horizon.

Mountains!

"Look there. I have been at least this far afield and have never seen mountains before."

Garen, the oldest amongst them, agreed.

"True. There have been naught but hills before Senfall."

"Are you sure?" Corma asked skeptically.

"I have hunted at their base. Herds of lum and saro were plentiful in my youth."

"Do mountains grow from hills?" asked Tru, the other woman in the party.

"Great spearcats grow from tiny cubs, trees grow from twigs."

"My spirit guide says you are correct. The young hills grew into mountains and reached up to capture Sen on their first hunt."

Jalex mentally shook her head at her companions' ideas.

"Rather than depend upon our spirit guides, let us use our eyes and noses and discover *for ourselves* what is there. There is still light remaining. *Forward!*"

* * *

Wisdom is not reserved for the wise.

> \- MORBO OF THE HOUSE OF SAGES

CHAPTER 4

Today – the desert

The flaky substance Foxx had found burned nearly as well as coal. They now had a good fire going, but still nothing to eat. The nights in this awful place seemed darker than normal. Usually the moon lit up the sky in her comforting way as a brilliant blue and brown orb. Here, Nyha was just a pale glow behind the clouds as it rose in the southeast.

"I still say it's getting dark too early," said Tresado, his furrowed brow making his conical ears stick out even more than they usually do.

"Maybe you should ask for your money back," quipped Foxx.

"Well, I don't have those famous Eryndi senses that you're so proud of," said Orchid, "but I think you're right. And, I can't believe I just said that out loud."

"I suspected as much." Tresado snapped his fingers. "That's it. The teleport spell somehow transported us into the future!"

"But only an hour or two?" mused Orchid, tapping her chin. "I suppose such a thing is possible."

"Sure, it's possible," said Tresado excitedly. "I knew a

Magician in Ostica, *a Worldly Magician,* mind you, that was experimenting with a time speed spell. She claimed it could compress the passage of time and effectively send you into the far future. She was kind of a crazy old bag, but it sounded like she was on the right track."

"What happened to her? Did it work?" asked Foxx, suddenly interested.

"I never did hear. In fact, I haven't heard of Kanardra in years. You don't suppose she actually did it, do you?"

"That would explain why you haven't heard of her recently," theorized Orchid.

"You think she accelerated herself into the future, don't you?" suggested Foxx.

"Maybe months," added Orchid.

Tresado's eyes went wide. "If Kanardra was using Magic to compress time, it figures you could use its processing power to calculate an exponential progression."

"She could be a thousand years in the future!" said Orchid with her hand to her mouth.

"Maybe *we* are a thousand years in the future!" exclaimed Foxx.

Tresado, Foxx, and Orchid stared open-mouthed at each other in amazed silence.

"Or . . ."

That calm voice of reason came from Serena, of all places. She had a look on her face that called all three of them idiots in no uncertain terms.

"You have some other explanation?" asked Foxx.

"This is a serious situation. If we're forward in time, then everything and everyone we've ever known could be long gone!" said Orchid.

"Orchid is right, Serena. With all due respect, this is a Magical problem," said Tresado condescendingly. "Maybe you should keep watch or something while we discuss this."

The stupidity slap to the back of Tresado's head smarted but did no real damage.

"You want to watch something? Try watching to the east. That's the direction that night comes from. This *telepunt* spell, or whatever you call it, sent us somewhere to the east—not into the future, *to the east!* That's the reason you think it's getting dark too early."

Serena could be annoyingly logical at times.

"Yeah, I suppose that's possible," admitted Orchid.

"What is it about you Magic mooks that makes you want to overcomplicate everything?"

"I think we have to award this round to the warrior," said Foxx gallantly. "Our apologies, My Lady."

"Hmmph."

"Still, it would have been cool to be in the future . . ."

* * *

Truth is harder and sharper than the finest steel blade . . . and just as tough to take to the gut.

\- General Prixus Scapulus,
Commander of the Treskan 12th Legion

Not quite 50,000 years ago

It took two days to scale the new mountains. As Jalex and her companions came to realize, these weren't really mountains so much as enormous piles of upthrust rock and soil. The ridge they were scrambling up now made Sentinel Hill look like a termite lodge. Huge boulders lay strewn across the ridge, a terrifying testament to the incredible force that formed these new mountains. There was little firm footing and the hunters lost two steps for every three taken.

There was no life anywhere in the vicinity, not even insects. Close to the top, even the occasional bit of firewood was scarce. At night, the usual pitch black was now offset by the strange glow emanating from behind this range. The purplish light shot straight up and was eventually lost in the thick dust cloud that hung in the sky.

The hunters had hoped to reach the summit before the second night, but decided not to risk the treacherous climb in the blackness. Jalex found herself a comfortable rock seat and pulled a bit of jerked clee-at meat from her pouch. There was not much food left and her water bag was less than half full.

"Early tomorrow should see us at the top."

"Agreed," grunted Garen, chewing on a ration of his own. "Then we release Sen from her enemies. She will be welcome in the sky again."

"Yes, the sun's return will be welcome," said Jalex softly.

The night passed softly, but Jalex was restless. There was something not exactly wrong, just . . . odd. The way the flame of their tiny campfire flickered, the taste of the air, the flow of water in her bag all seemed different somehow. Jalex's Ern senses were on edge, but there did not seem to be any danger. Perhaps it was just her hunter's instincts reacting to the bizarre happenings of the last several days.

The morning came in its now sluggish manner. The strange glow emanating from the ground beyond the summit was less noticeable in the dim daylight, but was still there. The last bit of climbing was the most treacherous of all. The rocks appeared

60

to have been very recently broken. The edges were sharp and slid perilously beneath their feet. Corma went down once and received a nasty cut along his thigh. Finally, the hunters tied themselves closely together with fiber to prevent sliding back down the dangerous slope.

The final ascent took longer than expected. It was nearly midday by the time they reached the top of the ridge. Tru was in the lead and scrambled up onto a large flat boulder. She gasped in astonishment at what her eyes saw.

"Tru, what is it? Do you see Sen?" called Corma anxiously.

She did not respond. Tru's open mouth could produce no more than the slightest sound. The others pulled themselves on top of the rock and peered into the valley beyond. The view was beyond anything the Ern hunters had ever experienced. The mountains they had scaled continued on to their right and left, curving away from them in an immense arc. This new range was formed into a great circle, many marches across. The far side of it could not be seen on the smoke-filled horizon. In the center of this circle of mountains, a sea of thick, boiling liquid roiled and fumed, ejecting great furious geysers of purple blobs into the air. These gigantic eruptions spewed up to dizzying heights, only to slowly splash back down, creating huge ripples of super-heated fury. Whenever one of these masses of molten material plunged back into the purple sea, an intensified ray of unnatural light shot into the air, adding to the freakish glow that had drawn the party of hunters to this strange place.

Garen was the first to find his voice as he pointed toward the writhing sea.

"That is not Sen. She is not here. Whatever plunged from the sky was not the sun. My spirit guide tells me there is great evil here. It will someday bring death to all Ern."

A particularly large eruption of material leapt into the air and sloppily splashed back into the fiery liquid. Again, the strange sensations Jalex had been feeling washed over her like a chilling fever. She couldn't help feeling that Garen was at least partially right.

"We cannot stay in this place. The people must move."

Today – the desert

Group Six huddled in their makeshift rock shelter, listening to each other's stomachs growl. The eerie silence surrounding them was unnerving. There were no sounds of beasts or insects coming from the dark night. Suddenly the campfire popped loudly, startling them all.

"I wonder what made the life disappear," mused Foxx. "As soon as it got fully dark, it all went away."

Orchid trembled slightly. "Not all of it. Listen."

Serena's hand edged toward her sword hilt. "Is there something alive out there?"

"It must be," answered Orchid in a strange, creepy tone. "But . . ." She shrugged as her voice trailed off.

Whoosh, snap. Whoosh, snap . . .

No one bothered to ask the obvious *what the hell was that?* question. The four froze as the strange sounds came out of the desert darkness.

"It's getting closer," whispered Tresado.

"Put the fire out, *quick!*"

Orchid immediately focused on the elements and, with her Worldly Magic, reduced the heat and called in moisture to the air surrounding the fire pit. The flames quickly died with little smoke, plunging them into darkness. There was just barely enough moonlight filtering through the clouds to see each other, but that was about it.

Whatever produced the strange sounds was getting louder and heading toward them. There was nowhere to hide. The small rock fortress Tresado had constructed was as defensible a position as anywhere around this place.

Whoosh, snap. Whoosh, snap . . .

They now felt vibrations in the ground beneath them. Whatever was coming was big.

"I'm going to have a look," declared Tresado. There was a strange steeliness in his tone. He cast his levitation spell and noiselessly rose into the air, disappearing into the darkness.

Serena's brow furrowed. Something about Tresado's demeanor bothered her. While he was certainly not a coward, he wasn't usually quite so eager to volunteer. It was more of a laziness thing.

The noises and vibrations were getting closer. Orchid squinted out into the darkness.

"Look. What's that?"

Something loomed above them. Were it not for the fact that it was moving, it could have been taken for a giant colossus tree. A strange shuffling could now be heard. It sounded like a plow being pulled through the soil.

Whoosh, snap . . .

Tresado suddenly appeared from out of the air.

"We need to get off the ground, fast!"

Tresado quickly expanded his levitation spell to include the others. Before they could even comment, Group Six found itself lifted high into the air. As they ascended, a towering form loomed in the darkness next to them. A deafening wind arose from an ominous shape that lunged at the airborne Group Six quicker than Tresado could accelerate them away. The pale, cloud-covered moonlight revealed an enormous mouth lined with rows of smooth plates. The wind was being caused by a powerful vacuum effect. The thing was trying to literally suck its victims into the gaping maw and grind them into bergalo burger with those teeth-plates.

Tresado poured on the Magic and tried to steer them away from the giant mouth, which was waving through the air on the end of a long, sinuous neck. When it realized its flying prey was escaping, the thing launched a snaking tentacle out of its maw, aimed at Serena's dangling ankles. But before it could grab hold, the tongue found itself severed by a half-reach of razor-sharp Northlands steel.

That slight distraction gave them the time they needed. The head drew back just long enough for Tresado to increase altitude to get beyond its reach. And that was no small distance. The behemoth below them was as large as the Imperial Palace of Tresk.

Whoosh, snap . . .

There was that noise again. Once he was sure they were at a safe enough distance, Tresado focused and created a luminous sphere that floated down below them and lit up the surrounding area. The thing could only be described as an incredibly huge walking starfish. It seemed to have no main body at all. It was nothing but nine serpentine necks connected to a central point. Each enormous neck terminated in a great mouth like the one that had tried to pluck Group Six out of the air. It plodded along the desert floor, stomping those mouths into the ground. Every couple of minutes, one of them would create a vacuum and suck something out of the sand.

Whoosh, snap . . .

The crawlers! The gigantic horror was sucking the rock crawlers out of the sand they had burrowed themselves into. Once it had captured one, those grinding plates clamped down upon it and cracked it open like a *koofa* nut. The shell and rich, chewy center were then swallowed to begin the lengthy trip down the gullet.

As soon as Tresado's Magical flare floated closer to the creature, it immediately turned and scurried away into the darkness. It seemed odd to apply the word *scurry* to something the size of a small village, but that's exactly what the behemoth did. Apparently, it didn't like the light at all. As a parting gift, the creature opened an orifice on its central hub and squirted a large, horrid blob of black, tarry liquid onto the desert floor. It then vanished into the dark night.

"I don't like this place," offered Foxx.

* * *

> *Home is where you feed your soul, not stuff your face; but it's nice to have a porch to scrape the dog crap off your boots.*

- Travelogue of
Dementus the Mad Treskan

Not quite 50,000 years ago

The people of the village had been wandering for more than two seasons. The bones of their ancestors had heartbreakingly been left behind in their graves, which could not even be found again. That included those of Jalex's parents, who had both been put to ground seasons before. They headed north, away from the strange, purple light that shone from the ground. The great herds of lum and saro had been dispersed. There was little food to be gathered, certainly not in any quantity to keep a village supplied. A new land with water, shelter, and hunting must be found.

It was growing colder. As long as anyone could remember, the land of the Ern had been warm and fertile. Now, the sky was a constant dismal brown and the sunless days and dark nights made for chilling temperatures. Two winters had come and gone since Senfall and warmth struggled feebly to return after each one. It was summer again, but the temperature had not come up enough to melt the ice and snow that many of the villagers had never seen before.

Since that frightful day of Senfall, nearly a third of the Ern had perished, half of that number in the disaster itself and the rest in the horrid time since. Malnutrition and exposure took most of them. Drana's child had just died of lung rot during the previous night. The boy had less than a hand of seasons. A tiny grave was laboriously scooped from the frozen soil and the body laid to rest. As was the custom, gifts of food and carved icons of family were buried with him. There was little to spare, but no one would think to deprive those following the Trail of the Dead of their provisions.

After the ceremony, Jalex pulled her fur wrap closer about her to cut the chilling wind. She walked away from the new grave and the grieving mother and approached Corma and Tru.

"Come. We must go out again."

Corma stood and looked down upon Jalex.

"Yes," he said, sighing.

Nothing else was necessary. Jalex knew the strong young hunter was bone weary and discouraged. She knew because she felt the same, but food must be gathered somehow. Tru picked up her arrow stick and followed silently along.

On the day of Senfall, Corma had been but a stripling. The past two seasons had grown him to his full height. He was thin, as were most of the hungry Ern, but was now a man-sized hunter, one of the few left. Chief Durat, Garen, and the only other elder hunter, Jooran, had all died the previous season. Their frozen bodies had been discovered on the bare prairie after a blizzard.

The hunting trio set out to the northwest away from the temporary camp. Tru had the best eyes, so she was tasked with watching the horizon as they moved. Jalex and Corma kept their gaze and their noses aimed at the ground, looking for spoor, roots, or anything useful.

Jalex spotted a bit of green on a rocky area of ground ahead of them. It was a small patch of what the Ern called tube brush. The pounded root made for a good pain balm. The buds could be eaten, but tasted awful. Still, nothing in these dark times could be passed by.

As they approached, Jalex signaled a halt. The other two froze. They didn't know if she had sensed danger or prey. Either way, caution was everything. Jalex slowly worked her way forward, focusing on the brush ahead. She waved two fingers a certain way, which translated as 'proceed carefully and stay alert.' Corma and Tru crept ahead and saw what Jalex had discovered. The buds of the tube brush had already been gnawed by something. Most of the edible parts were gone, which was something of a disappointment, but the fact that they had been gnawed meant there was something around to gnaw them. The hunters scanned the area with practiced eyes until a low whistle came from Tru, who was pointing at the ground. She knelt and examined the marks in the dry soil.

"Lum . . . lum with a calf, it looks like."

This was a major discovery, evidence of the first lum that any of the Ern had seen since Senfall. Before this, Jalex had wondered more than once if there were even any lum left in the world.

The tracks were nearly invisible. The edges were fuzzy from age. Clearly, they had been made more than a day ago. But the presence of the huge animals in the area could mean salvation for the starving villagers. They must be tracked at once.

"Spread out. We must pick up the spoor," said Jalex excitedly.

The stony ground gave up its secrets reluctantly, but eventually the hunters picked up the trail.

"They're heading east," Jalex said. "Toward the valley. We'll have to move fast."

The area ahead had been seen by the Ern only from a distance. It was a great, ugly rip carved in the land. The three hunters fell into a slow trot designed to eat up the distance, but not overtax the runners. Occasionally, they halted to verify the spoor they were following and take a sip from their water bags.

Nightfall came, bringing its usual chill. There was enough firewood around to stave it off, though. The hunters slowly chewed their meager rations, allowing the dried cherfa grain to soften in their mouths before swallowing. They stared into the fire, hoping to see the immediate future in the dancing flames.

"With only three of us, it will be difficult to bring down a lum," said Corma.

Tru nodded, "Our arrows must be cast perfectly."

"If we try to kill the calf, we would have a better chance."

"You forget about the mother," said Jalex, always the voice of reason. "If the calf is harmed, her rage will be great. A charging lum cannot be stopped with arrows and she will avenge her young no matter how badly we wound her."

"We must try somehow," Corma insisted. "The clan needs meat. Two lum will feed my sires and cousins for a season."

"Perhaps we could distract the mother away from the calf and corner her," suggested Tru.

"Then we find a safe place to hurl our arrows from. That is a good plan."

Tru grinned at the praise. "After the mother is dead, we go after the calf. Yes, that will be good!"

Jalex could not fault them for their exuberance, but had to get them to use sense.

"Yes, that is a good plan . . . *if* we can track the lum . . . and *if* we can get near them . . . and *if* there is a place to corner them . . . and *if* we can kill them safely."

Corma and Tru quietly grumbled at Jalex's pessimism, but realized she was right. A creature as large and powerful as an adult lum was usually taken by many hands of Ern. Three young hunters stood little chance of succeeding. Still, to not try was to not eat.

For three days, the exhausted party of hunters tracked their quarry over the desolate prairie. The spoor eventually became easier to follow. Deep footprints and broken brush plainly showed the way, even from a distance. The pace they maintained was consuming more of their vitality than their meager rations were replenishing, but they could tell they were catching up. Lum are large animals and take large steps. However, the two beasts were meandering about, searching for food, while the hunters were traveling in a relatively straight line. One thing that aided their pursuit was the slight downhill grade they were following. The pair of lum were definitely making for the head of that valley beyond.

These grass-eaters did not have fangs or claws to speak of, but were still very dangerous creatures. And it was well-known that they would fight back if threatened. Being the biggest animal around, they usually tried to trample whatever enemy was attacking. The three tiny Ern with their tiny arrows could be squashed like beetles if they weren't careful.

Normally, lum hunts had been organized, many-day events in which most of the villagers went afield with the hunters. If successful, there was the immense job of skinning, butchering, preserving, and transporting the meat and hides. Ern of all ages participated. Successful hunts could supply the village with enough meat for much of a season. During her young life, Jalex had seen several hunts take place in which a herd of lum were located, stalked, and driven to a pre-arranged kill zone where other hunters were waiting with prepared spears and arrows. The most animals taken in one hunt that Jalex had ever witnessed was five. That had been with four hands of hunters in the kill zone and two hands or more driving them.

But that was before Senfall. After that horrible day, there were no more mass hunts, because there were no more large herds of any animals left in the area. Equally, there were far fewer hunters in the world. The majority of villagers killed on Senfall had been the exposed hunters in the field. It had mostly been elders and children who had survived by the grace of Sentinel Hill's sheltering bulk. Now Jalex, Corma, and Tru were some of the few survivors still capable of wielding hunting weapons.

Dawn of the fourth day brought the first sound of their prey. As the brown sky began to lighten, a distant trumpeting could be heard. Corma cocked his cone-shaped ear in that direction.

"Mother lum is calling to her child."

"Telling it to let us kill them," added Tru, delighted with her own sense of humor.

The deep, warbling sound echoed out of the eastern mists once again.

"Whatever she's saying, it sounds urgent," said Jalex. "Let us find out."

The hunters quickly gathered up their weapons and set off after the sounds with Jalex in the lead. As they trotted forward, the calls of the mother lum repeated. With each new bellow, strange flashes of awareness rippled across Jalex's senses. She had heard lum cries many times before Senfall and these sounded the same. But now, it was as though she could almost understand the bellowing mother. Another loud cry, even closer, passed through Jalex's spirit and said *danger . . . protect . . . flee*! No words entered her ears, but she was somehow sure.

Jalex pulled up quickly and signaled the others to do the same as she realized other sensations. The frozen sod beneath her feet was trembling and a faint crashing sound was approaching fast. Up ahead, Jalex saw the top of a tall tree suddenly sway unnaturally.

"They're headed this way in a hurry!" she hissed to the others. "Find cover and be ready to throw your arrows, but only if she charges!"

Tru and Jalex ducked down behind a patch of low thorn bushes that any animal should avoid. Corma took the high road by scrambling up to the top of a rock outcropping that was only slightly taller than their giant prey.

Only a hand of heartbeats later, a beast came into view. The mother lum emerged from behind a rock ridge. Her short, thick legs propelled her along at a slow gallop, but upon entering open country, came to a quick halt. Her toenailed feet, nearly as wide as a hunter is tall, dug great furrows in the ground as her massive bulk slid to a stop. Mother peered about for a moment, her sandy, thickly-furred snout sniffing the air. She then turned her massive head to glance behind her. Her blubbery lips parted and bellowed out another urgent cry. This one, Jalex was certain, meant *hurry up!*

A moment later, a calf waddled out into view, moving his short little legs as fast as he could. He was just a little fellow, only as tall as two hunters. He was wheezing and honking in his efforts to keep up with his mother, who was ever so eager to get going again.

Jalex leaned over to whisper into Tru's ear.

"They're running from something. This might be our only chance. If you and I can herd them between these thorns and that rock, Corma can throw arrows into her from above."

Tru nodded and started working her way around to the other side of the thorn patch. Jalex silently signaled her intentions to Corma. He stood ready with an arrow in his stick and three more in his other hand.

The mother lum waited for the baby to catch up to her and took another quick look over her shoulder. She bugled a short note and the two of them resumed their trot right toward the narrow passage that the hunters had stationed themselves on each side of. As soon as the mother came abreast of them, Jalex and Tru leaped out of hiding, waving leafy branches and whooping like marsh birds. Mother saw it was only two pitiful insects making the noise. She normally would have just continued on course, or even trampled them. However, her inexperienced, easily frightened child veered away from the strange apparitions and headed right toward the rock spire where Corma waited. Mother lum swerved with her errant young, trying to shield him from the danger coming up on their right.

By now, Jalex and Tru had dropped the branches and had their arrow sticks ready. They ran after the retreating lum, just barely able to keep up with them. The mother and son were side-by-side as they passed Corma's rock. She was running at a slow pace, matching that of her young and trying to stay between him and the two Ern. But mother had no idea that a third one waited above on the other side. As they passed, Corma jumped out of his hiding place and launched his arrow with all the force he could muster, aiming for the mother's left eye. Hitting that small a target on moving prey was nearly beyond even experienced hunters' abilities. Even so, Corma's arrow hit impressively close to the target into the cheek of the mother lum. She bellowed in pain and looked to Jalex and Tru, the closest enemies she knew of, to take it out on. Her weak eyes picked them out at the same time another arrow from Corma's stick buried its obsidian head into her shoulder. Blood was streaming from both wounds, streaking the lum's tan fur with deep red.

Jalex had felt the pain of the arrows. And she also knew the lum were going to come after her and Tru. She was so in tune with what this creature was feeling, it was almost as if Jalex *was* the mother lum. That instinct probably saved their lives. Jalex signaled Tru immediately and the two of them were scattering to either side of the charging beast, even before the beast knew she was going to charge.

That tactic forced the animal to make a choice of which target to go after. It chose Jalex, who was running away at full speed back the way she had come. She quickly ducked behind a large thorn patch, trying to keep it between her and the enraged mother. The beast charged the prickly barrier and for a moment, Jalex felt the lum's near-decision to not brave the thorns. Her anger won out though, and the giant animal barreled right through directly toward Jalex. She dodged and swerved with all the agility of her Ern heritage, but it was ultimately hopeless. Jalex finally found herself cornered amongst the thorns and the lum's smashing feet were heading right for her.

CHAPTER 5

Today – the desert

It was a long night. Group Six had escaped the uber-starfish thing for now and Tresado lowered everyone back down to the ground. Simply because there was no better place to go, they returned to the shelter among the rocks. This time they elected not to have a fire, even though the desert was cold at night. Tresado's Magical flare had driven off the ridiculously large creature, but the concentrated light only tended to attract other horrors. Some things that looked like flying dinner plates with big pincers flitted around the lit area, snapping at anything that moved. They didn't seem to have wings, but rather hovered about using the power of Magic. Orchid tried to persuade them to leave, but they weren't having any of it. Serena managed to split one in two with her sword as it buzzed her. Foxx picked up one of the halves and immediately flung it down again in disgust. The inside of the creature was crawling with thousands of tiny worms with pincers of their own. Even as hungry as everyone was, they weren't that desperate yet.

"What the hell kind of a creepy-assed place is this?" demanded Serena.

"It's like nothing I've ever seen or even heard of," answered Orchid. "There is zero plant life, but plenty of insects, which is impossible. And these *animals,* if you can even call them that, just aren't natural. Nothing here makes any sense."

"We heard that the Crystal Palace was sending cheaters to some kind of monster-filled no-man's land," said Foxx. "This would seem to be it. Jakki is way overreacting, if you ask me. You'd think they could just serve some jail time."

"This is not Jakki's doing," said Tresado. "The teleportation spell that sent them and us to this desert was all up to the Palace itself. I wonder if there's a connection between the two."

Serena gave Tresado a withering look.

"Happy, now? Did you get everything you wanted out of your stinky experiment?"

"I would have if that rabble hadn't burst into the lab. And I still will, someday."

There was a sinister undertone to Tresado's response. Serena half-expected him to break into an evil laugh.

"The real trick to mastering that spell is not in learning how to do it, but controlling the reactions. When something teleports away, the object is instantly gone and that leaves a vacuum. Air rushes in to replace what is lost."

"But that's not the problem, is it?" interrupted Orchid, who was suddenly interested.

"No, the problem is what happens when something teleports in. The object begins as an infinitely small pinpoint of existence and expands rapidly. The existing air and small objects that happen to be in the target area could be thrust violently away."

"I noticed when Jakki blipped into the fight ring, there

was a rush of air," said Foxx. "Sparkly's toupee nearly blew off his head."

"*Exactly.* If there were pebbles on the ground, say, a poorly done spell could send them shooting off like bullets from a sling. A skilled teleporter like Jakki can make the transition smooth, while a crude spell might cause explosive damage."

The conversation continued on into the night. They were not menaced by any more dangerous creatures and the three Magicians debated technical details for hours. Serena moved away to the far corner of the shelter and curled up, sword in hand and seemingly asleep. She was not interested in what they were saying, but surreptitiously kept an ear on the tone of the conversation. Something about their attitudes was a bit disturbing.

When the sun finally came up, dim as it was behind the cloud cover, Tresado lifted himself up to altitude to have a look around. Again, he was very impressed with himself. He had never felt so powerful, so in command of the Magical forces around him. He hovered far above the desolate landscape and turned his body slowly, basking in the vista.

As he looked to the southwest, the direction they had come from, Tresado saw something familiar . . . not with his eyes, but with his mind. Tendrils of raw energy were emanating straight up from the distant horizon and disappearing into the high clouds above. Tresado's thoughts went back to the recent past when he and his friends stood atop the ruins of the great Arena in the drowned city of Mennatu. That huge structure was not an arena at all, but rather a gigantic collector designed by ancient Eryndi to concentrate and focus the Magic in the air. With the mysterious power of their psyches, Tresado, Orchid, and even Foxx were able to perceive the Magical energy being pulled from the sky. What Tresado was *seeing* now was similar, except for the direction of the flow. This was not Magic being drawn from the air, but rather the very heart of the power of Magic rushing from the ground into the everlasting sky.

He tore his gaze away and looked in the opposite direction. Far to the northeast was the tiniest hint of green land with a ribbon of blue sky on the distant horizon. If they wanted to eat, that was the direction they must go.

But the lure of what was behind them again drew his gaze. When he concentrated, Tresado could not only see but *feel* the immense energy emanating from the ground. It added great strength to his abilities. He had to get a better look. Focusing his mind on the power around him, he willed himself to gain even more altitude. His invisible cradle easily lifted the Eryndi further and further into the bleak desert sky. He had never been anywhere near this high before and the air was beginning to get a bit thin. Normally, Tresado's levitation ability was limited to only about a hundred reaches. But here, in this forsaken wasteland, the power of Magic flowed through his body like an overripe makara smoothie.

Soon, the land was laid out below him like a map. The other members of Group Six were no longer visible, even as dots on a page. To the southwest, Tresado could see a range of mountains with a strange regularity to them. These peaks were laid out in a great curving line. In fact, from this altitude, Tresado could tell that they formed an enormous circle, the far side of which faded in the desert mists. It was from the depressed center of this country-sized ring that the lines of energy emanated. Even at this great height, Tresado could still sense the flow continuing on far above him. As far as he could tell, the power was shooting straight up from this giant crater and into the great unknown beyond the clouds. A thought struck him as he watched the ethereal light show.

This is a major discovery . . . one that must not be shared.

* * *

I question thee - What may make thee idolized or shunned? A queen or a target? A tycoon or a pauper? What may thou desperately seek or bitterly regret to own? . . . Give up?

Thine answer is 'knowledge' . . . a curious possession.

- Pelonka Ke Dor,
Riddlemistress of the Court of Abakaar

Not quite 50,000 years ago

The enraged mother lum thundered toward the puny thing in front of her with the intent of pulverizing it. Jalex covered her head with her arms and prepared to die. A *thunk* sound followed by a pitiful bellow changed the beast's mind. At the last beat, she turned away and galloped back the way she had come. Jalex, amazed to be still alive, looked about for the reason. From atop the rock formation, Corma had cast another arrow, this time into the body of the calf. This arrow hit the young lum in the center of its back and buried itself in the spine. The calf's rear legs collapsed under it and it sat on its now useless haunches, bleating horribly.

As the mother lum swung her great bulk around to defend her young, Jalex saw something that froze her blood. The left side of the giant had a streak of blood running from a wound, but not one inflicted by Corma or the women. Protruding from the lum's left haunch was the thick, broken shaft of a large spear. Jalex and her friends had only their arrow sticks. They had not brought large spears with them.

There was no time to think of that though. The lum was heading back toward Corma with murder in her eyes, but Corma wasn't there. As soon as he had cast his arrow at the calf to distract the mother lum away from Jalex, he dropped down the other side of the rock.

The mother thundered up to her wounded child and nudged it with her snout, trying to get it to move. The baby bleated piteously, its ruined back legs refusing to obey its commands. The frustrated mother would have preferred to stay there and attempt to shield her young, but there was still the unfinished business of pulping Corma.

Now it was Jalex's and Tru's turn to do the distracting. The two women moved amongst the rocks, hooting jeers and trying to draw her off. The beast charged Tru, only to get a lightning-fast arrow to the face. Tru started running even before seeing the result of her throw. The mother reared in pain and fury, her giant front feet waving briefly in the air. She crashed back down, shaking the ground with the impact. Before she could pursue Tru, another arrow from Jalex thudded deeply into her flank. Now she was really pissed.

The three hunters picked up the strategy quickly. Surrounding the beast and launching attacks from all sides kept the lum confused and distracted, but Jalex realized they couldn't keep it up. For one thing, among the three of them, they probably had barely a hand's worth of arrows left. It would require many of these pinpricks from many hunters to kill this creature. It was so large and its fur so thick that their arrows were mostly just enraging it, rather than doing much damage. Slim chance, if any, of killing it, but starving bellies demanded nothing less.

"Out!" shouted Corma, indicating he had launched his last arrow.

Jalex didn't wait for Tru to yell the same.

"Scatter to cover!"

She saved her final arrow in case the lum needed to be distracted again to allow Corma and Tru to escape.

That didn't seem necessary though. The lum was noticeably slowing down and Corma and Tru easily outdistanced it. The wounded baby bleated once more. Its mother slowed to a trot and then came to a wobbly halt. Again, Jalex had a flash of awareness. The great beast had gone from feeling rage to sudden confusion and genuine fear. She began to turn back toward her young when she suddenly lost her balance. The great rounded head thudded into the ground, scattering the sand. The tiny eyes fluttered and rolled up. The giant mother lum lay helpless in the sand, twitching and making little honking noises.

The hunters cautiously approached the stricken creature. All three were baffled. The lum had taken several arrows and had that curious spear wound, but none of those injuries appeared to be life-threatening. Nevertheless, it appeared the unlikely hunt was successful. Both beasts could now be easily killed with no more danger to the hunters. The vast slabs of meat beneath those thick hides would feed the starving Ern for many, many days. The fur, bones, teeth, and even the intestines could all be put to life-saving uses. The time of troubles appeared to be over, at least for a while.

Jalex approached the stricken lum. Once again, the curious feeling of empathy overtook her. It was as though she could look into the creature's soul. She could feel the pain of the arrow wounds and the motherly concern for the calf. But the strongest sensations were those of confusion, fear, and a kind of sinking feeling, as though the animal was plummeting down a dark hole. It made no sense, but the priority was to dispatch the beast as quickly as possible. Jalex took her one remaining arrow and prepared to manually plunge it into the lum's eye socket.

"*HOLD!*"

The hunters turned at once to the source of the sound. Tru let out a high-pitched little gasp. At least three hands of figures stood watching them from behind rocks and brush. Many more were approaching from the east. They were obviously Ern hunters, well-equipped with spears and arrows, but no one the trio recognized. A tall, well-muscled man approached.

"The kill is ours," he said, gesturing with his obsidian-tipped spear.

"*GO!*"

* * *

Never be afraid to oversell your product . . .

- Professor Abadiah Generax, 21862

Today – the desert

Tresado slowly descended back to the ground where the rest of Group Six waited.

"See anything interesting?" asked Foxx.

"What do you mean?" replied Tresado quickly.

"I guess that *was* kind of a hard question. I should have used finger puppets."

The image of shooting Foxx in the ass with a flame spell crossed Tresado's mind. Instead, he ignored the barb and pointed.

"Off in that direction, I could see greenery, but it's at least forty or fifty leagues away."

"I'm all for greenery," said Orchid. "At least plants listen to me. I can't even sense the presence of these weird animals, let alone influence them."

"But when those mega-grasshoppers came at us, you got them to go away," said Foxx. "Which was really very impressive. I admire anyone so persuasive."

Orchid blushed at the compliment, not realizing that she had been buttered up by Foxx's Knowing Spell. "Well, thank you, but those locusts were simple, ordinary insects, despite being really large. I could sense their needs and motivations and influence those. But the rock crawlers, the giant, those flying things . . . it's like they . . . just don't belong here."

"Neither do we, so let's get moving," said Serena, taking the point. The Northlands warrior was in full survival mode. "We need to keep up a slow but steady pace. Nature Girl can always conjure water, but keep your eyes and ears open for anything we might be able to eat . . . beetles, grubs, anything. Just remember, the first one to die of starvation is food for the rest of us."

The scary thing was that she was completely serious about that last bit.

"It'll take us days to walk out of here, if that green area is as far away as you say," said Foxx, examining the state of his shoes.

"*I* may be able to help with that," said Tresado smugly. "Let me try something."

Tresado concentrated, *seeing* in his mind's eye what he wanted. That image traveled out into the ether, interacting with the mystical energy that permeated the world around him. For added showmanship, he made an overly dramatic display of focusing his thoughts. He did a little dance with plenty of elaborate arm gestures.

Foxx was surprised. They all knew such things were unnecessary for summoning Magic, and Tresado knew that they knew it. Still, Foxx the former showman was proud of his friend of many years for such a histrionic display.

The processing power of Magic coalesced Tresado's thoughts into four hovering blobs of semi-transparent energy. Another squirt of mental direction formed them into comfy easy chairs floating half a reach above the ground.

"There you go," said Tresado, quite pleased with himself. "These should scoot us along the landscape in no time. Have a seat, my friends, and leave the levitating to me."

Foxx needed no second urging. He gratefully sank down into one of the plush, non-corporeal chairs.

"Now this is more like it," he sighed. Foxx always did like his comforts.

Orchid clucked her tongue in obvious disapproval. "Such a blatant misuse of what Nature has given us. The future is going to be a bleak one, if you *Absoluters* continue to squander Magic like this."

"So, you'd rather walk?"

Orchid snorted, but gave in to his logic and sat down.

Serena prodded suspiciously at the floating apparition with the tip of her sword, but then hesitantly sat down.

"You couldn't have conjured up a horse and saddle? I feel like an idiot lounging in this padded throne."

"Just sit back and enjoy," beamed Tresado. "Here we go."

Tresado's spell engaged and shot the seated members of Group Six across the desert floor like arrows from a bow. The sudden acceleration sucked them all into their chair backs so they couldn't even draw a breath. Tresado could feel his lips pulling back over his gums as he struggled mentally to gain full control of his spell. Eventually he slowed them to a steady but still rapid pace. He found only minimal concentration was necessary to maintain this levitation spell, that being his specialty in the first place.

"I told you it would be all right!" he shouted gleefully.

The four Magical chairs zipped Group Six across the barren landscape as fast as a galloping horse could have taken them. At one point, a spherical balloon-like thing over three reaches in diameter bounced out of their way. The surface of the rubbery creature was disturbingly covered with at least thirty mouths bristling with teeth. It went bounding off across the desert floor looking for slower prey.

The hours passed. The good news was that there were signs the barren desert was coming to an end. Twisted tree trunks and scrub brush were starting to appear more frequently. There were also patches of long, bamboo-like poles growing here and there. Aside from watching for anything that could be eaten, there was nothing to do other than engage in conversation, an activity sure to cause trouble.

"Does anybody have any money?"

Three heads turned at Foxx's odd question. No one even had to ask.

"Yes, I know, it's not relevant out here. I just thought maybe we could pass the time with a friendly game."

A flick of his nimble wrist produced a deck of playing cards seemingly from nowhere.

"Tresado, you're out because you're driving the wagon, so to speak . . . ladies, what do you say?"

It's hard to say whose dirty look was dirtier. Orchid was the first to speak.

"I don't want to end up owing you my immortal soul."

"Perish the thought," replied Foxx with a smile. Even over the wind of their speed across the land, his voice was smooth and pleasing, almost melodic.

"It would be better if we kept our eyes on the lookout for danger or food, instead of your little toys," growled Serena.

"Ha, ha, good one," laughed Foxx, in the most charming way imaginable. "It's just a little game of Four-Card Blitzkrieg . . . a little something to lightly . . . pass the time."

Foxx looked deeply into the eyes of Orchid, then lingeringly on those of Serena.

"Oh, twigs . . . why not?" said Orchid.

"Excellent. Sir, if you wouldn't mind scooting our chairs a little closer together."

Tresado looked back at Foxx. He had seen this gleam in his eye before, like every time he was about to take advantage of someone. He shrugged, it not being any of his business, and mentally ordered the speeding chairs behind him to close up tighter. Besides, he had more important matters to think about.

Foxx manipulated the deck with his agile fingers, executing a couple of slick, one-handed shuffles. The blowing wind of their passage prevented him from tossing the cards out in the usual way, so he carefully handed out four cards each to Orchid and Serena, who warily took them.

"Now, I assume everyone knows how to play . . . of course

you do. Now this first hand is just for fun. Serena, the open is to you."

Serena managed to tear her eyes away from Foxx's gaze and glance at her cards. She held out two of them face up.

"No pair, same suit."

Orchid took the sixteen of squares and handed back one of her own cards face down. Serena kept the other one, the quad of squares.

"One . . . by me."

It was now Foxx's turn. He offered the eleven of stars.

"Open choice . . . by me."

Serena took his card and gave him back two face down. That gave Foxx the choice to keep either or both of them or trade them for two of Orchid's. He opted for the trade.

Orchid's face lit up blatantly for a moment, but she quickly composed herself.

"Withhold."

"Draw," Foxx sighed. He discarded his hand and drew four fresh cards, losing his turn.

Serena offered the solo of suns. Orchid snatched it up and spread out her hand.

"Blitzkrieg!"

"Well, that leaves me in the ditch," said Foxx, counting out his hand. "I show twenty-seven. Good thing we're not playing for money."

"Three for me," said Serena. "One more square and I would have had you, Nature Girl."

"Never happen, Diamond Girl."

"Another?" asked Foxx.

"Sure."

"Why not?"

The play continued for another several hands. Foxx won a couple of them, but mostly the wins were divided up between Serena and Orchid. Another round went to Serena, who was starting to get into the spirit of the game.

"HA!" she roared triumphantly, flashing a three-quarters Blitzkrieg.

"You've played this game before," smiled Foxx.

"Not till I came south. We don't do this sort of thing in the Northlands."

"No games of skill?" asked Orchid.

"Sure . . . just with axes instead of cards," said Serena, her deep lapis eyes meeting Foxx's brown ones. "You know . . . I happen to have a few copper gendrins in my pocket. Care to make a friendly wager?"

"Boy, I don't know," said Foxx hesitantly. "What do you think, Orchid?"

"I think you could both afford to lose a little lunch money to me."

"So be it," said Foxx, with a worried look. "Everybody ante up. We'll use my hat for the pot."

Foxx continued to deal the cards. The gendrins turned to silver paleens. Soon a few gold daurics made their way into the pot. Both Serena and Orchid went through periods of boom and bust while Foxx's funds always hovered just above the poverty level. At last came a hand that went through several cycles without a winner. The stakes rose until there was a tiny little fortune in Foxx's hat . . . pretty much the sum total of everyone's money. To drop out of the hand now would mean abandoning their stakes to the other two players.

"Hoo boy," Foxx sighed and dropped his few remaining coins into the pot. "What more do I have to lose? All in, I guess."

The turn came to Orchid, who needed a sizable bet to stay in. She had no other choice.

"All in," she said, and with a fearsome look in her eyes, offered up her precious oaken staff. This was the artifact that never left Orchid's sight . . . the one item valued by her over any other. It defined her Worldly identity. Reflecting her defiant mood, the enchanted object sparked and fumed, shooting out angry arcs of Magical fury. It didn't fit in the hat, of course, but the gesture was well understood.

That left Serena. The speed of their passage whipped her blonde hair about her face. She looked over at Orchid who glared back defiantly.

"What's the matter, warrior woman? Afraid your hand isn't strong enough?"

If there was one thing Serena couldn't let slide, it was a challenge to her abilities. Foxx didn't say a word, but continued to just watch both his opponents.

"If you think I'm afraid, shorty, you are sadly mistaken!"

As Serena's eyes unwaveringly locked with Orchid's, she reached down and plucked the fabulous diamond out of the hollow in her sternum.

"All in," said Serena with deadly calm. She leaned forward in her ethereal chair and slowly dropped the jewel into the hat.

"I guess that means we show our hands," said Foxx.

One by one, Orchid flashed her cards.

"Seven squares . . . seven suns . . . seven stars."

"Impressive," said Serena. "Not nearly good enough, but impressive."

Serena held out the four cards in her hand triumphantly.

"Run of suns . . . Empress high!"

Orchid's staff rumbled ominously and storm clouds began to gather above their heads.

"Try not to be too disappointed," said Serena, smugly reaching for the pot.

"Ahem."

Foxx expertly did a one-handed fan of his cards.

"Full Blitzkrieg. Looks like I finally won a hand."

Foxx sat back in his chair, his eyes lit with satisfaction. He clutched his hat to his chest, pulled out Serena's diamond, and held it up to the light. Even on this cloudy day, the gem winked at him with flashes of color, tickling his imagination with lurid hints of riches to come.

"Yo," said Tresado, who had been all but forgotten in the heat of gambling. "Are you sure that's such a good idea?"

"Shouldn't you be concentrating on your spell?" said Foxx out of the corner of his mouth.

"I was about to say the same thing to you."

Serena blinked and shook her head.

"Spell? . . . SPELL?!"

Orchid looked at her friend who had bested her fair and square. She took another look and saw instead the man who had just cheated her at cards.

Serena's hand went to her chest and felt the empty space that used to house her diamond. Then it dropped to the hilt of her sword.

"You have one chance," she said, drawing her scimitar halfway out of its hanger.

"There's no need for that," said Foxx, looking into Serena's eyes.

"Stop that crap *right now!*"

Serena stood in the seat of her chair with sword drawn.

"You heard her, you *Absoluter* low-life." Orchid clutched her staff in both hands and held it above her head menacingly.

90

The ornately carved piece of oak vibrated and thundered with the promise of divine retribution.

"Whoa, whoa, whoa!" yelled Tresado, turning around in his seat. "I've had enough of your ridiculous prejudice and your narrow-mindedness!"

"You stay out of this, Ernie!" yelled Serena. "This is between me and him."

"I don't like that term! I never did! You don't know who you're talking to! *I'm* the leader here. Now sit down and put that stupid knife away!"

Orchid now turned her staff toward Tresado. *"The leader?! Since when?"*

"Well, if you would look up from your little card game, you'll notice I'm the one saving everybody's asses at the moment!"

"Why you self-important prickweed! You want to save someone's ass? *Try saving your own!"*

Orchid called up her Worldly powers, which, like Tresado's Absolute Magic, seemed greatly enhanced in this bizarre place. Humidity increased, temperature dropped, and pressure fluctuated wildly. All these factors combined to create a miniature tornado which lifted Orchid out of her speeding seat and moved along with the caravan, hovering just above the others. The electricity in the air played about her head, giving Orchid a terrifying countenance.

Little lightning spears spat out of the vortex and aimed themselves at Tresado. He countered them with Magic of his own. He batted the attacking bolts away and shot back at Orchid with blasts of kinetic energy, which she likewise defended against. The demands on his concentration caused his four Magical chairs to lurch and weave frantically in their wild trip across the desert.

Foxx, being the weakest Magician of the three, simply covered his head and tried to use his influence to calm his pissed-off friends. Serena could do nothing but try to maintain her balance.

Far ahead of them, a pair of eyes watched the curious sight and narrowed ominously. A silent gesture later, it was joined by many others.

"You will pay the price for your arrogance!" Orchid was terrible to behold, her eyes full of righteous vengeance for Tresado's intrusive style of Magic.

"EAT THIS!" Tresado yelled back as he launched another blast of power at Orchid.

"Stop it! STOP IT, ALL OF YOU!" shouted Serena. She couldn't reach Orchid on her flying wind perch, but she tried to make her way to Tresado. If she could just wound him in the leg or something, it would break his spellcasting and bring this nonsense to an end.

Tresado upped the ante, however, and reached out with his kinetic force. He managed to get past Orchid's defenses and wrap a Magical tendril around her tiny throat. His face went red with fury as he poured on the power. Orchid's tornado subsided and vanished. Tresado held Orchid aloft by the neck as they flew along wildly. Her eyes bugged out of her head and she started to lose consciousness from the choking attack.

Serena needed to do something fast. Realizing the seriousness of the situation, she knew she had no choice if she was to save her friend Orchid. She made a wild leap from her chair to the one Tresado was in. Serena raised her scimitar high and shrieked out her Northlands war cry. She started her swing, aiming the flat of the blade for the point where his neck and shoulder met.

Before the sword could fall, however, the caravan of chairs passed between two patches of the bamboo. A sturdy rope suddenly snapped up in their path. It caught Tresado across his pudgy stomach, flinging him backwards barely in time to avoid Serena's descending blade. He collided with Serena, who collided with Orchid, who collided with Foxx. His concentration now completely shattered, Tresado's ethereal chairs vanished and the members of Group Six found themselves dumped onto the desert floor and surrounded by armed people.

CHAPTER 6

*It has been said that I wish no friends. Untrue!
It is merely that my position as future planetary leader
necessitates otherwise . . .*

-Imperator Merak – Commentaries:
Book 3, Chapter 11, paragraph 1

Not quite 50,000 years ago

The hunter holding the spear held his ground and once again demanded what was due him.

"This lum is down from Yulo's spear. We take the kill."

"Our arrows struck both beasts," replied Jalex in a purposely calm voice.

The man coolly regarded Jalex. He looked about and saw no other hunters than these three.

"Arrows may bring down a grassbuck or a longear, but not a lum."

"It was *my* arrow that crippled the calf!" shouted Corma brashly. He brandished his arrowstick, but without arrows, he was not threatening. "And a single spear to the haunch also does not kill a lum!"

"Corma! You must . . . we must be calm." With her tone, Jalex also tried to infer the words *because they greatly outnumber us.*

"I am Jalex," she said, holding her arms wide. "You and Corma both speak truth. One spear and a hand of arrows cannot kill a grown lum. There is a thing here we do not understand. But, as my friend says, the calf was taken down by our arrows. Perhaps we may claim the young animal to feed our people. The mother is yours."

The man remained silent for a few moments while he appraised the young woman before him. He was surprised by her words and pleased by her appearance. The rest of this band of Ern had all arrived by now. In total, there were about five hands of men to one of women hunters.

"I am Doran," he said simply. "And the lum is not dead. We must dispatch her before she wakes from *deathsleep.*"

Doran turned to one of the hunters behind him. "Yulo, the charge is yours."

Yulo, short and wide for an Ern, puffed out his barrel chest proudly. "It shall be, leader. *Muta . . .* bring the medicine bundle."

An aged Ern with bowed back and a scarred face toddled up carrying a bulky package wrapped in hide. He and Yulo approached the lum, which lay upon the ground taking rapid, wheezy breaths. Muta ceremoniously unwrapped the bundle. Inside was a large carved wooden bowl, a sharpened *morok* antler, and several small leather pouches bulging with unknown contents. Yulo picked up the antler and stood by. Muta took the bowl and held it aloft, facing his companions. The hunters began uttering a low humming sound. The bowl was then offered to the sky and to the ground and finally to the lum. Yulo stepped up to the beast's head and bowed his own in an obvious sign of respect. The humming stopped abruptly. He then deftly sliced the sharpened side of the antler across the massive throat of the lum. The great beast did not react, as though unaware of what just happened. A massive amount of blood flowed freely from the wound and was caught by Muta in the bowl, which quickly filled to overflowing. They both stepped back with bowed heads and respectfully allowed the animal to bleed out. With a final shudder, the mother lum expired. The calf, sensing the tragedy, bleated piteously. Muta stepped forward, struggling with the heavy bowl of blood.

"We offer our thanks to land and sky. We offer our thanks to the hunters. And we offer our thanks to the lum, who will now live forever in the bodies of the Ern."

Muta passed the bowl to Yulo, who lifted it to his lips and took a long swig. He then gave it to the other hunters, who passed it around, one by one. Finally, it returned to Muta, then to Doran, the leader, who took his draught and wiped his bloody chin upon his wrist. He turned once again to appraise Jalex and her friends.

"Where do you make your hearths?"

"Do not tell him, Jalex!" cried Corma. "These strangers must not know . . . um . . . because they would all be killed by our many hunters!"

"*Corma!*" hissed Jalex. It was time to change the subject. "I ask you again, hunter Doran, to allow us to take the calf." Corma continued to act as though he wanted to dispute the deal, but the abundance of spears and more warning looks from Jalex kept him in check.

"Does this sound fair to you, hunter Doran?" She made sure to keep her voice calm and undemanding.

There were immediate mutterings of dissent among the other hunters. Many of them were unwilling to give up the calf. While it did not yield as much meat as the adult, it was more tender and the hide softer, a rich prize.

"And I ask *you* again," said Doran, not answering her question, "where is your tribe?"

"Near," she said evasively. To let on that they were days away would be just asking for trouble. Many of the mostly male strangers were openly ogling both her and Tru.

"Why do you send only a small hand of hunters to bring down a lum?"

"Our hunters are brave and skilled, but we did not expect to find such a large prey."

"But still you hunted the lum."

"That is right."

Doran studied the three for another moment, then turned back to his companions. They conferred for a few minutes quietly. Jalex and the others cocked their conical ears, but couldn't make out exactly what was said. They got the gist of it, though. At one point, a difference of opinion was voiced by a couple of Doran's men. The matter was settled by Doran knocking one of them on his ass, while the other backed down. He returned and nodded to Corma.

"You disabled the calf with a true cast of your arrow and prevented it from escaping. You may dispatch it and claim the kill."

Corma swelled with pride at this acknowledgement from the stranger. He looked to Jalex, who gave him an approving nod. She also handed him her last remaining arrow.

"Strike truly again, hunter."

Corma took the arrow and went to the stricken calf, who bawled in fear at the approach of its enemy. It struggled to move away, but with useless back legs, it could do nothing but pitch about. Corma cautiously waited for his opportunity, then leapt up onto the animal's back. He locked his strong legs about the baby lum's neck and plunged the arrow into one of its eye sockets. He shoved with all his might, driving the shaft into the animal's brain. It gave a shudder and collapsed into a quick, merciful death. Once he was sure it was dead, Corma jumped down to stand next to his trophy in triumph.

"CORMA! CORMA!"

Jalex and Tru shouted out their village's traditional tribute to a successful hunter. They went to him, clapping him upon the back and congratulating him further. Doran and his hunters looked puzzled and upset.

"You do not pay proper respect!"

"The lum dies without honor!"

"You would deny its calling!"

"ENOUGH!" shouted Doran to his hunters, then turned to Jalex. "You would give honors to the hunter and not to the prey?"

Tru was imprudent enough to spontaneously laugh out loud at this idea, which did not improve the mood of the hunters. She immediately stifled herself at their reaction.

"Corma, strike a fire. Tru and I will prepare some small amount of meat for the trail," said Jalex, trying to change the subject.

"I must send Tru back to our . . . *tribe* . . . to bring back skinning and butchering parties."

"And many hands of your warriors, too?" shouted one of the hunters.

"Do not think us of no wits!" from another.

"To steal what few women we have left?"

"KATA!" roared Doran. *"Keep your senses keen and your mouths closed! ALL OF YOU!"*

Doran turned to Jalex and fixed her with a cold stare. His intense grey eyes were as two agate stones worn smooth by the rivers of her youth before Senfall.

"My hunters are brave of heart, but like me, are cautious. What their mouths say, my ears must hear. Speak truly. *Do you seek to bring back warriors to slay us?"*

There had been no formal word of honor given. That sort of concept had no words in the language of the Ern. But, in the way that all Ern are as leaves of the same tree, somehow Jalex knew he was asking such a thing from her. And Doran knew that he would receive it from her.

"We do not." Jalex paused and made a decision. "I will tell you. Our village and lands were destroyed by Senfall. Most of our hunters were afield when . . . it happened."

She still couldn't get herself to say *when the sun fell,* as so many of her friends would.

"We three are the only hunters left. The rest of our village is camped two or three days away. There are but nine hands of us left, mostly mothers, children, and our wise women. Our people are starving and need food soon. This calf will save their lives, but it must first be skinned and slaughtered and the meat preserved. To do that, we must bring our people here."

Doran nodded, satisfied. "I, too, must speak truly. These hunters you see are all that are left of *my* people. When, what you call . . . *Senfall?"* He raised his eyebrows at Jalex. She nodded back. "On the day of *Senfall* our homes and families were all taken from us. We hunters were afield among the Glen of Stones, hunting saro. The rocks and their caves were as shields against the storm. Our village was along the riverbank near the lake. When the storms passed and we could return, we could not even find where our lodges and hearths had stood."

"Where do you call home now, Doran"? asked Jalex sympathetically.

He turned to his party of hunters and gestured for them to gather round. They all clasped arms about each other's shoulders in a pre-rehearsed gesture. "Until we find another place to build our lodges, our home is each other, and it travels with us always. *Does it not, my brave hunters?*" The brave hunters all agreed vigorously.

"We were heading for the valley beyond, to search for hunting lands when we found the pair of lum. Their way was also for the valley. When we began the chase, the animals turned around and headed back in this direction. Yulo's spear was the only one to hit true. We then followed the animals to await *deathsleep*. You know all after that."

"What is this *deathsleep* which you say?" asked Tru. Her speaking for the first time caused many hushed comments among the young men in the group. Tru blushed.

Again, Doran paused. He slowly reached for a small pouch that hung from his neck. He unlaced it and tapped a tiny amount of brownish powder onto the stone tip of his spear. "This is *deathsleep*. It is made from a mushroom that sprouted near the river of our home. When it enters an animal's wound, it is soon robbed of its wits and lies as one dead for a time. We need only follow and slay. It is rubbed onto our spearpoints. *Deathsleep* is one of *The Great Gifts of the Land* . . . one that was taken from us by the storms. When our river home was lost, the mushrooms were as well. We have little of the powder left."

Jalex was intrigued. From the wise women, she had heard of certain plants that had strange effects, like taking away pain or increasing bravery. This powder that could bring down a lum was frightening to think of. She wondered if such a thing could be trusted to all people, but didn't voice that concern just yet. Right now, there were more immediate things to think of.

"I must see to the meat."

Corma had a fire going by now and Tru was busy cutting and sharpening some stakes. Jalex turned to the problem of how to begin removing some meat from the calf. It would be some time before her people could arrive and she didn't want to expose too much of the carcass to the elements just yet. There were also scavengers to worry about. She selected a section of the calf's rump and made a deep cut in the animal's flank with her knapped flint knife. The rich, red tissue beneath the hide steamed in the cold as Jalex sliced away a thick portion. All of the Ern gathered around, their mouths watering at the sight and smell of the fresh meat. Jalex realized what must also be done.

"Doran . . . will your hunters join in filling their bellies?"

It was a generous offer. The giant carcass of the mother lum would yield many times the sustenance the calf would provide, but Jalex wanted to make doubly sure there would be no risk of conflict with these hunters. They seemed to have some strange ways of doing things. Besides, Doran's much larger band had the power to take both animals if they should wish. It would be wise not to anger them. Again, Doran was surprised by this dark-skinned woman with her peculiar but intriguing ways.

"We are honored and must return the gift. Yulo . . . the ears."

The man whose spear had made all this possible nodded. Using the thick hair of the beast, he pulled himself up onto the head of the adult. Using his own knife, he expertly sliced off the beast's two tiny ears. Tiny from the point of view of the giant lum. For the Ern, they were just the right size for a pair of soft, furry hoods, the very thing to stay warm while traveling across the frozen prairie.

The hunters squatted together around the fire, roasting meat on stakes for immediate consumption and smoking more for the trip back to retrieve the rest of Jalex's people. Tru was popular and had no shortage of male offers to roast meat for her or fetch her water or any number of suggestions.

The next morning, clad in her new lum's ear hood and loaded down with a supply of dried meat, Tru set off across the frigid land to fetch the rest of her people. Yulo accompanied her to provide protection and keep an eye on her at the same time. Jalex and Corma stayed behind with the rest of Doran's hunters, guarding the kills and making plans for the future.

* * *

Yes, Porter, you have a question?

Professor, I was down at the docks the other day when a trade ship came in, supposedly the first one ever from someplace called the Treskan Coalition. They had a weird accent, but I could understand them. How could people from thousands of leagues away whom we have never seen before use the same words for things?

Porter, I can see how you, as a Macai, would wonder about that. But the simple fact is that all Eryndi know what all Eryndi know. Macai know what they have learned. Now, speaking of learning, everyone open your scrolls to the section on ethics . . .

\- Professor Hariel, Dean of Kadizio University
– 21056 to 21172 - New Calendar

Today – the desert

The members of Group Six all stopped rolling at about the same time. Orchid was still stunned and coughing from being choked. Tresado and Foxx were in not much better shape. Serena had come through the collision unscathed, thanks to her warrior reflexes. She had managed to come out of the roll springing to her feet and still clutching her sword.

The people surrounding them were armed with a strange assortment of clubs, staffs, and spears, most of which looked homemade. A couple of them carried small round shields and one of them wore a bronze helmet with a feather plume on top. Their attire was a mishmash of styles and materials. One fellow had on a kind of green toga that looked like it was made of fine silk, while another had his loins covered by nothing more than a filthy rag. Most of them wore shoes of some kind, but much of these people's clothing was torn and ragged.

"Everybody just take it easy," said a gruff-looking man who had some kind of odd crossbow trained on Serena. "Drop the sword, sweetie."

"Not gonna happen, chief," she said in a steely voice. "Why don't you put down your toy while you still have all your limbs." For emphasis, she whirled her scimitar around in a faster-than-the-eye-could-follow move.

"Tell you what," the man replied. "You hand over all your food, and I'll consider not putting a bolt through your little friend's gullet." He turned his weapon on Orchid, who was just starting to struggle to her feet.

Serena blinked at that. She had dealt with her share of ruffians and highwaymen in her time, but they always demanded money before everything.

"Well, now you're really shit out of luck. We don't have a crumb . . . so why don't you do the smart thing and move on. I got no time for you today."

There was something ominous in her voice that made the guy hesitate, but only for a fraction of a beat.

"GET 'EM!"

The other ambushers all charged at once, swinging whatever weapons they had. Serena was already moving, though. She had read the guy's intentions and had reacted faster than he ever could. By the time he pulled the trigger, she was already between him and Orchid. His bolt glanced off the broad part of Serena's scimitar. Her swing followed through in a sweeping arc and came down on top of his crossbow. The razor-sharp steel cut through the bowstring and knocked the weapon out of his hands. A quick reverse caught the man behind the knees with the back edge of the sword and he went down hard. Serena kept him down by standing on his chest and holding her sword tip to his throat. He was quite satisfied to not move. A quick kick under the chin put him to sleep and she jumped off.

Foxx was engaged with a couple of guys at once. One had a club and the other a staff and both were trying to brain him. He had no weapons other than a small belt knife and his rapier wit. But Foxx was an expert, not at fighting, but avoiding a fight. He could get out of harm's way faster than anyone. He ducked their clumsy swings with some defensive moves and kept backing up, forcing them to advance.

Tresado and Orchid had by now recovered from their falls and were on their feet. At first, their fury was still directed at each other, but the onslaught of the muggers distracted them from that. Tresado sent out a powerful wave of kinetic energy that slammed into two of the attackers with sledgehammer force. One man's skull was crushed from the impact, while the other was abdominally pulped, staining the desert floor with a crimson intestinal mess.

There were six more muggers to be dealt with. Orchid's eyes lit with emerald fury as she gathered the forces of weather around her. A small tornado formed, picking up stinging sand from the desert floor. It traveled unerringly to each one of the brigands, gathering them up into its vortex as easily as a child picking daisies. One by one the highwaymen, including the two attacking Foxx, were sucked up into the funnel. They were then flung high into the air, making squishy splat noises when they finally hit the ground.

Serena watched the brutal display with worried eyes. She had seen her fellow Northlanders go into berserk killing frenzies, but not her supposedly *civilized* friends.

The last of Orchid's victims landed on his back on top of a sharp rock, snapping his spine with a sickening crack. The maniacal look in her eyes lessened some, but she was still grinning in satisfaction. Serena had never seen her friends react with such extreme measures.

Tresado looked around, seemingly disappointed that there were no more villains to vanquish. His eyes fell upon Orchid.

"YOU! You tried to kill me with those feeble little sparks of yours!"

"And *you* tried to strangle me, you psycho bastard!"

Both of the powerful Magicians began once again to summon the forces at their command. In their anger, they did not notice that Serena had quietly picked up one of the attackers' clubs. She sidled up to Tresado's side.

"That's it, let her have it," she said supportively. A beat later, the knob end of the cudgel cuffed the Eryndi on the back of the head. Without losing momentum, the weapon flew through the air and unerringly impacted Orchid's noggin. Both of them stood there with stupid looks on their faces for a moment and then collapsed into the sand.

"Good work!"

Foxx emerged from cover, brushing off his scarlet jacket. He beamed a smile at Serena and began examining the bodies that were strewn about. He bent over one of the ones dropped from the sky by Orchid's tornado. The broken body had landed in a bamboo patch and impaled itself on a pole.

"Hey, I know this one! She was the gambler that I saw teleported away by the Palace for cheating."

"Speaking of cheating at cards . . ." said Serena humorlessly. She slowly advanced upon Foxx with outstretched palm.

"Ah . . . I think we should discuss that, my dear." His voice became melodious and pleasing. His glance was gentle and reassuring, until Serena's powerful right fist landed directly between his eyes. Foxx went flat onto his back and stayed there.

"Discussion over."

Serena reached into his pocket and retrieved her diamond, snapping it back into place in the hollow in her sternum. That being finished, she looked around at her unconscious companions.

"Now, what am I going to do about you turdheads?"

A shuffling sound caught her ear. The ground was shifting in several places as a herd of rock crawlers began burrowing out of the sand. Serena tensed for another attack, but soon realized they weren't going after her. There was much easier meat to be had in the neighborhood. Serena watched stoically as the crawlers began devouring the dead. These things always seemed to be hungry.

"Yeah, that'll work."

CHAPTER 7

> \- Travelogue of Dementus,
> the Mad Treskan

* * *

Not quite 50,000 years ago

It took a few days, but Tru returned safely with the rest of
their people. At first there was mutual suspicion and mistrust,
but Yulo spoke on their behalf. It seems he had developed a
. . . respect for Tru and these strangers. The decision was
made to combine the two tribes. Doran's people were capable
hunters, but mostly male. The survivors of Jalex's village had a
higher percentage of women. Each group had what the other
needed (or wanted).

The lum carcasses were stripped of everything of value.
For the first time since Senfall, there was enough food for all.
The huge supply of smoked meat and hides harvested from the
animals was invaluable, but it would not last forever and this

was not the place to settle down. The area was too desolate. Encountering these two animals had been a fluke. If the Ern did not find good hunting grounds, they would soon be on the verge of starvation again.

The older Ern and children were kept busy making temporary shelters among the rocks. The giant ribs and sinew from the lum were put to good use. The hunters meanwhile ranged far afield on scouting trips. One place they wanted to investigate was the valley to the east. From a distance, it was a forbidding place. Essentially it looked like an enormous crack in the land. The walls of this gigantic rift were striped with ugly shades of brownish-red like a jagged wound left untreated. Jalex, Doran, and a hand of hunters approached an arm of this valley after two days of travel. They nearly passed it by because it looked so desolate, but Jalex stopped in her tracks, sniffing the wind.

"Danger?" asked Doran, looking around with spear ready.

"No . . . there is nothing. I . . . see nothing."

That seemed to satisfy Doran.

"Come. We must move on. There are no hunting grounds here."

Jalex didn't answer, but moved to the sharp edge of the precipice ahead. She peered down cautiously.

"I cannot see to the valley floor. There is a ridge far below that blocks my sight."

Doran joined her and wrinkled his nose.

"There is a foul smell coming from this valley. It is as eggs that have spoiled. This is an evil land. Not good for Ern. Come."

Doran moved away from the sheer precipice and signaled the other hunters to take up the trail again. Jalex stubbornly stayed where she was. She looked up and down until she spotted a place where a broken fissure had fractured the cliff edge. It was still treacherously steep and strewn with loose boulders, but might provide a way down to the ridge.

"Wait. I would see closer."

Without looking back at the others, she immediately headed for the fissure and disappeared over the edge of the canyon wall. Doran sighed. In the brief time he had known this woman Jalex, one thing he learned about her was her stubborn streak. There was also her frustrating habit of being right all the time.

"Wait here."

The other hunters nervously agreed, but remained where they were. Against his better judgement, Doran followed the woman down the steep incline. Being lighter and more agile, Jalex was already far ahead of him. He could see her scrambling down the tortuous path probably faster than it was prudent to go.

What is her hurry?

Doran picked his way carefully and eventually lost sight of Jalex. He called out to her several times, but received no answer. It was unnerving the way his voice echoed back and forth in this evil canyon. His animal instincts told him to get away from this place fast. His legs didn't know that, though, and carried him down the same path the woman had gone. He scrambled down the boulder field, nearly slipping to his death a handful of times. At last, he stopped sliding just above the ridge and got a good grip on a scrubby bush that grew out of the rocks. He supported himself there and looked around. A slight fog was rising out of the chasm beyond the ridge. A dark figure was silhouetted against it. It was Jalex. She was standing still and peering down into the valley.

Prudence prevented Doran from calling out her name. There was something very disturbing about Jalex's body language. She was holding herself very still while looking down, but her demeanor was one of complete calm. He approached her quietly.

"This will do."

Doran walked up beside her and peered down. Below the ridge, which blocked the view from above, the whole valley floor was laid out. A river of blue water wound through a greenery-filled ribbon of forest and grasslands. The valley was narrow and winding, but extended far beyond the horizon to disappear into the mist. Here and there, steam was rising above bubbling pools of apparently hot water. There were areas of snow and ice, but the heat rising from the ground kept most of it at bay. But the most treasured sight, the one that lifted Doran's soul to the sky, was of the tiny dark figures moving across the landscape. Great herds of animals were grazing on the abundant grass. Saro, grassbucks, and yes, even gigantic lum wandered about freely.

"Yes, this will do," repeated Jalex quietly.

* * *

Macai are bigger and stronger, use more powerful Magic, and outnumber the Eryndi five to one. Of course Macai eventually win in the end . . . but does the Council want to listen to me? NOOOOO!

- Joculan the Third — Banishment Diaries, Chapter 6 — *Mathematics as Prognosticators* — 21659, New Calendar

Today – the edge of the Zone

Tarbor and Sensis goaded their horses just a tad faster. If they didn't, it would be dark before they returned from this patrol. Both of the soldiers lived in married housing and both feared their wives more than their Captain. It was a little hard on the string of infantry that trotted along behind, but the Queen's Guard had a reputation for toughness. That's what every army tells its troops.

"So, what's this I hear about you retiring, Sensis?"

"I don't know what you hear," replied the older man.

"That you're retiring. Whaddaya got now, twenty-eight, twenty-nine?"

"Thirty-four."

"*Thirty-four* years of fighting off raiders, patrolling the Zone, guarding the Queen. You've done it all, seen it all . . . think you're ready to give that all up and settle down at home every day with the Missus?"

"Hypothetically that might be a nice change."

"And what would you do, *hypothetically?*"

"Look."

"Look for what, your lost youth?" Tarbor guffawed at his own fabulous sense of humor.

"No, dumbass. I mean *look* . . . over there . . . that cloud of dust."

Tarbor shaded his eyes against the setting sun. "Hey, something's coming out of the Zone."

"No shit. They should make you a general. *Squad!* Form ranks and stand by for an interception!"

The foot soldiers quickly formed a skirmishing line and readied weapons. Bows were strung and swords were drawn.

They fanned out, taking advantage of whatever cover was in the area. Sensis pulled out his viewing tube and took a long look. He dropped the tube, rubbed his eyes, and took another look.

"What is it, Lieutenant?" asked Tarbor, automatically using rank now they were back on the hourglass.

"Remember when you said that I've seen it all?"

"Yeah."

"Well, now I can retire," replied Sensis, passing the tube to Tarbor.

Coming out of the zone was the most bizarre sight ever seen by someone not stoned on billy bark. It was some kind of . . . *sleigh* made of long *bola tree* poles lashed together with bark. And lashed to the body of this contraption were three people trussed up like Honor Day piglets. Projecting out the front of this thing was a triangular arrangement of long spars tied together at their tips. Dangling from the end of this was another tied-up man who hung by his feet like an upside-down figurehead under the prow of a ship. A wild-maned blonde woman stood atop the back of this desert dogsled shrieking an unearthly war cry. She was hanging onto ropes or something and apparently guiding it.

"Lieutenant . . . that's . . . um . . . that's weird."

"Yeah," replied Sensis simply.

As the craft got closer, Tarbor and Sensis could now make out just what was propelling this thing. Somebody had managed to capture six of those disgusting yellow crawlers that lived in the Zone and strapped this homemade dogsled thing onto their backs. Apparently the tied-up man dangling from the *bowsprit* was the impetus for them to scuttle along after him, but finding their lunch always just out of their blasting range.

"Like hanging a carrot in front of a plow horse," said Sensis.

Tarbor squinted his eyes. "It's slowing down."

He was right. The crawlers had noticeably backed off on scuttling speed. The driver continually yelled *hyah, hyah,* but rock crawlers don't know what that means. At last, the whole contraption came to a halt. The woman jumped down and gave one of her steeds a swift kick, but it was no use. The creatures were not only no longer moving, but actually starting to dry up and disintegrate. Bits and pieces were falling off of them, until at last, the sled dropped to the ground as the stone-crawlers turned into nothing but bits of flaky husks, blowing away in the dry wind.

Serena snorted in disgust and looked around to see what her options might be. Her warrior senses suddenly came alert. The reason was clear a beat later. Two mounted Macai flanked by twenty foot soldiers had emerged from cover and were advancing on her. They were not charging to attack, but their demeanor was not that welcoming.

"Halt and stay where you are!"

The older Macai on the horse was the one barking orders . . . obviously the leader. He would be the first target if it came to that.

"Identify yourself!"

Serena stood her ground, sword ready, but she saw the armored bowmen flanking out around her. They were well equipped, professional, and clearly had the advantage.

"I am called Serena the Free," she replied, not lowering her sword just yet.

"Indeed . . . that may change. What is your purpose in this area?"

"I and my friends are here by accident. We are trying to reach civilized lands."

Sensis regarded Serena's sleigh. "These tied up people are your friends?"

"They were . . . a little out of control."

The soldier indicated the upside-down fellow, who was whimpering softly. "And this one?"

"He attacked us."

"Do you practice Magic?"

The question caught Serena off guard for a moment.

"No."

"Do they?"

"They do. I don't know about him," she said, indicating the dangling captive.

"Lemme go . . . LEMME GO!" said Mister Dangly.

Tarbor dismounted his horse and cautiously approached Serena and her strange conveyance. He kept a wary eye on her as he examined the trussed-up figures of Tresado, Orchid, and Foxx. He had no need to draw a weapon. He and Serena both knew any aggressive move on her part would instantly bring a dozen arrows from the soldiers.

"Lieutenant . . . I think these three are dead."

They certainly looked that way. There was no sign of breathing and the woman's green eyes were open in a blank stare.

"Is that true?" asked Sensis.

"They are not dead," answered Serena. "I gave them a dose of sleeping powder from that one's herb kit. I . . . may have used a bit too much. I am a warrior, not a healer."

"And the upside-down one?"

"I needed him to be active so as to give my *steeds* more reason to run."

Sensis nodded in understanding. His own soldier's instincts told him Serena was speaking the truth.

"Sergeant, check all for buboes."

"Yes, Lieutenant."

Tarbor loosened the collar of Foxx's garish shirt and closely examined his neck. He then did the same for Orchid and Tresado.

"Nothing on these three. The fat one's a hook!"

That comment caused murmuring among the Macai soldiers. Tarbor then approached Serena and gave her a quick once-over, closely eyeing her open neckline and sparkling diamond. She was used to that, though. The fire in her eyes clearly warned against anything more. Tarbor did nothing more than look, however, and went over to the squirming captive, who was still pleading to be released.

"Hold still, this won't hurt."

The man had a bit of rag wrapped around his neck like a scarf. When it was removed, two large red lumps on his throat stuck out like a pair of hobo clams. Tarbor poked at them with his thumb, causing the guy to scream in agony.

"Okay, so it did hurt. This one's positive, Lieutenant."

"All right, step back." Sensis turned to three of the closest soldiers. "Reger, Nollan, Jorkill . . ."

The men called stepped forward with their bows. Sensis gave them a nod and they simultaneously drove three arrows into the chest of the hanging captive. He died with a strange smile on his face.

"Now, warrior," he said to Serena, "listen very carefully."

* * *

12,579 years from today

The bluish smoke from Vinnie's little pipe swirled around the interior of his ground car. He would have passed it to Derek right away, but his buddy held up a palm. To prevent the expensive jamba from burning away, he quickly covered the bowl with the bottom of the lighter.

"I'm tellin' ya man, history doesn't just unfold like a paper map."

Vinnie was intrigued. "Whaddaya mean, dude?"

"Okay, dig this," Derek said, staring fixedly at the van's dome light. "You take a road map like . . . like this one here . . . and you unfold it one fold at a time. And each time you do that, you reveal about a hundred more leagues of land at a time."

"Yeah."

"It's the same with a history textbook. As you turn the pages, it jumps you ahead centuries at a time, just like a road map. History . . . *real history* . . . is more like a . . . an endless linen scroll that's rolled up."

"Okay . . . okay . . . I'm totally diggin' that," said Vinnie in an epiphany. "As the history scroll *slooooowwwwly* unrolls, it exposes just a tiny bit more of itself as it goes."

"*Beauty* . . . every thread a new day, each day with the tiniest of changes, so gradual as to not even be noticeable. And then every turn of the scroll is a century."

"And the whole thing unrolled is all of Macai recorded history. If you could go back way before that to pre-cataclysmic times, you could actually see the point where the Eryndi are still there."

"The Eryndi? Dude, that would have to be one long-assed scroll."

"Totally."

Vinnie and Derek sat in silence and contemplated the enormity of what they had just discussed. They each took another toke from the pipe and Vinnie stashed it under the dashboard. He checked his watch.

"Dude, I gotta split. I have a class starting at one."

"Will we see you and your wife at the faculty dinner tonight?"

"No worries, man. I'll have to stop by the magic station and fuel up the van, but we'll make it."

"Pat and I will be there, too. We're sitting at the Dean's table."

"Far out."

Not quite 50,000 years ago

Jalex's back ached. This wasn't the first child she had carried, but she swore this one was either triplets or would be born fully grown. The terrain was rough, but not too steep and she took it slowly and carefully. She had all day. Doran had taken their other two children, Tarl and Shona, with him today. It would be their first longear hunt and they were excited to try out their first arrowsticks.

The weather was cold as usual, but today was different somehow. There was a tingling in the air that Jalex could swear she hadn't felt since she was a girl. Ignoring the advice of the wise women who warned her not to go tromping around the hills in her pregnant condition, Jalex continued the easy climb up to the ridge. She could do this and get away with it. She simply wanted to get out of the communal lodge for a while and it was a pleasant day. As she climbed, she remembered that other day in the past when she had been out by herself . . . the day the flaming orb plummeted to the ground . . . the day that changed everything . . . the day of *Senfall.*

That's it . . . this day . . . is that day.

She smiled to herself at the thought and felt a little silly. That day was nearly three hands of seasons in the past times. Jalex had always been known as the sensible one, the thoughtful one, the one who looked for reasonable answers to difficult questions. That was why she had been chosen long ago to lead the tribe. And a leader had no business thinking such ridiculous thoughts. Two days so far apart cannot be the same day.

For one thing, Senfall was the beginning of the most terrible storms and destruction ever known by the Ern. So very many of their people had died from exposure and hunger.

This day was nothing like that. The snows were actually melting on the ridge today. Icicles dripped from every tree in the unaccustomed warmth.

No, this day is not that day.

The valley below was warm, of course. The lodges had been built among the hot springs, which provided a constant source of warm, tangy-tasting water. This valley, sheltered by the surrounding hills and replenished by the underground water springs, had drawn every living thing in the area. Herds of saro, grassbuck, and even lum flourished here. The forests produced hardy strains of rockfruit and vine melons. The pools were full of shellfish that somehow flourished in the hot, steamy water and the river was home to fat clubfish and flipperpups.

Other tribes of Ern who called this valley home. Some lived in the forest hills and hunted birds and wild goats. There were others who stayed on the plains and lived a nomadic existence, traveling up and down the vast, winding length of the valley trading with other tribes. And there was the tribe of

Jalex who stayed close to the herds, as they had always done even before Senfall. There was plenty of room and resources for everyone to live peacefully in their own way and not have to compete.

Jalex reached the stony ridge at last. She sat down gratefully upon a large, flat rock and massaged her swollen feet. The land below stretched out as far as her eyes could see. This was the same vantage point where she and Doran had first gazed upon the valley many seasons ago.

That tingling sensation returned.

Maybe it has something to do with being pregnant, but . . .

Jalex had been having these occasional twinges since . . . well, for a long time. They usually occurred whenever she was excited or under stress. Many times during a hunt, she had felt like she was in contact with the prey. She thought back to the day she had met Doran. That enraged mother lum had communicated her feelings as clearly as if she had spoken aloud. Jalex had never put much stock in these strange twinges. They were probably just the result of the excitement of the moment. But today it was different. Jalex felt good. Her sore back and aching feet were forgotten as a warm, friendly feeling swept over her, filling her being with great joy. She realized with a start that the warm feeling was actually on her shoulders. As she shifted her weight on the rock, she noticed a movement directly in front of her. It was something she had not seen in many seasons – her shadow. She turned quickly and looked to the sky. The ever-present brown clouds had broken above her and bits of blue peeked out. But that was not what lifted her spirit and caused it to soar like an arrow hawk.

So that was why this day felt like one from the past . . .

Sen, the glorious sun, was back in the sky!

CHAPTER 8

Flowers turning petals to ash,
Fire turning ash to honey,
Oh newborn Ring, Oh perfect mate,
Newly wed to the circle of time . . .

\- Trianna of Sylvas,
Poetess to the Glades

Today – the edge of the Zone

"Just so we're clear," said Lieutenant Sensis, "we're going for a little hike and we won't tolerate any nonsense from you. Now cut your friends loose and let's be on our way."

"Where to?"

"You'll find out when we get there."

"They're still unconscious."

"Well, that's too bad."

The unsaid meaning behind that was not lost on Serena. She sheathed her sword and used her utility knife to loosen the strands of bark that held her sleeping friends to the sleigh. She then laid each one of them on the ground.

"Give me a beat."

She took Orchid's herb kit from which she had obtained the sleeping powder. There had to be something to counteract the sedative. Serena searched through the various vials until she found something she thought might work. It was an oil made from some kind of nut. She thought she remembered Orchid saying something about it being a stimulant. Taking a bit of cotton that she found in the kit, Serena put a couple of drops on it and rubbed it on Orchid's nostrils. The piercing scream that came out of the tiny woman's mouth was probably heard all the way back in the Northlands. Orchid came to immediately, writhing on the ground and rubbing her nose frantically, trying to get rid of the *saba oil*. The potent fumes penetrated her brain and convinced her body it was on fire.

"What the? . . . Where? . . . Oh, my head! I think I'm gonna . . ."

There was not much to throw up, since none of them had eaten in over two days. Still, her body spasms weren't pretty as she retched. When she was done, Orchid looked up with bleary, unfocused eyes.

"Serena?"

"Yeah?"

"What happened? Who are they?"

"Long story. I'll tell you later. Right now, we have to wake up the others."

Serena quickly filled her in on what she had done medicinally. It turned out to be kind of the right thing to do, just a bit of overkill on the stimulant. It should have been diluted, but Serena didn't know that. Orchid was still snorting and shaking her head, trying to purge the remaining full-strength saba oil from her sinuses. She took the herb kit and prepared the proper dosage for Tresado and Foxx. She also took a bit of analgesic to try to alleviate the pounder she had. Foxx awoke with a similar headache, but when Orchid went to tend to Tresado, Sensis interrupted her.

"Not that one!"

"I beg your pardon?"

"Keep the hook asleep.

"Now wait just a damn minute!" retorted Serena, her hand going back to her sword.

Sensis's finger went up. At the signal, the soldiers immediately drew beads on all of Group Six. The dry desert wind sang through the dozen tightly drawn bowstrings. That plus the ten drawn swords convinced Serena to back off. She knew that a drop of that finger would mean instant death. Even so, backing off was not something the Northlands warrior did easily.

"Tarbor, sling the hook over your saddle," Sensis said gruffly. "You, warrior . . . you won't be needing that funny looking sword for a while. Pass it up here."

Serena thought of several ways she would like to 'pass it to him,' but chose to do things the peaceful way. She handed the soldier her scimitar pommel first and he slid it under a strap on his saddle.

"All right you three, start walking," he said, pointing to the east. The two horsemen led the way, while the foot soldiers surrounded the captives and followed behind.

"Sorry about clobbering you, by the way," said Serena, noticing Orchid rubbing her temples as they walked.

"Huh? What do you mean?" replied Orchid, touching the bruise on her forehead. "You mean this? You did that?"

"You don't remember?"

"I . . . I'm not sure. It doesn't hurt much. A little tarrabor root took care of that, anyway. This headache is coming from inside my skull."

Foxx was also blearily trying to locate himself. "So . . . what were we . . . how did . . . ? I mean . . . Gods of Us All, I don't know *what* I mean."

"I know what you mean," said Orchid. "I mean I *don't* know what you mean! Oh, my head is killing me!"

"You mean Tresado was killing you."

"Huh?"

"You made a tornado? And the lightning? And then he was strangling you?"

"*WHAT?*" yelled Orchid, instantly regretting it.

"Maybe we should just forget about it," said Serena. "I don't think you two were yourselves back there and you're not thinking very straight right now."

"I gotta agree," added Foxx. "I swear there's a marching band with sledge hammers in my brain. So . . . who are your friends, Serena?"

Serena wanted to loudly retort something about their escort being a bunch of blundering morons. It wasn't their proximity that prevented her, but rather the fact that these guys had professional soldier written all over them. They were well armed, disciplined troops that kept close eyes on their captives at all times. The soldiers and their officers wore matching armor breastplates with red medallions on their chests. Serena didn't like being under their control, but admired the way they comported themselves.

"We haven't been introduced," she said instead. "By the way, they seemed pretty interested about who uses Magic. I wouldn't try turning them into frogs just yet."

"Don't worry," said Orchid painfully. "With this headache, I couldn't bend a dandelion stalk."

Evidence backing up that statement was the fact that Orchid's staff had gone completely dark. Usually when she carried it, the head sparked or glowed or rumbled or whatever. Now it behaved like any normal piece of intricately carved wood and did nothing.

Walking seemed to help. Eventually, Orchid's and Foxx's pains settled down to dull aches. As they trudged along, it was a pleasant relief to see the desert sands rapidly turning into grasslands. The change was in fact so rapid as to be startling. Just a quarter of a league behind them, the terrain was still sand, rock, a few of those bamboo poles, and some scrub brush. Now the ground beneath their feet was pleasantly soft and verdant. Wildflowers and succulent plants grew everywhere, which made Orchid feel better.

"Lieutenant," called Tarbor from up ahead.

"Yeah, Sarge."

"The hook is starting to squirm. Permission to let it walk on its own fat little legs?"

"Granted . . . your horse will appreciate being rid of that load."

Tarbor pulled on the end of the knot holding Tresado to his saddle. The rope came undone and the Eryndi slid off onto the grass in a heap. Foxx and Orchid helped him to his feet. The same look of confusion crossed his face as he tried to remember who he was and why he felt so weird. He soon recognized his friends, but there was no time for explanations before the soldiers resumed the march. A couple of prods from sword tips got the party moving again.

"I know, you've got a million questions," said Serena quietly to Tresado. "Save them for now until we figure this out." He was still too groggy to put up much of an argument, so he just fell into step with the rest.

"Anybody got anything to eat?" asked Foxx of his escorts. "We've been stuck in that hellhole back there for a couple of days."

Sergeant Tarbor looked back and gave them a nod. Some of the troopers dug into their packs and handed over a few bits of rations. They were some kind of dried meat wrapped in a rock hard tortilla and tasted like salty boot leather, but to the hungry Group Six, they really hit the spot. They were also given a skin of water to pass around.

Everyone was feeling better now that they seemed to be out of the desert and had a little food in them. The three Magicians still had little memory of events other than bits and pieces.

Foxx closed his eyes and strained every brain cell as they marched along. "I remember the locusts . . . and that giant starfish thing . . . but . . ."

"Yeah, and there were those stony creatures," added Orchid. "Did something else happen? I seem to remember playing cards or something."

"No, not much. There was a scrape with . . . some bandits," replied Serena quickly. "But that was about it."

"And I think I owe everyone an apology," said Tresado. "This was my fault. It was my experiment that got us here . . . wherever we are."

"Listen to that!" chortled one of the foot soldiers. "The monkey talks."

"Hey blondie, is your pet housetrained?" added another.

The platoon obviously appreciated good humor and broke out in chuckles.

"Pipe down, back there!" shouted Tarbor.

"Good advice, boys," said Serena. "You wouldn't want to say anything you'd regret."

"Just keep moving and keep quiet . . . *all of you!*" added Tarbor.

The walk continued on in silence. The trek became a bit easier as they topped a rise and started down a gentle grade. A well-used road appeared and the party followed it. In the distance up ahead, the green grassland was marred by a huge jagged canyon carved into the land. Reddish, striated rock lined the walls. Another two hours of marching brought them to the rim of this valley. A fortified stone wall guarded the entrance to the giant canyon. It was a quarter of a league wide, terminating at the sheer cliff edges on both ends. In the middle was a large gate made of solid stone. Each side of the door was flanked by a pair of enormous wooden columns with depictions of large animals adorning them. Sensis called a halt before the door. Several figures could be seen atop the wall, which bristled with defensive battlements obviously designed to launch weapons from.

This is one well-defended place, thought Serena. *I wonder what they're afraid of.*

"Patrol returning with four prisoners," Sensis called up to the guards on top of the gate.

"Recognition," demanded a voice above.

"Moonstar, seven-one-nine, red," the Lieutenant responded.

"Open the gate!"

The thick stone doorway began moving upward, accompanied by a heavy grinding sound. Sensis guided his platoon through, ducking below the still-rising gate. As soon as the party was inside, a command was given and the gate began dropping back down again. On either side of the door was a lumba wearing a heavy woven leather harness. The giant animals were hitched to a complex block and tackle system connected to the stone door and controlled the opening and closing of the gate.

"Look at those machines there," said Orchid. A pair of powerful giant crossbows were located just inside the gate. They weren't aimed outward, as one might think, but instead were both pointed at the lumbas. "What do you suppose those are for?"

Serena appraised the devices with her warrior's eye. "I'd say they're designed to instantly kill the lumbas in case of a siege . . . to keep an attacker from opening the stone gate."

"Heartless bastards," replied Orchid, coldly glaring at the soldiers. She received no response from them.

Ahead there were wide, short steps carved into the rock wall. The prisoners were led down a short distance to the top of a stone ridge. From this point, they saw the floor of the valley in its entirety. Group Six stared down with wide eyes at the most beautiful land they had ever seen. A winding river meandered through the twisting valley, irrigating huge tracts of rich farmland and fruit orchards on terraces carved into the canyon walls. The valley floor was covered with exotic-looking buildings interspersed with groomed parks and walkways. Pools of brilliantly blue water bubbled and steamed in the setting sun. A slight smell of brimstone wafted up on the gentle breeze.

"Prisoners," said Sensis, "welcome to the country of Abakaar. We hope you enjoy your stay, because this is where you will spend the rest of your lives."

Today – The Crystal Palace

Sparkly had to find some way to bring good news to his boss for a change. This being the bearer of gloom and doom was getting old. Once again he approached the glowing double doors to Jakki's inner sanctum. This time they didn't open on their own. He exhaled a long, shaky breath and took out his converser. He held the enchanted seashell to his ear and waited. After several beats, the voice of Jakundarana Slivershkanent Trystelliar answered.

"What IS it?"

The fact that she didn't address him as *hon* didn't bode well.

"Sorry to intrude, Boss . . . more problems, I'm afraid."

Something was said just quietly enough to not be picked up by the converser, but Sparkly could recognize the profane nature. The doors ceased their blue glow and swung open. Jakki stood there, both hands on the doors. Her clothing was disheveled and her hair looked like it hadn't been washed recently. She glared at Sparkly with bloodshot eyes.

"What . . . *now?*"

The slow, ominous delivery made Sparkly's toupee slip down over his eyebrows.

"Customers are complaining."

"Well, don't make me guess! *What* are they complaining about?"

"I have compiled a list, Boss, but nothing seems related. The water supplies in the upper rooms are slow to respond, lights in the exhibition hall are flickering, even the *DoubleDare* wheels in the casino are reported to be . . . sticking. One party has filed a complaint because their carriage came back from

Service still dusty from the road and their draft animals didn't get their feathers groomed."

Jakki simply glared back without saying anything. Sparkly couldn't tell if he was dismissed or not.

"Fortunately, nothing that's happening is dangerous in any way. It just seems like the Magic systems in the Palace are . . ."

"Slow?"

"Yes, Milady."

Jakki's demeanor softened just a tad as she looked back at something in her office for a moment. She dipped her chin slightly, which to Sparkly's experienced eye meant she was casting some kind of spell. There was no visible effect, but after a moment, she turned back to him.

"It's okay, hon. Actually, that explains a lot."

"Is there anything I can do, Boss?"

"Keep the guests as happy as possible, but let them know we're aware of the problem and doing everything we can. You know, all the usual BS."

"Right, Boss. Is the Palace all right?" he asked, genuinely concerned.

"No. Right now the Palace is working itself to death. I will try to verify, but I'd say it's so busy with . . . whatever it's doing . . . that its basic functions are suffering for it."

"Can we help it?" asked Sparkly naively.

Jakki gave him an ironic grin. "We'll do everything we can."

Not quite 50,000 years ago

The celebration had already started by the time Jalex made it back down to the lodges. Young mothers were pointing to the sky and telling their wide-eyed children about the old days. The wise women and elder hunters were weeping with joy at the return of the sun. Many of the younger Ern were coupling in the excitement of the moment. Doran returned from the fields with Tarl and Shona, who ran full speed into their mother's arms. Shona was so excited she peed all over Jalex, but nothing could spoil the happiness of this day.

Unfortunately, the event didn't last long. By the end of the day, the break in the clouds had filled in again and returned the patch of blue sky to the unending brown of eternal winter. That didn't matter in the slightest, however. Just knowing that Sen was up there, back in Her place, back where She belonged, filled every Ern with joy and hope for the future.

That night, Jalex nuzzled Doran's neck as he held her in his strong arms.

"All is well now, my mate."

"Yes," she replied. "All will be as it should."

As if testing to see if the Ern really could maintain that faith, the weather got even colder over the next season. The sun did not reappear after that all-too-brief taste. The land froze once again above on the plateau and on the canyon walls. Many of the fruit trees died from the heavy frost. The parts of the valley floor near the hot springs where the lodges were built stayed thawed. This made hunting a bit easier, because the animals also congregated around the warm pools where they didn't have to scratch their way through frost to find edible plants. Unfortunately, some of the other tribes of Ern were also drawn to those areas for the same reasons. Hunting may have been more convenient for the tribe of Jalex, but now there were many more mouths in the area demanding meat. That made the animals more wary and the predators more dangerous because of the competition. Many times, conflicts with rival bands of hunters resulted in altercations. There had been nothing serious so far, but those whose spirit guides spoke to them were unsettled.

Jalex's third child came with great difficulties. The wise women were with her for much of an entire day, coaching her and easing her pain with herbs. When finally the baby arrived in the darkest part of the night, Jalex was so exhausted that she passed out before getting to see it. In the morning, she woke to the worried eyes of her mate. Doran was holding her hand. Before he even said a word, Jalex read what was in his eyes. The baby boy had come into the world backwards. Now his tiny body was being prepared by the wise women for a traditional Ern burial.

Jalex was severely weakened by her ordeal and could not even rise from her furs to attend the ceremony. Doran would not have left her side, but for her insistence that he honor the memory of his stillborn son. He reluctantly did so and watched the wise women carefully add bits of food, water, and a layer of sweet-smelling *coba* flowers to the grave. Two icons carved from a morok antler were also added. One represented his mother, Jalex, and the other the likeness of his father. Doran had always thought the custom strange, but honored it nonetheless. The tiny boy's trip beyond would be comfortable and pleasant. Jalex named him Dren, after a hunter that had died not long after Senfall.

CHAPTER 9

Today – Abakaar

Group Six's first destination in this new country was not one of the exotic-looking buildings they had seen from above. Instead, they were taken directly to a stone fortress at the edge of the city. It was a massive, forbidding place whose entrance was guarded by several soldiers.

It was a short walk down the stone road to the blockhouse. This building had none of the elegance of the structures glimpsed below. It was a fortress, nothing less. Like the gate at the top of the canyon, it hadn't the ancient look of some of the military places that Foxx had seen in Tresk or the castles designed to defend against Northlands raids. This place was of fairly recent construction. The stonework still had sharp edges and was not pitted or encrusted with lichens. It looked like no more than a few years had passed since this place was built.

They were taken under a heavy iron portcullis that was raised, but on a geared release system designed to be able to drop the gate at a moment's notice. Ten soldiers were on duty there, apparently ever ready to do just that if required. Another fortified door lay just beyond as an added precaution. Serena noted all with an appraising eye. Foxx kept a close watch on how everything worked. It was an old habit with him to always stay aware of the way out of any situation. The second door took them into a stone corridor. Oil lamps kept the place lit and maintained a greasy petroleum smell in the air. The hallway branched off to the right, but Sensis called a halt before another door leading to a dark staircase.

"Take chubby boy down below," he ordered a trio of guards on duty there. "The rest of you this way."

"Hey, wait a . . ."

"Hood it!" shouted Sensis before Tresado could finish his objection. The guards were apparently expecting the order, because they had a bag ready in hand and complied happily. The hood, made of some kind of wooly hide, was whipped over his head and cinched with thongs around his neck.

"Where are you taking him?" demanded Foxx.

"The tigers are hungry," gleefully answered one of the guards. That brought a giggle from the other two, who each took one of Tresado's arms and roughly hauled him down the stairs. A moment later, Foxx heard the unmistakable (and familiar) sound of a heavy, barred door slamming below.

Foxx, Orchid, and Serena weren't given the opportunity to object any further. They were immediately hustled down the hall and taken through a set of double doors. All three were expecting anything from simple holding cells to a fully equipped torture chamber. Surprisingly, they found themselves in a comfortable sitting room with padded furniture and a cheery fireplace blazing away. Next to it was a sideboard loaded down with decanters and trays of crackers, meats, and veggies. A little mouse of a woman squinted at them from behind an oak desk at the other end of the room. Like the soldiers, she also wore an identical red medallion, but as a cameo on her choker.

"Thank you, gentlemen, I'll take it from here."

The soldiers exited the room and closed the doors behind them.

"Come in please," she squeaked in a pleasant voice. "Help yourself to drinks and snacks. My name is Naomi. I have several questions, but we should be able to get you processed and out of here in no time."

Foxx eagerly grabbed up some morsels to quell his acute hunger. Orchid went right for the liquor bottles. Serena strode quickly toward the woman.

"What in Crodan's name is going on here? Where's . . ."

Before she could reach the desk or even finish her sentence, Serena collided with something unseen, which flashed with a strange red light upon impact. She wasn't hurt, but was flung backwards a couple of steps. To Serena, it felt like she had bounced off a rubber wall.

"Oh, do be careful, dear," Naomi said without even looking up from her desk. "You need to stay behind that red line on the floor until we're finished with your processing. I should have told you."

"We're very sorry to have caused you any inconvenience, ma'am," said Foxx in his charming way. "My friend just wanted to know . . ."

"We shall start with you, sir. Name?"

"Um . . . Foxx. That's with two exes," he replied, with his signature gesture of crossed fingers on both hands and crossing his wrists across his chest.

"First or last?"

"I beg your pardon?"

"Is Foxx your first or last name?"

"Yes."

Naomi glanced up from her desk for the first time with a no-nonsense glare.

"Full name, please."

Foxx looked back at Orchid and Serena, who were suddenly both very interested in hearing his answer.

Foxx mumbled something unintelligible into his hand.

"Lucy?"

Despite the apparent seriousness of their situation, a pair of barely contained snickers came from Orchid and Serena. Foxx's reddened cheeks did nothing to help the situation.

"No, not Lucy. It's *Lieusé*. It's pronounced Lyu-say' Foxx."

"Would you spell that, please?"

Foxx did so very deliberately, making sure to mention the accent mark.

"Place of birth?"

"City of Parad, in the Land of Tur on the western ocean."

"My, we *are* far from home, aren't we?"

"I don't know . . . are *we?*"

The Macai woman was completely nonplussed by any amount of sarcasm, it seemed.

"Do you practice Magic?"

"A little."

"What variety?

"Technically it's Absolute, but it's kind of . . ."

"Thank you. And now you, please. My, that's a lovely bauble you're wearing," she said, nodding toward Serena's diamond.

"This old thing? I just threw it on."

"Full name and place of birth."

"Serena Brimstone. Village of Grannugh, Luftar Valley of the Northlands," she stated proudly.

"Do you practice Magic?"

"Magic is for healers. I am a warrior."

"Thank you."

Naomi's eyes went next to the final member of the group.

"Orchid," she said, stepping forward, staff in hand.

"Full name, please."

"There is no more name. I am known only as Orchid. I was born in the Withiman Forest at the junction of the Olani and Tintani Rivers."

"I see," replied Naomi in a strange tone. "Who were your parents?"

"My adoptive parents were called Mishanna and Revinal."

"Those are *Eryndi* names, are they not?"

"Yeah . . . *so?*"

Naomi clucked her tongue and made some kind of notation on a form.

"Now then, Mister Foxx. What was the nature of your offense?"

"Offense . . . what offense?"

"Come, come now, dear. Just tell me what crime you were convicted of . . . and please . . . surprise me by not saying you're innocent."

"I'm innocent."

Naomi sighed. "Why should today be any different, I suppose?"

"All right, that's enough of this crap," snarled Serena. "It's time for you to answer some of *our* questions!"

"I'll tell you what, dear. If I answer your questions, will

you cooperate and answer the rest of mine? It will make all of this go much smoother and quicker.”

“I suppose.”

“Splendid. I’m already working overtime this evening and would like to get home and make dinner for my kiddos. What would you like to know?”

“Like . . . what is this place? Who are you people? What have you done with Tresado? What do you think you’re going to do with us?”

“This place is Abakaar. We are Abakaarians. I don’t know of any . . . Tostado, was it? I think I’m going to question and process you as per my job.”

“*Tresado* is our other companion,” interjected Foxx. “He was separated from us and taken someplace else.”

“Was your *companion* an Eryndi, by any chance?”

“Yes.”

“Oh, well that explains it,” said Naomi cheerfully. “Eryndi are processed separately. Eventually he’ll probably reside in the Bythian Quarter. He’ll be much happier there with his own kind. Now if that answers all of your questions, let’s get going on these forms. A little more paperwork and we’ll be all done here. Now, back to my original question. What offense did you commit that led to your banishment?”

“He already answered that,” replied Serena. “We didn’t commit any crime. We weren’t banished. We ended up in that turd pile because our Ernie friend was trying some new recipe or something and the Crystal Palace sent us there. It was an accident.”

“*Ernie,* huh?” giggled Naomi. “That’s a new one. I’ll have to tell my husband that. He’ll get a kick out of it.”

“So glad I could help,” scoffed Serena.

Naomi reached into a drawer and brought out a separate form.

"And the rest of you . . . you also came from the Crystal Palace?"

"That's right."

"Yes."

"How would you rate your time at the Palace?"

Blank stares.

"Would you consider the time you spent there to be a positive experience?"

Serena fingered the diamond embedded in her chest. Her two friends nodded.

"Very much," answered Foxx.

"Excellent. This *recipe* you mentioned. I take it you mean a spell."

"Yes," said Orchid. "Tresado was trying to duplicate the teleport spell the Palace used to send cheaters and thieves away."

Naomi tsk-tsked. "Oh, those crazy Eryndi . . . or should I say *Ernies,*" she tittered. "They really shouldn't be allowed to play with Magic like that . . . especially Absolute Magic. It's just asking for trouble.

"Now, just a few more questions," continued Naomi, all business once again. "Do any of you have any knowledge of the Treskan Imperium?"

"Why do you ask?" inquired Foxx innocently.

"No need to be evasive, dear. It's just a standard question. What can you tell me? Have you visited there?"

Orchid and Serena both answered no. Foxx tried to read Naomi the same way he would if she were sitting on the other side of a card table, but he found his Knowing Spell still difficult to summon due to the bad effects the zone apparently had on him. Even so, she was just too bubbly nice to have ulterior motives. He decided it was best just to be truthful.

"I've been there . . . some time ago."

"What were your impressions of their culture?"

"A well-ordered place. It was always safe to walk the streets at night and Treskan citizens lived in relative peace and security."

"Did you travel in any of the eastern provinces?"

"No."

"And how were you, as a Macai, treated by the ruling Eryndi overlords?"

"Well enough . . . though I don't know if I would call them *overlords.*"

"While there, did you ever get to see Imperator Merak?"

"Once. He addressed the crowd from the Imperial Balcony."

"Thank you. That completes these forms. One moment while they are processed."

Naomi neatly gathered up all the papers she had been writing on and placed them in a shallow tray on her desk. It looked like a simple in/out tray, but a moment later, an eerie red bar of light tracked back and forth once across them. After about five beats, a gentle tone sounded. Naomi smiled, picked up the forms, placed them into a common paper folder, and secreted that away into a leather valise.

She stood, wrapped her shawl around her narrow shoulders and picked up the bag.

"There now, that wasn't so bad, was it?" said Naomi. "The guards will issue you your citizen's certification tokens and info folders on your way out. Don't lose those, now. You're free to seek lodging anywhere you choose. Just look for red flags over the doors. They indicate vacancies. And welcome to Abakaar. I'm sure you'll enjoy living here. *Ta-ta.*"

Naomi went out a door behind her desk and was gone. Group Six was left in the room staring at each other with their mouths open.

Not quite 50,000 years ago

The cold seemed as though it would never let up. Conflicts with the neighboring tribes had increased as competition for the prey animals became more serious. There had been several skirmishes between hunters from the tribe of Jalex and the hill tribes who were forced down from their rocky homes due to the ever-present ice. The herds of morok, their usual prey, had also fled the cold to be closer to the hot springs on the valley floor. Tensions rose and it looked as though all-out war would soon show its vile face.

But always it seemed when things were at their worst, war was shooed away by a welcome visitor. Sen made occasional appearances more and more over the next few seasons. Each time She showed her face, it was a cause for celebration and good will.

Such things never seemed to last, however. The current summer season, such as it was, was coming to a close. Doran had joined a group of hunters intent on tracking a family of morok that had been spotted near one of the more distant hot spring pools. The giant deer were an excellent source of meat and hides and the tribe needed all they could harvest for the upcoming winter. Tarl and Shona, now capable adult hunters in their own right, accompanied.

Their mother stayed behind. Over the last two seasons,

she had been receiving tutelage from the wise women in the proper preparation of medicinal herbs. Jalex was still healthy and strong, but lately was cutting back on her hunting trips to study the mysterious ways of these healers and advisors. Ever since losing her child Dren a hand of seasons before, she had been impressed and awed by the skill of the wise ones. She also realized that their wisdom was slowly being lost as the elderly women passed beyond one at a time. Jalex knew that their knowledge must be preserved for the future, perhaps even improved upon. Maybe the skill to avert such tragedies as she had borne could be discovered.

Today, she was with old Myela on a trek to retrieve a supply of *bubble lichen*. From it could be made a salve that drew out rot from a wound. The fuzzy, blue-green organisms could be found only on the trunks of a certain type of pine tree that did not grow on the temperate valley floor. Finding these trees was not difficult. Getting to them on the icy slopes of the canyon walls was.

Jalex was here to learn the proper way to harvest the lichen. According to Myela, it had to be scraped off the tree bark in a very careful manner. Cut too deep and bits of the tree's sap were gathered as well, fouling the salve's healing powers with poison. Cut too shallow and the essential layer needed was not gathered, making any salve useless.

The wise woman and apprentice wise woman struggled up the slippery slope north of the lodges. Jalex had to support her elderly mentor the entire way as they laboriously climbed to where the twisted trees sprouted out of the red stone walls. While she denied needing assistance, the old woman's legs threatened to collapse under her at every step. The frigid wind swirled about them, raising clouds of stinging ice crystals that blocked their vision as they ascended. At last they reached the elevation at which the *sling tree* grew. Myela found a good specimen that had an abundance of lichen growing upon its bole. She reached into her medicine pouch and produced a very thin shard of flint. The curved edge was sharp enough to skin a pebble grape. Her wrinkled hands were deceptively strong and dexterous as she demonstrated.

"Observe how I hold the blade between my first two fingers. This will allow you to begin your cut at the proper angle. Note the widening of the tendrils as they attach to the base of the lichen. Begin your cut just a hair's breadth below the widest point. A swift, upwards motion, and . . ."

Myela flicked her wrist almost faster than the eye could follow and a wide swath of the lichen was severed from its parent. She caught the piece before it could hit the ground in a bowl made from a large mussel shell. Being careful to not touch the sample with her fingers, she used her shard to turn the slice over and showed the underside to Jalex.

"See the blue spots? That is the source of the lichen's power. But if you cut too deeply . . ."

She took her blade and cut a little deeper on the same spot. The lichen layer below was streaked with yellow.

"The sling tree is of an evil nature. It enjoys the suffering of the injured and seeks to prolong their pain. It resents the lichen leaving home and sends along poison out of revenge."

Myela carefully cleaned the offending sap off her blade and handed it to Jalex.

"Hold it as I showed you . . . use your thumb to steady the blade from behind. Bend your wrist thus . . . and hold the edge at the base of the tendrils. Do not rest the blade upon them. That will encourage the tree to leech its sap upwards.

You must strike when it is not aware of you . . . good! Hold the bowl below and be prepared to snare your prey. Now . . . make your cut."

Jalex's piece of lichen was not as large as Myela's but was properly cut. It would yield the medicine just fine.

"Good, you have learned quickly."

Jalex and Myela continued to collect the lichen until their fingers began to stiffen up from the cold.

"That is enough for now. To do more is to anger the tree and it will attempt to seek revenge and foul the medicine."

Jalex inwardly smiled at the old woman's notions, but instinctively knew of what she spoke. Carelessness could be disastrous when dealing with such delicate matters. Myela shivered and gathered her fur wrap about her stooped shoulders.

"It is time to make the homeward march."

"Let us rest and prepare ourselves first," said Jalex. She did not wish to endanger her frail old mentor's health by taxing her too much.

"Come, there is shelter in yon rocks. I will strike a fire and we will warm up before starting back."

"Very well, apprentice . . . if you are tired."

Jalex helped the old woman to a hollow between two large boulders. She got Myela settled and snugged up her furs. She then gathered up several twigs and pieces of bark that lay about and arranged them into a neat pile. Digging into her pack, Jalex pulled out a flexible stick of lum cartilage bound with thin leather thongs. She bent it and strung on a long piece of sinew, creating a small bow. She then took a pointed reed that was blackened on one end and twisted it onto the bowstring. Then a small handful of dried fur from her pack completed her fire-making kit. She packed bits of the fur onto a flat stone beneath her kindling and began to spin the reed quickly with the bowstring. It was a long process to get the stick hot enough to catch the fur on fire. Also, her kindling was not totally dry. Myela started a raspy coughing fit that worried Jalex. She had to get this fire started and it was not cooperating.

If only the tinder was drier and not so cold, she thought.

A strange tingling coursed through her veins as she doubled her efforts to ignite the flame. There was that strange feeling again . . . like an instinct. It was something that happened to her occasionally during times of stress. It was nothing she could explain, but felt completely natural to her. Jalex allowed the feeling to guide her wishes as a hunter guides the flight of an arrow. The object of her wishes obeyed. Jalex swore she could feel the moisture within the firewood vaporize and whisk away. The cold within also moved aside and allowed the flame to ignite. She blinked her eyes and suddenly realized that a bright fire now blazed away in her pile of wood. It seemed like a dream. She could remember how it felt and what was necessary to do this thing. The friction heat created by the spinning reed was scarcely even necessary. The flame ignited practically by itself. It was astonishing and very frightening at the same time.

Unfortunately, there was not time to think on this act because an ominous sound reached her ears from the lodges on the valley floor. It was the urgent repeated tones produced by someone beating the hollow warning logs in the village. Something was terribly wrong below!

CHAPTER 10

Today – Abakaar

Foxx, Orchid, and Serena went back out of the sitting room the same way they came in . . . after filling their pockets with snacks from the trays. Orchid tucked a decanter of mulsum under her arm. True to Naomi's word, the soldiers were waiting in the hallway for them. As callous as they had been during their capture, these guys were now strangely polite. Serena's scimitar was returned to her. They then gave each of the newcomers identical pouches printed with their names and escorted them out of the fortress and into the open air.

It was a beautiful evening in the valley. The sun had set, but the buildings all had an abundance of lit lanterns hanging over doorways and from roof eaves. The pathways and streets were also brightly lit by enclosed bonfire pits. They glowed with pleasing bluish flames, probably from the burning of some kind of petroleum product. The meandering river, which they learned was called *The Serpent,* was also lined with lights shining through red-tinted glass in the lantern frames. The river seemed to be the main way to travel the canyon. Barges and boats of all kinds plied the waters, maintaining orderly traffic patterns.

Their pouches each contained a map of the country and a list of amenities such as rooming houses and eateries. There were also brochures listing art galleries, theatres, and sports arenas, as well as a large, folded-up color poster inviting one to join the Abakaarian Defense Force and defend the realm against all enemies. Foxx examined his map and whistled through his teeth.

"This is unlike any place I've ever seen. This country is more than five hundred leagues long, but completely within the confines of this canyon. In square leagues, it's probably not that big, but to travel from one end to the other would take weeks, especially the way the canyon twists and turns."

Serena looked at her own map and agreed. "There are a few small offshoots from the main canyon floor that look like they are inhabited, but basically, it's like a huge city with only one street . . . kind of creepy, if you ask me."

"All cities are creepy," said Orchid, not for the first time.

The one other item issued to each of them was a metal medallion. Unlike the all-red ones that the soldiers and Naomi wore, theirs were blue overlaid with a bold red X. The back was printed with the owner's name and a unique number.

"Hey, look at this note on mine," said Orchid indignantly. Her locket was slightly different. Below the red X was a green dot that read *non-traditional history.*

"Let me see," said Foxx. Orchid handed it over, but as soon as it left her hands for Foxx's, the red and blue metal turned gray.

"Whoa, that's weird," he said. He handed it back to Orchid and it immediately returned to its original colors.

"Why the hell would it do that?" asked Serena. "Wait a beat . . . here, take mine."

She handed her own medallion to Orchid and it did the same thing.

"I get it," Serena said. "This is to keep somebody from pretending to be somebody else. This place freaks me out. We gotta get outa here."

"First we have to find Tresado," said Foxx.

"The last we saw of him, they took him down those stairs in the fortress," replied Serena.

"What was it Naomi said? That he would probably be living in . . . the something or other quarter?" Orchid rubbed her temples, trying to remember. Her head still ached a bit. She took a good slug of her purloined honey wine to ease the pain.

"Pissy something," suggested Serena.

"Pithy? Swishy? . . . something like that," said Foxx.

"Wait a beat, here it is," said Orchid, looking at her map. "The *Bythian Quarter.* According to this, it's maybe about 160 leagues or so downriver from here."

"I'm looking at this list of places and things," said Foxx. "There's no description of it anywhere."

"Why don't we find a tavern or something where we can make plans," suggested Serena.

"Good idea," yawned Foxx. "We need to find Tresado, but I think we also need to rest up. Maybe a good night's sleep will help us with our Magic."

"I think you're right, my brain is fried," said Orchid, looking through brochures. "How about this one, the *Lumba Lodge?* It's supposed to have food, rooms, and, get this . . . *forty-nine varieties of ale!*"

"Yeah, that'll help your brain."

The lodge was about a twenty-minute walk from where they were. There were plenty of people on the streets, ordinary citizens who seemed well-dressed and prosperous. Their attire was quite varied with one exception. Most everyone they saw sported identical red medallions. There were a few that were blue with the red X like theirs. There were also some that were green with a red X. Some were worn as lockets, but others functioned as brooches or hat pins or belt buckles. Apparently, it didn't matter how one wore it, as long as it was visible. Walking the streets as well were numerous patrols of soldiers. The civilians seemed to be completely comfortable with this and greeted various individuals that they knew. One group of young folks even applauded when a platoon proudly marched by.

"This is the most advanced place I've ever seen," observed Foxx. "There doesn't seem to be any poverty or crime. Even Tresk has hobos and pickpockets hanging around."

"Now that's just not natural," said Serena.

"There is one major difference from Tresk," Foxx continued. "Has anybody seen any Eryndi since we got here?"

"Not since they whisked Tresado away," said Orchid. "Naomi didn't seem too fond of them."

"She asked about the Imperium, too," noted Serena. "Are we anywhere near it?"

Foxx shrugged. "There's no way to know. I have no idea where in the world we are."

"It's hot here and the sun seemed pretty high," said Orchid. "We must be fairly far south."

Serena looked to the night sky. "Look, there's Bruggenwahld the Berg Bear, but I've never seen him so low above the horizon before."

"We've got a map of the country," said Foxx. "But we need to find one that shows where this bloody canyon is."

The *Lumba Lodge* lay just ahead. There was a red flag above the door, which Naomi had said indicated vacancy. Some jazzy, flute-like music drifted out the doors. The trio entered and found it a comfortable enough place. The various foods available were a bit unfamiliar—lots of meats and cheeses, but nothing any of Group Six had ever eaten before. It was tasty enough, though. The silver and gold coins in their pockets seemed to be acceptable here, but drew some curious looks from the innkeeper.

The tables were full of people relaxing after work and the bar was busy. There were also various games being played, but again nothing they had ever seen before. One popular game involved a wooden wheel on the wall adorned with painted caricatures of Eryndi. Apparently, the goal was to gain points by throwing darts into their various bits of anatomy as the wheel spun. A butt or belly was worth two, the exaggerated ear cones five, the two eyes and tiny crotch were worth ten points each. The equivalent of a bullseye was the tip of the ridiculously long and pointed chin.

After they ate, Foxx inquired about the availability and price of a room for the night. The rates were fairly reasonable and he suggested to the two women that they get one room for the three of them.

"Think again, chief," said Serena. "Nature Girl and I will share one room. You can have one all by your lonesome."

"I'm just trying to save us money," he said innocently.

"And Serena's just trying to save your life," smirked Orchid.

Arrangements were made, nightcaps ordered, and three-quarters of Group Six retired for the night, each of them worrying in their own way about what had become of the fourth member.

* * *

Every new race of people I meet, every new country
I visit, every new city, has the same old bumholes . . .

- TRAVELOGUE OF DEMENTUS,
THE MAD TRESKAN

* * *

Tresado suddenly realized he had a really weird taste in his mouth. The last thing he remembered was having the hood pulled over his head. He could see nothing, so he assumed he still had it on. A few beats later, though, he realized it was gone and wherever he was, it was pitch dark. It was also cold and uncomfortable because he was lying on a stone slab. His left wrist was wedged under his butt, and that whole arm was asleep. Apparently, he had just been dumped there. Tresado pulled his arm loose and shook it to restore feeling. The pins and needles caused him to say, "Aaauugh!" That triggered (or maybe it was just a coincidence) a bright red light just above his head. A voice accompanied.

"State your name for the record."

He tried to sit up, but a pair of strong hands roughly pushed his shoulders back down onto the slab.

"Who are you? Where am I?"

The hands pushed down harder. A dark face was silhouetted in the light.

"State your name for the record."

"Tresado."

"What is your purpose here?"

"Purpose?"

The hands pushed him down again.

"What is your purpose here?"

"I don't have a purpose. I'm here by accident." Those words somehow seemed familiar as soon as they came out of his mouth.

"What Magical abilities have you?"

"My specialty is kinetic manipulation." Again, he had the odd feeling he had recently said something similar.

"Have you ever been to the Treskan Imperium?"

"No."

"Don't move, hook."

Tresado heard the sound of several sets of feet shuffling away. He lay there listening to muffled voices across the room. He couldn't make out much, but caught the phrases *that tallies* and *harmless enough*.

The footsteps returned. Two pairs of hands hoisted him up by the armpits and the hood was once more roughly tied about his head. There was a chemical smell and then nothing.

Not quite 50,000 years ago

Jalex could have made it back down to the lodges three times faster, but she couldn't leave Myela to battle the treacherous slopes by herself. Coming down was actually more difficult than ascending. At one point, Myela slipped and started going down. Jalex just managed to prevent her tumbling to her death by snagging the hood on her wrap. Finally, they descended past the snow line and onto the steamy hot spring-warmed valley floor.

"I am able to track on my own, apprentice," wheezed Myela. "Go, return quickly to the lodges."

Jalex squeezed the old woman's hand and took off for the village. The warning log had been silenced, but a wailing cry could be heard ahead. There was also something burning. From out of the smoke a small person appeared. It was Traka, the youngest son of the hunters Yulo and Jalex's lifetime friend Tru. The boy was running away from the lodges, sobbing and breathless. Jalex tried to intercept him, but as soon as he saw her approaching, he screamed in fear and fled in another direction.

"Traka, stop! What is the matter?"

She managed to catch up to the child, who was limping, and snag him by the arm. He had a scrape on his knee as though he had fallen, but it didn't look too bad. The boy whimpered and struggled at first, but finally calmed down when Jalex soothed him and assured him he was safe.

"Traka, what is it? Why do you run?"

"Chief Jalex," the boy whimpered and pointed back toward the lodges. "Hunters!"

"The hunters have returned?" Jalex asked slowly.

"Bad hunters . . . throw stones and fires."

Jalex looked about quickly. She could still hear shouted voices coming from the village, but could not see any details due to the smoke in the air. She picked up the child and carried him over to a small grove of trees. She laid him down in the undergrowth and gathered some leaves and branches around him.

"Now listen, Traka. You stay right here and be very quiet. You're safe here, but do not move until I or someone else you know comes for you. Just stay right here and be very quiet. Try to go to sleep. Do you understand?"

152

"Yes."

"Good. Here's a bit of dried fruit. Try to eat this and go to sleep."

"Yes."

Jalex didn't want to leave the child alone, but needed to know what was happening back in the village. She ran to the source of the shouting, approaching cautiously, not knowing what she might be running into. The first lodge she came to was a communal home to several individuals, older hunters who no longer had mates or who had been injured in the past. It was deserted. Jalex continued into the village. The source of the fire and smoke was ahead. Two of the lodges were collapsed piles of charred ruin. A third was still vigorously burning. Several elder Ern were desperately trying to throw dirt on top of it, but it was useless. The lum hide from which it was made was fully engulfed with flame.

"Garna!" she shouted to one of them. "Garna, what happened?"

"Tribe . . ." Garna responded breathlessly. "Tribe of Sodak . . . from the hills. They came . . . stole food . . . and children!"

"Where are they now?"

"Gone. Our hunters fought them . . . terrible . . . terrible."

At this point, the old Ern dropped to his knees from exhaustion.

"Rest yourself, Garna. Get away from the smoke and take some water."

Jalex left him and ran through the village. Everywhere she found injured or hysterical members of her tribe, including her friend Tru. She quickly told her panicked friend where to find her son, Traka. Tru grasped Jalex's hands gratefully and ran to retrieve the boy.

A still body lay in the dirt ahead. Jalex quickly turned it over and looked into an unfamiliar face. It was a man with distinctive markings on his neck and shoulders. None of Jalex's tribe shared the curious habit of tattooing themselves. Only the hill tribes did this thing. The man's cause of death was apparent. His temple was caved in by some small but heavy object, most likely a sling stone. Next to the body was a broken arrow stick, also with identifying marks on it. This hunter was definitely from the hill tribe of Sodak.

The tribe of Jalex had had run-ins with them before. Sodak was known to be a most disagreeable Ern, given to bouts of madness and uncontrolled rage. His tribe was one of the ones who tended to stay in the cold heights of the valley hills. They hunted the morok and mountain sheep that also preferred the lofty slopes. Mostly they kept to themselves, but the last few seasons had been bitterly cold and conditions were harsh. That was no excuse though. This raid into Jalex's village could not be tolerated.

Jalex quickly moved through the whole village, assessing damage and casualties. Five lodges had been destroyed, including the smokehouse, where large stores of dried meat and fruit had been kept. Witnesses said this had been the first target of the raiders. Bands of hill hunters had crept up on the village and created distractions of mayhem while baskets of food were carried off. The lodges were then fired to cover their retreat.

There were also nearly two hands of children missing. The raiders had apparently gone after mostly young girls and carried them off. Several hunters of Jalex's village had immediately pursued the raiders into the snows, but had not returned yet. Jalex would have preferred to lead the pursuit herself, but for her late return to the village when there was not a beat to be wasted. Yulo and the others had done the right thing by setting out at once. He was the best tracker in the tribe. They would succeed.

Jalex's mate Doran, her children Tarl and Shona, and others were still out on a hunt of their own and could not know about the raid. For two days, she and the wise women worked to repair damage and assist the injured. The healing techniques she was just now learning were put to good use. Many of the tribe were burned or wounded from arrows and stones.

At midday of the third day after the raid, a shout sounded from one of the lookouts.

"Be alert! People approach!"

Jalex quickly issued orders for her people to prepare for anything. This could be another raid. Their anxiety was soon relieved, though. The party of hunters that had pursued the invaders was returning. They were moving slowly. Several of them were carrying heavy burdens.

The somber group of hunters entered the village. Jalex soon recognized two figures in the center. They were Tarl and Shona, who were helping two other hunters carry something laid out on hides stretched between wood poles. An awful feeling came over Jalex.

CHAPTER 11

Today – Abakaar

Orchid and Serena came down the stairs to the common room of the Lumba Lodge. They were both wearing their newly-issued citizen's certification tokens. Serena made it very apparent with her expression just how much she loathed the idea. The place was crowded with folks getting breakfast and beverages before heading off to whatever jobs they had. Foxx was already sitting at a table and waved them over.

"Morning, ladies . . . how'd you sleep?"

"Well enough," replied Orchid, who took a seat and leaned her staff against a post. "Although Serena snores like one of her berg bears."

"And Nature Girl smells like earthworms," Serena fired back.

"Pretty mild compared to that crust you scraped off your tunic before you got in the bath."

"Blame that one on Tresado, wherever that Ernie bumhole got himself to."

"I have a few thoughts on that," said Foxx, pushing his empty breakfast plates away from him. He took out his standard-issue map of Abakaar and pointed to the area marked *Bythian Quarter.*

"I've been sitting here for a while, talking to a few folks and listening to a lot more. I'm pretty sure Naomi was right. What few Eryndi live in this country are confined . . . well, maybe that's a harsh word . . . *encouraged* to live in Bythia."

"Are Eryndi banned in public or something?" asked Serena.

Foxx shook his head. "I don't see that in so many words, but . . . from what I read and what I see, it seems that way. I don't know, it's just a feeling."

Orchid signaled to the tavern keeper, who sent one of his serving staff over to the table. She ordered a fruit plate with a beer chaser, while Serena decided on a shank of mutton for breakfast.

"There's a copy of the local laws in our folders," said Orchid, after the server left.

"I've looked it over," said Foxx. "There's hardly anything mentioned about Eryndi. It's almost like they don't exist. The only exception I can find is an ordinance about vendors having to apply for a permit to deal in the Bythian Quarter."

"All the time I was growing up in Grannugh, I never saw an Eryndi," remarked Serena. "Not because they weren't allowed, but because there just weren't any around."

"I don't think that's the case here," said Orchid. "As you know, I grew up around Eryndi. I know them and their tastes. These buildings around here are like no place I've ever been, but they still have an Eryndi kind of a style. They were here once, that's for sure."

"Did you notice the server?" asked Foxx. "Pretty exotic looking, wasn't she?"

"No doubt you already have a date this evening," said Orchid dryly.

"That's irrelevant for now," replied Foxx. "My point is that a lot of the people I've seen around here seem to be from different places."

"A lot of them, but not most of them," said Serena, looking around.

"True. You see that table over there, the one with the four workmen-looking types? Now I'd say they represent the typical Macai from around here—tan skin, stubby fingers, fairly long noses. But mostly, I'm going by their similar accents. Naomi looked and spoke like that, too. But our server has completely different features and accent. She has those narrow eyes and her skin color glows like the inside of a seashell. And that couple that's just getting up to leave—they're as dark as any Macai I've ever seen. I've even seen some redheads and blondes that look like they might be from your neck of the woods, Serena."

"Now wait a minute," said Orchid. "I would think that every city has different-looking people living in it."

"Sure a few, but I've been to a lot of cities. This place is *unnaturally* varied. Just as a test, I struck up a conversation with some of the other patrons. There are people from all over this part of the world living in this country. Did you know we're not the first visitors from the Crystal Palace?"

"Naomi did seem to recognize the name when Serena mentioned it," said Orchid.

"I still don't know where it is from here, but obviously it's within traveling distance. I heard a third-hand story about somebody's cousin's friends who once went there to gamble."

The server arrived with the women's breakfasts. They ate

while Foxx made small talk with the waitress. She mentioned several times that she had other tables to wait on, but didn't seem to get around to it for the longest time. It was only when the innkeeper bellowed at her that she was able to tear herself away from this charming fellow in scarlet. Orchid and Serena just kept eating all through the display of smarm. They'd seen it before.

"So I take it the plan is to go to this Bythian Quarter and see if Tresado is there?" asked Orchid.

"But we don't know if Tresado even left that fortress," argued Serena.

"True," said Foxx. "We were released just last night because we evidently passed some kind of test or qualification. But I'm betting that an Eryndi has a harder time with that one."

"I'd say he's more than likely still in there. If somebody's a scumbag in your eyes, you hold him and beat the crap out of him, not let him go with a goody bag."

"Northlands wisdom," quipped Orchid. "How do we find out for sure?"

"We have to talk to as many people as we can, learn as much as we can," replied Foxx. "There's something about this place that makes me nervous. As nice as it is, there's just something . . . *wrong* about it."

"Well, BS-ing with people is what you do best. I'll try and find a library or archive and find out more about this valley and the city."

"I'll go talk to the soldiers at the fortress," said Serena.

"And I also want to check out the travel potential," nodded Foxx, who held up a brochure from his folder. "I think I'll start with *Remy's River Taxi* service. Let's meet back here at Midday."

"Are you sure about everything you heard?" asked Orchid. "Maybe they were just stringing you along."

Foxx smiled. "Yeah, I'm sure . . . which brings up a point. We need to be at our sharpest around here. I think I'm pretty much back to normal. How are you feeling?"

For an answer, Orchid glanced at the vase of drooping flowers that decorated their table. She concentrated for a moment. The stems stiffened up, the petals regained their texture and color and, in about three beats, there was a vase of fresh, healthy flowers standing proudly on the table . . . just like Magic. She leaned forward and confidently looked Foxx in the eye. The head of her oaken staff glowed and sparked healthily.

"I feel just fine," she said.

Today - Abakaar - Orchid

Orchid had to admit that, for a city, this place wasn't all that bad. The walk paths and riverbanks were lined with pleasant, even wholesome, plant life. Most of the bushes and trees were not only beautiful, but covered in tasty fruit and berries. There were also many different animals in this place. Many of them, like the lumba they had seen at the military gate, were being used for some purpose. There were plenty of horses being ridden and pulling carriages and wagons, of course. There were also large deer and a kind of buffalo being put to work in the tracts of farmland. Gloriously-colored flame geese and booger birds strolled around the riverbanks, begging for morsels tossed by passersby.

According to her map, the Hall of Remembrances, Abakaar's great library, was some distance upriver. Orchid could have taken a carriage and saved a couple hours' walking, but decided she would see more if she hoofed it. It also saved money. As she came to know more of this peculiar country, she realized that such a concern was mostly unjustified. While it did cost money to patronize upscale places such as the Lumba Lodge, basic shelter and food was available to any citizen who needed it. Nobody was homeless. Bread and cheese were provided at food banks throughout the city. Nothing fancy, but it was free. And of course, fruit grew everywhere.

The library lay ahead. The entrance was guarded by five huge pedestals topped with marble statues. There were a giant moose-like creature, a huge cat of some kind, a behemoth rodent horror, a fierce rhino-looking animal, and the head and shoulders of an impossibly big lumba. Orchid wondered if these were the product of somebody's active imagination or if such magnificent creatures actually existed. The incredibly detailed and disturbingly realistic statues stared defiantly down at her as she climbed the stairs between them and entered the Hall of Remembrances.

Orchid's footsteps echoed in the enormous hallway. Shelves five times her height lined both walls. They were filled with books and scrolls. Researchers stood on high catwalks searching through what seemed like an infinite number of volumes. There had to be some kind of guide to all this chaos. The hallway eventually led to a central hub with an information desk. A withered little wisp of a man sat poring over a faded scroll. When Orchid cleared her throat, he jerked his head up immediately. The magnifier strapped to his head blinked back at her with a watery, bloodshot eye three times its normal size.

"Eeyesssss?"

"Good morning," said Orchid with a little bow. "I am a newcomer to Abakaar and would like to learn something of its history and culture."

"Reference Corridor Red, Sections 10 through 25," he said unerringly, while pointing with his stylus. "Number, please?"

"Pardon?"

"Your certification number . . . on your token."

"Oh." Orchid fumbled with her medallion and read it to him.

"Thank you," he said, returning to his scroll as though she weren't there.

Orchid thanked him and headed down the hallway indicated. As soon as she was out of sight, the librarian scribbled something down on a note. He handed the paper over to an intern with a whispered instruction. The girl hurried down the main corridor and out of the building.

Today - Abakaar - Serena

Be the Hero You Were Meant to Be! Join the Abakaarian Defense Forces!

Signs with similar messages were posted all over the area surrounding the fortress where Group Six was initially brought. They hadn't noticed them before because it was dark at the time. During daylight hours, there were also a handful of recruiters who passed out brochures to people who wandered by. Serena sat down on a bench and watched the process for a while. She had seen military recruitment in her homeland and elsewhere. They were usually of a more aggressive nature. Many regimes used involuntary conscription to boost their ranks of soldiers. And the unfortunates who were pressed into service usually didn't enjoy such an honor, nor had asked for it. That did not seem to be the case here in Abakaar. The soldiery were looked upon with respect and envy. It seemed like every teenager's dream was to join the army.

Being from the Northlands, Serena's martial experience was primarily in defense of her homeland against barbarian attack. There were offensives, to be sure, but usually in the form of small unit raids against neighboring countries and ships at sea carrying more treasure than was good for them. It was less about organized conquest and more about maintaining an enemy's fear and respect for Northlanders, not to mention the acquisition of booty.

"Good morning, care to learn more about the ADF?"

Serena looked up into the smiling face of an immaculately uniformed young soldier. His gleaming breastplate armor, polished boots, and shiny medals of accomplishment showed him to be one of Abakaar's finest. There was nothing on this person that was not spit-shined, including his regulation red certification badge, properly worn on the center of his chest.

"As a matter of fact, I would," answered Serena.

"Outstanding. This pamphlet will give you the basics. And I can answer any questions you might have. Or, if you like, I can take you to our recruitment center . . . show you around . . . even introduce you to my C.O."

"Thanks," said Serena, taking the brochure. "Maybe I'll stop by later. For now, I'll just read up on it."

"Any time. My name is Corporal Narbo. I'm always around this neighborhood during morning shift. Say, that is one fine-looking . . . sword you're packing."

Serena was sure he considered making a remark about her diamond-studded cleavage. She let it slide . . . this time.

Settle down, warrior, you're here to learn, not to pick fights, she told herself.

"I've never seen a blade quite like that," Narbo whistled. "Is that folded steel?"

"Twelve times," Serena answered proudly. She stood up and loosened her weapon from the scabbard, slowly drawing the blade out. She didn't hand it to the soldier, but merely presented it for his inspection.

Narbo respectfully didn't touch it, but clucked his tongue in approval. "Beautiful. I love the pattern of the layers. That reverse-curve grip is sure something. That should add some heft to the swing, am I right?"

"And speed," said Serena, stepping back to demonstrate. She executed a fast whirl around both sides of her body. The sword was nothing but a blur.

"Impressive. How does it fare against close-in short sword opponents?"

"I've not had much experience against short swords," admitted Serena. I'm told that they can be dangerous if you allow your foe to get in too close. I notice that you folks favor straight blades."

Narbo drew his own weapon. Just like the rest of his equipment, it too was immaculately polished. He handed it to Serena, pommel first.

"Standard issue."

She nodded her thanks, sheathed her own sword, and accepted his. She made a few practice swings with it.

"Nice," she said. It was not as long and heavy as the swords most of her fellow Northlands warriors carried, but it was still a fine weapon. "My people use double-edged blades, too. My scimitar is a bit of an exception, but it works well for me."

"Well, *we're* your people now," he said with a charming smile. "And you and your skills are very welcome."

The two soldiers continued to amiably chat about death and destruction for more than an hour. Serena had to admit to herself that, for a foreigner, this guy was all right. He was kind of cute, too, but she thrust that notion aside.

Today - Abakaar - Foxx

It was the strangest thing. Foxx had never been to this part of the world, but it had a nagging feeling of familiarity. It didn't seem to be the people or the climate or anything else, but he somehow felt accustomed to something around here. He was still not even sure just where in the world he was.

He spent his day perusing the people and business around the riverbanks. This seemed to be a very old country, but with many modern elements. Some of the buildings had an ancient look to them, built from blocks of stone hewn out of the red cliffs that surrounded this valley. They were mostly located close to the river. That seemed to be the quaint *old town* section. Other buildings, especially the ones up on the terraces, were of a more modern design, using more brick and wood in their construction. Orchid had been right. There was a definite Eryndi influence in the design of the place.

But what happened to them?

The Macai here were the cleanest people Foxx had ever seen. The hot mineral pools that bubbled up from the ground were plentiful and these people took full advantage of them. Bathhouses were a common sight.

Foxx strolled through the crowds, using his Knowing Spell to read their mood and watch for deceit or threats. He found nothing but happy, contented citizens who went about their business with nary a serious worry. There was a deep confidence in the military's ability to protect them and most people seemed satisfied with their lives. Nowhere had Foxx encountered such universal contentment, and yet there was still that persistent feeling of familiarity with the whole setup.

After an hour of sightseeing and people watching, Foxx eventually came to a large wharf area. A great many boats of all kinds were berthed here. There was an industrial area equipped with cranes and hoists where barges took on and unloaded cargo. Other dock areas were dedicated to large ferries that carried up to a hundred passengers up and down the Serpent River. Private pleasure and fishing craft also had their assigned berths. Evidently this was a transport hub.

Just what I've been looking for.

Foxx knew that such a crossroads was the very thing to take the pulse of the country. People of all walks of life and professions passed through here. In a country that was very long and narrow, river travel defined their lifestyle.

Remy's River Taxi service was based here and seemed like a good place to start. He found the office easily enough. The brochure from his folder advertised charter travel of any distance. They charged by the quarter-league with group discounts, off-peak hours pricing, and other specials. It was all laid out on a slate chart on the wall. The latest rates were written in temporary chalk, as they were currently in a price war with other charter services.

Along with the prices per distance were fixed rates to popular destinations. Many were tourist attractions like Serpent River Zoo, the Museum of Antiquities, and Zanteryne Castle. Foxx noticed with disappointment that the Bythian Quarter was not listed among the possible destinations. It wasn't hard to figure out the exact cost to get near there, though. There was a large map of the country on the wall of Remy's Depot that was even more detailed than the one in his information folder. Foxx studied it and determined that the Bythian Quarter was 164 leagues downriver from here. That would translate to about eight paleens and three of west coast money per passenger; expensive, but affordable.

Curiously, it was cheaper to go downriver than up. It made sense when Foxx learned just how the river taxis and other vessels were propelled. Except for the ones with sails or oars, most boats were powered by Magic. Each boat had what was known as an *impetus box*. Essentially, it was an invention that could store the power of Magic and transmit the energy to a propulsion screw or a paddle wheel. There were sites at intervals along the river known as *Re-enchantment Stations* where one could replenish their boat's Magical fuel supply. The stored energy was broken down into set quantities known as *packets* and sold to boat owners to propel their vessels.

Tresado would love this.

Watercraft were not the only things powered in this manner. Heavy machinery such as the loading cranes and farm equipment also ran on Magic. Animal power was still widely used, of course. It was the cheaper method and many traditionalists still preferred a good old-fashioned draft horse to this new-fangled Magic stuff. That was an opinion that Foxx picked up on a lot, mostly from the older folks around.

He learned that Magical fueling was a new government-run service, so a packet of Magic cost the same anywhere on the river. Proceeds from the sale of Magic were used to purchase foodstuffs from the farmers for distribution as well as to maintain other infrastructure such as levees, bridges, and lighting. It was a tidy arrangement, one that benefitted everybody, or so the publicity stated. There was no need for taxation, if the sale of Magic continued.

All this was not answering Foxx's questions about the status of Tresado and the Eryndi. He decided that the best thing to do was to find someone who was likely to know and simply ask them. Foxx's experience told him that around here the best person for that would be whoever ran this depot. Anyone who had that much contact with those who frequently traveled the length of the valley would be savvy of the way things are. He went to the main building and inquired within. A clerk told him that Grel Fondren, the Depot Manager, wasn't in his office. As usual, he was down at the wharf.

Foxx thanked the fellow and headed to the river. He found Fondren down at the barge docks personally supervising the unloading of a shipment of horse grain. Apparently he was a hands-on kind of an administrator who didn't manage from his office, insulated from the rank and file. Fondren was a barrel-chested Macai with a rapid-fire speech pattern that didn't waste a single word.

"Swing the crane smoothly this time!" he hollered at a rookie operator. *"Quick, but not jerky! A little more . . . THERE! Hold it. You! Bring in the wagons. Keep 'em tight and be ready to move after each load is secure! . . .* Yes, what can I do for you?"

Foxx was uncharacteristically taken by surprise. Fondren had been so focused on his work that he did not think the Manager had noticed him. Apparently this guy did not miss a trick. Carefully tuning his Knowing Spell to read Fondren's demeanor, Foxx adopted the man's mannerisms and speech pattern to form an instant trust, something he did very well.

"Good morning. My name is Foxx and I've got a couple of quick questions for you." He had considered fabricating some story about a news interview or research project, but his Knowing Spell told him not to waste this guy's time.

"Shoot," Fondren responded immediately, not taking his eye off his work.

"Could you tell me the best transport to take to get me to the Bythian Quarter?"

"*Watch the spillage, or you'll be sweeping the dock with a toothbrush!*" For a beat, Fondren took his eyes off the unloading operation to appraise Foxx. "You're a little overdressed to go to Bythia, don't you think?"

Here again was the same contempt for Bythia that Foxx had read in everyone else in this country. Automatically, he adopted the same kind of sneer. "It's not a trip I'm looking forward to. There's a particular *hook* I have to find." Foxx didn't care for racial terms, but in this case, his spell told him that was the best approach.

"Friend of yours?"

"Yeah, right. This guy owes me money." Technically, that was true. Tresado had borrowed a gold gendrin back at the Crystal Palace to buy supplies for his experiment and had not paid Foxx back yet.

"Good luck with *that! . . . All right, that's enough for this load. Get that wagon moving and bring in the next one!* Most of the regular charter boats don't go to Bythia. If you're still set on going, you'll have to hitch a ride on one of Floozy's scows. She makes regular runs to Bythia . . . Dock 27."

"Thanks a lot. Appreciate the help."

"No worries. Watch your back down there. *Move it, you slug! We got three barges waiting behind you!*"

Foxx left Fondren to his work. He glanced up at the sun. It would be ten o'clock soon. He better start back to the Lumba Lodge for his Midday meeting with his friends. On his way back to the lodge, he talked to some people and listened to many more. Little did he know that at the same time he was using his Knowing Spell on the Depot Manager and others, Orchid was researching Eryndi history in the Hall of Remembrances. Little did either of them know that deep in the bowels of Zanteryne Castle, two red indicators on a Magical board were flashing their citizen's certification numbers.

CHAPTER 12

Life sucks, boy. It'll kick ya in the nuts. It'll stick it in and break it off. Life will beat the crap out of you, leave you layin' in the gutter, and laugh its ass off at you. But the show must go on . . .

- Professor Abadiah Generax, 21861

Not quite 50,000 years ago

Jalex was the strongest of women. She had the most courage, the best abilities, was the wisest and most learned of women in all the village. But right now, she was absolutely shattered. Her knees were as those of a newborn as they hit the ground and she had little faith they would ever bear her weight again. The image of Doran's bloodied body and sightless eyes burned into her soul like a brand from the fire. There was not even breath enough in her body to ask her two children what had happened. All she could do was to hold them and never let go.

Tarl and Shona let two other hunters take over for them carrying the poles which supported their father's body. They helped Jalex to her feet and the three of them accompanied the somber party into the village where Doran could be cared for in the proper manner. Eventually the initial shock eased. Jalex once again became the concerned mother and strong leader.

"Are you two all right?" she asked, checking Shona and then Tarl for injuries. She found only minor scrapes and bruises. "What happened?"

"We were on our way back to the village," replied Tarl. "Our pace was slow. We were carrying meat from a morok we had taken as well as several longears. Suddenly arrows and stones fell upon us. Tasik and Fren were struck and went down. It was then that Sodak and many hands of his hill hunters leapt from hiding places and charged us. We fought them, but they were many. Brunan and Forria were also killed. Doran fought like a wild beast and killed two of the enemy. But then Sodak himself went for Shona. I believe he meant to capture her. Doran turned away from the brute he was fighting and pushed her out of the way. He and Sodak battled, but the hunter he was fighting before came up behind him and . . . Doran was speared in the back. He went down. It was then that . . ."

Tarl looked into his mother's wide eyes, not wanting to say any more.

"Tell me, Tarl. Tell me everything," she said immediately.

"I killed him," interrupted Shona grimly, relieving Tarl of the burden. "I cast my arrow into the neck of the coward that killed our father. He will not kill anyone ever again."

Jalex regarded the face of her young daughter. It seemed only a day ago that Shona was nursing at her breast. Now a fierce warrior stood before her, proud of taking the life of an enemy.

"It was then that Yulo and the other hunters appeared over the hill," added Tarl. "Sodak and his band ceased fighting and fled."

"Did you see any of our missing children?"

"No. We did not know of such a thing until Yulo told us," said Tarl. "The captives must have been hidden from us. We had wounded and dead to tend to. The decision was made to return to the village."

"We should have pursued and slain them all!" shouted Shona viciously.

Hearing her youngest child utter such words was as shocking and painful to Jalex as if the arrow had pierced her own body.

This must stop. This must stop immediately.

The wounded were tended to. The worst of them was Barexa, who took a spear thrust to the thigh. The wound was severe, but she would live. The bodies of the dead were prepared according to Ern tradition. Doran had been raised in a different tribe who did not have such elaborate death rituals. Even so, he was buried along with the traditional gifts of food and flowers.

When these necessary duties were finished, Jalex brought her people together to plan strategy.

"Hunters, you all know what has happened. Our people have been killed and our children have been taken. This cannot go unchallenged."

"We must attack the tribe of Sodak!"

"Kill them all!"

"Make them suffer and die!"

This last comment came from Shona. Hearing it shot a pain through Jalex's heart.

"Hunters!" shouted Jalex. "Hear me. We will attack Sodak. We will retrieve our children. We will teach them to not do this thing again. We will *not* become worse than they are!"

A murmur rippled through the hunters. Many were not satisfied with this idea. But more of them than not trusted Jalex and would abide by her decision.

Yulo set out immediately to track Sodak's group and find where they camp. He would leave signs for the rest of the tribe to easily follow. The other hunters spent the remainder of the day preparing weapons and provisions for the expedition.

When the dim light broke the darkness in the morning, the war party set out. They made good time. Yulo had left a series of blaze marks on the trees to quickly guide them. The trail took them up the snowy slopes of the canyon wall. Two days later, he was found waiting on the trail for them.

"Sodak and his tribe are camped among the rocks up there," he said quietly, pointing to a frowning projection of stone. "They make shelter beneath that overhang."

"Can they be approached without being seen?" asked Jalex.

"No, My Chief," he replied. "Many of their hunters hide among the stones to give warning of any who approach. I was able to creep close enough in the dark to smell the smoke of their fires, but could not see their camp. Once I heard the voice of Sodak himself as he roared at someone in anger."

Jalex shaded her eyes and examined the overhanging cliff that sheltered Sodak's camp. She noted with interest that there were many *lerpa vines* snaking out of the treacherous layer of snow and ice that covered the rocky projection. Something stirred within her.

Such vines could be useful.

"We cannot approach from below," Jalex whispered to her hunters. "This is what we shall do . . ."

Today – Abakaar – The Lumba Lodge

Foxx met Orchid coming the other way up the street as they approached the tavern. Each read in the other's expression that they had made discoveries. Foxx held the door and they proceeded in.

The lunch crowd was just arriving. As with everyone else that Group Six had seen in this country, all were happy and contented. People drank, but not out of depression or hopelessness, or even to excess. Those who were going back to work after the Midday meal had one or two; just enough to get a happy buzz on before returning to their jobs. It was all perfectly normal for this place. Serena sat at a table, sipping an ale. The whole thing was unnatural. To her, a bar should be a loud, raucous place with a fist fight every few minutes, but maybe that was just a Northlands thing. She waved over her two friends when she saw them enter.

"So, who wants to go first?" asked Orchid.

"You seem eager enough, go ahead," said Foxx. She was about to, but was interrupted by Foxx's favorite waitress. She had spotted him as soon as he came in and hurried right over to take their, or rather *his*, orders, bypassing a couple of tables who had been waiting longer.

"Good day, Melicia . . . how is your day going?" he asked, oozing charm.

"Can't wait for it to be over," she replied with a wink.

Orders were placed and Melicia scurried away to fill them. As usual, Orchid ate healthily, Serena heartily, and Foxx exotically.

"I found the library," Orchid said when they were finally alone. "What an astounding place! It's immense. It must be one of the largest archives in the world. There are books and records that go back thousands of years. The older ones are all Eryndi."

"So they did build this place," said Serena around a mouthful of venison.

"There was a section on ancient cities. Abakaar, Tresk, Kadizio, and a dozen others I've never heard of are all Eryndi in origin."

"Kadizio?" said Foxx, wide-eyed. "I thought that was just a myth!"

"So did I. Apparently it's thousands of leagues down the western coast somewhere. I even found mention of Ostica and the Northlands, too. It seems like the ancient Eryndi knew a lot more about the world than we do today. Don't ask me what happened to that knowledge, but I don't think anyone from this part of the world has traveled there in a very long time . . . except for maybe one person. I'll give you three guesses who."

"Dementus? Has he been here, too?" asked Serena.

"It would seem so. I was researching local laws, trying to find out why the Eryndi are so despised here. I found a scroll written about ten years ago that referred to an Eryndi arrested for public lewdness, of all things. It didn't give his name, but apparently there was a scandal involving *an insane Treskan,*" Orchid explained, using air quotes to emphasize. "It had something to do with two of the Queen's daughters being snatched up by a naked Eryndi riding a lumba and singing sea chanties at the top of his lungs."

"Are you sure it was him?" asked Serena skeptically.

"The scroll went on to say that, after he steered the lumba into a bakery, he was seen talking to a large book that he had in a knapsack."

"Sounds like Dementus, all right," smiled Foxx.

"The two princesses managed to get away and the Treskan was arrested. The incident sparked outrage against the Eryndi minority, especially after the man disappeared from his holding cell and was never seen again. There was talk of an Eryndi conspiracy against the Queen."

"Talk by who?" asked Serena.

Orchid pulled out a note she had taken. "The official chronicle stated that, *The Eryndi presence is eroding and corrupting the inborn decency and endangering the safety of the Macai citizens. For the good of the State and welfare of the people, those of Eryndi birth are prohibited from the following activities: the holding of public office, enlistment in the Defense Forces, employment in the fields of education or administration, use of public bath houses, etc, etc, etc.* The proclamation is signed by Administrator Rastaban, Grand Vizier to Her Majesty, Queen Minore."

"Sounds like there was some kind of purge," offered Foxx.

"Not all at once, but that was the beginning of it. As time went by, Eryndi lost more rights every year, until finally they were all relocated to this Bythian Quarter, *for their own safety.*"

"And I found one more thing . . . look here." Orchid dug into her satchel and pulled out a faded parchment scroll.

"I found this old map in the archive. It's about a hundred years old."

"They let you check that out?"

"Not exactly . . . I kinda stole it."

"I'm so proud. I taught you well," said Foxx, examining the map. "So that's where we are. Looks like we're maybe about nine-hundred leagues or so southeast of the Crystal Palace. That teleport spell is really something to send us so far."

"Apparently that has something to do with this circle thing here," said Orchid, pointing to a spot on the map. "That's the really interesting part. Some ancients called this *Witchheart Crater*. It's also known as *The Fountain*. Here in Abakaar, the whole area is just called the *Zone*. The physical crater is about 50 leagues across, but the whole zone spans hundreds of leagues. It's supposed to have been there since the dawn of time."

"Looks like a big hole in the ground," said Serena.

"There are different schools of thought on what it is. Some scholars say it's an enormous volcano. Others believe it's a kind of gateway to an evil underground realm . . . I don't know about *that* one. One old Eryndi sage wrote that it's the source of Magic on Lurra. The only thing everyone agrees on is that the area surrounding it is a pretty unhealthy place. There are high concentrations of raw Magical energy in the area, which is what the Palace's teleport spell is attracted to. Somehow it makes it easier to lock onto from great distances."

"Looks like this mountain range separates this part of the world from the west coast," said Serena, pointing with her table knife. "Look, this must be the Talus River that we followed through the mountain pass to get to the Palace. Ostica isn't shown on here. It must be off the map."

"Yeah," replied Orchid. "That's all I've found for now. I would like to go back to the library and keep digging, though."

"My turn," said Serena. "I found out a few things about this *Zone*. It seems you were right this morning when you said there were people here from lots of different places. Most of them are brought in from the Zone, just as we were. A big part of the local defense forces are deployed along its edges to watch for *immigrants*, as they call them. It sounds like the Crystal

Palace is not the only place that sends its garbage here. The soldiers have orders to bring in as many of them as possible, but they have to get to them fast."

"Why is that?" asked Orchid.

"Because if you're in there for too long, something starts to happen to you . . . some kind of sickness or something. That's why they shot down that one guy."

This drew blank stares from Foxx and Orchid. "Oh yeah, you guys were still kind of out of it at the time." She then explained about how the soldiers had checked all the captives for something called *buboes* on their necks. That man had been coldly executed for it.

"It sounds like we got out of the Zone just in time," said Foxx. "I still don't remember much about it, but apparently if you spend enough time in that awful place, something happens to you."

"Well, if you remember any more," said Serena slowly, "be sure to let me . . . *us* know."

"It doesn't make any sense. It seems like all the people here are sickeningly honest and stalwart citizens. The Palace was sending cheats and thieves to the Zone. You'd think Abakaar would be a den of iniquity if it keeps importing criminals."

"The Zone isn't the only place they import people from. The soldier I talked to said that patrols are stationed along every border, rounding up everyone they can and bringing them to this valley."

"But why bring them in at all?" wondered Orchid, looking around at the crowded tavern. "There's no slavery and there doesn't seem to be a people shortage in this country."

"They must have value. Why would you bring people here if not to use them for something?" said Serena coldly.

"And everyone is so bloody happy to be here," said Foxx, looking around at all the smiling faces in the tavern. "If thousands of people are being abducted, why doesn't anyone want to go home again? I know *I* certainly don't want to stay here."

Orchid suddenly got a horrible look on her face. "That soldier said we'd be spending the rest of our lives here, but nobody is stopping us from trying to leave. Maybe after a while, *we won't want to go home, either!*"

CHAPTER 13

Tra-la-lee, Tree-la-lame;
Come on down and play the game;
The players all look the same;
It's Red's turn, move your Queen;
Blue stays under where he can't be seen;
But most of the board belongs to Green;
Choose your color, choose your side . . .
Oh, shoot, what's the next line, Octavia?
It's 'Fight or flight, Stay or hide.'

- Travelogue of Dementus,
the Mad Treskan

Not quite 50,000 years ago

Jalex led her war party up the slippery slope far to the side of the rocky projection that sheltered the band of Sodak. As difficult as the ascent was, it was even harder due to her orders to stay hidden and silent the whole way up. At last the Ern were higher than the enemy. Now came the even harder part of moving laterally and still remaining unseen. Several times, Jalex silently signaled her hunters to freeze and wait for an enemy sentry to move out of sight. On several of those occasions, neither she nor her hunters saw the enemy. Somehow Jalex's heightened senses just knew they were there and when it was safe to proceed.

Finally, the war party was directly above the rock overhang. The lerpa vines snaked their way down the face of it to dangle above the heads of Sodak and his brutes. The grey-green tendrils were much like the Ern: resilient, unyielding, and adaptable to harsh conditions. That's why they stubbornly insisted on surviving the bitter years since Senfall. There were many plants and animals like the lerpa. There were so many more that were not. Since that terrible day, much of the life of Lurra was never seen again. Only the smart and cunning, strong and fierce, and the prickly and poisonous seemed to still be around. Perhaps after many, many seasons that would prove to be a good thing.

Jalex signaled one final silent instruction to her hunters: *stay quiet.* As per plan, they grasped the dangling vines and began to lower themselves over the icy outcropping that sheltered the enemy. Jalex's senses were at a fever pitch. She could feel the anxiety and anticipation in her fellow hunters. At the same time, she was also in tune with the colony of screech divers that made their mud nests on the nearby rock faces and the primitive but tangible *thoughts* of the lerpa vines themselves. Even the air and ice surrounding her seemed to speak to her soul. Such all-encompassing awareness was exhilarating.

As they descended, the Ern could now begin to hear the voices of their enemy. It became apparent that the tribe of Sodak outnumbered the hunters of Jalex. This would be a difficult and bloody business if they did not maintain the element of surprise. As they silently lowered themselves hand-over-hand down the cliff face, the gruff tones of the brutes became mixed with whimpers and cries of pain.

Their captive children!

At last, the attackers reached the low point of the overhang. The vines they were clinging to dangled over the edge, just over the enemy's heads, their little yellowish fingers seeking more rock or anything to cling to, but finding nothing but empty air. Jalex peered cautiously over and caught a glimpse of some of Sodak's hunters moving about. Now was the time. She waited until all her people were in position, then emitted a shrill whistle as a signal to attack. The hunters all roared their lungs out as they swiftly slid down the vines to land on the surprised heads of Sodak's band. Many of the brutes were caught without weapons in their hands. They were soon laid low by the cudgels and stone axes of Jalex's hunters. The object was not to kill if at all possible, but to disable and cripple the enemy.

Jalex and her hunters fought bravely, driven by their need to save the captives. At first, Sodak's band was on the defensive, having lost several of their number in the first few beats. A few of them actually did themselves in by stumbling off the edge of the cliff in an effort to get away from their attackers.

The tide turned quickly, though. They regrouped from the initial surprise and began to overwhelm the outnumbered tribe of Jalex. Sodak was the most dangerous of the lot. He was wielding an enormous, knotted cudgel with a large river stone lashed to the end for extra effect. He had downed two of Jalex's hunters with it. One had taken a hit to his thigh, shattering the hunter's hip, while the other had his skull crushed from a direct strike to his temple. Sodak roared like a spearcat in triumph.

Shona saw that man go down with a sickening crunch. A red mist fell before her eyes, robbing her of any remaining control. She let out a primal scream and launched herself at the huge man, hoping to plunge her sharpened antler into the brute's throat. Jalex had just disengaged with her defeated opponent and saw the tragedy about to unfold.

"*NOOOOOO!!!*"

Jalex's cry and her frantic effort to get in between the two seemed to slow to a crawl. Her legs simply would not propel her fast enough to get where it was impossible for her to be in a too short amount of time. Shona, half the height of the towering Sodak, made her flying leap and took the upswing of his immense cudgel under the chin. Her head snapped backwards at an impossible angle and her slight body made a complete flip in midair. Shona was dead before she hit the ground.

The horror and blood-red vengeance welled up in Jalex like an erupting geyser. She wanted nothing more at this moment than to violently twist the ugly head off of Sodak's hairy body. The primal urges shot out of her and were picked up by the hanging lerpa vines that she was still unconsciously in contact with. It was unintentional and unexpected, but quite as natural as breathing. The vines sent internal sap and nutrients flowing through their veins, obeying the forces in the air being directed at them. The tough tendrils snapped downward, wrapping themselves snakelike around the bull neck of the grinning Sodak. Jalex was still unaware of her control of them on a conscious level. All she knew was what she wanted done, and the vines did it. More and more lerpa gathered themselves together, ensnaring Sodak by the neck, wrists, legs, and torso. He tried to cry out a guttural call for help, but his mouth and nostrils were being forcefully invaded by clinging vines. Jalex glanced at the lifeless body of her daughter upon the ground and another wave of vengeance poured out of her and into the obedient vines. They tightened and stretched until Sodak's head and limbs were violently ripped from his torso and flung in all directions.

The battle paused as the other hunters from both sides saw this astounding thing and gaped in astonishment. Jalex turned to them all, a terrible aura of destructive power playing about her visage. Her voice rang out with absolute and undeniable authority.

"*STOP!* Drop your weapons . . . *ALL OF YOU! NOW!*"

Storm clouds began to gather behind Jalex, blowing up a fearful whirlwind of ice crystals to add weight to her booming command. Clubs and spears clattered to the ground on both sides. Many of the combatants fell to their knees in the presence of such powerful authority.

"It is over! Sodak is no more. The dead and the taken have been avenged. There is no need for more of our loved ones to die! The food of all hunts will be shared with all. We are warring tribes no longer. Do you hear me? We are not the tribes of Jalex or of Sodak. *We are Ern!* Let there be no more war between us!"

Some of the hunters on both sides were simply stunned by such a surprising statement and stood there with their mouths open. Others were awed to the point of cheering. A few even wept in joy.

The electric whirlwind about Jalex eased. The storm clouds began to dissipate. And in a magnificent grand finale, Sen the Glorious Sun broke through the high clouds, bathing all in Her Eternal Warmth.

* * *

Dinday, Awan 33-21876 — We all spent the rest of the day in the archives learning more about this country we have found ourselves in. Everything we

- ORCHID's JOURNAL

Today - Abakaar – On board Floozy's Folly

"So, Floozy, how'd a nice girl like you get into the . . . *waste transport service?*" That was the best line Foxx could manage.

The scow's captain cackled gleefully, showing off the fact that she had more teeth missing than present. Her matted, salt-and-pepper hair sprouted out from her head like wilted sea urchin spines. She itched the third-largest mole under her right eye with the spitty stem of her pipe and glanced back at her passenger.

"By being used to hauling a lot worse in my time."

"I can tell by your accent that you're not from here, but I can't place it," said Foxx.

"Nah . . . I ain't from here."

Floozy's voice rattled from the phlegm in her throat, but it was soon hocked out.

"As a tadpole, I come from a wee fishing village called Roria, what lay on the eastern coast of the Amoran Sea. Haven't been there since I was caching contraband weapons for my brothers."

"How'd you come to be here?"

"Was running Craymon Nightroot out of Nurea to some dealers in Graysod Bay. Powdered gold, that were! One little vial the size of yer pinkie fetched at least twenty coin o'gold. On one trip we carried a full two stone of 'root. Aye, rollin' in lucre in them days we were. But the sea gods were agin us on our last run. A storm blew up and we lost our mast. A Jerikan Freesailor tacked round Scar Rock Point and come after us. I only had five men with me, but we managed to scull her into a cove and scuttle the boat. The Jerikans chased us through the hedgerows for days. We set snares and spike pits, dipped in Nightroot, mind ye, and took out a fair share of the buggers. Managed to slip across the border into Luxean territory, but they didn't like us much neither. They had no evidence against us and no cause to execute us, but Prince Antine had us declared as criminals anyway. The court Magicians sent us into exile. Next thing you know, here we be making a fine living in Abakaar. Life be pretty sweet, don't she, mates?"

Her crew, most of whom were apparently the ones teleported here with Floozy, whooped enthusiastically in agreement.

Floozy's cheerful anecdote sounded as innocent as though she were telling Group Six about a trip to the park. This woman who had dealt in deadly drugs and illicit weapons rattled off her stories with nothing held back and no apparent guilt or fear of disclosure. Apparently one's past was unimportant around here.

Once again, while talking to Floozy about her sordid misadventures, Foxx felt that curious sense of familiarity that had teased him ever since arriving in Abakaar.

What is it about this place, anyway?

Floozy's Folly had a visible cloud of funk that perpetually followed it as it putted its way up the Serpent River. The Magical impetus box that propelled the boat was a fairly new component, having been installed only a handful of years previous. It was not one of the more powerful or expensive models available, but it got them where they wanted to go.

The aged scow's charter was to make a regular run up and down the river collecting manure, bones, hides, farm waste, and any other organic products that nobody wanted. It was all taken to some facility where it was reconstituted into fertilizer and sold back to farmers and gardeners. The boat was actually headed *away* from the Bythian Quarter where Group Six wanted to go, but Floozy's deal was if you wanted a ride, you had to go on the full route. She claimed it had something to do with which bank of the river the stops were on.

Sounds flimsy, thought Foxx. *Flimsy Floozy.*

The *Folly's* last pickup before heading back downriver was at a feed lot for cattle and mountain swine at the southern tip of the valley. This head of the canyon marked the end of the country of Abakaar. Beyond these narrow canyon walls to the south were other lands, other countries unknown to Group Six. Foxx, Orchid, and Serena gazed upward and noted the ever-present fortified gate that guarded every entrance to this place. They scanned the sloping walls and agreed that, while treacherous, it wouldn't be too difficult to surreptitiously climb out of here and escape the country of Abakaar. They discussed it, yes, but only as a possible future plan. There was no thought of attempting it now while one of their own was still missing.

Floozy remained here for several hours while her barge was loaded with troughs of hog crap, cow manure, and rotten silage. As paying passengers, Group Six didn't have to aid in the loading, but the smell was their constant shipmate. They tried to stay upwind as much as possible.

Over the next three days, *Floozy's Folly* made more than twenty stops at various farms and businesses. Each place was glad to see the ex-pirate turned business woman. She was popular and enjoyed a jaw at each stop, despite the generous fee she charged to haul away their refuse. During the course of their trip, the scow passed a major fork in the canyon. At the conflux of the winding Serpent River with another tributary, there stood a looming, ancient structure that towered over all around it.

"Aye, that be Zanteryne Castle." Floozy pointed out the massive structure with a shrug of her shoulders. "I ain't never been in there. Never had no cause to be."

"Is that the seat of government?"

"Queen Minore's throne is in there if that be what you mean. She runs the whole country."

"I've read a lot about the Queen," said Orchid, staring up at the massive castle. "It's said she can tell the future. Any truth to that?"

"Well now, don't know about that, but . . ."

Floozy took a long puff off her pipe. Foxx was not sure what was in it, but it smelled like burning tar.

"... everyone around here knows that the Queen be the wisest ruler that ever walked on two royal legs. She knows everything what happens in her country all the time."

"Does she get out much?"

"Occasional she tours the country on the royal barge. They stop all river traffic whenever she does. Don't want no stinky-ass honey scows upsettin' her delicate nose, do they?"

Floozy's cackle was raspy and mucous-filled, but a delight to listen to.

The next stop was some distance downriver, so the barge made good time. The pickup was at a large lumba ranch. Here the great beasts were bred, raised, and broken for all number of heavy work duties. Such a place produced many wagonloads of what they referred to as *lumbanure*. The less said about it, the better. Floozy informed her passengers that this was her biggest scheduled load and would take more than a full day to secure onto her giant barge. She wouldn't be pulling out until morning two days hence. The lumba ranch was actually a short walk from the Museum of Antiquities and maybe they would enjoy a day ashore to hit the museum and have a nice dinner. Orchid noticed there was also a hot spring bathhouse nearby. Foxx and Serena thought that an excellent idea.

The *Folly* docked and Group Six got off. Three hours later, soaked, scrubbed, and fed, Serena, Foxx, and Orchid gratefully slept in clean beds in a comfortable inn.

After breakfast the next day, they walked up the steps into the Museum of Antiquities. The first thing that greeted them in the large gallery was the reassembled bones of an impossibly large animal. The creature must have stood seven reaches tall. The great rounded skull was two reaches wide by three long. Its mandible was hanging open, showing huge, flat teeth as large as fruit baskets.

"What the hell . . . that thing can't be real!"

Serena stood next to one of the creature's lower leg bones. Even though they were relatively short for the animal, they towered over Serena's head. The immense flat foot could have stepped on a horse and covered it completely.

Orchid stepped up to read a plaque beneath the behemoth's ribcage, which was the size of a small house.

"Prehistoric male lumba – now extinct."

"Damn," said Foxx. "They made 'em big in those days."

Group Six continued through the natural history part of the museum. There were other skeletons of strange creatures, who thankfully didn't seem to exist anymore. There were deer with antlers wider than three grown men, gigantic tiger-like cats, and bears with teeth and claws like short swords. The most terrifying-looking creature couldn't even be compared to anything living today. Known as a *clee-at,* it was a two-reach tall, spiny rodent-like thing that walked on two legs. Thin, curved fangs hung out of its jaws and its talons were as long and sharp as stilettos.

"Gods, that's something out of my nightmares!" observed Foxx, who shivered at the sight of the horrid predator.

According to the descriptions on the plaques, all of these creatures existed in this very valley, now called Abakaar, in the distant past. The bones had all been found in an immense, natural cave trap in the northern end of the country.

There was one curious exhibit that seemed to contradict the notion that ancient creatures were far larger than their contemporary descendants. Displayed in a glass case were the bones of a winged, reptilian predator with a long, snakelike tail. The inscription read *Primitive Dragon.* Everyone today knew that dragons were huge, fierce creatures with hypnotic Magical powers. The members of Group Six had all seen one — the giant, silver mascot of the Crystal Palace, Gleam. The skeleton in the case was no bigger than an eagle.

The tour through the museum continued. Other rooms contained displays of antique tools and artifacts spanning hundreds and even thousands of years. The whole glorious history of Macai civilization in this valley was laid out chronologically. There were displays and framed written texts detailing the line of rulers all the way up to the present queen, Minore. Achievements and inventions were reproduced in miniature, or graphically illustrated. The Eryndi were not forgotten. In fact, all of these brave accomplishments were said to have come about *despite* the interfering presence of the Eryndi, not because of them.

Foxx, Orchid, and Serena concluded their museum tour and returned to their quaint inn for the night. They retired early, because Floozy would be loaded and ready to shove off by dawn. And shove off she did. Group Six had barely stepped aboard the fully laden barge when its captain gave the order to cast off and proceed on its mission.

"Thought maybe you folks had give up on me. See you got yourselves all cleaned up. Don't put much stock in baths meself . . . bit of a waste of water in my case!"

Floozy punctuated her point by kicking a big, round lumba turd the size of a boingball across the deck.

Evening came once again and the *Folly* pulled up to a berth at an out-of-the-way pier that seemed to be reserved for Floozy. Other craft kept their distance. Floozy snugged her down for the night and gave her crew of five the rest of the night off. They immediately went ashore to frequent their usual watering holes.

"You lubbers be back here before sunup, you hear? The mornin' sees us bound fer Bythia on the wings of dragons!"

Again her cackle echoed off the canyon walls.

"Did I hear right, Cap'n?" asked Foxx. "We reach Bythia tomorrow?"

"Aye we do, and we'll unload there. We've got a fair load . . . should pay well."

"I didn't realize our . . . *cargo* went to Bythia as well," said Orchid.

"Aye, that be where the processing plant is. We unload the raw, take on a load of processed, then downriver to the terraces to deliver it."

"How long do you stay in the Bythian Quarter?"

"Take near a day to offload, warsh down the decks, load the goods, and be off agin."

"That should give us enough time to find Tresado," said Serena.

"What be this Tresado thing yer lookin' fer, anyway?"

Orchid started to answer, but Foxx butted in. Automatically, he adopted Floozy's speech pattern.

"A certain hook what owes me coin."

"Arr."

(Translation: "I understand your plight. I am much skeptical as to whether you can accomplish this goal, given the Eryndi predilection for nefarious activity.")

Morning came. The early sun's slanting rays illuminated the upper terraces first as it climbed higher in the sky. The colored rock strata sparkled with glorious bands of scarlet and brown.

"This sure is a nice place," mooned Orchid, drinking in the vista.

"Yeah, a fellow could have himself a fine life in this valley," answered Foxx.

"That from the world traveler," scoffed Serena.

Foxx's eyebrows knit together. "Yeah, I can't believe I just said that . . ."

By the time the valley floor was lit, *Floozy's Folly* was well underway again with its cargo of evil-smelling waste. A sharp rock crag jutted into the right bank ahead. Beyond it lay a large stagnant area of water cut off from the river's flow by the giant boulder's eddy. The man on the tiller put her hard over and the scow turned sharply past the rock to head up this side road in the river. Sheer cliffs lined both sides of the water, leaving no beach. A twin pair of squat buildings flanked each side. Between them was a sturdy iron gate that spanned the whole waterway. Floozy picked up a large animal horn and blew a long, mournful note. Several uniformed soldiers emerged from the buildings and took a careful look at the approaching barge. One of them held up a hand, which Floozy recognized right away as the signal to stop for inspection.

"I figured this would happen. Usually they just wave me through, but with strange faces aboard, they'll have to check us out. No worries, should only take a few beats."

She ordered the impetus box shut down and the barge brought to a halt. Six troops boarded and took long ganders at the three passengers, paying special attention to Serena and the sword that swung at her hip. Group Six's certification tokens were examined and their numbers recorded. Floozy was obviously familiar and on good terms with the officer that was questioning her. After a moment of serious conversation, both were snickering at some unheard joke. He called off his troops and the soldiers disembarked. Someone shouted a command.

The gate was quickly unlocked and swung open. The soldiers held their noses as the *Folly* slowly proceeded through.

Once again, Serena nodded in appreciation of this country's soldiery. Even at what seemed to be a pretty crappy post to be assigned to, they maintained efficient discipline at all times.

Floozy filled her pipe with some horrid brownish mass and lit it with a brand from the onboard incinerator hearth.

"Welcome, me hearties, to *The Bythian Quarter.*"

CHAPTER 14

Leadership can't be taught in school or learned in books. A true leader earns his rank on the battlefield.

> \- GENERAL PRIXUS SCAPULUS,
> COMMANDER OF THE TRESKAN 12TH LEGION

Not quite 50,000 years ago

The land was slowly healing. Over the past several seasons, Sen showed Her face more than half the time. The winters were still cold, but each season brought new green buds that poked their way through the retreating ice. Food, both animal and vegetable, was more plentiful. The warm, scented water from the hot pools seemed to breathe life into whatever it touched.

The tribe of Jalex had grown in several ways. In addition to the former tribe of Sodak, many other clans entered the valley after so many seasons of wandering. They were welcomed as new members to a very large and growing family. Each new group of people brought new ideas. Enormous gains were made in the methods for making stone tools and hunting weapons. One clan was extremely adept at building efficient lodges that maintained comfortable temperatures practically by themselves simply because of the way they were made. Each new tribe had their own versions of the wise women who were knowledgeable in the art of plants and healing herbs. Everyone learned from everyone else.

Two entire generations had come into the world since the day of Senfall. There were not many Ern who even remembered that terrible day. Those that did made sure that the young knew of that event and of the days before . . . *Magic.*

The extraordinary power that Jalex had developed over plants, animals, and even the weather itself had manifested itself not only in her, but in several other select Ern. She was undisputedly the most adept, but it seemed the ability could be taught to others. Jalex, as ruler of all the Ern of the valley, happily plunged her every effort into doing that very thing. As she taught them, she learned more herself. No one knew from where this power came; there were many theories, most of which were simply guesses. The only thing anyone could agree on was that Magic did not start to happen until after Senfall. Clearly the two were related somehow.

Jalex originally began to sense these abilities during times of stress and danger, such as a hunt or battle. But eventually she learned that the ability was not dependent on those things. It could be brought on at will with the proper concentration. She found that the most important thing was to treat that power with respect. Manipulating plants and animals did not work if one tried to force things. As a former hunter, Jalex understood the value of patience.

One day, two young girls were gathering tender eyepod shoots out of a patch of ground where they grew profusely. The baby plants were tasty, to be sure, but if picked, would not grow to adulthood and produce the large, fleshy green orbs that were filling and even tastier.

"Do you mean to pick all of those?"

The girls looked up to see their revered leader, who had silently approached.

"Chief Jalex! We are gathering these shoots for our meal tonight. Our fathers sent us."

"This patch of baby eyepods will feed your families for one night, but if allowed to grow to adulthood, will feed you for many nights."

"But if we do not pick them, we will have to find other food to eat tonight."

"That is true, Goa. What about the rockfruit trees that grow upon the middle slopes?"

"The slopes are hard to climb and we would have to carry the fruit a long way back to the lodges. The eyepods are easier."

"Goa is right. Gathering the rockfruit is harder. The eyepods are near the lodges and easy to gather. But they can only be gathered once. Is it so with the fruit?"

Daya's face brightened with an idea. "No, Chief. The fruit returns to the trees."

"Do the eyepods return to the soil?"

"Yes, if they grow and drop their seeds."

"Will these eyepods you've picked drop seeds?"

"No, Chief . . . unless . . ."

"Yes . . .?"

"Unless some are left in the ground to grow."

"But how will you feed your families if you leave some in the ground?"

"By . . . gathering both eyepods and rockfruit?"

"Very good, Goa. You have learned well today."

"Thank you for your help, Chief Jalex."

"I wish to become a wise woman like you, Chief."

"Daya, you can all be whatever you want, whether it is a wise woman, a hunter, a builder, or anything. Now, let us give the eyepods a little help to grow into what *they* want to be."

The girls looked confused. "What do eyepods want to be?"

"Why a tasty meal for your families, of course."

Jalex closed her eyes and concentrated on the power of the world around her. Changes occurred in the ground beneath her feet. Water and nutrients flowed. Pores opened in the delicate plants' roots. The internal pressure in their cells lowered, helping to draw the liquid food into their systems. The green sprouts turned their heads to face Sen, gathering Her warmth and accelerating the whole process. Jalex had no knowledge or even understanding of all these details. She simply knew what it was she wanted done. Her thoughts connected to the Magic in the air, which connected to the plants and the soil. The plants knew what they needed. At Jalex's urging, the Magic processed all that information and allowed it to happen faster than normal.

"Look, *look!*" The girls watched in delight as the unpicked eyepod sprouts quivered and snaked their way above the ground. Curled up leaf buds appeared and spread. Within only a few hands of beats, there was a patch of healthy, half-grown eyepod plants, where there were only tiny sprouts before.

"Now go to fetch a few rockfruit. On your way back, gather of few of these plants for tonight's meal to go with them. Be sure to leave some fruit on the trees and some plants in the ground for the future or for others to gather. Your parents will no doubt bring in good meat and you will provide plants to eat with it. Your meals will be tasty tonight. Go now, girls."

"Thank you, Chief Jalex."

"Thank you, Chief."

The girls giggled delightfully as only little girls can and scurried off. Jalex looked down at her handiwork. The patch of half-mature plants surprised even her. She had been developing this new skill for several seasons now, but the potential of it still left her in awe. She looked up at the glowing face of Sen as She smiled down upon the world. Jalex could not help but wonder about the meaning of it all.

The eyepods' growth spurt had slowed by now. Some of the plants even had the beginnings of tiny seed pods starting to develop. The wise women had taught her that plants grew from the seeds their parents produced. Jalex stared at the ground for several more beats. As with the eyepods, an idea began to sprout in her mind.

* * *

Weeny peeny, greeny go;
Hookie crookie bergalo;
Make 'em sorry, make 'em pay;
Make 'em gone so Red can play.

- Popular Abakaarian playground verse

Today – The Bythian Quarter

Floozy's Folly slowly picked her way through the narrow canyon. The narrowness was not caused by the proximity of the rock walls. It was actually because of the multitude of floating shanty houses that lined both sides of the tributary. Eryndi of all ages and sexes peered at them out of dilapidated windows and from rickety walkways. Eventually the sheer rock gave way to increasingly wide beaches. On the left ahead was a large, warehouse-looking building with one open side. The barge sailed in and berthed at a special dock. A Macai supervisor blew a shrill whistle as soon as the barge was secure. About twenty Eryndi scurried aboard with shovels and brooms. A large wooden hopper on a hoist was swung into place and the workers began filling it with cargo. As soon as it was full, it was swung away to be emptied into a large pit and swung back for another load. Floozy explained the procedure as it went.

"This be the processing plant. The raw is dumped into yon pit. Some kind of witch's brew is mixed in – got no idea what's in it. That goo breaks everything down, be it animal or veggie-table. After three day of fermentin', the workers syphon it into a tank fed by a hot spring what comes up under the building. The Ernies turn cranks to keep everything stirred up. That goes on for another day. Then they use hand pumps to send it into molds and them goes into kilns. Two hours later the cake is done."

Floozy took a cackle break and lit her pipe.

"Crap go in, fertilizer bricks come out. Make anything grow. Turnin' crap into food. This be the best job in the world. Make a body feel powerful good."

With a warning that the scow would be pulling out again by early evening after the offloading was complete, Floozy bid good luck to Group Six in this hopeless search of theirs for the Ernie that they foolishly expected to collect a debt from.

The three Macai stepped ashore and strolled along the riverbank. The word *squalor* did not quite apply, but it was close. Foxx had seen slums before in many cities, most with worse conditions than this. The one thing that stood out here was that all the Eryndi were working. They were sweeping and shoveling and repairing and doing any number of menial but necessary jobs, but nobody was idle. As Group Six continued to wander the Bythian Quarter, they also saw a lot of manufacturing being done by the Eryndi. There was the fertilizer processing plant of course, but there were also blacksmiths and potters, basket weavers and brick makers. Nothing that was being made here had much aesthetic value. All of the industry being done by the Eryndi was of the basest, most utilitarian quality. Abakaarian officials in uniform patrolled around, but were not slave-driving the workers. They just seemed to be directing what work was being done by whom. None of the Eryndi were getting chastised or abused. They just had crappy work to do in a crappy environment and they all seemed okay with that. Aside from their race, the Eryndi stood out in another way. They of course had certification tokens, as did all Abakaarian citizens, but instead of red, theirs were green with a red X.

A building signed *Administration* lay just ahead.

"Let's check in there," said Foxx.

Several uniformed Macai were working at counters and shuffling paper forms. Group Six got odd looks from all of them when they walked in.

"Good day, gentlefolk. Might we trouble you with a few questions?"

"They must be important for respectable-looking people like you to come here," replied a stern-faced woman who was filling out progress reports on paving stone production.

"We're looking for an Eryndi who's new to this country . . . fair hair, fat little sod."

"What'd this hook do that you need to find him so bad?"

"Welshed on a payment."

Another uniformed Macai spoke up with a sneer. "You must be new here, too. When you tourists gonna learn that you don't do business with throwbacks?"

"We learned all right," said Orchid in a phony harsh voice. "No more dealing with these . . . Eryndi *stinkers!*"

Foxx and Serena surreptitiously rolled their eyes. Orchid was a skilled Magician, but a terrible actor.

"Tokens, please."

"Come again?"

"Your certification tokens. You really are new here, aren't you?"

Foxx, Serena, and Orchid were strangely reluctant, but handed over their medallions in turn. As each one left its owner's hand, the color vanished and turned grey, as before. The woman laid the three tokens in a tray similar to the one they had seen in Naomi's office when they first arrived. The same line of red light passed over them and the tokens were handed back to them. They immediately returned to their red and blue colors.

What's your buddy's name?" asked the woman.

"Tresado," replied Foxx. "He should have arrived within the last few days."

"One moment . . . Brikal, bring me the four-two-seven file."

Another uniform dug into a cabinet and fetched a folder. A few beats of examining it and Foxx had his answer.

"This Tresado isn't here. He's been assigned to an outworker position."

"Outworker? What's that?" asked Serena.

"Issued a special mandate to operate outside of the Quarter."

"Can you tell us where?"

"Sorry, we don't have that info. Your boy's under the jurisdiction of the regular army now."

"Anything else you can tell us?"

"Just that if you're planning to collect whatever debt this fellow owes you, you're probably hosed."

"We probably are," said Foxx. "Thank you, ma'am."

Group Six left the building and made their way back toward Floozy's barge. They had plenty of time, so they took a different route back, just to see more of the Bythian Quarter. Again, they saw many things being manufactured: building materials, clay piping, road paving gravel, and other commodities. There were no food or beverages being produced here, no fine silks, no delicate artwork, no high-quality items of any kind. Apparently, that sort of work was reserved for the Macai living along the luxurious riverbanks of Abakaar.

Group Six strolled past all the busily engaged Eryndi and noted that, however hard they worked, spirits were good. Families laughed and joked together while they worked at their jobs. Whether it was breaking up rocks with sledgehammers or shoveling crap off of Floozy's barge, the Eryndi of the Bythian Quarter apparently lived happy, contented lives.

There was nothing more to be done here. Group Six went back to the fertilizer plant. Floozy's barge was being loaded with stacks of fertilizer bricks. Orchid asked to see one.

"I can see why this will grow anything," she said, sniffing the powdery cake. "This is loaded with nutrients and enhanced with good old Worldly Magic. You could stick an acorn in this, throw it into a pile of rocks, and have an oak tree growing within a week."

Loading was complete and *Floozy's Folly* chugged out of the narrow channel. The gate was opened for them and the barge moved back out onto the Serpent River.

"Ahh, that's better," sighed Serena. "Fresh air. It was a bit stagnant in that backwater canyon. Still, the Ernies seemed happy with it."

"And it's good for them," added Orchid. "They all looked well enough fed and it's probably for the best to keep them separate from the Macai. That way they stay safe and out of trouble."

Foxx didn't say anything, but when the ladies made these comments, again there was that weird feeling of familiarity. It was like hearing the notes of an old song, but not being quite able to place it. He almost had it when Floozy interrupted his concentration.

"Gonna pull into the re-enchantment station ahead. If you folks want to get off here, there are more *genteel* modes of travel to be had. Not that I don't enjoy yer company or yer money . . . just thought I orta tell ye."

"Thanks, Floozy. I wouldn't have missed it," said Orchid.

Serena also chimed in. "Yeah, thanks. Your boat stinks, but it got us where we needed to go."

The resulting cackle was the loudest one they had heard yet.

"Stand by on the bowline, there."

One of her crew scurried up forward and prepared to jump off onto the slowly approaching dock. Floozy eased her pride and joy into the berth, the bow gently kissing the rubber bumpers on the pier.

"Make 'er fast, ye scalawags! After we fuel, the first round is on me. The rest of 'em are all on ye!"

The stinky crew tied off the stinky barge and hopped ashore to begin the Magical fueling process. There wasn't much to it, really. They went to the stern and removed the protective cover from the top of the impetus box. One crewman wiped it down with a cloth, while another disengaged several connecting rods that ran to the paddle wheel. A man came out of a small building and warmly greeted Floozy and her boys.

"Ahoy, you old bag!"

"Ahoy, Chintzy, you son of a sick bergalo! 'vast that *old* talk. That ain't no way to make converse with a lady."

"My apologies, Floozy. I shoulda said *middle-aged bag.*"

"That be more like it."

The two apparent old friends exchanged hugs.

"Don't need the usual eye-dropper of packets today, Chintzy. You can top off the *Folly* for me. We had a good run."

Chintzy wrinkled his nose as their hug broke. "Yeah, I can tell. Who's your friends?"

Group Six was just climbing onto the dock and getting ready to take their leave of Floozy as soon as she was through with business.

"They be the other reason I can afford a full charge . . . payin' passengers!"

"They don't look like typical hitchhikers . . . especially the one in the fine red suit. Gotta say I like the look of the other two," he said, eyeing Serena and Orchid.

"Shush, Chintzy. What would yer wife say?"

A sturdy, redheaded woman called out from down the dock. "She'd say he'd never have the stones to carry through on his lechery. Besides, if he did, he knows it'd be his last day on Lurra."

"Ahoy, Gracie. How be the little'uns?"

"So-so. Gorno wants to be a lumba when he grows up."

"Good to have goals, I expect."

"All right, enough female gossiping," smirked Chintzy. "Let's get Floozy fueled up and out of here before I'm tempted to leave you and run off with her."

"Promises, promises. Hook her up, honeybuns."

Chintzy pulled a curious spiral hose made of a silvery metallic material off of a reel and plopped the rubber suction cup on the end to the top of Floozy's impetus box.

Gracie produced a small, hinged box and opened the lid. Inside was a recessed circular depression.

"Sign your life away, please."

Floozy pulled her certification token from around her neck and placed it in the box. The familiar red light played across the disc, which never lost its red color, apparently because she kept her thumb on it. When that was done, Gracie nodded to her and the token was removed.

"Start the flow."

Chintzy turned a handle on the top of the hose reel and a repeating Magical glow flowed down the hose and into the impetus box. A line appeared near the bottom of the box and rose slowly.

Group Six watched the procedure with interest.

"Pure, refined Magical energy being stored and transferred," said Foxx with awe. "Amazing."

"Those rock crawlers in the zone did something similar," said Orchid. "I wonder if that's where these guys got the idea."

Before the ascending line got halfway up the side of the impetus box, it halted and the pulsating glow in the hose stopped.

"Ah, nuts," said Chintzy. "Half a minute while we do a recharge." He pulled a whistle out of his pocket and blew a shrill note.

"Boy . . . BOY! Terminal seven's run out. Get your ass out here!"

"Coming, boss . . ."

A plump figure wearing a hooded robe hustled out of the building and ran over to the hose reel.

"Sorry, boss . . . I was just taking a . . ."

"Don't need to hear any lame excuses. Just do your job."

"Right."

A pair of soft hands extended from the oversized sleeves and hovered over the reel. The figure froze in concentration and evidently began some kind of spellcasting. A few beats later, the glow returned to the hose and resumed filling the *Folly's* impetus box. A quick breeze swirled off the river and blew back the figure's hood, revealing a pair of cone-shaped ears and a pointed chin. Foxx gaped in astonishment.

"TRESADO!"

"LUCY!"

PART II: THE QUEEN

CHAPTER 15

Today – Zanteryne Castle

The windows of the East Tower were lit with a scintillating glow of Magical energies. It was comforting to the populace whenever they witnessed this event. In fact, Abakaarian citizens considered it an omen of good luck. It meant that Queen Minore was hard at work for their benefit.

There were few in the country who knew exactly what went on up there. In fact, there was only one. Grand Vizier Rastaban stood quietly outside the royal chamber. As soon as the glow faded from below the great double doors, he nodded to the guards, who swung them open and allowed him to enter. He was a tall, thin Macai with piercing black eyes that seemed to be all pupil. His short, immaculately trimmed brown beard came to a needle point below his gaunt cheeks. His robes were of the finest red silk, belted at the waist. He wore no jewelry, save for matching gold bracelets, each set with a large, brilliant ruby. Right now, his habit of grasping his wrists inside the opposite sleeves kept them out of sight.

Queen Minore's back was to him. She stood in front of an enormous tapestry which hung on the far wall from the door.

The heavy material was embroidered with scenes of carnage and warfare. Mounted troops and endless columns of green-armored soldiers were depicted marching across fertile basins and leaving barren wastelands behind them. Great generals in plumed helmets beckoned the troops on, pointing short, thick swords. Standard bearers carried long poles topped with the golden head of a bear.

Rastaban approached his ruler softly, as was his style. His slippered feet made no sound. Nevertheless, Minore acknowledged his presence without turning her gaze away from the tapestry.

"My Lord Rastaban."

"By Your will, My Queen."

"This is a disturbing picture, would you not say?"

"Most disturbing, Your Grace."

"Our forces must be adequate."

"I assure you, My Queen, recruitment figures are at an all-time high."

Minore turned quickly, her thick, black, waist-length braids whirling about her toned body like a nest of striking onyx snakes. Her nearly milk-white eyes with the faintest hint of blue flecks pierced Rastaban like two opal arrowheads.

"You guaranteed me one hundred percent compliance. Even now, after ten years, the ranks are not back up to full strength!"

"My Queen, the internal Eryndi problem has been fully dealt with. There is no further risk of . . ."

The Vizier's words were cut short by the blast of flame at his feet. Rastaban held his ground, as though he expected such a near miss. The Queen's icy stare made it clear that she was in no mood for excuses.

"I shall read the tapestry again in another eight days. I trust I will be pleased with what I see."

"Of course. By Your will, My Queen."

Rastaban backed out of the room and the guards closed the double doors behind him. He motioned to an assistant, who stood unobtrusively at the end of the hall.

"Bring the latest data to my chambers. This will be a late night."

Late that night – Zanteryne Castle

Rastaban stood in his ultra-private alcove in the back of his private chambers in his private mini-tower. Not even the ancient Eryndi builders of the castle would have known of this room's presence. The Magically created alcove didn't exist back then. There were no chairs. Rastaban was a man who preferred to stand. His tall frame was surrounded by curved consoles that glowed with strange figures. He was currently examining a bar graph set against a depiction of the river valley of Abakaar. Tiny, colored squares and triangles appeared at different points on the map. Some were larger than others, some were blinking, some not. If the Vizier touched one of them, several lines of illuminated figures appeared under the graph and the height of the bars changed accordingly. After examining several points all up and down the river on the map, Rastaban touched another section of console and the map disappeared. He stood in silence for a few beats in deep concentration and at last exited his alcove.

He went to a shelf in his living quarters, picked up a decanter filled with a thick, yellowish liquid, and poured a small amount into a glass. He took his drink to the only piece of upholstered furniture in the room, a low divan with a table next to it. On the table was a glass bottle with a metallic funnel at the top. Set evenly around the base of the bottle were several small vials containing different powdered substances. Rastaban slowly spun the bottle around on its bearings until he found the vial he wanted. He removed a small pinch of brown powder and placed it in the funnel. The bottle was spun again and he selected an even smaller pinch of another powder, this time rust-colored, and mixed it with the other. After a beat's concentration, the substances in the funnel glowed with heat. A flexible rubber hose with a copper fitting on the end went into Rastaban's mouth and he inhaled slowly and deeply. The water in the bottle bubbled and sent the cooled smoke into the Vizier's lungs. He held it there and drained his glass in one swallow. Reclining on the divan, Rastaban closed his eyes and held his breath for a period of time that would make a pearl diver jealous. Finally, he slowly exhaled through his nostrils, expelling a thick cloud of billowing smoke. They were not visible to the untrained eye, but Magical energies were summoned from the air and played about the Grand Vizier's head. His thoughts were of the data he had just reviewed, his Queen, and of lands beyond this one. He lay there for nearly an hour, motionless but for the throbbing vein on his temple.

At last he rose from his bed and re-entered his alcove, this time making sure the sophisticated hatch behind him was doubly secured, both physically and Magically. He touched a hitherto unused section of console and entered a series of commands. A light emanated from a glowing red gemstone set in the surface. From it a sphere of luminescent gas swirled about and began to take shape. The globe became mostly light grayish-purple with patches of brown. Then, spider silk-thin filaments began to circle the sphere, each one intersecting with a glowing figure of either blue, red, or green. The figures were tiny representations of various objects. There were depictions of swords, ships, towers, trees, mountains, buildings. A single blue fish and a green bear and a red serpent pursued orbits of their own, constantly slowing, stopping, or changing course. There were crowns of all three colors, small silhouettes of cityscapes, images of shields and flowers, fire and birds. Every pictogram that circled the ephemeral globe was shown in either blue, red, or green. But for every colored symbol that actively circled, there were five times as many that were unmoving and colored gray. As Rastaban pondered the display, his eye caught one of the static grey city symbols as it suddenly turned green and began moving in an orbit of its own.

Grand Vizier Rastaban observed the complicated display for several minutes, then touched the console. The globe vanished and he exited and secured his alcove. He signaled his ever-present assistant who maintained vigil in the hall.

"Prepare my launch. I would travel the river in the morning."

* * *

My brother Cyrus used to say, 'Home is where you hang your hat.' But I don't wear a hat — makes my hair funny.

 - Travelogue of Dementus the Mad Treskan

Today – Abakaarian Re-enchantment station 12

"Cover yourself!" shouted Chintzy. "You think decent people want to see that?"

"Sorry, boss." Tresado hurriedly pulled his hood back over

his head to cover his Eryndi features.

"Where's your escort?"

"Uhm . . ."

"CORPORAL!"

A uniformed soldier sheepishly appeared from behind some casks on the wharf. Several crumbs formerly attached to a sandwich dropped from his breastplate armor. There was also a dab of sour sauce at the corner of his mouth.

"Aren't you supposed to be keeping an eye on your charge?"

"I apologize, sir," said the soldier. "I have no excuse, other than this one is a workaholic. He actually seems to enjoy this Magic business. He recharged nearly every terminal on the wharf before he finally headed for the outhouse. I . . . hadn't eaten since breakfast and thought I'd take the opportunity for a quick bite. Who'd have thought a hook would have a work ethic?"

While this banter was going on, Foxx sidled up to Tresado.

"You all right, bro?"

"Sure," replied Tresado cheerfully. "It's good to see you guys."

"What happened to you after we were picked up? We were worried."

"What are you talking about?"

"Those thugs dragged you down those stairs in the fortress," added Orchid.

"WHAT?!"

"Are you saying you don't remember?" asked Serena.

"I . . ."

Tresado paused before finishing his thought. A look of calmness came over his Eryndi features, still half-hidden beneath the hood. "I was assigned a case worker who evaluated my skills. That's how I managed to get this choice job. What did you guys get into? Serena, I bet they made you an ambassador," he chuckled.

"Actually, I think I'm going to join the defense forces. Somebody's got to keep the Ernies at bay. And if this job is what snaps your bowstring, then more power to you. You're really lucky to have it. Don't screw it up," she replied sternly.

"Yeah, Tresado," added Orchid. "I'm glad to see you're happy in your work, but don't you think you should get back to it?"

"You're right, ma'am. I hope to see you guys again. If I don't, good luck in whatever you get to do here."

Foxx blinked his eyes, but that was the only reaction that showed on his face. A wave of understanding had just washed over him. He concentrated intently on his Eryndi best friend.

"Tresado, keep the faith. Don't let anyone talk you into anything you shouldn't be doing . . . *know what I mean?* C'mon ladies, let's get out of here."

Tresado stared back at Foxx for a beat, but noticed the evil eye of Chintzy, his employer, and hurriedly resumed charging the terminal.

Orchid and Serena went over to Floozy to give her a final departing hug. They had come to like the hideous-smelling ex-smuggler. Foxx was left staring down at his citizen's certification token.

* * *

Give a man a loaf of bread and he eats for a day;
Teach a man to farm and you also better teach
him to use a sword.

- GAISERAN – CHIEFTAIN OF THE
BERYNGIAN BORDERLANDS

Not quite 50,000 years ago

This season's planting was doing very well. The rows of eyepods and conegrass were thriving and should yield a harvest in not too many days. In the past two hands of seasons, the Ern had also learned to maintain orchards of rockfruit trees and to cultivate large patches of vine melons in the boggy lowlands. All this new learning was from the active mind of Chief Jalex. It was she who had first conceived of the idea of deliberately seeding and growing food plants instead of just gathering those that sprouted on their own.

The days of suffering and want since the long-past Senfall seemed to finally be over. Food, both meat and vegetable, was plentiful. All the tribes of the valley, however far apart they lived, were now as one – the tribe of Jalex. Occasionally, clans of Ern from outside the valley arrived, having heard of the land of plenty in the great crack in the ground. All newcomers were welcomed, provided they were willing to contribute in some way. This had never been a problem. When conditions were good, Ern were hard workers with a sense of fair play.

Then, one day near the end of the summer season, change came. There was a party of Ern hard at work near the northern end of the valley. The clay soil at this end of the canyon was friendly for planting *coryal,* a leafy vegetable with fleshy roots. They were using a new technique recently developed to dig up the ground to prepare a new field. It involved the cooperation of a giant *milk beast,* a gentle creature that smelled just awful, but had great strength and was willing to work for a handful of rockfruit, all the grass it could eat, and occasional itching behind its great, floppy ears. The shoulder blade bone of a morok was tied behind the beast with braided leather ropes.

The handlers guided it back and forth across the field, the sharp end of the morok bone digging into the hard-packed soil and turning it over, making the ground ready for seeding.

The furrowing had to be stopped while a large subsurface rock was dug out of the ground. Two brothers, Karrol and Drook, and Drook's mate, Shemin, had already snapped off two pry sticks trying to extricate the boulder. A movement on the canyon wall caught Karrol's eye.

"Look there."

A little way up the slope was a patch of short, scrubby bushes growing out from between the red rocks. Peeking out from just above one of those bushes was a hand. The hand waved.

Karrol picked up one of the pry sticks as a makeshift weapon.

"Come, let us see who that is."

The two brothers quickly scrambled up the slope. Lying on her side in the bushes was a woman. Her wrap was torn and bloodstained. Her arms and legs were bruised and bleeding, possibly from having tumbled down the canyon wall. She looked up weakly. Her dry, cracked lips opened.

"Beware!"

The woman's head dropped. Little wisps of dust weakly blew away from her nostrils.

"She still lives," said Drook. "Shemin! Bring water quickly!"

The brothers gently picked up the injured woman and carried her down the slope to the valley floor. She did not appear to have any life-threatening wounds, but was terribly bruised and scraped.

"She may have been beaten," said Drook. "We must bring her to the lodges quickly."

While Karrol and Drook cut some branches to carry her on, Shemin ran up from the river with a large leaf cone filled with water. She cleaned the woman's injuries as best she could.

"I do not recognize her tribe," said Shemin. "She has skin markings here on her forehead and her hair is closely cut in a way I have never seen. She must be from outside the valley."

The crude stretcher was quickly lashed together and the brothers loaded the unconscious woman onto it.

"Shemin . . . Karrol and I will take her back to the lodges. Release the milk beast and let him roam. Then join us quickly. Stay alert for danger!"

"I shall."

There were only a handful of permanent lodges at this northern end of the valley. The main grouping where Chief Jalex and most of the Ern dwelt was far away near the southern end. What few families lived here had arrived only three seasons ago.

The injured visitor was taken to a shelter and placed on a comfortable bed of furs. Broth and fruit mash were brought and fed to her as though she were a newborn. With time and care, the woman eventually returned to consciousness. Suddenly realizing she was surrounded by people, she woke with wide eyes and cowered with fear.

Shemin and her mother, who also shared this lodge, comforted her and assured her there was no danger. After a few minutes the terrified woman calmed down.

"I am called Shemin; this is Arma. You are safe here. Who are you?"

The woman clutched the torn remnants of her wrap to her chest.

"My name is Kray."

"Are there others with you, Kray?"

"I . . . I alone escaped. I ran and ran until I found this valley."

"Escaped? From what did you escape?"

Kray looked at all the Ern faces surrounding her in the lodge. Her eyes widened and her voice trembled.

"Demons!"

* * *

Work will set you free . . .

- MINORE, QUEEN OF ABAKAAR

Today – Abakaar

Foxx, Orchid, and Serena were feeling refreshed and well-fed. After taking their leave of Floozy and Tresado, they stopped at one of the many bath houses along the river and had a pleasant soak in the mineral-rich thermal water of this delightful country. Foxx had suggested that all three of them use the unisex pool in the facility, but was threatened with beheading by Serena. The men's pool was not as much fun, but still it felt good to rid his body of the remaining vestiges of their days on Floozy's honey barge. After they cleaned up, their growling tummies demanded satisfaction, so they dropped into a charming eatery whose specialty was a sautéed clam dish served over vegetables. An hour later, three cleaned plates and three empty flagons of ale sat on the table. The flagons were in front of Orchid. Foxx and Serena had only drunk a glass of rockfruit wine each. The conversation turned to plans for the future.

"Are you sure you want to do this?"

Foxx stared across the table at Serena. She was perusing the literature she had gotten at the fort from the young soldier she had talked to not long after their arrival.

"Yeah, I am."

"Explain that to me, if you would."

Serena motioned to the waiter to bring her another glass of that delicious wine.

"Oh right, like you'd understand."

"Actually, that's what I was hoping for."

"Okay, fine," she said while holding up her glass for refilling. "Because I like this place. I like the food, the weather, the people . . . I like that river and the hot springs. I like the fact that everybody else likes it here, too. There ain't no malcontents, nobody trying to stir up trouble or *change everything.* Nobody here feels the need to *compete,* to be better than anybody or rule over anybody. This is as perfect a country as you're ever gonna find. But there's only one problem with that. Anyplace this perfect is gonna have enemies that want to try and take it from them. That's why they need a strong military to protect it. I wanna be a part of that."

"Okay, fair enough," replied Foxx. "But haven't I heard you say that you don't care for hot weather? And didn't you once mention how you loved betting on the weapons competitions and daily brawls back in your home village?"

"So? Ain't a girl allowed to change her mind?"

"Oh, leave her alone," snapped Orchid. "Just because you've been run out of everyplace you've ever lived doesn't mean we don't want to settle down!"

"*We,* huh? I take it you want to stay here, too?"

Orchid took a breath. "Maybe."

"But you don't like cities." Foxx stared at both the ladies intently.

"There you go again," said the annoyed Serena. "Telling everybody what they like and don't like! And stop that starin' mumbo jumbo! Just keep your creepy spells to yourself!"

Foxx had to admit to himself that he was indeed trying to use his Knowing Spell to influence Serena and Orchid. He also had to admit that he had failed. In the past, the spell had been useful in calming the distinct personality conflicts among the members of Group Six and guiding the headstrong characters away from stupid decisions. This time, however, Foxx sensed that his self-taught version of Influential Magic bounced right off them.

It's like my spell ran into a stone wall.

"Okay, you're right . . . and I apologize. Who am I to try to run your lives?"

Orchid paused for a beat then said, "You know, sometimes I can't tell when you're being cynical and when you're serious."

"I'm always serious . . . never cynical."

"See what I mean?"

Foxx smiled, then actually got serious. "It's just that . . . if we do stay here . . . and . . . it chokes me to say it . . . *got jobs* . . . then that's the end of Group Six."

"Well, if you remember, we became *Group Six* to get rid of my love spirit problem," said Serena, tapping the diamond in her chest. "No more problem."

"Actually I joined because Leader paid like a drunken fool," retorted Foxx. "But later I kind of thought the four of us made a pretty decent team. Tell me, Orchid, what would *you* do in this place?"

"You've probably noticed that there are lots of animals here, both domestic and wild. I'm sure I could find something."

"How about you, chief?" asked Serena. "Any ideas on how a cheap carnival con artist might make himself useful?"

"Whaddaya mean, cheap? I don't know, there doesn't seem to be much in the way of gambling houses here."

"Maybe you could start one."

"Yeah, maybe."

Foxx paused to think. He had never felt so conflicted before. His past life was a history of using up a place and quickly hitting the road . . . usually before the local constabulary caught up with him. This place was different though. The country and the culture seemed to call to him, just as it did to the others. His buddy Tresado was apparently happy and content. Orchid and Serena seemed to be fitting right in as well. But still he knew something was not right here. He would make one more subtle attempt at unraveling this riddle.

"Tell you what . . . before we make any quick decisions, what would you ladies think about seeing the rest of the country first?"

Foxx pulled out his standard issue map of Abakaar. "We haven't been to the northern end of the valley yet. How about it . . . one more adventure as *Group Six?*"

CHAPTER 16

Today – Zanteryne Castle

Queen Minore was surrounded. Not by an army of enemies, but by an army of body servants, secretaries, scribes, gown makers, dressers, hair stylists, perfumers, makeup artists, manicurists, tooth polishers, apothecaries, chefs, wine stewards, confectioners, musicians, singers, acrobats, and dancers. Minore was not preparing to attend a major state function. She was merely heading down to the main hall for the nightly court appearance. After all, it wasn't like a girl could just throw on any old thing and run down to dinner.

"Borla," she said to one of her advisors, "what is the status of the new dock works on the Yenna estuary?"

"Ahead of schedule, My Queen. We added an additional two hundred laborers to dredge the banks. We now have sufficient depth to accommodate our biggest barges. We have only to finish the walls of the redoubt and we will be able to deploy regiments to our western flank quickly and efficiently."

"What was the cost in laborers?" Minore asked while closely monitoring the application of her toenail varnish by a pair of servants.

Borla consulted a small notebook. "Eleven Eryndi dead from accidents . . . five of those from drowning, three from unknown collapse, two by dragon attack, and one who attempted to run away and was shot down."

"The one that was shot was not an accident."

"Your pardon, My Queen. That Eryndi blatantly defied his handlers and fled the work area. He foolishly tried to climb the canyon wall to escape the valley. The arrow fired by the guard struck him a non-fatal wound in the leg, but caused him to tumble down the cliff face and impale himself on a spear bush. That's why it was classified as an accidental worker loss. I'm told it was quite an amusing sight."

The Queen's retinue of servants tittered in appreciation at the anecdote.

Pelonka Ke Dor, the Court Riddlemistress, sat on her usual stool in the far corner of the room. She was a frail, elderly woman dressed in robes covered in mystical symbols. Her sightless eyes lifted to the ceiling, as though she were actually seeing something undetectable to all others.

"I question thee . . . I have an infinite number of definitions. I am disappointing to friends, amusing to enemies, condemned by the righteous, and praised by sinners. What am I? . . . Give up? Trick question . . . I, of course, am *sin.*"

Once again, Minore's servants snickered in amusement.

"Silence!" she snapped in an effort to maintain discipline. The laughter ceased immediately. "The loss of workers is nothing to joke about. Our very way of life may be soon threatened by the hordes of the Treskan Imperium! We cannot afford to waste or needlessly lose any usable asset."

Minore maintained an icy stare to enhance the intimidation. It worked like a charm, as usual. As soon as all the servant's eyes were down in submission, it was back to business as usual.

"Now, finish me up and get me down to the receiving hall. The Court is waiting."

The finishing touches involved the royal jeweler. It was her job to select just the right set of pearls, the right brooch, the right gold armbands, the right everything to go with today's gown. The culmination of the work of art that was Queen Minore was the placing of the royal crown upon the royal head. It was an incredibly ornate and ancient masterpiece of gold and jewels, handed down through the generations of Abakaarian rulers. On the front of it, not really matching the ancient filigree, was a modern addition, a circular metallic disk. As the crown was lowered upon Minore's head, the token glowed a Magical bright crimson. Before heading out, she called an attendant to her side.

"Go at once to the Vizier's quarters. Have them searched once again. Bring me the results in one hour."

The servant bowed and scurried out. Queen Minore turned to her Chief of Staff.

"I am ready."

* * *

How strange and wonderful is the life of Lurra . . .

- Mama's notebook – Day 4

Not quite 50,000 years ago

The strange woman who called herself Kray had been tended by Shemin and Arma for a full three days now. After her initial few words, she once again lapsed into semi-consciousness. The weakness from the pummeling she had evidently received was worsened by a bout of some kind of fever. The nausea made it difficult to keep down any food, which delayed her recovery even more. She also suffered from terrifying dreams. Many times she awoke from a delirium crying out about strange invaders and their monster servants.

As Sen sank below the western rim of the canyon, Karrol and Drook returned to the lodge after working in the field all day.

"You are a coward, Karrol."

"I am not," he replied to his older brother. "I am cautious. I do not leap out of the bushes and try to chase down my prey like a boy hunter. She will evade and outrun me like a grassbuck."

"But if you do not pursue, Lani will run to the lodge of some other hunter. I do not want you living with my family for the rest of your life."

"Lani will be *my* mate. You will see!"

"Perhaps by then, my eyes will be too old to see *anything.*"

Karrol picked up a dirt clod and threw it at Drook to finalize his position. The two brothers entered their lodge to a somber sight. Shemin and Arma were hovering over the bed of furs that Kray had not left since arriving here. Her skin was wet with perspiration and her mouth gaped open like a fish from the river. Arma daubed at the woman's lips with a soft leaf. It came back with traces of blood on it.

"Drook," said Shemin with relief, "at last you are here. Kray is much worse."

"Her bruises were not serious. Is she injured inside, perhaps?"

"I do not think so. Her body is very hot. We do not know what more to do. Kray needs a wise woman. We must summon Chief Jalex."

"But it is many days' travel to those lodges," replied Drook. "And it would take many more days for her to arrive. The Chief is elderly. I do not know if she can come so far."

"Kray may die if we do nothing."

"I will make the trip to Chief Jalex," stated Karrol.

"*You,* brother?"

"I shall run. I can run all day with but short rests. I shall bring help for Kray."

Drook looked proudly at his younger brother. "Lani shall have herself a fine mate, Karrol. You have worked the field all day. Tonight, you shall have a long rest and start your journey when Sen returns."

Unfortunately, that night there was little rest to be had. The woman Kray was delirious much of the time. She would wake in a feverish state, babble about many strange and horrible things, then pass out again, only to repeat the actions several times. Finally, morning came and Karrol prepared for his long journey.

"I shall prepare a bundle of food to take along," said Arma. "It will keep those fine legs moving, Karrol."

She went outside to retrieve some dried meat and fruit from their storage dugout. As Arma emerged from the hole, she began to cough.

Today – Abakaar

Foxx knew the ladies were under the influence of a spell. It had finally come to him why this country of Abakaar had that familiar feel to it. The Magic being used was closely akin to his own self-invented Knowing Spell. The strange satisfaction and sense of contentment they were feeling were being introduced into them by an unknown agency. Something in the back of his mind told him that this was not a good thing and he should continue to try to counteract it. It wasn't that easy, though. What he wasn't consciously aware of was the fact that the spell was working on him as well. After his initial attempts to influence Orchid, Serena, and Tresado, it had increased in potency. His own psyche, accustomed to this form of Influential Magic, fought back subconsciously, but the power of the outside spell inhibited his ability to fully resist it.

Group Six (minus Tresado, of course) strolled down the pathway that bordered the Serpent River. It was a beautiful day, as usual. Up ahead was another large travel depot similar to the one Foxx had visited farther upriver. There were hundreds of people out and about; most of them were either disembarking or on their way to board one of the many water taxis and river transports.

Foxx glanced over to Orchid, who was currently engaged in smelling a planter full of colorful flowers. It was right in the middle of the walkway and she was being somewhat jostled by the flow of people moving back and forth. The expression on her face was one of happy contentment as she inhaled the fragrances. Foxx had seen her in crowd situations before and she usually hated it. Cities and crowds offended her Worldly Magic ways. Orchid had always preferred the quiet solitude of a woodland glade to an urban sprawl. Foxx noticed one other alarming thing. The citizen's certification tokens issued to all of them used to be blue with a red X. Orchid's was now fully red.

A large water taxi was getting ready to head downriver. Group Six paid their fare and waved their tokens over a box, as was required. There were about thirty other people on board. You could easily tell the tourists from the commuters. They were the ones looking out the windows and taking in the sights. The regular passengers, who were going to and from jobs, kept their noses in books or on their knitting. The boat made several stops, dropping off and adding passengers. Nothing so far interested Group Six enough for them to get off until the next stop took them to the Serpent Valley Zoo.

"Ooh, let's check that out!" said Orchid, not surprisingly.

Foxx had seen a zoo once before in the Treskan Imperium. It had essentially consisted of rows of cages filled with miserable animals. This one was quite different. There were elevated walkways that looked down into spacious habitats with free-roaming beasts of all kinds. There were herds of black-faced mountain sheep with spiral horns. They reminded Serena of the grilk of her native fjords, but smaller. Several huge, caged-in areas contained varieties of exotic, colorful birds. Some areas had gentle creatures for the kids to pet, while others contained some very vicious, dangerous animals. Group Six was at just such a place, overlooking a habitat for something called a spearcat. These were frightful long-legged felines with gray and white stripes designed to blend in with grasslands. Their long, needle-sharp fangs extended six fingers below their lower jaws and their claws were as long as one's hand. The information placard on the walkway said these fearsome cats had survived virtually unchanged since prehistoric times.

There were several people on the walkway above the spearcats' enclosure marveling at the magnificent beasts. One woman was holding a fussy and overactive toddler in her arms as she leaned on the railing trying to get a better look. Suddenly, the little one grabbed hold of the citizen's certification token which hung from his mother's neck. The overly-strong tyke gave it a good yank and snapped the thin chain, sending the metal token plummeting down into the enclosure. The woman let out a panicked scream, dropped her son on the walkway, and vaulted over the railing to fall over three reaches to the ground. The bones in her left ankle gave an audible pop as they shattered from the impact. Ignoring the pain, the woman desperately scrambled on hands and knees after her lost token, which had bounced into a bush.

Four of the spearcat inhabitants, sensing it was feeding time, started circling the injured Macai. The grinning, drooly expressions on their cat faces signaled intentions that were less than friendly.

The other visitors gasped with horror at what was about to happen, but Group Six reacted as one. Serena and Orchid both vaulted the railing. Serena landed between the woman and the cats in a somersault move, coming to her feet in a rolling motion, sword out and ready to defend against attack. Orchid began a spell in mid-plummet. Before she reached the ground, a small whirlwind enveloped her and suspended her just above the stricken woman. Foxx began a spell of his own. He reached out to the woman below and *suggested* that she cease her ridiculous search for her lost medallion and worry instead about saving her life.

Several things all happened at once. Two of the spearcats launched themselves at their intended victim. One of the predators caught the razor-sharp blade of Serena's scimitar right between its open, slavering jaws. The beast's thick skull was nearly cut in two, but the sword lodged in the bone, wrenching it from Serena's grip. She immediately shifted her stance, whipped out her secondary weapon, a thin stiletto, and stood ready for another cat attack.

The woman was still trying to stretch her arm into the bush to retrieve her lost token. Her skin was being terribly scratched by the thorny stems, but she paid no more attention to that than to the dangerous animals. The other cat would have landed directly on top of her, but for a furious wind that enveloped it and flung the animal backwards. Orchid had directed a portion of her tornado spell down onto the savage beast. It landed several reaches away and shook itself, but was uninjured. It and the other two cats regrouped and began a coordinated stalking of their intended victims, fanning out to surround Serena and the woman.

Foxx, watching from above, concentrated for all he was worth. His recent revelation about the nature of the Magic at work in this place gave him an advantage. He now understood, at least partially, at what *frequency* this form of Influential Magic operated. It was similar to his own, but reached more deeply into the mind of the victim. His Knowing Spell reached out to her, appealing to her common sense. Foxx detected some feedback in the spell, as though she were fighting back. He fine-tuned the Magic, trying to get under the more powerful spell. He realized that her sense of self-preservation was his ally and he pinpointed his efforts on that aspect of her mind. Finally, it worked. The woman looked confused for a moment, looking first at the edge of her now gray medallion which was peeking out from under the thorn bush just beyond her reach. She then looked around her and realized the danger creeping up on her in the form of three vicious spearcats. The woman yelped and hobbled for an access door that was used by the zoo employees for maintenance. Fortunately, those wardens had also reacted quickly when she fell in. They were even now releasing the bar that kept the door locked. The terrified Macai stumbled for the door and flung herself through it, knocking down one of the zoo wardens.

With the loss of their intended prey, the remaining three spearcats concentrated their attentions on the lone Northlands warrior that stood before them. The stiletto in her hand seemed pitifully inadequate against the combined fangs and claws of the beasts. Still, she met their hungry gaze with a steely eye, ready to do battle. A wind tousled her blonde hair as Orchid dissipated her whirlwind and gently deposited herself on the ground next to Serena.

"Get out of here, you meathead!"

"Quiet! I need to concentrate . . ."

Orchid called upon her Worldly talents and reached out to the minds of the spearcats. Unlike Foxx's Knowing Spell, which was a variety of Absolute Magic and invasive, Worldly Magic was passive and took the path of least resistance. As a Macai, Orchid lacked the innate connection with other higher animals that the Eryndi all possessed naturally. In fact, because of this, most Macai Magicians didn't practice Worldly Magic. Orchid was an exception, having been raised by Eryndi. Influencing animals had always been difficult for her. She was much better with plants. She had managed the feat only once before in her life, when she had been driven by desperation. That one time had taught her a few things, though. The notion of saving her friend Serena was the motivating factor. It had worked that other time, back when Group Six was fighting the water spirit. It had to work now. Beads of sweat appeared on Orchid's brow as she concentrated.

All three spearcats were very close now. They were crouched with butts in the air, gathering their clawed feet beneath them. Serena tried to read their intentions, gauging which one would pounce first and planning her defense. Suddenly, one by one, the cats shook their heads, as though to rid their tufted ears of a troublesome insect. They paused and relaxed their muscles. A beat later, all three turned and trotted to the opposite end of their enclosure and entered the small opening to their artificially-created den.

Serena almost looked disappointed. She glanced over at Orchid, who was making some kind of ritualistic gesture. The warrior shook her head as usual at this mumbo jumbo and went to retrieve her sword. She placed one foot on the face of the dead spearcat and pried her beloved scimitar loose from the cloven skull.

Orchid completed her ceremony, turned her attention to the thorn bush, and made a quick request. The bush animated one of its larger branches and reached into itself. A beat later, it *handed* the lost medallion to Orchid and then went back to being a normal bush.

"Are you two going to stay in there all day? Thinking of becoming the latest exhibits?"

Foxx's dry question came from above. He was leaning casually on the railing, looking down on them as though nothing extraordinary had just happened. Orchid and Serena fist-bumped each other and exited the enclosure to the growing applause and cheers of the onlookers. As soon as they were back on the walkway, all three were surrounded by people, clapping them on their backs and congratulating them.

"There's the woman who fell," said Orchid, pointing. "Let's make sure she's all right."

"And then kick the crap out of her," added Serena.

They made their way to the lady, who was seated on a bench and having her purple, swollen ankle tended by a healer in the crowd. She was holding her young child with one arm, and she embraced the members of Group Six in gratitude with the other. When Orchid handed her back her citizen's certification token, it immediately returned to its red color. Her eyes flickered strangely as she gazed at it in her hand.

Foxx felt his Knowing Spell, which had been successful, suddenly lose its influence on her. He sensed the ever-present, more powerful spell once again take hold of the woman and push his own spell away. She was clutching the medallion to her breast as though it were a priceless family heirloom. This taught him more about what he was facing and confirmed something he had suspected earlier. He would have to think on it, but first he turned to the others.

"Well done, you two. Orchid, especially you. That was impressive, getting rid of those nasty critters. What did you say to them?"

"I just told them to go home."

"You didn't do so bad yourself," added Serena. "If you hadn't talked that dumb-shit into running, we couldn't have protected her in time."

Orchid was beginning to feel her old discomfort with crowds as the people continued to cheer and congratulate the trio.

"Come on, let's get out of here."

Foxx was a little reluctant, with his love of love of applause and adoring audiences. He had picked that up during his time with Professor Generax's Traveling World of Wonders. But right now, he had more important things to consider. They started to head for the zoo's exit. Since they were apparently leaving, the following crowd dispersed quickly. But before they could get out the zoo's gate, they were met by an oncoming crowd that was accompanying some other popular figure. A flash of red appeared amongst the throng. A tall, bearded man, dressed in robes just as scarlet as Foxx's silk suit, approached and stood before them. He opened his arms wide and addressed Group Six.

"Greetings, my fellow citizens! I have just learned of your marvelous deeds. Allow me to praise and congratulate you! I am Rastaban, Grand Vizier to Her Majesty, Queen Minore. I invite you to be the Queen's guests in Zanteryne Castle, where you shall receive just rewards for your heroic actions!"

Not quite 50,000 years ago

Karrol rested little and ate sparingly on his quest. He adopted a slow trot that was designed to cover great distances, but not to overtax himself. He tried to run in as straight a line as he could, but ultimately had to follow the twists and turns of this immense river valley. Many times he was endangered by predators. Twice, prides of spearcats chased him up trees and once a horrid clee-at leapt out of its den and nearly grabbed him with its spiny fingers. All of these encounters were irksome delays, but Karrol doggedly carried on. Finally, after several days he passed through groves of fruit trees and fields of vegetables and soon arrived at the large group of dwellings where Chief Jalex lived. The sweating young Ern was immediately escorted to her lodge. He was met by Tarl, Jalex's only son, who was now an elder leader among the clans. Karrol gave Tarl a brief description of events and his mission.

"Rest here, grower," Tarl said. "Bring water and food for this Ern. I will speak to the Chief."

Karrol sank gratefully before the hearth. A young boy

brought him some refreshments. He had barely taken a sip of water and nibbled a bite of rockfruit when Tarl returned.

"You may enter, grower."

Karrol was ushered through a hanging curtain of soft hide and into Jalex's chamber. The Chief sat upon her bed of furs with two great-grandchildren on her lap. They were listening wide-eyed and open-mouthed as she told them stories of adventure in the old days. She looked up at Karrol with eyes surrounded by wrinkles, but still bright and full of life.

"My Chief," said Tarl, "this grower would have words."

"Dran, Melli," she said to the two children, "you must sleep now. Go to your mother and tell her to give each of you a sweet fruit before bed. Tell her it is a command from her Chief. Go now."

The two youngsters squealed with delight and scrambled out of the lodge. Jalex looked up at her visitor.

"What is your name, grower?"

"Chief Jalex, I am Karrol of the Clan of Tarben."

"You have come a long way. What has brought you here?"

"My Chief, my brother and I were preparing to plant a new crop of coryal. As we worked the field, we found a strange woman from outside the valley. She was injured, so we brought her to our lodge. My brother's mate and her mother tried to treat her, but the woman, who called herself Kray, did not get any stronger. Her skin was hot and she could not hold food or water."

"What were her injuries?" asked Jalex.

"She seemed to be bruised and scratched only, no broken bones or deep cuts, but still she suffered from strange waking dreams. During those times when she was able to speak, she told of her clan being hunted by people she called *demons*. Her clan, she said, lived far to the north, next to a great body of water. Their stories of hardship after Senfall sounded much like our own. Many families journeyed far to try and find new hunting lands. Her own clan had been following a herd of *berga* south for several seasons. Then one day they encountered a band of strange hunters. They were large and ugly, she said, with broad, square faces and tiny, brutish ears. The woman described these demons as looking like giant, hairless *trimians*. They wore strange wraps made of water and carried weapons of ice. They moved as people, she said, but are animals because they do not speak as Ern. They made sounds to each other, but no words were said."

Karrol paused, as if debating whether to continue.

"Was that all she said?"

"There was one thing more, My Chief. Once during the night, the woman woke screaming in terror. She warned that these demons traveled with strange creatures who did their bidding. Some would attack upon command. She described them as winged snakes with vicious claws and fangs that would perch upon the shoulders of these giant brutes and whisper in their ears. There were also large animals that carried the demons upon their backs and could run with the fleetness of birds."

Jalex's facial expression mirrored what Karrol had felt when he heard these tales the night before he started on this journey.

"I know, My Chief, these things cannot be true. They must be dreams of fear such as when one's sleep is being stalked by night hunters."

"Perhaps . . . Karrol, can you tell me what methods your wise women used to treat the woman Kray?"

"My brother's mate and her mother are not wise women,

My Chief. No Ern in our small clan knows the healing arts. All they knew to do was to clean the woman's skin and give her food and water."

Jalex reached for her staff and pulled herself to her feet with a small grunt.

"The story that the woman Kray has told you is probably a false trail. But whatever the truth, she needs the help of a wise woman."

Jalex went to a rack on the far wall. From it hung a variety of small pouches and gourds. She made several selections and placed them in her well-worn travel pack.

"You and I shall travel back to your lodge, Karrol. I would see this woman for myself."

Karrol hesitated, as if he were afraid to answer his Chief. Her eyes twinkled with amusement.

"Unless you are too fatigued to make the journey."

"No, My Chief. I was concerned for you . . . that is . . . for your *safety.*"

"You are actually concerned I am too old and feeble to walk such a long way."

"*No!* My Chief, I . . . it is not . . . *yes* . . . I am concerned."

"And you are correct, hunter. My legs can barely take me to the river. Fortunately, that is as far as I need go."

CHAPTER 17

Today - Abakaar

Rastaban's private launch was the height of comfort. It featured an enclosed cabin lined with open windows. An upright mesh of plant fiber sat in front of each one and was kept filled with bits of ice. The hot breeze filtered through them and kept the cabin delightfully cooled. Five smartly-uniformed crewmembers efficiently operated the vessel and acted as stewards. Group Six found their glasses kept ever full of the beverage of their choice, much to the delight of Orchid. The boat's sophisticated Magical impetus box differed from those of other river craft they had seen. It did not power a screw or paddlewheel, but simply propelled the whole vessel swiftly through the water, creating a very smooth and quiet ride. Its speed outpaced every other boat on the water. The other river traffic always pulled over and respectfully allowed the Vizier's distinctive red launch to pass.

"You are recent immigrants to our country, are you not?" Rastaban scrutinized every detail of the three members of Group Six. Serena privately likened it to an expert in horseflesh checking over a potential mare purchase.

"Yes, that's right," replied Orchid. "We arrived here from the Crystal Palace."

"I am pleased to see you are adapting well to our culture." Rastaban noted the two women's now all-red citizen's tokens. His gaze lingered for a beat on Foxx, whose medallion was still blue with a red X. "Tell me about yourselves and how you came to be here. The Queen will be fascinated."

"Go ahead," Orchid said to Foxx. "You're the storyteller."

Never one to pass up an audience, Foxx related Group Six's adventures in the months since they had met. He described in histrionic detail how the mysterious Leader had gathered them together, ostensibly to escort him safely up the danger-filled Talus River to consult with a legendary powerful Magician far inland. That had been a lie, of course. Leader's real motive had been to bring Serena to his master, the water spirit that inhabited the ancient drowned city of Mennatu. It wanted the fabulous diamond imbedded in the Northlands warrior's chest that housed another spirit, one that thrived upon love. Foxx's overly-dramatic descriptions of fighting giant river crocs and malignant pygmies brought grunts of derision from Serena. His details were enhanced quite a bit, but essentially the truth. He wasn't sure why, but Foxx chose to omit the detail about finding Dementus the Mad Treskan's journal.

Rastaban was especially interested to hear the story of how they finally came to discover the Crystal Palace and meet its steward, Jakki. The story of Tresado accidentally getting them teleported into the deadly crater zone actually caused the Vizier to chuckle in amusement.

"It would seem you enjoyed your time in the Crystal Palace."

"Yes, Vizier," replied Foxx. "Let us say that *it was my kind of joint.*"

"And it solved my problem by getting rid of my unwanted passenger," added Serena, tapping her diamond.

"Quite a pleasant, Magical place," said Orchid.

Rastaban paused for a beat while he took a sip of Abakaarian Fire Nectar.

"Yet I believe you will find a very good life here among us."

"We've certainly gotten a good taste of Abakaarian hospitality," said Orchid, motioning the steward for yet another refill.

Rastaban smiled enigmatically. "We wish our citizens to be happy here. Now, you've told me of your adventures as . . . what did you call yourselves, *Group Six?*"

"Leader came up with that moniker," said Serena, who was popping water peas into her mouth one by one. "We never did know why."

"Perhaps someday you will find out. Now I would like to know about each of you before you joined together in this . . . interesting band. Tell me about your early lives."

"Ladies first," said Foxx after a pause.

"Which one of us is more of a lady?" asked Orchid.

"You are," responded both women at once.

Serena shrugged. During the years when she was inhabited by the love spirit, she had gotten grudgingly used to talking about herself. Her admirers expected it. She had learned to tolerate it, if not like it.

"I was a Northlands warrior. I *am* a Northlands warrior. Like others of my kind, I took the four Trials of Snow and Ice at age thirteen to become apprentice shield maiden. After two years of tutoring with my mentor, Katrina the Defiant, I was granted the status of full warrior. I defended my homeland many times from barbarian attack and embarked on many raids, mostly upon foreign ships in our waters . . . or *close* to our waters, anyway," she said with a wink to Orchid.

"You are proud of your profession . . . most admirable. I hope you can be of equally valiant service to your new home here," said Rastaban. His black eyes bored into Serena's lapis-colored ones. A calm expression came over her face.

"That is my hope as well, Vizier," she said slowly.

Rastaban flashed a satisfied smile and turned to Orchid. "And you, my dear . . . I believe you were raised amongst the Eryndi and practice Worldly Magic. Tell me, how did that come about?"

"I never knew my Macai birth parents, Vizier. I was told they were fungifarmers in the Withiman Forest, which was mostly inhabited by Eryndi. I was still a baby, so I don't remember, but apparently one day they just disappeared. I was found in their cabin all alone."

"Were they abducted by the Eryndi?" asked Rastaban.

"No, Vizier. No one knows what became of them."

"I see. That would seem to be impossible. They disappeared in an inhabited area . . . inhabited by *Eryndi*, did you not say? It seems plausible that someone there had to have been responsible. *Would you not agree, Orchid?*"

The tall man in scarlet robes held Orchid's gaze for several beats.

"Yes . . . I suppose anything's possible, Vizier," Orchid said slowly.

"Tell me," he quickly interjected, "was it difficult for you to grow up amongst people so different from you?"

"I never knew any different, Vizier. After I was discovered by a forest warden, Mishanna, who was a judge, and her bondmate Revinal, a healer, were granted custody of me. They became my guardians and raised me along with their own children."

"Ah, both powerful and influential members of Eryndi society. You must be proud."

"Later I was tutored in the use of Magic."

"By the Eryndi?"

"Yes, Vizier."

"Well, judging by your splendid performance rescuing the woman at the zoo, I would say your skills are equal if not superior to any Eryndi."

"I had a marvelous tutor, Vizier. His . . . He was . . ." Orchid looked down at the last of the ale in her mug and downed it quickly. She turned to the steward.

"Do you have anything stronger than this?"

* * *

I needed to insert a double-walled etheremite drainage tube obliquely into a left-threaded Rizzonian compustator without collapsing the containment mesh, so I just created a tool to do it. The next thing I knew, I was a zillionaire . . .

- Interview with Filo J. Wainwright, inventor of the Filotron©, Popular Astronautics, Issue #435

Not quite 50,000 years ago

Jalex moved down the trail from her lodge to the river. She leaned on her stick the whole way, but refused Karrol's offers to assist. Several Ern were working on some kind of construction. Tak, eldest child of Tarl, was in charge.

"How does your work go, Granddaughter?"

"My Chief! This logfloater is finished. We are now building a frame in the water so that the stores may be loaded easier without fear of wetting them."

"You hear this Ern, Karrol?" Jalex said with a smile. "She would believe that her chief is nothing but a skin full of seed grain. But I do appreciate not being made wet."

"Grandmother?" said Tak in a confused voice.

"Today you are not transporting supplies to the other clans. You are taking me and this hunter far to the north to the Clan of Tarben."

"My Chief! You would be carried by the logfloater? It is only for moving heavy loads to the new growing lands!"

"Then it should be able to move your chief to the Clan of Tarben. I am not that heavy."

"But My Chief, we tie the skins of seeds tightly to the logs to prevent them falling into the river! The pots of dung are covered with hides to keep them dry and also lashed down!"

"Are you saying you would tie your chief to the logs like a pot of dung?"

"No, Grandmother!"

"Do you tie yourself down while guiding the floater down the river?"

"No, My Chief. But there are places where the water moves swiftly. There are sharp turns and large rocks. I and the others who guide the floaters must keep our balance and hold on tight."

"Then I shall hold on tight, also. This is Karrol. He shall assist you on the journey and if needed, he shall help me. How soon can you start?"

"The stores lie there. We were just finishing up the ramp before loading them."

"Very well. Finish your loading and be ready to begin the journey quickly."

Jalex said no more, which everybody knew meant the conversation was over. The cargo in this case was several skins of eyepod seeds and two hands of rockfruit saplings with their roots bound in marsh grass. When everything was secured, Jalex carefully climbed onto the contrivance and settled herself between two sacks of seeds. The logfloater was essentially just several straight poles of lodgewood tied together. Two short cross poles kept the raft from tipping over (most of the time). The idea was when the supplies reached their destination, the floater was dismantled and the poles used in whatever construction was needed on site. Bringing the rafts back upstream was just not feasible.

One final attempt by Tak to warn her grandmother about the hazards of such a trip went unheeded. Chief Jalex merely smiled and urged her to get moving. The floater was untied from the ramp and pushed into the slow-moving river current. Tak and her assistant, Auran, guided the raft with long poles.

Karrol was a brave and strong Ern, but was unnerved by the bizarre idea of being out of control on this floating thing at the mercy of the waters. Despite the fact that the floater was moving very gently at this point, he held on with a white-knuckled death grip. Tak glanced nervously at Jalex and then motioned Karrol to her.

"What do you wish me to do?" he asked. He looked almost panicky when he saw the pole in Tak's hand.

"Auran and I shall guide the logfloater. I charge you with protecting Chief Jalex. You are not to leave her side. Her safety is more important than all else. Do you understand?"

"I shall guard the Chief with my life," said Karrol proudly. Guiding the floater was beyond his abilities, but this was something he could relate to.

The first few days of the journey were relatively easy. The river was gentle and passed through areas where many clans of Ern made their homes. Each evening, Tak would guide the floater to one or the other bank to spend the night. The first three nights Jalex was able to sleep in lodges graciously vacated by Ern who were more than happy to give up their bed to their beloved Chief.

The nature of the land then changed. They were passing through large tracts of bubbling pools that emptied their hot, pungent waters into the river, creating clouds of steam. The land was not good for growing plants, so no Ern lodges were nearby. There were, however, many animals that congregated around these pools to drink of the healthful, mineral-rich water. That made for prime hunting grounds for the larger predators in the area. Karrol, Tak, and Auran took turns during the night keeping a close watch over their sleeping chief. Jalex had at first volunteered to take a shift, having been a hunter herself in her youth. The others would not hear of such a thing though, and insisted that she sleep through the night.

Chief Jalex grudgingly agreed, although she seldom slept all night. She was just enjoying herself too much. In her youth she had several times traveled the whole length of this winding river valley that they had called home for so many seasons. It had been a long time since she had ventured out this far, though. Her responsibilities as leader and her own failing body had kept her close to home these last seasons. Jalex lay in her furs, her ear cones quivering at the various calls and growls that made up the night sounds. She stared up at the stars and happened to catch a glimpse of one of them that suddenly decided to streak across the night sky like a spearcat chasing prey. It brought her thoughts back to that terrible day so long ago when the great fiery ball roared across the sky over her head. She had nearly died from the resulting storms that swept across the land. Were it not for the sheltering cliffs of Sentinel Hill where her clan's original lodges were, she would have. That entire area had been rendered nearly lifeless after Senfall. Jalex often wondered if it would ever return to the lush grasslands it had been. A small group of travelers that had recently arrived in the valley from the southwest reported seeing strange and completely unfamiliar creatures in that area: bizarre multi-legged things described as looking like little walking hands with biting mouths on the tips of the 'fingers.' Jalex shuddered and shook off such disturbing thoughts.

The next day's travel brought the logfloater to its original intended destination. Beyond the hot pools was a settlement of Ern clans who were farming in the rich soil where another river joined the main channel. They happily welcomed the cargo of seeds and saplings and the unexpected visit from Chief Jalex. They wanted to prepare a feast, but when she explained her urgent mission to the north end of the valley, they saw to it that the stores were quickly unloaded and the floater immediately sent further downriver. They did provide a few comfortable furs and other small gifts of food for the remainder of Jalex's journey.

The next few days on the river made Tak a nervous wreck. They passed herds of great lum and milkbeasts grazing on the banks, as well as the fearsome predators that hunted them and watched the occupants of the raft with hungry eyes. The waters of the river grew narrower and therefore swifter. She and Auran had difficulty controlling the logfloater in places and she ever feared for her grandmother's safety. Karrol was right beside Jalex the whole time, keeping a tight grip upon his chief. He was ready to give his life if necessary to save hers. Several times he was sure that was going to happen as the raft bounced off the occasional jagged boulder that protruded from the swiftly moving water. Tak pleaded with Jalex to abandon this mission. Every day brought the aging matriarch further from her lodges that she would have to eventually walk back to. Jalex was unyielding though, and said she would deal with whatever life threw at her. After all, what else would one do?

Finally, after two hands of days upon the river, the logfloater, which was now beginning to fall apart, arrived at the lodges of the Clan of Tarben. An eerie quiet greeted them. No one could be seen working the newly plowed fields. There was no smoke coming from any of the lodges. Tak guided the raft up to the sandy bank and it slid to a slow stop. Jalex was helped ashore by Karrol.

They proceeded up the bank to the lodges. Jalex checked the ground the whole way, her hunter's instincts of old kicking in. There were no signs of recent activity, whether animal or Ern. A bit of hide hanging from a drying rack flapped in the breeze, the only sound coming from the small village.

"DROOK! SHEMIN!"

There was no answer. Karrol continued to call out, but there was no answer from his brother or anybody else in the village. He immediately ran to the lodge where they lived and entered. A few beats later, Karrol slowly emerged, his face white with horror.

"Dead . . . they are all dead!"

Today - Abakaar

At the swift speed that Rastaban's launch could travel upriver, it only took a day and a half to reach Zanteryne Castle. They stopped the first night near an establishment known as the Ecstasy House. It was a high-class venue with gourmet food, luxury rooms, and even a floor show featuring dancers and Magical lightshows.

Seventy-five percent of Group Six ate and drank well that night. Tresado, on the other hand, had just been ferried back to the Bythian Quarter where he was issued a ration of grain porridge and suet. It was bland food, but plenty of it. He was generously allowed to drink all the river water he wanted. It was a satisfying life for him, but there was always a nagging thought in the back of his mind . . . something that Foxx had said a few days ago. He was reminded of it when he saw that fancy launch speeding up river. If only he could remember.

Several times during the trip, Rastaban attempted to persuade Foxx to speak of his past the way Serena and Orchid had done. He was jovial and polite, but Foxx the master wordsmith always managed to subtly change the subject. He spoke much but said little. Orchid and Serena had seen this before when they were in the Crystal Palace. They knew that much of Foxx's past could be considered *extralegal*. It was probably just his usual way of not incriminating himself to anyone. He did mention once that he and the Eryndi Tresado had long been friends. That was when Rastaban changed the subject.

"Ah, we have arrived."

Coming into view ahead was the looming bulk of Zanteryne Castle. Group Six had seen it once before as they passed it on board *Floozy's Folly*. Rastaban began reciting the history of this ancient structure.

"The first foundations were laid over nine hundred years ago. Over the centuries, additions were made and expanded upon. The secondary tier was completed during the Third Dynasty by King Harius I, who was a direct ancestor of Queen Minore. The most recent addition is the East Tower, from where Her Majesty can overlook the Serpent River, the lifeblood of our country."

Orchid wrinkled her brow and looked slightly confused. Foxx quickly moved to her side and spoke quietly to her.

"Something doesn't quite ring true, does it?"

"I read about Harius when we were in the library . . . he . . ."

Orchid struggled, as though she had to fight to say what was in her mind. Foxx finished her thought for her.

"He was an Eryndi, wasn't he?"

"Yes, but . . . I don't understand. Minore is a Macai, isn't she?"

"Do me a favor," whispered Foxx. "Keep that in your mind, but don't mention it aloud."

"Okay."

Once again, Foxx felt resistance to his Knowing Spell. He knew that Orchid was aware of the actual history that ancient Abakaar was built by Eryndi. The ascendency of the Macai and subjugation of the Eryndi were relatively recent events. He was coming to realize that all the Macai citizens of this place were aware of the same thing, but were being coerced into simply not caring and pushing the truth from their minds.

Rastaban's launch pulled off into a side channel that led directly to a large portal in the castle. The heavy door rumbled up, allowed them access, then immediately closed behind them. Group Six found themselves in a huge indoor lake. Docks where a variety of vessels were moored lined every side. There were cargo barges, personnel carriers, and even small dinghies. Many of these were military craft bristling with weapons. Clearly the most impressive craft was Queen Minore's Royal Barge. It was a massive, single-hulled vessel decorated with colorful streamers and lined with gold railings. It had a relatively narrow beam, due to the restrictions of travel on the river, but made up for it in length. From bow to stern, the barge, named *Serpent Arrow,* measured sixty-one reaches in length. The hull was broken into three identical sections and connected with massive hinges to negotiate tight turns, much like a snake. Otherwise, the winding Serpent River would have to be artificially widened to accommodate the lengthy craft.

Steering that must be a bitch, thought everyone.

The launch pulled into its assigned berth and several dock hands secured the moorings. A carpeted ramp was lowered and Rastaban descended to the pier followed by his three guests. An escort of guards met them at the main castle entrance and accompanied them through a maze of passageways. Another man appeared at Rastaban's elbow as they entered the castle. Apparently he was an aide of some kind. He carried a thick sheaf of papers on a clipboard and quietly discussed them with Rastaban as they walked. The vizier either attended to or ignored each one at his discretion. Group Six couldn't hear what was said as they followed behind, but several times the assistant glanced back at them.

After a hike up through the levels of the castle, Rastaban finally led his entourage into a long hallway. He nodded to the guards at the end who snapped to and opened a set of double doors for him. An enormous receiving hall lay beyond, filled with many guests. There were decorated army officers and guild leaders, cabinet members and citizen officials. Musicians and dancers entertained the crowd, while colorful, levitating banners and Magically-lit spinning chandeliers created dazzling effects. Long tables filled with exotic food and beverages were kept well supplied by an army of servants. Rastaban was greeted with many bows and respectful salutes as he moved through the room.

"Are all these people being honored by the Queen, too?" asked Serena, gazing around. The royal receiving halls she was used to usually had a big vat of beer to dip from surrounded by belching warriors who got into fistfights a lot.

"This is a normal day at court," replied Rastaban. "Ah, looks like we are right on time."

Just then the barrel-chested Royal Herald entered from a vestibule followed by trumpeters. He mounted his podium and gave a signal to the guards, who proceeded to open the large doors to the Queen's chambers. The notes blared out, drawing everyone's attention. The man's stentorian voice boomed out to today's guests of Zanteryne Castle.

"Announcing Her Royal Majesty, Defender of the True Way, Holder of the Orb of the Valley, Daughter of Sensang, and Unquestioned Sovereign, Queen Minore!"

Once more, the trumpets sounded and the Queen made her grand appearance. What the court did not see was that, a fraction of a beat before entering, Minore's stern visage that she used on her retinue of servants morphed into a radiant smile. Her opal-colored eyes twinkled in a bright, almost mischievous way as she pleasantly greeted the room with a nod. Heads bowed. Ladies curtsied. Soldiers saluted. Fops checked their coiffures. Queen Minore swept into the room like a regal zephyr, her long shimmering braids swirling behind her like an escort of black serpents.

"Thank you for that introduction, Harold. Once again, you flatter me with your magnificent prose."

"I live but to serve, My Gracious Queen," responded Harold the Herald with a deep bow.

Minore gave him an affectionate pat on the cheek and moved into the room, greeting select guests personally and exchanging pleasant banter with them. Eventually that chore was complete and she sat at her place. The Court followed her example and dinner was brought in by an army of servants. It took the form of great racks of meat and trays of fruits and vegetables. Casks of ale and the finest wines were on every table for all to choose from. Minore picked delicately at her meal, as befitted her regal self.

At an adjacent table to the Queen sat an official from the City-State of Linn and her retainers. Minore greeted her warmly.

"I do hope you are enjoying your stay in our country, Ambassador Kurrean."

"Thank you, Your Majesty. This magnificent meal is a welcome treat . . . very much appreciated after so many days of travel."

"I'm sure our humble fare in no way compares to that of your homeland of Linn."

"You honor me, Your Majesty."

"And you honor us with your trade proposals. I look forward to hearing the details."

"I am anxious to discuss them with your Vizier, Your Majesty. Might I inquire if he will be joining us this evening?"

"I am sure Grand Vizier Rastaban is anxious to speak with you, Ambassador. In fact, here he comes now."

Rastaban, with Group Six in tow, approached the Queen with both hands over his heart, as was his style. His two ruby-studded gold bracelets glittered in the Magical light around him.

"My Gracious Queen, it is with great joy that I am able to join your court this night."

"My Lord Vizier. Your presence is comforting as always." Minore's opal eyes regarded Rastaban's black ones. Neither gaze wavered.

"You know, of course, Ambassador Kurrean of Linn?"

"Indeed," replied Rastaban, bowing formally. "Welcome to Abakaar, My Lady."

"Thank you, Vizier. I look forward to our negotiations."

"As do I. My aide shall make the arrangements."

With that, Rastaban turned his full attention back to his Queen, where it belonged, leaving Kurrean to awkwardly withdraw.

"You bring visitors, it seems," said Minore.

"I bring heroes, My Queen. These three citizens performed an incredible act of bravery in rescuing a fellow Abakaarian from a most unfortunate circumstance and I would hope to honor them here tonight."

Minore nodded. Rastaban handed Harold a slip of paper and then gestured to Group Six to come forward and be recognized by the Queen and court.

Harold glanced at the paper, then his deep voice rang out. "Attention, attention. All pay heed. Introducing to the court and Her Majesty these brave souls that would have your praise and thanks . . . Orchid, Healer and Magician, Serena

Brimstone, warrior and protector, and . . ." He squinted at the paper, *"Lu-see* Foxx, Entertainer and Ambassador."

The court responded with applause, even though no one knew why they were applauding. It was just the thing to do.

"Your Majesty, if you will allow me . . ." said Rastaban. At a nod from the queen, he turned to the waiting crowd.

"Citizens of Abakaar," he intoned. *"This* is a tale of skill and courage . . ."

Rastaban proceeded to narrate to the court the events at the zoo. The story was full of hyperbole and greatly exaggerated details. There were twenty spearcats instead of four and the distance jumped into the pit was equally increased. As he told the tale, his huge black pupils tracked the crowd and fixed on every member. The court drank it all in like fine wine. They listened in rapt attention and finally erupted in cheering when his story came to the exciting conclusion.

"A fine tale, worthy of remembrance," said Queen Minore. "Come, sit here at my table."

At Rastaban's quick glance, three of Minore's closest staff immediately vacated their seats at the Royal Table. Serena was about to take the seat to the Queen's right, but Minore held up a hand.

"Why don't you sit here?"

The command was issued to Foxx, whom Minore had scarcely taken her opal eyes off of.

"I am honored, Your Majesty," he said in his most charming voice. It was not a difficult duty. The Queen's brown skin, ebony hair, and milky eyes were very easy to look upon. Foxx had made it his business over the years to take in as much feminine beauty as was Macaily possible. He had certainly known his share of it and more, but the Queen of Abakaar was one of the most stunning women he had ever seen. She even rivaled Tildy the fan dancer and that was saying a lot. As he sat next to her, many men of the court elbowed and winked at each other. Evidently this was not the first man to catch the eye of their queen.

Minore glanced at Foxx's citizen's token, which was still blue with a red X.

"You must be a recent arrival in Abakaar. Are you not enjoying your time here?"

"My Queen, I have never enjoyed myself more than at this moment."

Minore's unbelievably attractive eyelashes dipped once. "Indeed, perhaps we can change that."

Foxx's Knowing Spell had kicked in almost automatically. That usually happened whenever he was hitting on or even just around attractive women. It was something he used to gauge the mood and desires of a potential conquest. Wooing women was like a game of Blitzkrieg. Reading one's opponent was just as important as the strength of the cards. The spell could also be used to manipulate the other player or the woman, of course. In Foxx's case, that was seldom necessary. Nor was it now.

"Conduct Master Foxx to my private chambers where he shall await my further pleasure."

Two splendidly uniformed guards appeared behind Foxx seemingly out of nowhere and gripped him by both arms. They were fully prepared to grip firmly, but it wasn't necessary. With a naturally charming smile, he went as a willing prisoner.

Minore then stood and the attentive court immediately followed suit. "My subjects, I shall retire now, but I bid you all a very pleasant evening and beg you to accept the hospitality of my hall."

The Queen's servants hastened to gather about and form up for escort. Minore turned magnificently, her silken garments swirling about her taut form as she strode sensuously through the same hallway where the guards had escorted Foxx.

Serena and Orchid performed a synchronized eye roll and shoulder shrug and turned their attentions to the cute members of the court who had been eyeing both of them. Several interested men were hovering about, one of them literally. A young Magician named Finnis levitated himself around the other potential suiters and floated above the table. Orchid liked his pretty eyelashes.

"You know, I might ask you to join me in a mug if you would just come down to Lurra and have a seat."

The man needed no second invitation and floated gracefully onto the seat next to Orchid. As he did so, her ever-present oaken staff cooed and glowed with soft pastels.

There was also a devilishly handsome army captain who seemed particularly interested in Serena. The multiple decorations for valor on his breastplate jingled and sparkled in hypnotizing patterns as he approached. He stood directly over Serena's shoulder and cast an appreciative glance from above at her glorious diamond and impressive display of cleavage, then met her lapis eyes as she looked up. Flashing a perfect smile that rendered her totally disarmed, he held out a small dish full of colored candies.

"Something sweet?"

CHAPTER 18

Not quite 50,000 years ago

Karrol's brother Drook and his mate Shemin lay in each other's embrace upon a woven mat in their lodge. From the foul odor and cloud of hideous flies, it was clear they had died at least a hand of days ago. Jalex examined the bodies while holding a bit of fur over her mouth and nose. The most notable signs were the rings of dried blood around the mouths and large, red lumps on the necks.

There was no sign of Shemin's mother, Arma, or of the strange woman they had been tending to. Jalex, Karrol, Tak, and Auran moved somberly through the small collection of lodges that had formerly housed the clan of Tarben. They found no one alive.

Jalex left the bodies and examined the ground with a practiced hunter's eye. "The freshest spoor I can find heads this way, toward the south rim. What lies in that direction?"

Karrol bowed his head and tears streamed from his eyes. "That is the Cave of the Dead. We found it not long after our clan settled this end of the valley. Tarben, our clan leader, chose to honor the cave with our dead. There they can feast well for all time."

"Feast?" asked Jalex.

"The Clan of Tarben have always put their dead under the ground with as much food as they can carry. In times past, often there was not enough and they were in danger of starving."

The Chief nodded in understanding. All the clans of the Tribe of Jalex had their own customs for preparing the departed. Back when she lived in the shadow of Sentinel Hill, her people placed family icons and token bits of food in their graves to take on the Trail. Now with so many clans living together, no custom was considered right or wrong, but all were respected.

"The Cave of the Dead is near the bottom of a steep slope. It is a deep hole in the ground. Many animals of all kinds lose their footing on the loose rocks and fall within. Even if they survive the fall, the walls are too steep to climb out. Those Ern buried there have meat always. We have only buried two of our own in the Cave since we have been here . . . but there will be more now."

Karrol once again was overcome by grief. He slowly walked to the riverbank and sat upon a flat stone, his head buried in his hands. Jalex's heart ached for the man, having lost many of her own loved ones in her many seasons. She reached into her travel pack and produced a small pouch of powdered herbs. Jalex took a pinch and mixed it with a bit of water in a leaf cone.

"Drink this, Karrol. It will make you brave."

Karrol swallowed the bitter mixture and got to his feet.

"Thank you, My Chief. We have work to do."

Thus began the disagreeable work of bringing the bodies of Drook and Shemin out of the lodge. This job fell to Karrol and Tak. Jalex had not the strength for such lifting, so she and Auran gathered lum leaves to wrap the bodies according to Tarben clan customs. There were several other Ern who had perished in whatever this disaster was, including Tarben himself, who had been a strong and virile man.

Jalex again examined the dead carefully. There were no signs of wounds on the bodies, except for traces of blood around the lips and the swollen red lumps on their necks. So this was some kind of sickness. The closest thing Jalex had ever seen was the lung rot that so many of her people had died from when the skies were full of dust after Senfall. She didn't think that was the case here, though. Many of the dead were bundled in heavy furs as though they were freezing cold. This told her that their blood had become too hot, which did not happen with lung rot. Sometimes young children became hot and nauseous, but these sicknesses usually abated after a few days of treatment with nakra root poultices. Whatever killed these people struck quickly and passed from Ern to Ern. Karrol had said that Kray's skin was warm after they found her. That told Jalex that Kray had brought this illness from outside the valley. Karrol was fortunate not to have been afflicted, possibly due to his leaving to travel upriver.

There was one other curious thing that had Jalex perplexed. The clan's animals were apparently untouched by this sickness. The milk beasts that pulled the plows and the *culots* that were kept for their meat and fur were all healthy. However, in the lodge of Tarben, a dead trimian was found with the bodies of the Ern. Karrol said the funny little tree creature was kept as a pet by the clan leader. It so resembled a hairy little Ern that they had even given it a name. They called it Chichi because of the sounds it made. Chichi, too, had apparently died of this strange illness.

There were three hands of bodies to be prepared. They were all carefully wrapped in the lum leaves along with water skins and pouches of food. Since the Cave of the Dead was a new burial place with new circumstances for the Clan of Tarben, skinning knives and fire rocks were also included with the provisions. Fresh animals were sure to tumble into the hole, so they must be butchered and cooked in the afterlife. Ern were practical people even in death.

There were woven hide ropes near the entrance to the Cave of the Dead. The signs indicated that some departed had already been lowered within. Evidently, the rest of the Clan had become ill too swiftly to bury everyone. No doubt Arma and Kray had been the first to die and the rest of the village soon after. The names of the dead and final farewells were spoken aloud and, one by one, the bodies were turned face down and lowered into the crevasse where they would have food and comforts for all time.

It was a sad party of Ern that finally completed the task of burying the dead. They returned to the village, but since someone had died in all of the few lodges, there was no thought of Jalex and the others sleeping in any of them. A temporary lean-to was constructed for the Chief. Karrol and the others stretched out on furs to sleep in the open air. A bright fire was kept burning to keep any predators away.

The next morning, Jalex closely examined everyone for any sign of the sickness but did not find any. Karrol was concerned about how they would be able to get their infirm Chief back up river to her own lodge so many days march away. Jalex just shook her head.

"It is not for me to return. My purpose is clear. I must find the source of this sickness before it can kill more Ern."

"How shall you do that, My Chief?" asked Karrol.

"The woman Kray spoke of *demons*. We must find them."

* * *

WANTED FOR QUESTIONING
AS SUSPECTED CHAIRMAN OF THE
MARCOLIAN ASSASSINS' GUILD:
MOLNEK
AKA The Uncle, AKA Femmie Face, AKA Fatboy

Known quote - *No matter how overwhelming or dangerous the job seems, you can always see it through with the proper application of technology - and venom . . . lots of venom.*

- CITY OF RENNIK POLICE BLOTTER -
32147 NEW CALENDAR

Today - Abakaar

Foxx awoke in the predawn hours. Usually he was a late sleeper, but this night had been a rough one. He was sore in a couple of sensitive areas due to the intense bout of lovemaking with Minore. Foxx had known many women, but few if any with such a voracious and insatiable appetite. He managed to extricate himself from her grip and slide out of the huge feather bed. Sneaking out of a tryst without waking his partner was one of Foxx's many skills. Silently dressing in the dark with a pocket of loose coins was another.

Foxx picked up his shoes and padded out the door into the outer rooms of Minore's chambers. He knew that beyond the main doors stood a trio of guards. He put his ear to the thick wood and could hear them quietly conversing. He concentrated. His thoughts reached into the ethereal envelope of Magic that was in the air around him to create his Knowing Spell.

The organizational and processing power of Magic is what makes it work. It is simply a matter of natural law. Magic functions for the same reason that water runs downhill; it takes the path of least resistance. It is not a conscious entity, but it has been said that Magic *wants* to be used. A Magician sends out a command (Orchid would say *a request)* into the universe. Magic expends energy to alter and manipulate the environment around it to satisfy the demand, whether it's creating fire or morphing an enemy into a tree sloth. The skill of the Magician is a factor. Not just anyone can use Magic. It takes years of study to learn the mental disciplines necessary. Few people are capable of that. Or more accurately, most people are too stupid and self-absorbed. That is much the reason that Foxx's abilities worked as they did. He could read what others feel or want and use that knowledge for his own purposes.

In this case, Foxx's Knowing Spell reached out and gauged the moods of the guards. They were generally happy in their work, but a bit on the bored side. Drawing guard duty for the Queen's chamber was considered an easy assignment, but being soldiers, they each yearned for a little action to break up the tedium. Foxx could use this. Although his self-taught spell was usually meant just to discern emotions, it could also be used to manipulate them. That was quite a bit harder, but Foxx had learned a few tricks since taking on the role of self-appointed referee within the often-quarrelsome Group Six.

First, he subtly and slowly began to build the idea in their minds that someone was watching them. He was patient, not wanting to alarm them into full readiness. The guards' conversation halted as they slowly felt their hackles rising. Foxx included a suggestion that something was going on in the corridor to their right. When he felt that all three guards' attention was focused in that direction, he planted a non-existent sound of scratching in their minds. That brought their attention up full as all three turned to the right and moved away from the door. At that same moment, Foxx silently opened the door and slipped out to the left behind their backs. He made it to a nearby intersection and ducked around the corner. He flattened himself against the wall and concentrated again, this time implanting a distinct *meow* sound in their minds. From their feelings of relief, he could tell it worked. The guards chuckled and again took up their positions in front of the door.

Foxx smiled to himself and silently proceeded on his exploration. He wanted a closer look at the inner workings of the East Tower of Zanteryne Castle. The place just reeked of the powerful Influential Magic he had been sensing. He was sure that something or someone in the castle was the source. He was also certain that the spell was transmitted to the people of Abakaar via the metallic citizen's certification tokens that everyone wore. His own medallion had now turned a dull grey, despite his still wearing it. Foxx smiled as he realized he had completely thrown off its grip upon him. Apparently, the spell included a possessiveness that inhibited citizens from removing them. That was why the woman recklessly jumped into the spearcat pit when her infant accidentally tore it from her neck. The spell was not infallible, though. Foxx had been able to influence her enough to come to her senses and run from the danger rather than continue to try to retrieve her token. She was only one person, though, and it had taken everything he had to counteract it. Once she had her token back again, the spell seemed unbreakable. The amount of power necessary to continually control thousands and thousands of people in this country was staggering. Foxx couldn't conceive how such a thing could be possible, but he was going to find out.

Foxx passed several locked doors along this corridor. He listened and sensed at each one. Some had occupants and some didn't. They seemed to be living quarters, probably for high-ranking officials. The hallway ended in a large set of double doors, which were far more interesting because of the powerful Magic emanating from behind them. This was Foxx's target. He closely examined every detail of the doors, looking for any kind of alarm trigger. He saw none, but discovered they were locked. From a hidden pocket within his undervest, he produced a leather packet of fine tools. There were tiny files, saws, and hardened steel hooks bent at various angles. This type of lock was unfamiliar to him, but all locks basically function in the same way. A bolt holding the door fast is manipulated by a unique combination of pins and/or gears. It took several beats, but Foxx's nimble fingers and precise tools eventually found the right combination of pressures necessary. The bolt slid back with a satisfying click. Foxx quickly checked the corridor and listened at the door to make sure he had not been discovered. He slowly opened the door into a large, ornate room dimly lit by a series of Magical domes in the walls.

The most prominent feature was at the far end of the room, an immense tapestry which took up the entire wall. The detail was amazing. It depicted thousands of green-armored soldiers marching across a war-ravaged landscape. Foxx had seen them before. The uniform markings and the bear-headed standards they carried marked them as Eryndi troops from the Twelfth

Legion of the Treskan Imperium. There was one other familiar feature. In the lower right corner of the tapestry was a stylized circle next to a jagged crack in the ground. Foxx was certain it depicted the deadly crater area and the river valley of Abakaar. Evidently this tapestry was meant to show that the valley was on the verge of an invasion by Tresk.

There was Magic in this great tapestry. Even Foxx, who was not nearly as skilled or powerful as Tresado or Orchid, could sense it. There was kinetic energy involved and a strong dose of the same Influential spell he had sensed all along. Even now, he felt that power surge. The hackles on his neck rose as he turned. A pair of very familiar eyes glared back at him.

"So it's you . . . you're the source."

Before Foxx could say any more, there was a flash of light. His eyes widened as he felt a sudden pressure on his chest. A feeling of cold crept into his limbs. Foxx dropped to his knees and pitched forward onto his face. A tiny blackened hole in the back of his shirt matched one that had just appeared on the tapestry behind him.

* * *

Scents of Omen Waft Across the Beach
To Warn the Lonely Footprints;
Joined But For a Beat of Eternity
'Til the Second Set Walks Alone . . .

- Trianna of Sylvas, Poetess to the Glades

Not quite 50,000 years ago

Despite Tak's objections, Jalex insisted on leading an expedition out of the valley. Karrol suggested that he run upriver again and find some volunteers at the closest settlement to help them. She would not hear of it, however.

"We must backtrack where Kray came from," she had said. "If there is a spoor to be followed, it is already growing faint. We can waste no time."

Supplies were gathered, including weapons. There may be a need to hunt and to defend themselves from predators . . . or even demons. Jalex, Auran, Karrol, and Tak set out at once.

The climb out of the valley went slowly. They made the ascent at the same point that Kray had been found. It was a relatively gentle slope compared to other spots and much lower than upriver, but Jalex's legs still did not like climbing. Tak helped her grandmother as much as she was allowed to. Jalex leaned heavily on her staff as she struggled up the treacherous canyon wall. Karrol and Auran stayed close behind her, ready to catch their chief in the event she slipped. It was difficult for her, but Jalex was as determined as ever. At last they came to the rim of the great canyon that had been their home for many hands of seasons. This was the first time since Jalex and her deceased mate Doran had found the fertile valley that she had been out of it.

The plain was still barren compared to the lush valley floor, but much had recovered from the total devastation of Senfall so long ago. For many seasons after that awful day, snow and ice had covered the land, killing the plants and driving most of the animal life away. Now the grassland had returned and trees had struggled their way out of the devastated soil.

The search for a trail to follow did not take long. Lying in the open at the edge of the rim was a pole of wood. There were hack marks along its length, indicating twigs had been trimmed off. One end was worn and caked with dirt. It had obviously been made and used as a walking staff by someone -- if not Kray, then whoever or whatever she had been running from. There were imprints of it in the dirt that led to a small grove of trees.

Jalex shaded her eyes and scanned the horizon. There was nothing in sight immediately.

"Granddaughter, climb that tallest tree and have a look around. Karrol, Auran, spread out and search this grove."

Tak did as she was bid and nimbly climbed to the uppermost branches. Sen was just past Her highest point. The plains stretched out for marches from Her morning home until lost in the shimmering distance. A slight hint of movement on the horizon caught Tak's eye. She noted the direction and climbed back down. Jalex was several paces away examining the ground near another tree.

"My Chief . . ."

"Yes, someone was treed by a spearcat," interrupted Jalex. "By a *mated pair* of spearcats. They waited for two days for their prey to fall out of the tree until they were finally driven off by a very strange animal."

Tak looked at the base of the tree. The tracks were faded with time, but several remained in a patch of hardened mud. They were strange, disturbing, resembling nothing any of them had ever seen before. Whatever creature made them walked upon four feet, but did not seem to have toes, hooves, or even flippers. The print was almost circular and about the size and shape of a vine melon, but the circle was open on the trailing end.

"I see no prints of a spearcat, Grandmother."

"Neither do I," Jalex replied. "But use your nose as well as your eyes."

Tak did as she was told and, to be sure, detected a very slight sour smell coming from the east.

"Droppings," said Tak. "But how do you know there was a mated pair?"

"Look over here," said Jalex, moving several paces away from the tree. There in a group were several piles of dried dung.

"Note how half the piles are separate turds, but the rest are clumped together. That tells me they came from a female spearcat in heat. The others are from her mate. The amount shows they stayed in this area for two days. They did not wish to mask the smell of their trapped prey, so one cat would come here to relieve itself while the other stood guard below the tree."

Tak could not help but admire the fine hunting skills that her aged chief still retained.

"What of the strange tracks, Grandmother?" asked Tak.

"They came from somewhere out there. Perhaps . . ."

A whistling hunter's call sounded through the trees.

"Perhaps we are about to find out. Come, Granddaughter. Karrol signals us."

Jalex headed off through the trees. She was moving better all the time, the thrill of the hunt lending forgotten strength to her limbs. Auran and Karrol were on the other side of the grove peering at the ground.

"Have you young, sharp-eyed hunters found something?"

"Yes, My Chief," replied Auran, who kept nervously looking over her shoulder. "But we do not know *what* we found."

The ground they were examining was a bare area surrounding the remains of a small pond that had mostly dried up earlier in the season. The soft soil was cracked and flaked and marked with the tracks of many animals that had crossed recently. There were impressions of spearcats, grassbucks, runnerbirds, and many other smaller creatures that came to drink from the diminishing water. Amid the jumble of familiar prints were those same mysterious circular tracks that Jalex had discovered in the grove. It was this unknown that was making Auran and Karrol nervous.

"Ah . . . yes."

Jalex focused her attention on the multitude of marks on the ground, muttering to herself and moving back and forth, crossing and re-crossing her path.

"Now we know what happened, do we not, my young ones?"

Tak, Karrol, and Auran stood with slightly embarrassed looks on their faces. None of them wanted to admit that they knew nothing other than many animals had been here. Jalex let them squirm for only a few beats before her twinkling eyes smiled at them.

"It is all right. Many young people do not have the hunting skills of us old ones. Karrol, you and your family were growers. Tak and Auran, you have grown up to become builders. Others have the skills to weave baskets and create stone tools. Wise Women know of herbs and healing. Life in the Valley is more than just hunters and warriors. No Ern can know all things . . . except for your Chief. Do not forget that."

Once again, Jalex's mischievous smile calmed her nervous followers' fears and reinforced the absolute faith they had in her leadership.

"Now, shall I tell you the story that the ground is telling me? The woman Kray came from the east. Here you can see imprints of the staff she walked with. Her gait was hurried and erratic. She may have stumbled right here as though exhausted.

Eventually she was treed by the spearcats for two days, possibly without water or food. The large animal with the strange feet followed her and the spearcats ran away. Kray then went to the edge of the valley rim, where she dropped her staff. Karrol, did you not say that the woman looked as though she had been beaten?"

"Yes, My Chief. She was bruised and scraped."

"Might she have gotten those wounds from falling down the canyon slope?"

"Perhaps." Karrol's face lit up with a realization. "That could be why she did not have her staff with her when my brother and I found her."

"Very good," nodded Jalex. "She may have slipped at the edge of the cliff and dropped it."

"As though she was running from something," said Tak.

"The strange animal!" added Auran.

"But that animal did not pursue," said Jalex, pointing at the ground. "These tracks show that the creature went in that direction along the rim of the canyon. And it left more swiftly than it came. The departing tracks are spaced farther apart."

Jalex traced the faint trail a little farther and pointed.

"It was followed . . . by a *pack* of spearcats and then turned back to the east. It may have frightened off the mated pair, but it seems they gathered the rest of their pride. The hunter became the hunted."

"Grandmother," said Tak. "when I was in the tree I saw something far off in that direction. It looked to be circling *skreets.*"

"Skreets?" said Auran. "That means something is dead."

"Yes," replied Jalex. "Let us track this fleeing animal as far as we can."

The hunters filled their waterskins to the top from the pond and set off slowly. Jalex was in the lead, constantly watching the ground. The grassy plain did not show the spoor as clearly as the dried mud and to Karrol, Tak, and Auran it was all but invisible, but occasionally Jalex found a slight print or a broken plant to indicate their quarry had come this way.

The daylight soon ran out and the four took shelter for the night among a grouping of boulders. Again, the chief's word was overridden when it came to standing watch. A bright fire and Jalex's loud snoring kept predators away and helped calm the jittery young hunters. In the morning, Sen rose in the very direction they were headed, as though She was guiding them to their destiny. Looking right into the rising sun made things a little more difficult, but eventually Jalex announced their search had come to an end.

"Stay alert."

The white ribs of an animal carcass peeked out from behind some tall grass ahead. A skreet took off with a flapping sound and angry gargling call. Several more of the repulsive birds stood atop the scattered remains, their beaks dripping with gore. A cloud of buzzing insects pushed and shoved their way to the head of the line.

Karrol charged the cowardly skreets, shouting and waving his spear. They complained a lot, but were used to being at the bottom of the feeding line and flew off to some distance to wait for another opportunity to eat.

The bones had been here for some time and were mostly picked over. Only dried remnants of hide and fur were left along with some putrefying innards that the skreets had been feasting on. The corpses were torn apart and scattered, but it was clear there were the remains of three different animals here.

A grinning skull with immense long fangs was easy enough to identify.

"A spearcat," said Auran.

The other two corpses were more mysterious. One was a large, deer-like animal, not as big as a morok, but similar in build. The other at first glance was that of an Ern. That was the one Jalex was interested in. She took note of the broad ribcage and long, thick leg bones. The skull was strangely misshapen with a wide, flat forehead and stubby, rounded chin.

"I wonder who this Ern was," said Tak.

"Not an Ern," replied Jalex. "This was Kray's *demon.*"

CHAPTER 19

Plants lived on Lurra long before Eryndi. Their ancient wisdom shall always be greater than ours . . .

- Jennick, Associate Instructor – Melosian Academy of Worldly Arts - 21863

Today - Abakaar

It was the wee hours of the morning. The pair of guards escorted Orchid down one of the many labyrinthine corridors of Zanteryne Castle. She busied herself with making final adjustments of her hastily donned clothing. At a junction, she was met by Serena, who was also under escort and also looking like she had just gotten out of bed.

"You too, huh?"

"Yeah," replied Serena. "They tell you what this is about?"

"Not a word. Just that I had to come with them right away . . . so, you get any sleep?"

"Not much . . . you?"

"I got off eventually."

The two smirking women and their escorts arrived at a large set of double doors with more soldiers standing guard. At a nod from the leader they were allowed access to a large room with an elaborate tapestry at one end. It was decorated with a pleasant forest motif and depictions of fawns and baby bunnies. A couple of civilians were crouching down attending to an unmoving someone on the floor. Serena recognized the gaudy red suit jacket lying next to him right away.

"Foxx!"

One of the civilians looked up. "Ah, you would be this man's friends? Which of you is the healer?"

"I am," replied Orchid. She immediately rushed forward. Foxx's shirt and jacket had been removed and he was lying on his side. There was a small black hole in his upper chest and a matching one on his back. Obviously, he had been punctured through by something, but curiously, there was no blood.

"What happened to him?" Orchid listened for a heartbeat and checked his breathing. Both were faint.

"We do not know. He was found in this room with the injury you see here. My name is Zuko. My colleague Leefen and I are the castle healers in the service of Queen Minore and were tasked with treating him, but we have never seen a wound like this. Obviously, your friend has been run through by some very thin weapon. He is still alive, but we see little hope for his recovery. His citizen's token has gone gray, a sure sign of impending death. It was then I sent the guards to fetch you. I am told your skills are . . ."

"I need my herb kit and my staff!"

A guard was quickly sent. He went to the wrong room at first, but was soon enlightened by knowledgeable staff. They redirected him to Finnis the Magician's quarters, who was well known for his entertaining talents. Orchid's gear was right where she had left it. The guard hurried back and turned the stuff over to her.

276

Orchid took the herb kit first. Inside were several different vials of powders along with a tiny collapsible bowl and several tools. She selected a long, thin probe and carefully dabbed at the wound. The thin point slid surprisingly easily into the hole in Foxx's chest. It did seem to be an actual tunnel drilled right through his chest cavity. The edges were blackened and hard with no soft tissue or blood exposed.

"Whatever did this was very hot," she muttered to herself. "The flesh is cauterized."

"Like he was shot through with a white hot arrow or dart," said Serena.

"Whatever it was, it's the only reason he's still alive, but it's still serious. His left lung is penetrated . . . and it drilled a hole right through one rib without breaking it."

Orchid took another look at the wound on Foxx's back. "From the angle, I'd say it missed his heart and just barely missed his spine. Serena, quickly . . . get me the vials marked *perimasis* and *saltleaf!*"

While Serena was retrieving the medicine, Orchid took out the little bowl along with a tube containing an oil extracted from the crushed seeds of a colossus tree. She squeezed exactly seventeen drops into the bowl and coated the sides with it. The herbs were carefully measured out and sprinkled over the oil. Orchid moved the bowl around in a circular motion, not stirring the chemicals, but allowing the oil to swirl about, carrying the powdered herbs with it. Four turns of the bowl achieved the proper consistency. She took the probe and carefully moistened the tip with the mixture.

"Lay him on his back again, placing your hands under his shoulder blades," Orchid instructed the two court healers.

"Now lift him up, so his back is arched, but don't cover

the wound . . . *good.* Now hold him like that as still as possible. Serena, get out two of those *bandi* leaves and the pouch of *boreroot.*"

Orchid took the probe and once again inserted it into the hole in Foxx's chest. The herb-enriched oil on the tip moistened the sides. She held the probe with one hand and with the other, very slowly poured a thin stream of the oil onto the wound. It flowed down the shaft of the probe and deeper into Foxx's chest. When gravity would drag down no more, Orchid removed the probe and placed her mouth over the wound. Her cheeks puffed out as she slowly but firmly blew for about two beats.

"Boreroot . . ."

Serena dug into the pouch and pulled out what looked like a piece of string about three fingers long. Orchid inserted one end of the root into the wound as far as it would go and poured more of the oil onto it.

She made a ceremonial gesture, one she had learned from her Eryndi upbringing. It wasn't Magical in itself, but helped prepare her mind for the spell she was about to invoke.

"Staff . . ."

When placed in Orchid's hands, her intricately carved oaken staff seemingly came to life. It glowed with lucent energies and emitted a low hum, as though signifying it was ready for whatever it was that it did. She grasped it tightly, hugging the wood close to her body. She closed her eyes and concentrated. Her mind reached out into the envelope of Magical energy that permeated the environment. She did not command. Worldly Magic was not forced. It was more like . . . *an agreement . . .* between Magician and Magic. Her wishes were read and energies were directed into the still-living strand of boreroot sticking out of Foxx's chest. The cells in the plant matter began to divide as they were stimulated and energized. The tip of the boreroot began to grow, extending itself deeper into the wound. As it traveled through Foxx's chest cavity, it passed through the rib and muscle tissue for a short way, finally breaking through and entering the lining surrounding the perforated lung. Orchid continued the spell. Her staff, attuned to her brain, glowed with a healthy green color. Small sparkles of light popped and fizzled from its carved top. As the growing boreroot continued on its path through the lung, it coated the inside of the wound with the herb-infused oil. At last, the tip of the root wriggled its way out of the hole on Foxx's back, sloughing off tiny blackened bits of burnt tissue that it had gathered on its journey. The spell was slowly backed off. The root stopped its growth. Orchid opened her eyes. She nipped off the protruding root on both front and back with her thumbnail, leaving it flush with the skin.

"Leaves . . ."

Serena handed them over. Orchid dipped them in the bowl, coating them with a bit more of the oil mixture. She covered both wounds with the leaves, which loosely adhered to Foxx's skin. Then she took up her staff again, took a deep breath, and began another spell. Once again the staff glowed, but with a slightly different color. Deep within Foxx's body, changes were happening. His immune system was stimulated to fight off infection and the burnt scar tissue within was being broken down and absorbed by the strand of boreroot. Healthy new cells began to multiply to replace the destroyed tissue. Orchid's spell was allowing her to commune with the plant matter of the herbs. She didn't actually know the exact chemical changes that were happening. Not even her Eryndi instructors knew that. All they and she knew was that Worldly Magic was being asked to release the healing power of the herbs and root. Such knowledge had been learned slowly over uncounted centuries and passed down to succeeding generations.

This spell took longer. Zuko and Leefen, the two healers, were dying to ask questions, but wisely concentrated on holding Foxx's body still as this strange procedure was performed. After nearly an hour of spellcasting, Orchid's eyes finally fluttered open and she collapsed back, exhausted, into Serena's waiting arms.

"Peel . . . peel off the bandi leaves," she muttered.

Serena gently pulled on the leaf on Foxx's chest. It came off easily. Beneath it was a circle of pink puckered skin, but no hole remained. The wound on his back was identical.

"You can take him to a bed now. I think I got to him in time. If I did, he should be all right in a few days. If not . . ."

Orchid started to get up, but had no power in her knees. Serena wrapped a strong arm around the small woman and hoisted her to her feet.

"I think you need to hit the sack too, Nature Girl."

"But I'll need to monitor him and maybe recast the spell . . ."

Orchid slumped again as a wave of dizziness and headache pain swept over her. The stress of Magical concentration for such an extended period was taking its toll.

"You're not gonna do anybody any good if you conk out," said Serena. "You done all you can for now."

"We shall see to their needs," said Zuko. "Guards . . ."

Foxx was loaded onto a stretcher. The guards had originally brought it in because they thought they would be hauling a dead body away. But now they used it to take the still-unconscious Foxx to his assigned quarters. Orchid followed slowly behind, supported on each side by the amazed castle healers, who plied her with questions all the way out the double doors and into the hallway.

"That was an amazing demonstration . . . what are the herbs used in this technique? What becomes of the root that is still within?"

Orchid was still drained, but recovering. The praise from her healer colleagues made her flush with pride in her Eryndi training.

Their voices faded as the doors closed behind them. Serena remained in the tapestry room with the two remaining guards. Whereas before her demeanor was nothing but concern for Foxx, now it was turning to anger.

"All right, what happened here? Who did that to him?"

"You must return to your quarters now," replied one of them, all business.

Two of the guards started to grasp Serena by her muscular arms to escort her out, but she broke free and backed up quickly. She didn't have her sword with her but was prepared to put up a fight, if necessary. These soldiers were the ones she had come to respect in this valley country. She admired their professionalism and comradery and had even been prepared to join their ranks. But now, even as she stood in a defensive stance with fists raised, Serena felt that sense of belonging ebbing away and her own self-reliant personality reasserting itself. Her citizen's token, which hung on a chain just above the brilliant diamond in her sternum, was losing its red color and becoming a lusterless grey.

"I'm not going anywhere until I get some answers! What is this place? What was Foxx doing here? How did he get wounded? Who found him like that?!"

"I did," said a commanding voice from behind. Serena spun and found herself lapis eye to opal eye with Queen Minore.

* * *

There is nothing stranger than a stranger . . .

- KING FAISRICK THE CAUTIOUS

Not quite 50,000 years ago

"Grandmother, look at this!"

Jalex looked up from her examination of the strange corpse. Tak was clutching something and approaching.

"I found this bit of hide caught on a bush."

Tak handed the shredded bit of material over to Jalex. The pelt was finer and smoother than any they had ever seen. There was no fur, just the impossibly thin skin.

"No animal was ever that bluish color," said Tak.

"None that we have seen, Granddaughter. Perhaps it comes from a fish or lizard, something without fur or feathers. I have made some curious discoveries as well. This rib bone here has a deep cut on it. Does that look familiar to you?"

"It looks like the mark left by a blade when an animal is butchered for food, but this is from the body of the man."

"And men do not butcher men for food . . . only in war. This man was stabbed."

"My Chief . . . My Chief!"

Karrol was several paces away examining the body of the large animal and waving frantically at something among the remains. This creature was the one most picked over. Apparently, the pack of spearcats had found its flesh to be tastier than that of the man. They had fought over the meat, each predator claiming its own morsel and withdrawing with it.

"What have you found?" asked Jalex.

"Many things of which I do not know, My Chief. First, there is this."

Karrol held up a gnawed foreleg of the animal. Most of the flesh and hide had been stripped off by various scavengers.

"This is the animal that made the strange tracks, but . . ." Karrol trailed off, completely at a loss for words. The foot of the creature ended in a pointed hoof, much like that of a morok or a milkbeast, but the bottom was in the shape of that open circle print they had seen in the grove of trees.

"This part of the hoof is as hard as stone, My Chief," said Karrol. He demonstrated by clacking a pebble against it. "And right here it seems to be coming loose from the rest of the hoof."

Jalex took the severed limb and pored over it with her still-keen eyes. This animal was indeed what had made the tracks.

"This . . . *thing* is not part of the animal," she said. "You are right. It has been attached to the bottom of the hoof by these long thorns."

Jalex pulled a little piece loose. It was a thin, pointed piece of the same hard material the object was made of. Several of these things had been driven into the bottom of the animal's hoof through holes in the object.

"I have never seen such a thing in all my seasons," said Jalex slowly. Tak, Karrol, and Auran had never seen their chief so in awe before.

"That is not all, My Chief . . . there is more."

Karrol led them over to a brown lump a few paces away.

"Here is another . . . *thing*. I thought it at first to be another body part of the animal, but it seems to be *made* from thick hide in the same way we make strong ropes woven from strips of leather."

The object lay in the dirt. There were several deep gashes and punctures in the hide. Possibly a spearcat had worried the thing, thinking it to be edible. It was indeed made by an intelligent hand. There were thick overlapping layers of curved hide connected to one another by strong threads looped over each other. Broad straps of leather with regular holes punched in them trailed from each side of the thing. Attached to some of them were more objects of the same hard material as the thing found on the animal's hoof. These were smaller and thinner square pieces with moving pins looped around one side. There was a separate pouch-like bit of leather attached to one side of the object. A shiny cylindrical item protruded from it. Jalex gingerly touched it, as though it might bite her. When it didn't, she pulled gently and it came free in her hand. The cylinder made up half of the object. The other half was shiny gray and flat as a piece of bark, but smooth and very hard. Though completely alien in its material and shape, it was apparent what the thing was. The opposite end was pointed and one side of the flat part was very smooth and sharp. The half that had been encased in leather was coated in dried blood.

"This is a knife," said Jalex simply. "Perhaps the one the man was stabbed with. But it is so smooth and thin. It was not knapped from toolstone as our scrapers and arrowpoints."

Auran's eyes went wide. "How can such things be made? Leave it, My Chief! These are the tools of demons! Let us go from this place!"

"Be calm, Auran. There are no demons." Jalex's voice was

calm and reassuring. "A demon could not be killed by spearcats. This was a man . . . not a man like our friend Karrol here, but a different kind of man."

The small party spent the rest of the day searching the remains and the general area. Jalex's reassurances convinced her people that, however strange, the artifacts they were finding were not supernatural in nature. By the time it got dark, they had gathered a very curious little pile of objects. There were three more of the hard objects from the feet of the big deer, the leather thing with the straps and loops, the curious knife, and several other small objects made of a combination of wood, the hard material, and something that looked to be clear as ice, but was not cold and did not melt with the touch of a hand.

Karrol had been sent afield to rustle up some dinner. He returned with a pair of runnerbirds. By the time he got back, Jalex, Auran, and Tak had a campsite set up some distance from the corpses. The birds were soon plucked, gutted, and roasting over the fire. By the time the bones were picked clean, darkness had fallen. This time, Jalex would not be denied keeping watch, which she did with Tak. Karrol and Auran took their turn together later in the night.

When Sen arose in the morning, Jalex set to examining their finds. Some of the objects were so foreign that even she with her analytical mind could not fathom their purpose. She snorted in disgust with herself, dusted off her hands, and stood up.

"Karrol, you shall carry the deerfoot objects because of their weight. Tak and Auran, you take the knife and the other things. We must leave the leather object as it is too heavy for any of us to carry for a distance. We shall bury it and perhaps come back for it later."

"It will be good to be back in the valley," said Auran with a sigh. "I do not like this open prairie that has such strange creatures."

Jalex looked fleetingly sad, but immediately returned to her usual authoritative Chief-face.

"We are not returning to the valley . . . we are here to track these strange people."

"And to find out what killed my family," added Karrol grimly.

"Such a thing must not be allowed to spread," said Jalex. She looked into the eyes of each of the others. There were no dissentions.

"Come, the river has turned to the northeast ahead in the direction the . . . *this man* was headed. That is the best place to try to pick up the trail again."

When all were loaded and ready, the small party headed toward the river that had carved out their beloved valley and saved the Ern from Senfall. Out here on the prairie, the water flowed wide and slow as it exited the high walls of the valley. There were great expanses of bare soil encrusted with layers of white residue, no doubt remnants of the cataclysm of Jalex's youth. When the storms hit, the waters were clogged with dirt and debris that had rolled across the land. It was only the continued supply of underground hot spring water from the depths of the valley that kept the river running at all after Senfall.

Jalex and the others kept up a slow pace all day, searching for more sign of the strangers. The trail had ended at the sight of the spearcat kill, but the man and his beast must have come from somewhere. That night they camped near some trees some distance from the water. Jalex taught them it was not wise to sleep very near the water, for everything on two or four legs came to the river to drink. Trees offered quick refuge in the event of a predator attack, at least those predators that couldn't climb trees.

The next morning, they set out again following the river. Jalex divided them up so that two of them were on each side of the water. The going was slow, as they painstakingly searched the ground for any trace of their quarry. That was all right with Jalex. While her aged legs had regained some of their former strength, she still tired quickly and welcomed any chance to rest. The younger members were glad to let her. The farther they got from their home, the less they liked it.

Immediately upon starting out on the third day since finding the corpses, the hunters came across a small herd of lum who were bathing their giant bodies in the shallow waters. A mother lum was tending to her calf, making sure the young one did not get into deep water or stuck in mud. The sight brought back ancient memories of the day Jalex had met her mate, Doran.

Such a long time ago . . . such terrible and happy times . . .

There was no thought of trying to hunt the huge beasts. Jalex and the others had found plenty to sustain themselves in the form of fish, waterfowl, and various grains that grew along the riverbanks. They were content to simply give the lum plenty of room as they detoured around them. It was still early and the group had not yet deployed to both sides of the river. They moved quietly through the squatty trees that grew in profusion here.

The weather, which had been very fine for the last few days, showed signs of changing. Dark clouds heavy with water were moving in from the east; nothing to threaten them, but rain might obliterate the strangers' tracks if there were even any to find. Sen hid her face for a moment, casting the morning into shadow. At the same time the wind shifted, chased by the approaching clouds. One by one, the lum lifted their huge round heads and sniffed the air. The young ones were immediately hustled into the center of the protective adults, who milled about nervously.

"They must have picked up our scent," whispered Jalex. "Come, stay behind the trees and keep moving. We shall get farther away."

Jalex led her party several more hands of paces away from the agitated lum, whose bawling cries could still be heard behind them. She did not quite understand why the animals were so upset with them. Then it suddenly hit her and she felt foolish for not realizing it sooner.

Something else is stalking them!

However, before she had time to communicate that thought, something crashed through the greenery in front of her. There was a laughing, high-pitched animal scream, the likes of which she had never heard. A mass of brown fur loomed in her face. She caught a glimpse of a long snout and quivering nostrils. More creatures flanked it and for a beat, an impossible image of a man's face hovered above the frantic scene. The creature reared up and the last thing Jalex saw was one of those hard, circular objects heading for her face. Then blackness closed in.

CHAPTER 20

Sacrificing a major game piece need not be a defeat. That move can draw out your opponents and leave them vulnerable to attack . . .

- Mama's essay assignment to Merak – *The Psychology of Ascendency Play* - Intervoid Educational Program – level 11

(Teacher's comment – *B+*
Well enough written, but work on your spelling)

* * *

Foxx was in a room . . . a very red room. The stone tiles he stood upon were red . . . red like blood . . . hot . . . the floor was hot. The walls did not meet the floor. The floor curved up to become the walls . . . red . . . all was red. The ceiling was red . . . hot . . . it was so very hot. The blistering heat poured down upon him. No sun . . . no sky . . . just the heat . . . and the red. Hard to breathe . . . can't inhale . . . pain . . . to breathe was pain . . . make it stop. The floor sloped down in the center . . . hole . . . hole in the red floor . . . like a funnel. Down there, no more pain . . . down there, no more heat . . . go down there and make it stop. Take a step . . . difficult . . . another step . . . afraid. What is down there? Foxx had often wondered.

Afraid . . . maybe one more step . . . pain . . . heat . . . make it stop. The hole was before him. It would stop . . . go down the hole to make it stop . . . but . . .

A cool breeze . . . just for a moment. Foxx lifted his gaze away from the hole . . . still red . . . the heat returned. It would be so easy . . . just go down the hole. Another breeze . . . from somewhere ahead. The red on the far wall was fading. Green . . . there was green . . . beyond the hole. The floor was still hot . . . still hurt to draw a breath. Beyond was a tree . . . so very far away . . . more trees . . . a forest . . . a very green forest. But to get there, Foxx would have to move away from the hole where it hurt less. Another cool breeze from the forest . . . but to move there would be painful. The forest was cool, but the pain . . . step to the side . . . go around the hole . . . pain . . . the pain of a thousand flames . . . but the cool forest . . . another step toward the trees. PAIN! Screw the forest . . . the hole was so much easier. The hole would stop the pain. Foxx conquered his fear and headed back toward the hole . . . soon . . . the pain would stop soon. Another cool breeze . . . scent . . . sweet scent. There were flowers clinging by tendrils to the lower branches of the trees . . . large, curved white petals . . . green centers . . . chocolate brown leaves . . . fragrant, Magical flowers. Foxx was not into flowers, but somehow knew what these were . . . *Orchids.*

Come closer.

Why were they here? It felt like an intrusion. These flowers were always doing that. This time was different.

We shall help.

The flowers wanted to help. Foxx snorted with the absurdity of it all. Place one's faith in flowers when the easier solution was right behind him?

Do not look back.

Indeed, the hole was behind him now. Foxx didn't remember going around it.

We are good for you.

Will you stop the pain?

Eventually.

Not right away?

Soon.

Hurts now.

This will help.

Foxx was now fully within the forest. The flowers stared at him.

Eat this.

The flowers handed Foxx a bowl of greens . . . and a fork.

What kind of dressing would you like?

Got any bacon bits?

No.

Flicken strips?

No.

Hard-boiled eggs?

Shut up and eat.

Foxx shrugged and ate the salad. It tasted like crap and gave him the worst case of heartburn he'd ever had. The dressing was oily. The croutons were soggy. And he had no choice.

Good boy.

Salad always makes me sleepy. I'm going back to the hole for a nap.

Holes are for losers.

I'm not a loser. I'm a gambler.

You bet your life you are.

Double or nothing.

Come back here, you grasshead.

Foxx looked back into the red hole in the red floor. Inside was a soft feather mattress with red silk sheets. Just a quick nap.

Stop.

Now what?

Drink this herbal tea.

What's in it?

Some of my petals.

The huge steaming mug in Foxx's hands smelled like fragrant flowers with a hint of rotten potatoes, but since there was no choice, he drank it down.

Turn your head and cough.

Cough, cough . . . COUGH, COUGH

That's it.

COUGH, COUGH, COUGH

Keep it up.

That tea's gonna make me . . .

That's right, get it all out.

The hole was gone . . . no longer an option . . . now I'll never get to sleep.

Later.

The red room broke apart brick by brick.

Time to wake up and go to bed.

Okay, okay . . . I'm awake . . . I'm . . . awake . . .

About time.

Yawn . . .

Today - Abakaar

Orchid wearily sat back from Foxx's bedside. Her bowl slipped out of her hands to clatter onto the spotted loperskin rug, spilling the remains of the herbal oil. She had just reopened his wounds slightly to apply more of the oil and cast the healing spell again. Foxx continued to cough and heave, emptying the contents of both his stomach and his lungs onto the floor to join the oil on the rug.

"Amazing . . . simply amazing."

"I would never have thought anyone could recover from a wound like that."

The two castle healers vigorously competed with one another in patting Orchid on the back.

"Okay . . . all right, give me some room here, boys."

Orchid clutched her chest, still reeling from the phantom pain. It was beginning to fade. Though not real, it gave her a humbling idea of what her friend that she sometimes couldn't stand had gone through.

Foxx coughed a couple more times, hacking up tiny bits of dead tissue. He gradually settled down and drifted into a much more peaceful, curative sleep.

"At one point, the patient seemed on the verge of passing on, but you managed to pull him back," said Zuko.

Leefen finished his thought. "Was it the increased potency of the herb mixture that you administered?"

Orchid pulled herself together. The praise and attention were appealing to her ego. "That second dose was to give the boreroot additional incentive. The herbs are assimilated into the remains of the root, which carries them to the damaged tissue. Eventually, the entire root is broken down and absorbed. But his body was seriously damaged. It didn't have sufficient life energy left to heal itself, even with the herbs."

"So you supplemented with some of your own," said Zuko, noting Orchid's trembling hands.

"Yes . . . it's . . . rather draining."

"Incredible. We have nothing like that," said Leefen. "Where did you learn this method?"

"Part of my Eryndi training. We learn all about the use of herbs and their interaction with Worldly Magic. In extreme cases, we are forced to *connect* with our charges in a metaphysical way."

It was as though a door suddenly opened within Orchid . . . or to be more precise, *closed.* The suggestions within her mind about this valley of Abakaar and its way of life were shut off, blocked by her strength of will and belief in herself. At this moment, Orchid's citizen's certification token changed color. No longer was it red like everybody else's in this country. Now the metal was uniformly gray, and it felt damn good.

The two healers both had confused looks on their faces. Leefen was shaking his head as though to clear it from the effects of skunky beer.

"*Eryndi training.* I have heard of such things, but it is not . . . seemly to . . . speak of them."

"It is in bad taste," added Zuko, equally confused. *"Isn't it?"*

"Foxx will sleep now," said Orchid wearily. "He needs *quiet rest."*

"Of course, of course. If there is anything you need, please let us know. Come, Leefen."

The two healers left, each full of questions that they were reluctant to ask. Foxx drifted off into peaceful sleep. Orchid plunked down in the bedside chair and soon dozed off. Outside the room, a full squad of armed soldiers was approaching from down the hall.

Not quite 50,000 years ago

Jalex's eyes popped open and she immediately regretted it. *Bright light . . . pain.* Her head ached inside and out. Right now, it hurt as much to think as it did to move her head, so she closed her eyes again and used her Ern discipline to settle down the confusion and fear that were creeping into her mind. She began to remember a series of terrifying images. There were several of the large animals with the objects on their hooves. They were screaming . . . no . . . *laughing* at her. There was also a voice . . . a strange, deep voice, loud, shouting.

A few beats of controlled breathing and a meditative technique taught to her by old Myela, the wise woman Jalex had apprenticed under so many seasons ago, eased her pain and her fear. An amusing thought tickled her mind. *Old* Myela was about the same age then as Jalex was now. Her head still throbbed, but she could think a little better. She gathered as much information as she could without opening her eyes again.

Sound . . . voices, muted, from varying distances. Birds . . . wind . . . the galloping sound of a four-legged animal on soft ground, and occasionally a strange high-pitched whistling sound she couldn't identify.

Scent . . . meat cooking . . . smoke . . . a *perima* bush. Its fragrant berries were unmistakable and useful in soothing burns.

Touch . . . she was lying on her side . . . grass beneath her body . . . something cold wrapped around her ankle. Jalex moved her leg, but not very far . . . resistance . . . She reached her hand up and felt the tender knot on her forehead. She remembered. That animal had struck her with its hoof.

She felt ready to open her eyes again, which she did slowly. A blurry face greeted her.

"Grandmother . . . Grandmother, can you hear me?"

Tak.

"Yes . . . yes. Are you all right?"

"Me? Grandmother, you were struck in the head and have been in deathsleep for half a day!"

Tak shifted around to help her chief sit up. At the same time, something tugged upon Jalex's ankle.

"Yes, we have been tied together by the demons."

Jalex looked down at her leg. There was a thin loop of rope coiled around her left ankle. The other end was around Tak's left ankle. The rope was strange-looking and heavy.

"Help me up."

Jalex struggled to her feet, assisted by Tak. The short length of rope connecting them made it difficult. They could not stand side-by-side unless facing opposite directions.

"My Chief."

Karrol and Auran stood nearby. They were similarly tied together with the strange twine. It seemed to be made up of very thin strands of the same hard material as the other objects they had found. It was not tied in a knot, but held tightly together by a hard loop. Even Karrol with his strong grip could not loosen it. He was sporting a black eye and his hide wrap was torn.

"What has happened?"

"We were surrounded and captured by the demons, Grandmother. Karrol put up a tremendous fight. He managed to knock down two of them before he was finally overpowered. We were all tied by the hands and forced to walk to this place, where we were hobbled with this rope. We are free to move about, but we cannot go far tied as we are."

Jalex looked around. They were in a camp. Peculiar conical tents were set up, a fire pit, people milling around. On the far side of the camp, two hands of the large animals were standing in a group. They stood munching on the prairie grass. Now Jalex got her first real look at them. They were tall, with deep chests and strong legs. Long manes of thick hair hung from the backs of their necks. Their tails were also hanging with long hair, which they used to flick away the biting flies that seemed attracted to them. They were all tethered to a rope stretched between two trees by means of elaborate leather straps wrapped around their long snouts. Two of them had something on their backs. They were heavy leather things tied around their bellies by means of straps. Jalex realized they resembled the object they had found among the corpses. She could not fathom the purpose of them until she saw two men approach the animals. They were some distance away and she could not make out their features, but they were large men. She watched them untie the two animals wearing the objects. They then went to the left sides of the animals. They each placed a foot in one of the hanging loops, hoisted themselves up onto the animals' backs, and sat on the leather objects. The men grasped a pair of straps that were attached to the animals' chins, who had no apparent objections to this astounding action. Together the creatures turned and galloped off across the prairie with the men clinging to their backs.

Jalex turned to her friends, a look of astonishment on her face.

"Yes, My Chief," said Karrol. "And I thought it was crazy to ride a logfloater down the river."

"They are so swift," Jalex replied. "Already they are nearly out of sight."

"Look there," said Auran nervously.

A woman was approaching. She was large and broad-shouldered and to Jalex's eye, ugly, even brutish. She had a wide flat nose, stubby chin, and hideous wrinkled ears flattened against the sides of her head.

The most terrifying thing about the woman was the bizarre creature that rode upon her shoulder. Its feet had sharp talons with which it hung on, but never poked into the woman's skin. Mostly it stabilized its ride with a long whip tail wrapped around her neck, its tip constantly in motion. It was snake-like in its face and shiny blue-gray scales. The sinuous head constantly looked at everything about it. It was very aware. Every small movement or sound, whether from the people around or a blowing leaf, was noted. Occasionally, the beast issued the warbling hiss Jalex had heard earlier. As the woman stopped in front of the prisoners, the creature displayed its most startling attribute. From its front feet, it unfolded a set of very thin, nearly transparent featherless wings, which it displayed to Jalex and the others with obvious pride.

The woman was wearing a most curious skin. It clung closely to her form, accenting the woman's muscular shoulders and large breasts beneath. Jalex looked closely. This was no animal skin. As with the leather objects on the backs of the animals, this garment was somehow *made*. Parts of it were stitched together with tiny loops of threads. The shimmery blue material resembled the piece found near the corpses. It was worn. There was a hole over the woman's belly and the edges of the sleeves which reached just above her elbows were frayed.

The rest of the woman's attire was more familiar. She had leggings obviously made from the hide of a grassbuck. Her sandals were also fashioned from some kind of rough leather. The design was odd, but not all that different than those of the Ern.

In one hand the woman carried a short stick with a pointed head tied to one end. It somewhat resembled the war clubs that some of the Ern carried, but this one was not capped with stone, nor was the shaft even wood. Both were clear as water! The handle was completely smooth and cylindrical with not a blemish or dimple. Capping it was another piece of a larger diameter, sharpened to a fine point on one end. It had a groove in the middle which slid into a perfect slot in the shaft and was secured with a thin strand of woven rope similar to that which held the captives' feet.

In her other hand she carried a skinbag, which she tossed at Jalex's feet. It landed with a squishy sound.

"*Kerna.*"

Jalex didn't move, but maintained eye contact.

"*Kerna,*" the woman repeated, pointing at the bag with her weapon. Jalex slowly picked it up, untied the neck, and sniffed. She took a small sip, then a good swallow. She passed the bag to Karrol, Tak, and Auran, who also drank.

"Water," said Jalex, looking calmly back at the woman. "Water."

"*Wah-der.*"

"It seems these demons can learn to speak, after all," Jalex said.

Auran looked suspicious. "My Chief, I have heard redbirds imitate hunters' calls and even the roars and howls of predators. This demon is merely doing the same."

A shout came from one of the other women, who was tending the fire pit. The one who had given Jalex the water turned and shouted something back.

"We have heard them make those noises, My Chief," said Karrol. "They sound like words, but say nothing."

"They seem to say something to each other . . ."

"*Los . . .*"

The woman motioned for the captives to follow her.

"Los," she repeated. *"Navarray su mat."*

"Yes," said Jalex, nodding her head.

The woman turned and headed for the fire pit. The captives followed slowly. Because of their bindings, Jalex and Tak were forced to walk in step in close single file, as were Karrol and Auran. Running was out of the question. Several women were gathered around the pit. A newly killed carcass of a *striper* lay next to it. Jalex had not seen this type of animal since before the days of Senfall. They didn't exist in the valley. Her younger friends had never seen one. There was not much meat left on the bones, but some of the less than choice cuts remained. One of the women handed Karrol four sharpened sticks. She then took out a knife, one similar to the remarkable one found on the dead man, and cut four slices of gristly meat from the carcass. These were passed out to the captives who were allowed to roast them over the fire under the watchful eyes of the women. The Ern hungrily ate the meat and drank their fill of water. When finished, the woman who had given them the water summoned them again.

"Los."

Jalex stood, followed by the others. This time they were led to one of the conical tents in the center of the camp. Two men stood outside, evidently guarding.

"Tella . . . u dur?"

"Aon u shukares et tabor dunsis."

"You see, Tak?" said Jalex quietly. "They are talking to one another, but in a way we cannot understand."

One of the guards went through a flap in the tent and entered. A hand of beats later, he emerged.

"Kabahee . . . Los."

He held the tent flap open and the woman motioned Jalex and the others to enter. It took a moment for their eyes to adjust to the dim light. A small flame burned in a central fire pit over which hung a black pot emitting a strange smell. A pair of eyes peered at them from beyond the flame. The slight figure sat huddled by the fire, wrapped in a black-furred pelt. A wrinkled, bony hand extended from below and beckoned with trembling fingers.

"Come . . . sit."

CHAPTER 21

My boy, the most important thing to ascertain about your prospective marks is their basic profile . . . what they need, what they want, what they value. Most of the time they don't know these things themselves. Once YOU know them, you got 'em by the balls, you have . . .

- Professor Abadiah Generax, 21862

Today - Abakaar

CLOMP, clomp, clomp, clomp, CLOMP, clomp, clomp, clomp.

"HALT. Assume guard positions."

The clomping halted upon command and the door swung open. The Lieutenant in charge entered the room, his armor rattling and startling Orchid awake from her nap. Stiff from sleeping in the chair, she rotated her neck, the crackling sound rivaling the noisy soldier's entry.

"What is it?" she yawned. "Wait a minute . . . I know you."

"Lieutenant Sensis, ma'am. First Brigade, Company Six."

"You were one of the ones who brought us in from the Zone . . . rather forcefully, as I recall. What are you doing here?"

"Orders, ma'am. You and your friend have been placed under our protection."

Orchid, now fully awake, suddenly remembered Foxx. He was still sleeping peacefully in the bed next to her.

"Protection? Protection from what?"

"From anything that may threaten, ma'am," replied Sensis, with a confident grasping of his sheathed sword hilt.

Orchid gave the Lieutenant a combined confused and worried glance and went to check on Foxx. She noted his eye movement, indicating dreaming, and his improved color. His breathing was regular and steady . . . all good signs. Her own body gave her some signs as her stomach growled. From the angle of the daylight streaming into the window, it was well past Midday.

"I think it's safe to let Foxx sleep for a while. I'm going to go and find something to eat."

"Your pardon, ma'am," replied Sensis. "I cannot allow you to leave these rooms. Let me know your needs and we shall send a messenger for whatever you would like."

"I don't think we'll need to do that," said a familiar voice. Serena strode into the room, her faithful scimitar swinging at her left hip. "I brought lunch."

The warrior woman went to the bedside table and plunked down a jug of wine and a heavy bag which immediately tipped over. Various fruits and a loaf of dark bread spilled out. There was also a big undercooked shank of roast mutton, which Serena claimed for her own. She ripped off a long strip of dripping red meat with her strong white teeth and gulped it down heartily.

"Wanna bite?"

Orchid chose not to make a culinary comment and instead gratefully munched on some fruit and wine, with the wine taking priority, of course. Then came a shout from the guards outside.

"ATTENNNN-SHUN!"

Twenty soldiers snapped to with chests out and stomachs in. They were identically equipped and noticeably without citizen's tokens. Queen Minore strode down the hall resplendent in her royal armor. Her custom-made silvery breastplate was form-fitted to her already impressive form. A jewel-encrusted double-edged sword and matching dagger hung from a belt of fine leather and her greaves and gauntlets also shone with polished gems. Magnificent colored plumes from a great *chromorapter* bird adorned her war helmet. Even her long braids of thick black hair were bristling with pointed spikes designed to be swung as weapons. Despite the pretentiousness and spotlessness of her war accoutrements, Minore never for a moment gave the impression of someone unfamiliar with their use. There was a deadly earnestness in her opaline eyes as she surveyed the readiness of her troops with a steely gaze. At a signal from Sensis, the assembled soldiers drew their swords and in unison saluted their ruler and general.

"All hail Queen Minore!"

Nodding in approval, the queen flowed into the room like an irresistible flash flood. Serena and Orchid bowed their heads in respect for the royal presence. Minore looked Serena in the eye.

"Well my barbarian friend, are you ready?"

Serena grasped the hilt of her sword and raised her chin.

"Ready, Your Majesty!"

Orchid looked confused. "Ready for what?" she whispered out the side of her mouth.

Minore smiled in amusement. "There has been a great crime perpetrated in our land. We are about to make it right. *Are we not, my loyal soldiers?!*"

"For the Queen!" came the shouted soldiery response.

"Hey, could you keep it down?" came a weak voice from the bed. "I'm trying to get a little sleep over here."

"Foxx . . . you're alive!" Serena moved over to his bedside and offered a hand. Foxx took it and instantly regretted being pulled upright in the grip of the muscular shield maiden.

"Careful!" warned Orchid. "You'll tear open his wound again."

"You don't recover from a few scratches by layin' on your ass." Serena cleared her throat and raised a finger. *"A wounded warrior heals best when back on the battlefield!"*

"Where did you get that gem of wisdom?"

"The Credos of Hrolvad the Berserker. Had to memorize 'em in second grade."

"And that's why Northlands warriors make such terrific doctors," snorted Orchid.

"Yeah, that's right, small fry. He don't need to be coddled like a baby. He'll end up a bigger puss than he already is."

"Well, we don't want that to happen," interrupted Foxx. He struggled the rest of the way out of bed and woozily stood on his feet, grasping the post for support.

"It's all right, Orchid. Serena is right. I've had enough sleep. So . . . what'd I miss?"

"You missed your own execution for leaving the Royal Presence without permission . . . but we can reschedule."

A stern face with nearly white opal-colored eyes glared at him from beneath a fearsome-looking silver war helmet.

"Minore! I m-m-mean Your Majesty! My Queen, I can explain . . ."

Serena smirked at seeing the usually silver-tongued Foxx stammer like this.

"Do so then. Explain."

"I was . . . investigating, My Queen. There is an unscrupulous force at work in this land. I was seeking to uncover . . . the truth."

"And your first thought was to keep this knowledge from your Queen and slither from my chambers like a shadow serpent?"

Foxx briefly considered using his skills to calm the situation, but came to the very wise conclusion that attempting to use his Knowing Spell to influence Minore at this time would be the worst mistake of his now precarious life. He therefore opted for the little-used path for him. He told the truth.

"Yes, My Queen."

Minore regarded him silently for all of two beats, but to Foxx it felt like a headsman's axe was hovering over his neck for an hour.

"Good. You shall join us as we take back our land and people. The Vizier shall pay for his treason."

"Your Majesty, you know about Rastaban and the tokens he controls?"

"I am the Queen. I am not exactly oblivious."

"Of course not, Your Majesty."

"The traitor Rastaban has disappeared from the castle. But I have a way to locate him. Then I and my loyal soldiers shall go out into the city and rip those accursed medallions from the necks of our citizens one by one if necessary. *Follow me!*"

Not quite 50,000 years ago

The voice that spoke occasionally hinted of a once deep and resonant tone. But most of the time, every mucous-rattled word the man uttered came out a painful whisper.

"It is all right . . . sit. Have some food."

The slight figure leaned forward, pulling the fur pelt away from his face. The wide cheekbones threatened to burst out of his ancient skin, which was wrinkled like a dead seed pod and nearly as transparent. He gestured to a wood pedestal which held a variety of dried meat and some berries.

"We were given food out there by your warriors," answered Jalex.

"*Ma swayna dukross* . . . we are not warriors. Why do you say this?"

"We were attacked by the beasts with stone hooves," replied Karrol defiantly. "Our feet were tied together like birds to be roasted. Your demons carry strange weapons and bring sickness and death to our kin . . . to *my kin!*"

The wrinkled demon bowed his head. A single tear formed at the corner of one of his milky eyes and ran down his face. His whisper could barely be heard.

"What are your names?"

"This is Jalex, Chief of all the tribes of the Valley Ern . . . her granddaughter Tak, and Auran of the Builders. I am Karrol the Grower of the clan of Tarben . . . the clan you demons destroyed with your sickness curse!"

Karrol rose from his crouch in a half-threatening manner, but was prevented from anything more by the tight binding connecting his ankle to that of Auran, who grunted in pain when it pulled tight.

"Steady," said Jalex calmly. "Let this . . . *man* speak."

"Thank you, Chief . . . *Jalex,* was it?"

She nodded silently and appraised the being in front of her. He scarcely made a move as though any expending of energy was taxing on him.

"My name is Tella. You are here for . . . *kosera*"

The man Tella dipped his head in thought for a moment.

"*Per . . . pro-tection.* That is the word. You are here for protection."

"What are you protecting us from?" asked Jalex.

"Not you . . ."

Jalex thought for a moment. "You are protecting the rest of our people . . . from the sickness," nodded Jalex.

"We are trying . . . we tried . . . but . . ." Tella's watery eyes met Karrol's angry ones and then dropped in remorse.

"Yes . . . I . . . have been trying to . . . pro-tect the Ern for . . . *evvy et ev urvat* . . . you would say, *three hands of hands* of . . . uh, what is the word . . . when the snows melt and *Arktorr* is high in the sky?"

Tella concentrated on the ground and seemed to forget about the Ern in the tent with him as he mumbled to himself with his strange words.

"I think he means Sen," Jalex said quietly to Tak.

"We try to stay away from Ern," Tella muttered. Once again, he looked Jalex in the eye. The old man's attention span came and went like a feather in the wind. "Stay away . . . but when your people meet my people . . . your people die."

"And who are your people? What is your tribe?" asked Jalex.

"We are called *Ma Kahy.* In your *dermot* the name simply means *people.*"

"I do not know what you said. What is *dermot?*"

"You know no word for it. All Ern speak with one dermot . . . quite remarkable. My people speak many *Ma Kahy* dermots. This is the dermot I speak . . . *Ke los, Jalex Tor. Dren ke pro du.* I just said, 'Come with me, Lady Jalex. I need your help.'"

"Why would anyone want to speak in this strange way?" asked Tak. "No one can understand you."

Tella smiled, revealing all five of his remaining teeth. A chuckle was begun, but soon degraded into a raspy coughing spasm.

"You are correct, my dear. None of the Ern understand us. That is why I have tried to learn your words and speak your dermot. It has taken me many *urvat . . . uh . . .*"

Even as he spoke, Tella seemed to be slipping back into another world deep within his own mind. Jalex needed to keep him talking and focused if she were to get any answers about these strange folk.

"Tella . . . *Tella!*"

The ancient Ma Kahy slowly brought his head up and focused his bleary eyes on Jalex. It seemed as though he didn't recognize her at first.

"*Seasons* . . . it took you many seasons to learn our . . . dermot. Is that right?"

"What? . . . oh, yes. Forgive me Chief Jalex. Sometimes my mind wanders."

"Tella . . . we have never seen people like you before. Where do the Ma Kahy come from?"

"My mother used to sing a song to me when I was still in *primerallar* . . . uh, First Home. It went . . . *nonde skoona de ransera nee . . . hai yai, bow ma det fee.*"

The singing brought on another coughing fit. Jalex instinctively moved to try to help him, but he waved her off.

"Thank you, *Jalex Tor* . . . but I am all right. Believe it or not, I used to be a very good singer. The song tells that Ma Kahy are from very far away . . . that there was another First Home even before my First Home."

"Where?"

"It sings of *Night dances in the sky* and *Rainstorms of stars,* but it is just a silly song sung to children. No one believes it. No one even believes my tales of *primerallar.*"

"You said that means *First Home,*" pressed Jalex. "Tell me about First Home."

Tella's eyes lit up. Clearly this was something he enjoyed talking about.

"Primerallar was a *doonsa* place. There was always food . . . there was always water . . . whenever we wanted it. You didn't need to go find it. Mother just opened the *neekom* and it was there. I can remember the day I was finally tall enough to reach the *neekom* myself. I ate all the *fennies* at once. Mother scolded me because she usually only let me have one *fenny* a *tern.* I threw up and cried. I ran to Father, but he said I deserved to be sick and made me go to sleep without seeing *korba* that night."

Tella continued with his strange tale of his first home. It was full of unfamiliar words and ideas. He told of how his home had no sky and the ground was flat everywhere. There were many other of the Ma Kahy in this home with him. They lived in family groups and met in great crowds for strange events. He spoke of hearing music, being taught lessons, and seeing many great adventures and marvelous things. These were concepts familiar to the Ern, but Tella also said that such happenings weren't real and were only seen in connection with something called *korba.* The Ern had no idea what he was talking about. It all just seemed the ravings of a very old man with very distorted memories of his childhood.

Tella related these tales with a happy gleam in his eye. To him, those were good times, however unlikely. Then his features fell.

"Everyone was very happy because we would soon move to Segonallar . . . uh, Second Home. But one day, there was an awful noise. Mother and Father were scared. All Ma Kahy were scared. Korba told everybody to go places. People were running and shouting. I saw Treffi's mother fighting. She got knocked down and another Ma Kahy stepped on her. Father picked me up and we ran and ran. We went into a crowded place that shook and roared. There was fire outside the *berstas*. People were crying and shouting. The animals were scar . . . uh, screaming. Finally, the shaking stopped. We left that place and then we were here. That was the first time I had ever seen the sky. It was dark and filled with dust for many . . . seasons, yes. Many Ma Kahy died from cold and hunger . . . and from . . . *esok* . . . uh, *quarrels*."

"With Ern?" asked Karrol.

"Sometimes . . . other times with . . . ourselves. We tried to live with Ern, but they became sick. My mother called it *syndrome*. She said it was from her *primerallar*."

"What do Ma Kahy do to fight this sickness?" asked Jalex.

"Mother said she tried to fight it at her *primerallar*, but it was hopeless. Ma Kahy there died of syndrome. She and Father came here to Segonallar. Here we do not die, but Ern do."

Tella's voice trailed off and his head bowed again.

"When Ern find us, we do not . . . cannot let them leave . . ."

"It is as I said," muttered Karrol.

"Hush, can you not see this man wants to help?" hissed Jalex.

"This man is asleep," said Tak.

It was true. Tella's stubby chin lay upon his frail chest and he was snoring lightly.

"My Chief, you do not believe this story, do you?" Karrol pointed to the tent flap. "Those demons out there are not trying to help anyone. You did not see what happened after you were struck on the head. We were seized by warriors, threatened with their water weapons. They tied our feet together and forced us here. They . . . are . . . *demons!*"

"I agree that some things he said are false. A land with no sky? But there are parts of his story that sound true. You young folks don't remember the days of darkness and cold after Senfall. I do. Those times could turn good Ern into bad. Tak, your father's sister was killed by Ern of the valley. It was those days of cold and hunger that caused such things."

At this moment, the tent flap was pulled back. One of the guards peeked in and noted his sleeping, ancient leader. He motioned to the Ern with his weapon and whispered hoarsely.

"*Conunda . . . los!*"

He stood aside as Jalex and the others hobbled out the opening. When they had exited, he crept in and gently pulled Tella's fur wrap more snugly around the old man's shoulders.

The Ern were taken across the camp to a large, squarish tent. This one was guarded by two full hands of warriors, all of them armed with the strange spears and axes tipped with the water stones. The walls of the tent were also fortified with heavy, sharpened stakes driven into the ground on all sides. It seemed to be designed to keep whatever was inside – inside.

The guards stopped Jalex and the others at the entrance.

One of them pulled out a curious tool of some sort and applied it to the bindings on their ankles. The tight loops opened and released them. Karrol was watching for a chance to make a break for it, but the guards pressed close, weapons ready. Jalex knew what he was thinking and shook her head at him. They were then sent through the opening and into the tent.

The interior was surprisingly lit. Strange, shiny smooth objects hung from hooks in the ceiling. They glowed with warm light and emitted an oily aroma. At least five hands of Ern lay upon hide mats on the dirt floor. Many of them were coughing . . . and many of them lay disturbingly still.

Jalex moved slowly among the Ern. Most of them nodded to her grimly with a pitying look on their faces. She stopped in front of a woman who was caring for a very sick little boy. He was sweating profusely and his breath was raspy and painful. There were large red bulges on his neck. A hacking cough wracked his small body and the mother wiped a fresh spray of blood from his lips with a bit of hide.

Karrol did a double take as he recognized something familiar about the woman.

"My Chief! Her skin markings and hair . . . I have seen such before! On the woman my brother and I found. Her name was . . . was *Kray.*"

"You know of Kray? Is she safe?"

Karrol's face gave the woman the answer before he could speak.

"What is your name?" asked Jalex gently.

"I am Yeny. Kray is my sister," she said sadly. "She and her mate Goru were helping us cross the high plains to visit the clan of Derin in the mountains. We encountered many demons, who captured all of us. Goru fought them, but was struck down by one of their sharp ice axes. Kray escaped and ran away. A demon and his beast pursued, but I never saw her again. My son Bodie and I were brought to this place, as were many other Ern over many days. Some got sick right away and others much later. I thought we would not, but now Bodie is very sick. We are all very sick. Two more died last night. I do not know what to do."

"I am Jalex. May I help?"

Yeny looked at Jalex with eyes that had been cried out for some time. She had no more tears left, only a sense of hopelessness.

"I have herbs that may help. Let me try."

The woman's expression brightened slightly at this slim ray of hope. Jalex took her medicine pack, which she had been allowed to keep, from around her waist. When the Ma Kahy captured them, only their weapons were taken. She dug several pouches out and began her preparations. Other Ern in the tent sat up and watched the procedure.

"A wise woman!"

"She is a healer!"

"Help us!"

The tent was filled with desperate excitement now. Tak interposed herself between the Ern and her grandmother.

"Calm . . . calm yourselves. Chief Jalex is a skilled wise woman. She has ways to help. Let her do it."

Karrol and Auran assisted Tak with crowd control, while Jalex did her work. She knew of many ways to bring down a fever, which seemed to be the boy's worst symptom. She applied *penna root* and *tosta leaves* to his chest. She also had him drink a mixture of mushroom and vine flowers that was known to be soothing, but nothing was helping. This sickness fought back with the strength of a spearcat. Jalex worked on the boy and several others in the tent for two full days. She wanted for nothing. She already had all the herbs and medicines that she knew of and the Ma Kahy provided adequate food and sanitary care, furs, firewood, everything they needed. The only restriction was not being allowed to leave the tent.

Finally, with an inevitability that others in the tent were painfully familiar with, the young boy Bodie breathed his last. His mother Yeny, who had now become too ill herself to care for him anymore, howled in agony. Jalex, who had not slept the past two days, collapsed from exhaustion into Tak's arms. Tears of remorse creased her face.

"My Chief, you did everything you could. You did everything *any* wise woman could do."

Jalex looked up into the face of her granddaughter. Her still-sharp eyes noticed a tiny spot of blood on Tak's lip.

"I must find the answer . . . *I must!*"

Her exhaustion took over and Jalex's eyes closed in much-needed sleep.

CHAPTER 22

*Malday, Brel 5-21876 — Foxx has recovered
nicely. I have to say, this is the touchiest healing I have
ever attempted. Oh, I can set a broken bone and use
the herbs for fever and illness easily enough. But true
Eryndi healing — actually connecting on a spiritual
level, combining your own strength and essence with
your patient - that's a tough one. Unless you're an
Eryndi, of course.*

\- ORCHID'S JOURNAL

Today - Abakaar

"Follow me!"

Minore spun around, the armored fringes of her battle
skirt billowing out. Sensis and his squad of soldiers turned as
one and fell in behind. Group Six followed, Orchid helping
Foxx and Serena guarding their rear. The Queen's entourage led
them down a familiar corridor of the East Tower to the room
where Foxx had been attacked. It was heavily guarded by more
loyal soldiers who had also been divested of their tokens. The
double doors were opened and the giant tapestry hung before

them. It was curiously blank. When Orchid and Serena last saw it, a pastoral scene adorned it. Foxx had seen images of Treskan warfare woven into the fabric. Minore nodded to Sensis and he issued orders.

"Secure the room."

The soldiers took positions in the hall and the door was closed. Group Six started to join them, but was stopped by Minore.

"You may stay and observe if you wish. Consider it debt payment."

Foxx, Serena, and Orchid looked at each other with confusion at this cryptic remark, but said nothing.

"Sensis, you also will stay . . . consider it a benefit of your new position as Captain of my personal guard."

The soldier's mouth dropped for but a beat, then he snapped back to attention.

"My Queen . . . I live to serve!"

There goes my retirement.

Minore now moved before the tapestry and prepared herself to commune with Magic. The world of Lurra swam through a self-produced sea of metaphysical energy in its circular dance around Sensang, the eternal sun. A Magician of skill such as Queen Minore could tap into that envelope, bending it to her will, directing its processing power as she chose. She formed the image of Grand Vizier Rastaban in her mind along with the desire to know his location. Magical energies coalesced and filled the room, invisible to Serena and Sensis, but Orchid and Foxx picked up on it. It began with a far-reaching intuitive Magic. It took in the information that was sent into it and its natural organizational tendencies took over. It was not a plea or request of any kind to be granted by an intelligence. Magical energy processes because it is natural for it to do so. Once in full communion with that sphere, Minore summoned powerful kinetic forces. Both disciplines hovered about each other and finally merged to become one spell, giving the Queen the desired effect.

The great tapestry shivered as though chilly. All across its face, various colored threads unraveled themselves, moved about, changed places. The process accelerated, the threads re-weaving themselves into a totally different pattern. The plain pattern of like colors swam about and began to form a scene. An image of Zanteryne Castle from above took shape. The river, the surrounding city, and valley walls -- all were being drawn by the snaking colored threads. At last the spell was complete. A portrait of Rastaban surrounded by an ornate circular frame appeared above the river downstream of the castle. The rest of the scene had fully rendered and was still but this image of the Vizier was slowly moving, being carried on the backs of still quivering tapestry threads.

"There," said Minore, pointing. "He is fleeing. Sensis, order pursuit craft to intercept Rastaban's launch."

The new Captain hustled to the door and started snapping orders to the squad outside.

"Wait," came a voice still weakened by recovery efforts. "There is a manipulation . . . I can feel it." Foxx shrugged off Orchid's supportive arm and moved in front of the tapestry.

"It's the spell . . . like my own Knowing Spell. My Queen, it's infiltrating your own spell and creating a false effect."

Minore's opal eyes widened briefly in anger over such an outrageous notion.

"It was what I detected when we first came to this country. It was just a tickle at first, hardly there at all. My own mind was being dulled by it, so I had not the awareness to question it. As time went on, I began to recognize the pattern, so very similar to what I have taught myself to do, being sent out through the thousands of citizen's tokens that all your people wear. It made them think the same, feel the same. It was why everyone is so happy and content here, even those who would be malcontents or criminals anywhere else."

Minore's command voice softened a bit. "What would seem to be a ruler's greatest wish."

"And I am feeling that same spell at work among us here, Your Majesty. Much more powerful and directed at your spell and the tapestry."

"Are you saying that the locator image of Rastaban is not as it should be?"

"Correct, My Queen. I believe it is a diversion. The Vizier is elsewhere, but he is using his spell to influence yours and change the result."

Minore stared silently at her personal construct that had guided her decisions over the many years that Rastaban had been here. If he had been altering the impressions from the tapestry and hence interfering with her plans, especially those involving military force . . .

"We must find him . . . commit a single craft only downriver after this . . . image . . . just to make sure. The rest of the loyal forces must begin a search immediately."

"Yes, My Queen."

Foxx had retreated and was quietly concentrating. "Your Majesty, I may be able to help. I have no way of knowing where Rastaban is, but I might be able to find out where this spell is coming from."

"By all means."

Foxx closed his eyes and focused on the familiar feel of what he called his Knowing Spell. He used the passive mode, similar to what he did when playing Four-Card Blitzkrieg. He was not trying to control or influence the person on the other end of the spell. He did not wish to draw attention to himself at all. It was meant to learn the emotional state of his opponent. Were they overjoyed at having a good hand, or fearful and likely to bluff or fold? What he was picking up now was a sense of bemused superiority.

It was all so very easy.
Done this so many times before.
She can be re-educated easily enough.
The Game is not lost.

There! That was the thought that was driving the caster of this spell. Whoever it was, and Foxx assumed that had to be Rastaban, was most concerned with some sort of game he was playing. Maintaining control over Minore and this country was crucial to that aim. Foxx narrowed his vision upon this desire and began to get a sense of direction and distance. His eyes opened slowly.

"My Queen, the spell is coming from within the Castle." He turned slowly toward the tapestry, hand out.

"Here."

The area he was pointing to showed a small, relatively new-looking tower just below the main East Tower where they were now.

"Rastaban's tower," sneered the Queen. "I have had it searched many times, but never found anything but the man's private living quarters. I cannot believe he would be so foolish as to think to hide in his own chambers. Well, we shall see. *Captain!*"

"My Queen."
"Bring your men. We go to visit the Vizier this day."

* * *

Old star, old star, you were so good to us,
Smiling down from mighty perch;
So lonely we shall be, she says;
The feet and fins and wings that stay shall miss your friendly
  play;
Not us, not us, not us, said the few that got to go;
To the night dances in the sky among rainstorms of stars;
Some of us to little home, some of us to big.
Minor opened arms and said, Come let's play;
Arkship, arkship, why do you weep so?
Cry, cry, cry, fuss, fuss, fuss;
Segonallar Major teases you so.
Shuttle, shuttle, shuttle, shuttle;
Cover your face, cover your face.
Major and Minor have to do it, too;
Cold and dust and naught to drink.
Someday someday, we'll join again and have another picnic.
Anybody home?

\- Translation of children's song
Our New Home into native Ern language.
Written and performed by Tella Maneret on
the occasion of the funeral of Frader Maneret,
his father. (Note: phrasing, meter, and
rhyme necessarily distorted)

Not quite 50,000 years ago

Jalex floated in a sea of dreams, dreams that feinted and probed in the form of a tiny spider battling a large wasp in her web, patiently trying to get in a bite without being bitten back by wakefulness. Her mind was that wasp, weary and obsessed with searching for a cure. She was trapped amongst repetitive visions and thoughts. Images that seemed relevant, yet not. Her herb pouch, opening and closing by itself and exposing all the little separate parcels she had assembled over the years. Now they were unfamiliar, but endlessly repeating in a one-by-one manner. In her semi-conscious state, Jalex knew such things were unimportant and played no part in her quest, but the dance of herbs would not stop repeating. Accompanying them were snatches of phrases and sounds: the crackle of the fire, the tent flap, some common words that her guards used much. Even Karrol's grumbling about their 'demon captors' would not stop repeating in her mind. It kept her from getting the rest she needed, but somewhere in the tumult was commonality. Something was saying to her that this disease was no different than many other afflictions that she had seen amongst the Ern. Lung rot was stubborn but could be treated, or at least eased by certain poultices. Young children suffered frequently from rashes and hives and could be treated with a brew or paste of bitterleaves. At last the spider withdrew its endless mind dance as she was fully awakened by the sound of loud coughing. Her eyes snapped open as she realized it was Tak. Jalex pulled herself to her feet and rushed to the side of her granddaughter.

"How long have you been like this?"

"It started last night after you retired, Grandmother. It just won't . . ."

Tak was interrupted by another rasping bout of coughs, each one leaving a spray of blood upon her hand. Jalex ordered her to lie on her side and try to remain as still as possible. Her heart ached as she saw the young, vital woman slipping further away as she had seen so many of the other Ern in the tent do. With each coughing spasm, Jalex felt a spear go through her own chest. Her head dipped in sorrow. The coughing subsided for a moment, giving her a slight break.

Then a tiny bit of relief. For a moment, for just a moment, Jalex's spirit lifted and the slightest of smiles curled her lip. It had naught to do with Tak or anyone else in the tent. No image formed, no voice uttered a word, but something good had just occurred back home in the valley concerning her son, Tarl. Not an unfamiliar occurrence at all. Whenever those closest to her underwent an important or extreme experience, Jalex knew of it. Not the details, just the feelings that went with it. It could be anything. There could have been a successful hunt or the birth of a baby, even the gratification of a good meal. That's all it took. What happens to an Ern happens to all Ern in some minute way. Her love and closeness to her son amplified it, of course. The closeness and connection that Ern had to themselves and the world around them was a source of great strength. In times of stress and hardship, Ern could usually find a way to survive together.

Connection . . .

That's it . . . the one factor needed to fight this affliction.

Jalex stood and gathered her medicine pack. She took a careful inventory of her remaining supplies and separated out the ones she wanted. She also made a request to her Ma Kahy guards for a few other specifics, as well as asking for samples of as many different fresh fruits, grains, and vegetables as they might have. Most of them grumbled in a surly manner, possibly because they simply did not know what she was saying. There were a few of the Ma Kahy who could understand a smattering of her words and gestures and managed to scrape together most of what she wanted. Finally, she set the cooking pot over the fire pit to boiling. Everything was together and ready. Jalex took a deep breath and stood amongst the dying Ern in the tent. She knew what had to be done.

"My sisters, my brothers . . . it is time to end this suffering. It is time to return to the world of light and health. But I need your help. I need all of you to help me in this. *Are you ready?*"

Today - Abakaar

Rastaban's assistant was just exiting the Vizier's chambers with a tray of empty dishes from the Midday meal when the floor began vibrating beneath his feet, strengthening with every beat. His eyes widened to pie plates as he beheld Queen Minore in full battle gear followed by a score of soldiers equally armed. He had no words and no other choice but to stand aside as they strode past him to the locked doors. Even though he possessed the key around his neck, the soldiers didn't demand it from such a non-person. Sensis and another brute simply seized the handles and wrenched them open with hardly a grunt. The intruders began pouring through into the room and the little man made the wise decision to not get involved. He quickly scurried past the trailing three citizens who gave him a bemused look as he passed.

"I think someone might be out of a job," said Orchid.

"The spell is still being cast," said Foxx. His eyes closed briefly as he intensified his concentration. "In fact . . . *it's increasing*. Rastaban is ramping up the power. He's putting a huge boost on the token control spell!"

"What does that mean?" asked Serena.

For an answer, from the lower levels of Zanteryne Castle came the unmistakable sound of yelling, charging soldiers.

"My Queen! Attack coming from the rear!"

Foxx and Orchid were not sure if Serena's warning was true or not, but she tended to have an instinct for this kind of thing, so they got the hell out of the way. She immediately drew her curved scimitar and took up a battle stance. Minore and the soldiers joined them a beat later and formed up. The hallway then filled with charging soldiers of the Abakaarian Defense Force, each of the attackers wearing their citizen's tokens that were brightly glowing red with power. Serena's fearsome battle cry echoed through the halls and she launched herself first into the fray. Her speed was amazing. Serena fought unarmored, as was her wont. Before any of the attackers could swing a weapon, the Northlands Warrior made a flying leap into the horde, which put one down immediately with a cloven collarbone and a second one clutching a deep wound to his thigh. The spurting blood meant he would bleed out within a minute.

The attacking soldiers pressed forward to be met by the Queen's loyalists. The corridor was narrow and only about three abreast could fight at a time. The close quarters made for messy work. Serena's scimitar was longer than the double-edged swords the Abakaarians carried and there wasn't much room to swing once the battle was fully engaged. She used her speed to best effect. Every time an enemy swung or stabbed at her, she was not there. She whirled and thrust, somersaulted out of the way of a blow aimed at her midsection, recovered and counterattacked in the same motion. For his trouble the man had his jawbone nearly severed from an upswing of Serena's sword.

Steel blades clashed against steel armor. Three of Sensis's men went down in the first rush, but they gave as good as they got. The attackers lost men too, as sword points sought out the unarmored faces and limbs. Sensis swung a tremendous blow that caught an enemy right on the side of his battle helmet. The blade cut cleanly through the steel and lodged in the man's temple. His sword was pulled from his hand as the man dropped to the ground like a sack of stones.

Queen Minore, glorious in her dazzling armor, waded right in with her soldiers, scoring several telling hits. Her black braids whirled about, the steel barbs raking across unarmored faces. In addition to her swordsmanship, the queen fought with Magic. Bursts of flame erupted among the attackers, blinding and burning them. The battle would have seemed to be on the side of the loyalists, but for the fact that the attackers with the glowing tokens seemed inexhaustible. For every one cut down, another five came racing up the hall to replace them. And Minore's forces were down by a quarter now. Still they fought valiantly on. A united push of Sensis's troops drove the attackers back into the corridor for a precious moment.

"Soldiers! Rally behind me!" shouted the Queen. Serena leapt back with the rest, extending the point of her sword behind her as she did, resulting in a lost eyeball for an attacker.

Minore stood focused for a beat. Her speed in summoning Magic was most impressive to Foxx and Orchid, who, being not much good in an all-out melee like this, had retreated behind some pillars. When outdoors, Orchid was an imposing foe. In this stone room, without even a potted plant or a window, there was little for a practitioner of Worldly Magic to do. Foxx's Influential Magic was useless in a fight as well. The Queen's spell was launched at once. Just as the attacking troops started forward, a tremendous wall of kinetic force blasted them back, flinging bodies against bodies. Over forty Macai projectiles shot back down the corridor, their armor and loose weapons creating as much mayhem as if they had been wielded by an enemy. The spell came to a close, leaving a long smear of gore along the walls.

"Seal the doors."

Sensis nodded to his remaining troops, while nursing a deep wound in his forearm. They closed the broken double doors to Rastaban's quarters and braced them shut with whatever materials they could find. Orchid had already come out and started tending to the wounded.

Minore looked around at the room. Aside from the single divan, the lack of any other chairs struck her as odd. There were few items devoted to leisure or comfort save for the curious water pipe and decanter. A shelf containing books and scrolls on philosophy and politics, astronomical charts and instruments, maps of the country, a chair-less desk with paperwork depicting Eryndi populations and deployment as workers, clothing in the closet, toiletries. All the normal possessions of a man who aided in the running of a country, but very little else.

A slight sound of groaning and shuffling about began outside in the corridor as the few soldiers who had survived were pulling themselves together. Whether they were in any kind of fighting trim was for no one to say.

"Your Majesty, the spell is still being broadcast," said Foxx. "I would say we should expect another attack as soon as reinforcements can be summoned."

"The traitor is not here," snarled Minore. "Where is it coming from?"

Foxx's focus was pulled to the wall opposite the doors. There was only the small shelf where the decanter and a few other glass items sat.

"Behind here, My Queen."

"Then let us see what is behind there!" She angrily swept the bottles onto the stone floor, shattering them. Her opaline eyes burned bright and soon, so did the stone wall. Minore concentrated on the thin mortar between the stones, which burned away quickly, but there was something much more resistant on the other side. White hot sparks shot out from between the blocks, and by the smell, they were now burning through something other than mortar. The pinpoint of intense heat she had summoned moved slowly, following the pattern of the stones.

"Here they come again!" shouted Serena, peeking through the barricaded doors.

Another large wave of soldiers, many of them armed with crossbows and spears and fully under the control of their boosted, glowing tokens, was plunging down the corridor, outnumbering the depleted defenders five to one. This time, it looked like nothing could stop them.

CHAPTER 23

It has been more than six Segonallar years (nearly seven Casal years) since landing here. There has been no trace of syndrome among the colonists, at least the groups we did not lose contact with. Unfortunately, contact with the indigenous Ern has proved disastrous. It would have at first seemed the screening procedures were ineffective. Even a brief interaction initiates a condition highly resembling syndrome. But now, after years of research, I have determined that the disease did not, in fact, accompany us. The energy being released into the atmosphere by the destruction of Arkship is mutating a common rinovirus inherent in our systems. I begin to wonder if perhaps the syndrome on Casal was caused by something similar. Vorennium power had been used for decades on the homeworld. By itself the virus is relatively harmless and not dissimilar to many indigenous strains here on Segonallar Major. The Ern, unfortunately, have no resistance to it. It is my great fear that our arrival on this world may spell genocide for those fascinating people who evolved here. Of course, if the terrible climatic conditions caused

Not quite 50,000 years ago

"Ern!" called Jalex to the sickly in the tent. "Do you hear me?"

There was a murmur of voices, many very weak.

"Yes." . . . "I hear." . . . "Yes."

"You *must* hear me! *Do you hear me!?*"

"We hear you . . . we hear you."

"Do you feel me? *Do you FEEL me!?*"

"We feel you!"

"And I feel you. I feel your pain, your fear. That is good. That we are together is good."

As Jalex spoke, she slowly began to gather her special herbs and medicines and add them to the boiling pot. She continued to commune with her sick charges while the medicine cooked. At last she picked up pieces of the fruits and vegetables one at a time and held them up for all to see.

"This is a *flava* stalk. You all know it. You have picked it, you have eaten it, it is part of the world that sustains you, is it not?"

"Yes, yes."

"Feel the flava stalk. It is part of the world, it is part of you. Do you feel the connection with the flava?"

"Yes, yes."

Jalex dropped the vegetable sample into the broth and picked up another.

"This is eyepod. Very tasty. It grows from the ground, as do all plants. Do you know the eyepod? Do you feel the eyepod?"

"Yes, yes."

One by one, each of the vegetables and fruits were displayed to the sick and added to the broth. Bits of dried morok and milkbeast meat were also added, as well as a variety of birds and fish. The entire tent was in a light trance by now, in full communion with this wise woman who was bringing them and their world together.

At last, Jalex was satisfied. She gave the pot a final stir and transferred the broth to a bowl. She went to each person in the tent, spooning out doses. The herbs made for a bitter taste, but taking a taste herself, she could tell it was it was exactly what was needed, but for the final ingredient.

"My Ern . . . we are now all as close as any family can be. We are one. That is strength. Such strength is what we need to defeat the sickness. We are part of this world . . . sickness is among us in this world. Our strength, our *connection* to all around us . . . to each other . . . to the food we eat . . . the water we drink . . . the air we breathe . . . can rid us of sickness. We in this tent are as family. We are as one. Even now, the medicine is fighting the sickness. Alone it would fail. But we can help it. It needs our *strength*. I know some of you are weak from sickness. But it can be fought. That's it. Feel it. Feel the health returning to your bodies. You must have strength! Strength and all our world gives you! My Ern . . . feel the strength in this tent, the strength of those around you. Feel *my* strength! Use it! Use my strength. Add my strength to your own! Gain all I have. And when you have it, reach out. Reach out to your own families, your own clans, your own tribes . . . everyone you can. And they must reach out as well. We must spread this connection to all Ern everywhere. That's it. Use what you have learned. We are Ern! We are as one! Use it! Use it! . . . *USE IT!*"

Jalex stood silent for a moment, her arms raised, her eyes closed, her open lips trembling slightly. The Chief of all the Valley Ern slowly went to her knees, then sank gently to the ground.

Today - Abakaar

The defenders were fighting heroically, but were slowly losing ground to the ranks of attacking soldiers that continued to surge up the corridor toward the barricaded chambers of Rastaban. Four more loyalists were now either dead or incapacitated. Nearly all the remaining half of their original force were sporting wounds, including Serena, who had taken a deep slash in the calf from a half-parried spear thrust. Foxx and Orchid helped out where they could, whether it was maintaining the barricade of furniture and the now-shattered doors or helping wounded defenders. The red tokens on the breasts of the attackers continued to glow brightly, imparting to them what Serena would call almost a berserker rage. They were frothing at the mouth, wild-eyed with bloodlust in their attacks.

Minore's spellcasting power could not be spared from burning into the walls where Foxx said the spell was originated. That evil Magic controlling the soldiers had to be stopped at all costs. She kept her focus on maintaining her white-hot pinpoint spell. Whatever it was burning through on the other side of the stone blocks was no ordinary armor.

One of the attackers, in a suicidal leap, catapulted himself over the writhing pile of his fellow soldiers into the front of the fray. He quickly leveled his crossbow and fired from the hip directly at the back of Queen Minore. One quarter of a beat after his finger touched the trigger, his head was separated from his body by a lightning-fast swing of Serena's scimitar. He never knew the result of his shot. Sensis, the new Captain of the Queen's Guard, had been pulled back and was being tended by Orchid for a half-score of serious wounds in every extremity. His experienced eyes saw the danger and despite his weakness, he wrenched himself out of her healing arms and heaved his body upwards. The crossbow bolt buried itself deep in his chest with a dull thunk.

"For . . . the QUEEN!"

The old soldier dropped down and breathed his last breath with a slight smile on his face. The sight of their fallen Captain spurred the rest of the defenders to action. They responded with a flurry of blows that not only kept the attackers out of the room, but actually drove them back for a moment. The narrowness of the corridor helped, but even so, it would be but a temporary victory with the odds against them.

"My Queen!" exclaimed Foxx. "The spell . . ."

"GET BACK!" shouted Minore simultaneously. She flung herself to the side just in time as stone blocks exploded outward, shattering against the far wall and off the bodies of soldiers, both dead and alive. Brilliant rays of the late aftermidday sun began to filter into the room through the settling dust. It appeared the whole western half of Rastaban's little tower had blown away. A strange, bronze-colored shape was slowly moving up and out of the wreckage. It was strangely organic looking, but obviously artificial, hovering against the backdrop of the blue Abakaarian sky. As large as a small river taxi, it resembled a curved leech with strange protuberances

like spider spinnerets at each smoothly tapered end. It hovered vertically, its bottom half revealing a burned hole half the size of a man, obviously the result of Queen Minore's spell. A head and shoulders appeared and the bearded face of Grand Vizier Rastaban scrutinized them with his coal-black eyes.

Minore, stunned by the explosion, looked blearily up at the strange sight. Before she could even get to her feet, let alone pull herself together to cast a spell, an eruption of yellowish Magic power rushed from the neck of one of the protrusions on the bottom half of the object. It struck the queen, enveloping her for a beat. Her body tensed in agony and very nearly crumpled.

Serena had seen this before. The bizarre rock crawlers she had encountered in the zone attacked with a weapon just like this. The spinneret began to glow again. She leapt forward to defend the queen and caught the second burst on the blade of her sword. The impact knocked the weapon from her hands and she lay back, stunned, both arms numb to the shoulder, just as it had happened in the zone.

Yep, same thing, all right.

Queen Minore was struggling to get her wits about her. The beginnings of an offensive spell started forming in her mind, but before she could bring it off, another burst of evil, yellow light shot from the craft and struck her. Every nerve in her body was on fire and every muscle tensed, her mouth frozen in a silent scream.

"Good aftermidday, My Gracious Queen."

Rastaban's oily voice dripped with the venom of a needle snake.

"And a good day to the rest of you. I trust you are enjoying your brief stay in Abakaar."

Foxx had emerged relatively unscathed from behind a pillar and was pulling Orchid out from beneath some rubble. She was alive and coughing and covered in a thick coating of rock dust.

"That light . . . the same . . . the same as . . ." stammered Serena.

"Yes, my warrior friend," replied Rastaban. "There is much to learn from the creatures in the vorennium zone. But I'm afraid I have little time for discussion at the moment. There is much to be done. Control must be reestablished."

"Your control can be broken," shouted Foxx. "We've proven that much!"

One of the loyalist soldiers started painfully pulling himself upright from the debris and reaching for a discarded crossbow. Rastaban's black eyes flickered briefly toward him for a moment.

"My dear Master Foxx, you were supposed to die. Can you do nothing right? Perhaps you remember this item."

Rastaban pulled one hand from inside his opposite red silk sleeve. It clutched an object vaguely like a tapered hammer grip ending in a thin tube. A small movement of the Vizier's thumb and a very thin, red beam instantly appeared from the tube. A tiny flick of his wrist and the beam moved down through the top of the soldier's helmet all the way to his armored crotch. Two halves of the loyalist, each holding half a crossbow, fell in opposite directions.

"Usually, just a single pulse shot is sufficient. A sustained beam such as that consumes more power, but how I do love dramatic impact!"

Rastaban demonstrated his passion by random passes about the room. Stone and furniture and bodies were bisected, causing more of the ceiling and walls to collapse. Foxx, Orchid, and Serena did their best to shield themselves from the falling debris. By now, most of the remains of the tower were exposed to the open air. At last Rastaban ceased firing and leveled his weapon at Minore, who still lay weakly on the floor. With a bloody scuff on her gorgeous brown cheek, she pulled herself up onto one elbow and glared back defiantly at this evil man she had trusted for so long.

"And now, My Gracious Queen, it is time to destroy you all and repair this insignificant, though irksome, setback you have caused me."

Just as Rastaban's thumb began to move toward the trigger, a high-pitched whistle sounded from above. A glowing Magical sphere of heat and kinetic energy hurtled from the sky trailing sparks and smoke. The fist-sized projectile struck the Vizier's weapon and erupted in a small but violent explosion. Rastaban disappeared behind a cloud of smoke. A beat later, a second projectile was launched into the opening of the strange craft and also exploded, ejecting fire and smoke. Those in the room looked up and beheld a hovering figure. There was no mistaking the long, pointed chin, the cone-shaped ears, and the chubby belly.

"*TRESADO!*"

Foxx whooped like a circus daredevil rider at the sight of his friend.

"Hi, guys, good to see you!" the Eryndi yelled back, cracking his knuckles. "But we've still got a bit of work to do!"

"*You bet we do!*" shouted Orchid. This open air was just what she needed. Her Worldly Magic went to work and summoned a violent little tornado that enveloped the hovering craft, buffeting and twisting it. Short bursts of lightning followed, striking into the opening and onto the outer skin.

"And you shall not deprive your Queen of . . . how shall I say it? Getting in a few licks of my own!"

Tornadoes and lightning and kinetic bombs and bursts of fire Magic blasted and pummeled Rastaban's strange object. Foxx even threw a rock at it. Pieces came off, holes appeared, but ultimately, the floating craft leveled itself and painfully rose into the sky, slowly picking up speed and disappearing over the limb of the canyon wall to the north. The dust settled and the smoke cleared. On the floor lay the melted, smoking remains of Rastaban's weapon. Clutching the handle was a charred hand and wrist still bearing a gold bracelet set with a red ruby.

Tresado lowered himself in his invisible harness to light on his feet. Foxx and Orchid bearhugged him and even Serena planted a big kiss on his cheek.

"Ahem."

"Oh, forgive me," said Foxx, immediately adopting a formal tone. "My Queen, may I present our friend and traveling companion, Tresado of Ostica. Tresado, I present you to Queen Minore, Ruler and Sovereign of the Country and Valley of Abakaar."

Tresado wasn't sure of exact protocol, but he gave a low bow that seemed to be sufficient. Minore regarded him carefully. His Eryndi features were not something she had been accustomed to seeing the last several years. Since Rastaban's arrival, the nature of interracial relations had changed. She now realized that Eryndi had been separated and shielded from most citizens' eyes and relegated to little more than slave labor. Despite her new knowledge of how they had all been manipulated, it was still a strange sensation to stand face-to-face with what had been considered a lesser being. After a few beats, she extended both hands and gripped Tresado about his soft shoulders.

"My friend, I owe you nothing less than my life and the safety of my realm . . . to all of you," she beamed to the rest. "And you shall find me grateful."

* * *

Rest in Bed of Yearned Deed,
Wrapped in Soft Contentment;
Sleep, My Gentle Mother,
Thy Children E'er Nurtured . . .

- TRIANNA OF SYLVAS, POETESS TO THE GLADES

Not quite 50,000 years ago

The disease had sloughed away from the Ern like the dried husks of feather nettles in the wind. And they *knew.* As Jalex had imparted to them, they now all *knew* it had worked, that the sickness could be stopped.

There was no sadness, no remorse. Only great gratitude and respect. All knew. All the Ern knew that this was what she wanted. This was what she had voyaged out of the valley to do. She herself had known it at the time.

The body of Chief Jalex was reverently gathered up and wrapped in furs. A litter was fabricated for transport back to her beloved valley.

The Ma Kahy that guarded the tent had oddly drifted away. Tak and the others paid them little mind while tending to their own. They were making final preparations to return to the valley when a strange processional approached them. Several Ma Kahy were solemnly leading four of their riding beasts, which in their *dermot* they called *horses*. The animals were tethered to a bizarre construction: a platform of poles that sat on top of two round wooden objects that strangely turned as the horses pulled it along. There was a wrapped bundle secured on the object.

A familiar Ma Kahy man signaled for them to stop and approached the Ern. He had no weapons and raised his hand in a sign of peace.

"Parolan," he said, pointing at his own chest.

Tak repeated the gestures and recited her own name, as well as introducing Karrol and Auran.

Parolan pointed to the bundle. "Tella, Tella *du* . . . *uh,* Tella is . . . die. Tella . . . last . . . last, *uh,* old from . . . Primerallar."

"The last from First Home?" Tak asked.

"Yes. Yes. . . . Tella want Ma Kahy . . . and Ern . . . *trazos,*" he said hesitantly, while clapping his hands together.

"Tella wanted the Ma Kahy and the Ern to be . . . *together . . . or friends?*" replied Karrol.

"Yes . . . *friends.* Friends in . . . alive, friends in die. Tella want you take."

Parolan took the leads of the animals and handed them to Karrol. "Take horses, take *cart.* Tella and Jalex . . . *trazos* in die." Once again, he clasped his hands.

Tak understood. All that was needed was a simple farewell bow and a *yes.*

"We shall take them both back to the valley." Tak and Auran lifted Jalex's body onto the cart alongside the body of Tella and turned to leave. Karrol remained a moment longer with Parolan.

"What will Ma Kahy do?"

"*Unh?*"

Karrol pointed to the people in the camp, who seemed to be packing up to leave.

"Ma Kahy . . . where?" He gestured in all directions.

"Ah. Ma Kahy . . . look . . . find . . . *gotema llar . . . uh,* home good. Water good, food good . . . *hava* . . . make . . . Ma Kahy place."

Karrol's eyes narrowed. Despite what had happened, he had little trust in these strangers. Tella had seemed to be a caring, thoughtful man. But these others were of a different generation. Despite what Tella had said, they were warriors and well-armed. He thought of his lush and fertile valley and what a tempting home it might make for these . . . *beings.*

"I, Karrol, say this. You are strange people; you bring strange beasts, strange tools, strange ideas. I fear for Ern . . . *and for Ma Kahy,*" he added with emphasis. "What will happen?"

He didn't know how much of that Parolan understood, but he left him with it and turned to join Tak and Auran, leading the horses along.

The horses and cart made the journey much easier. Within a few days, they returned to where the river exited the valley. The walls rose on each side until they were back to where the one-time Clan of Tarben, of which Karrol was the sole survivor, had tried to make a home. They guided the cart with its sacred cargo to the Cave of the Dead. There, the bodies of Jalex and Tella were laid face-down with clasped hands and wrapped together in furs along with carved icons representing their ancestors, a layer of coba flowers, and bundles of food to be feasted upon. The two *friends in death,* as Parolan had called them, were lowered into the giant cave to lie together as companions and fellow Chiefs for all time.

CHAPTER 24

Today – 300 leagues west of Abakaar

It wasn't the best road on Lurra. There were rough spots and a few washouts on the road to the Land of Yenna. But the ride was as smooth as twenty-year-old *Patria,* aged in the keg, which was exactly what Orchid was sipping on. The luxury coach bearing the royal crest of Minore of Abakaar had been but one of the lavish gifts granted to Group Six for their heroism in defending Queen and Realm. Elaborate leaf springs and cushioned wheels floated the now open-carriage along as if it were Magic. In fact, it was Magic. Permanently implanted kinetic spells in the frame added to the stability. Behind the rig rode a matching trailer, which bore chests and boxes filled with supplies of all kinds, gourmet foods, a triple-redundant stock of spirits, and lots and lots of money.

The only flaw was its color. Like everything Rastaban had controlled, the coach was painted a scarlet red. It normally would have been very striking, but Group Six had had enough of red lately.

"Maybe when we get to Tresk, we should have it repainted," said Tresado.

"Maybe like a nice forest green," offered Orchid.

"With metallic flakes and some gold pin striping," added Foxx.

"Yeah, and you could add pink ribbons and dingle balls too," said Serena in her usual sarcastic tone.

Foxx, whose turn it was to drive, gave the reins a slight twitch, goading the matching team of four magnificent white horses just a wee bit faster.

"Getting kind of warm," he called back to Tresado and Orchid. "You want to put the top up?"

"I like the Senlight," replied Tresado. "I didn't get much of that during our stay in Abakaar."

"Yeah, me too," yawned Orchid lazily. "Drive on, my good man, drive on."

"How about you, Serena?" Foxx called ahead. "Sure you don't want to ride in the coach for a bit?"

The Northlands Warrior turned to face her companions behind her. As she did, the aftermidday Senlight caught the magnificent diamond embedded in her sternum, firing off brilliant glints of color.

"I'm fine where I am. My butt wasn't made to sit on soft pillows."

"I know, you've said it before," said Foxx. "You're happy to be back in a saddle again."

In answer, Onyx, the spirited warhorse she had been given, snorted in defiance, as if itching to get into a scrape as much as his rider. Serena, like the others, was sporting new clothes—though not garish like Foxx's outfit. Hers was a sky blue, form-fitting jerkin made of the finest doe suede decorated with silver-threaded edging. It was, of course, cut low to properly display both her jewel and impressive cleavage.

Slung across her back was a splendid short bow that, among the four of them, only her muscles could draw, and a quiver of arrows. At her left hip swung her familiar, razor-sharp scimitar with the layered pattern in its deadly blade.

Tresado shielded his eyes and pointed to the south. "You can't see it from here, but Witchheart Crater is that way. It's huge. When I saw it even from a high altitude, I couldn't make out the whole thing."

"And, according to that map I found, the zone that surrounds it is even bigger," added Orchid.

"Nasty place . . . that raw power shooting up into the clouds. When I was in there, it was so . . . confusing. I couldn't . . . connect. I wasn't even sure which direction was which. Unsettling for an Eryndi."

"That reminds me," said Foxx. "Rastaban called it something odd. What was it he said . . . the *vorniam zone?*"

"Something like that," nodded Orchid. "I didn't quite catch it."

"I still don't remember much about what happened in there," said Foxx.

Tresado scrunched up his face, trying to think. "Same here. I just remember being there and feeling really powerful . . ."

Orchid wasn't having any better luck. "And there were some very strange forms of life in there . . ."

"It gives me a headache just to think about it," said Foxx.

"Then best not think. You might hurt yourself," interjected Serena, changing the subject. "Tresado, I been meaning to ask, how did you manage to be right where we needed you in the nick of time?"

"Yeah, that's not like me at all, is it?" he replied sarcastically. "Actually, I think you can blame Foxx. Remember that day at the charging station when we ran into one another? You gave me some kind of a mental boost, didn't you? After you guys left, I just kept thinking about my situation. My confidence improved and I started thinking that the whole Eryndi thing in that country wasn't quite fair. I still accepted it, though. But on the day of the battle something happened. Soldiers all around suddenly got real antsy and were shouting about having to get to the castle. Something big was going on. Right about then I seemed to snap out of it completely. My token went dark and I was myself again."

"From what I found out later, the same thing happened all over Abakaar," interrupted Foxx. "I wager that, when Rastaban sent out the power surge on the controlling spell to the soldiers, there wasn't enough left to continue controlling the rest of the population. He lost his grip on everybody in favor of super-control on the military."

Tresado nodded. "He must've figured once he had gotten rid of Minore, he could spread it out again and restore everybody to the mindless contentment. Probably install some puppet ruler in her place. Anyway, to answer your question, I knew something big was happening at the castle. Pretty soon I could sense all the Magic being flung around. Naturally, I figured you troublemakers were in the middle of it somehow, so I just zipped over there to see what was going on."

"He built a castle of cards," Foxx continued. "Rastaban was collecting people into the country, as many as he could. It had something to do with whatever game he seemed to be playing. Kind of like amassing points or tokens or something. Maybe it made his position stronger. The more people he brought in, the more there were to control. If there was a glitch, it increased the chances of something failing. I still can't fathom how he could control thousands of people. The amount of Magic needed would be staggering."

"So, what caused the glitch?" asked the ever-curious Tresado.

"Well, in all modesty . . . *me.*"

Orchid choked a bit with a near spit take on this remark.

"My Knowing Spell was so similar to his that I was able to recognize and fight it."

"That's why he shot you," said Serena.

"I guess he figured that once I was out of the way and not causing ripples, he could reestablish full control."

"So, you gonna take credit for foiling his whole plan and saving the day?" asked Orchid.

"I'd love to. You know my fondness for taking a bow, but I'm afraid this time I have to share billing with the rest of you. Each of you came through in your own way."

"At least Rastaban is dead now," said Serena with a sneer.

"Is he? That floating worm of his must have been controlled by someone," said Orchid.

"Not necessarily," said Tresado. "It could have been Magically coded to retreat on its own, a lifeboat. Not that hard."

"Aw, he's dead," chuckled Serena grimly. "With the pounding that thing took, what was left of him must've ended up a red smear of jelly . . . all but his hand. Minore kept it as a trophy and had it displayed in her receiving hall. I love that woman!"

"If he *was* playing a game," mused Orchid, "unless it was solitaire, that implies he had an opponent."

"Or *opponents,*" added Tresado.

Foxx narrowed his eyes. "So, *who* is he playing against? And for what stakes?"

Today - Abakaar

At the very moment Group Six was considering this question, Queen Minore was thinking about them, those four foreign oddballs to whom she owed so much. Naturally she had invited them to stay in Abakaar as honored citizens. But they had all expressed a wish to get on the road, Foxx especially. That little charmer had tickled her fancy more than she liked to admit and the thought of his touch sent royal quivers up her spine and elsewhere. The Queen would lament his departure.

It wasn't just Foxx. Orchid would have been of immense benefit to the healing arts in Abakaar. To Serena, Minore had offered the position of Captain of the Guard to take over for the heroic Sensis. And Tresado, the hook . . .

No, Tresado the Eryndi, she corrected herself. *This will take a while.*

He could have been instrumental in healing some very deep wounds in her land. But the queen reluctantly granted their wish and bid Group Six good journeys. They were on their way to the Treskan Imperium. Foxx had expressed a desire to see the Eastern Provinces, which were apparently not as hostile or as close as the vile Rastaban had tricked them all into believing. Group Six had been gone for a week now.

Eight days is plenty of time for that lot to get into trouble.

A whim seized her. Queen Minore rose from among her throng of retainers and advisors in the middle of an audience and headed for the tapestry room to check up on her saviors.

Meanwhile, 1000 leagues away
at the Crystal Palace

The blue crystal doors to the Steward's sanctum flew open. Jakundarana Slivershkanent Trystelliar hustled out, sticking a wad of spent chewing gum to the wall and replacing it with two fresh pieces. The lights in the room as well as throughout the entire palace were flaring in brightness and color. Bells and whistles sounded and many of the self-operated Magical gambling machines in the casino and exhibition hall paid off in silver coins, bringing grins to the wrinkled faces of little old ladies. Gleam the Dragon, on his perch above, unfolded his massive silver wings and let loose a joyous roar for what reason, nobody knew.

"Sparkly . . . SPARKLY!"

Jakki's aide tripped on the leg of his chair rushing to answer the call, but did not get too badly bruised.

"Yes, Boss."

"Gather the Principal Casters. Have them begin a communing at once. Someone somewhere has cast a spell involving Group Six. The Palace has detected images and a probable locus. We've got to help it tap in and retrieve the exact coding."

Sparkly scurried out, speaking rapidly into his seashell *converser.*

Jakki looked about at the blue walls around her.

"Well done, my friend . . . well done."

Today – 300 leagues west of Abakaar

"You'll like the Imperium," said Foxx. "I have to admit that Abakaar was a pretty nice place, but there's something about a huge empire. I've only been to the capital, Tresk, and a couple of other nearby cities, but there is something for everyone. People from all the provinces, every shape and color you can think of. The weirdest and most exotic food you can imagine, fabrics and inventions that just defy descriptions. Tresado, specialist Magicians in disciplines you've never even thought of. And then, of course, there's the arena. Tens of thousands of people watching gladiators and Magicians square off against criminals and captives, wild beasts, dragons, even each other. A lot of it isn't my game, but the gambling is great. Serena, you think the Abakaarian Defense Force was impressive? I once saw a full legion marching twelve abreast down the Arterio Treska. Ten thousand Eryndi Legionnaires all in perfect step."

"Off to conquer somebody else's country, no doubt?" This from Orchid, who tended to be a damper sometimes, to Foxx's annoyance.

"Well, I guess. You don't get to be a world empire by just asking people to join you. Imperator Merak likes to say, 'Inclusion is Order.'"

"Rastaban could have said the same thing," replied Tresado bitterly. "He just went about it a different way."

Orchid sighed in contentment. "Well anyway, we're home free. We're rich, we've got all these goodies, and we're on our way! This calls for a toast!" Her oaken staff glowing with satisfaction, her chocolate hair waving in the slight breeze, and her emerald-green eyes shining, Orchid grabbed a fresh amphora of mead, quickly knocked away the wax seal, and held it high.

"To Group Six!"

The clay jug was within a finger of her lips when a strange and suddenly familiar bluish glow enveloped them all. The carriage came to a slow halt as the reins dropped to the ground. The amphora followed, shattering and spilling its contents upon the floor boards.

Suddenly relieved of the weight on his back, Onyx pondered the other horses.

So, what do we do now?

I'm gonna eat grass until I hear otherwise.

Today - The Crystal Palace

"Contact verified, stabilization spells in place, it's up to the Palace now . . ."

Jakki's face reflected the bluish light coming up from the viewing crystal she was hunched over. There was a loud pop of her gum at the same time as a louder pop on the crystal platform. Foxx, Orchid, Tresado, and Serena blipped into existence with nary a whisper of wind. It was a perfect teleportation, except for the fact that Group Six appeared a full reach above the floor . . . and completely naked. Four bare butts hit the floor unceremoniously. A half a beat later, they were followed by their clothes, which fluttered down on top of them. As a finale, Serena's great diamond dropped onto the top of her head and bounced to the floor. A cheer went up from the surrounding crowd.

"Thank the Gods of Lurra!" shouted Jakki. "You've been rescued!!"

EPILOGUE

12,627 years from today

Finally tonight, we bring you a story from the oldest continually occupied city in the world – Rajanagari. Paleontologists have once again opened up the famous Abakaarian Grotto for further study. The grotto, dubbed after the ancient name of the city, is what is known as a natural cave trap. For millions of years, unfortunate animals stumbled into this great chasm located near the bottom of one of the steep cliffsides of Rajana Canyon. Treasure troves of fossils dating back as far as twenty million years have been unearthed, providing scientists with an invaluable look at ancient life. Researchers have made a remarkable, if puzzling discovery. For more, we go to our science correspondent, Jules Black.

Thank you, Garrett. In this latest expedition, the steel gates protecting the grotto from weather and amateur fossil hunters have been removed. The team of scientists, who perilously descend every day by ropes, has unearthed a previously unexcavated section of the cave. Radiocarbon dating is considered inaccurate for the age of the fossils found, but it is estimated that the layer uncovered is between sixty and sixty-five thousand years of age. Instead of the fossil remains of giant cats and primitive buffalo, scientists have found a regular burial ground. Hundreds of bodies have been uncovered, all showing signs of ritualistic death practices. Many of the dead were wrapped in hide or plant matter. There were also many artifacts buried with them. Bits of tools, strange carved figures, even the remains of fruit seeds and the bones of small birds were buried with them, suggesting that foodstuffs were taken with them into some sort of afterlife. The bodies are that of the extinct Eryndi race. It has been long believed that, during this period, the Eryndi, a separate precursor species of man, were little more than upright beasts and did not evolve into sentience until many thousands of years after modern Macai arose. This new evidence would seem to contradict that. Still, most scientists agree that the Eryndi learned their eventual civilized ways from existing alongside the more sophisticated Macai. But here's the astounding discovery. One of the bodies unearthed is that of an adult Macai male. Evidence of osteoporosis indicates that the man died at an extreme old age. He was found wrapped together with one of the female Eryndi skeletons. The bodies were laid face-down with their hands clasped together. One of the scientists, speaking on condition of anonymity, suggested that perhaps this Macai man and Eryndi woman were mates. The expedition leader, Professor Jaacav Dreiser, refutes that theory. He suggests, since the man has been the only Macai found so far, that he lived among the primitives, educating and possibly civilizing them, which could explain the sophisticated burial ritual among beings that could not have had an inkling of such a thing naturally. In any event, it is probably a mystery that will never be solved. Back to you, Garrett.

Thank you, Jules. Quite a tale. That'll do it for tonight. I'm Garrett Sondchi. Good night from World News.

LEXICON

ABAKAAR ('ă-bə-kär)
A country in central Aris.

ABSOLUTE MAGIC
A powerful form of magic mostly practiced by Macai. Alters and recombines, controls and directs.

AMORAN SEA ('ă-mor-ən)
A mostly landlocked sea in northwestern Aris.

ARIS
Second largest, but most heavily populated continent of Lurra.

BEAT
An indefinite span of time approximately equal to a single heartbeat.

BERGALO
A large, buffalo-like creature.

BILLY BARK
Bark from the silly billy tree which contains a psychotropic chemical. The bark can be smoked, chewed or used as an herb in tonics. The effects depend on potency.

BOINGBALL

Eryndi sport.

CLEE-AT

A horrid, bipedal rat-like predator that lived in ancient times.

COLOSSUS TREE

An enormous conifer of northern climes.

CRAYMON NIGHTROOT

A dangerous narcotic used to alter mental processes. It is banned in most civilized countries.

CREDOS OF HROLVAD

A guide by which Northlanders live their lives.

CRODAN

War god of the Northlands.

CRODAN'S KEEP

The afterlife where valiant Northlanders aspire to go.

CRYSTAL PALACE

A fabulous gambling casino/resort in the crater lake of Mount Boronay.

DAURIC

A common gold coin used throughout central Aris.

DRAGON

A huge, reptilian flying predator.

ERN

Prehistoric name for the Eryndi race.

ERNIE

A racial epithet for Eryndi.

ERYNDI (ə-'rĭn-dē)

Race of people on Lurra.

FINGER

A unit of measurement equal to 1/100th of a reach. It is approximately the width of a man's finger. (about ¾ inch)

FLICKEN

A common, domesticated food bird.

FOUR-CARD BLITZKRIEG

A popular card game.

GENDRIN

A common copper coin.

GRANNUGH

A town on the western coast of The Northlands. Birthplace of Serena.

GRILK

A hippo-sized wild mountain sheep inhabiting northern climes.

HOBO CLAM

A small shellfish found in ocean shallows, considered a delicacy.

HOOK

A racial epithet for Eryndi.

JAMBA

A plant-based narcotic used, among other things, as an aid to Magical concentration.

JASPERIA

Territory in western Aris, capital: Ostica.

KADIZIO

A large port city of southwestern Aris.

LEAGUE

A unit of measurement equal to 1000 reaches. (about 6000 feet)

LUFTAR VALLEY

An area of the Northlands encompassing several villages and fjords.

LUM

Gigantic prehistoric ancestor of the modern lumba.

LUMBA

A huge, slow-moving herbivore inhabiting temperate forests.

LURRA ('lə-rə)

Name of the world.

MACAI (mä-'kī)

Race of people on Lurra.

MAKARA ('mä-kə-rä)

A tart citrus fruit.

MAGIC

A form of metaphysical energy that permeates Lurra.

MOROK

A large, moose-like creature now extinct.

MOUNT BORONAY

An inland extinct volcano, the location of the Crystal Palace.

NORTHLANDS

A cold, mountainous country on the northwestern tip of Aris, inhabited by tribes of fierce Macai warriors.

NYHA ('nī-yə)

Large moon in the skies over Lurra; also known as The Orb.

OSTICA ('äs-tĭk-ə)

A large port city on the Talus River. Capital of Jasperia.

PALEEN ('pā-lēn)

A common silver coin worth ten copper gendrins.

REACH

A unit of measurement equal to about six feet. (or a normal man's fingertip to fingertip reach.)

ROCKFRUIT

A hardy fruit that flourishes in all mineral-rich climes.

SABA ('sä-bə)

A nut from which a powerful stimulant can be made.

SENFALL

A terrible catastrophe in prehistoric times resulting in massive destruction and climatic change.

SENSANG

The Sun, also called Sen.

SERPENT RIVER

Winding river running through the center of Abakaar.

SILLY BILLY TREE

A conifer with medicinal bark.

STONE

A unit of weight equaling approximately eleven pounds.

TALUS RIVER ('tă-ləs)

A large slow-moving river on the northwest corner of the Arisan continent.

TORMAC

A common gold coin worth twenty silver paleens.

TRESKAN IMPERIUM

A large empire of western Aris consisting of dozens of conquered lands. It has been ruled by Imperator Merak for the last hundred years.

TRIMIAN

A small, prehistoric, tree-dwelling primate.

VORENNIUM

A meteoritic substance capable of producing great power.

WORLDLY MAGIC

A nature-based, conservative form of Magic mostly practiced by Eryndi.

THE LURRAN YEAR

10 MONTHS OF 40 DAYS EACH

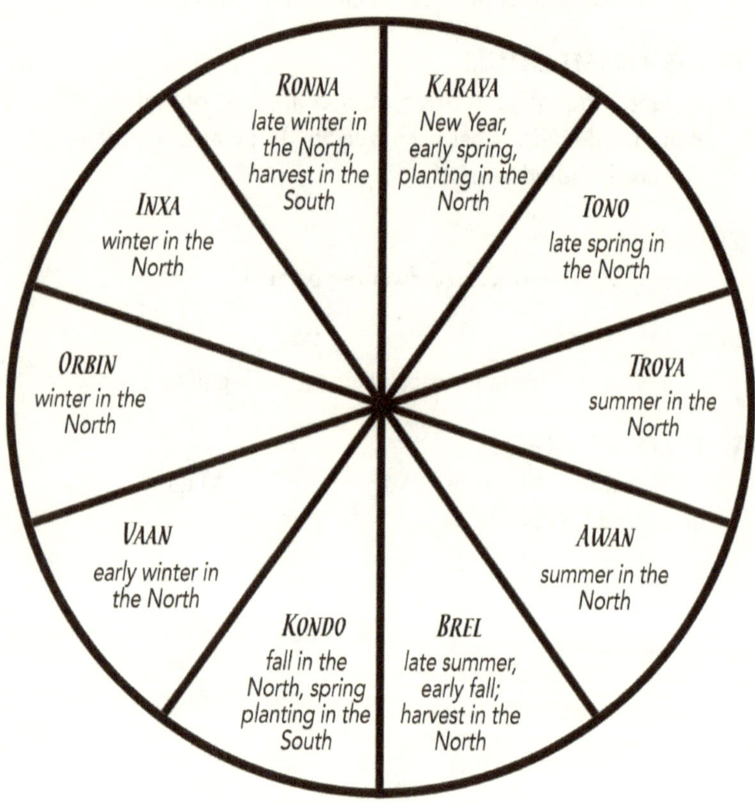

Each month consists of five 8-day weeks. Days 4 and 8 of each week, called Honor Days, are treated like weekends; everyone honors who or what they want, such as a god or ancestors or Magic itself. The numbering of days is the same in each month (i.e., Dindays are always the 1st, 9th, 17th, 25th, and 33rd). Each day is 20 hours long.

Dinday	Gleeday	Teerday	Midweek Honor	Malday	Kevoday	Vinday	Weekend Honor
1	2	3	4	5	6	7	8
9	10	11	12	13	14	15	16
17	18	19	20	21	22	23	24
25	26	27	28	29	30	31	32
33	34	35	36	37	38	39	40

In Group Six and the Crater, "today" is the year 21876.

Dates are expressed as "month day-year (last 2 digits)" – so Karaya 6-76 is the sixth day of Karaya in 21876.

ACKNOWLEDGMENTS

Much of this book was written while I was recovering from a lung transplant I received in 2017. My eternal thanks go out to far too many doctors and nurses to list here. Suffice to say, I owe my life to these scrubs-wearing heroes and especially to the young soldier who donated the organs that kept me and many others alive.

Also, the usual thanks go out to Suz the publisher, who is overflowing with good advice, and also, of course, to my beloved wife, Pat, who tackles every annoying detail that I have not the strength, wisdom, intelligence, charisma, dexterity, or constitution to handle – *THE RIGAMAROLLER*!

ABOUT THE AUTHOR

Ron Richard spent much of his life painting double yellow lines for the City of Casper. He is a Wyoming native, stage actor, woodworker, cat owner, and has written several plays and readers' theatre scripts designed for a planetarium setting. He also portrayed the bad guy in Crime Stoppers commercials.